PRAISE

MW01088128

"Meadows and Po boundaries of urban fiction with this fast-moving, entertaining novel. Part love story, part prison-life expose, *CONVICT'S CANDY* will keep you turning pages. The story, language, and writing deliver powerfully."
—Max Rodriguez, *QBR: The Black Book Review*

"Gripping...A gritty, scandalous story about brothers behind bars. Keeps you on the edge of your seat!"
—Aisha Gumby, *Don Diva*

"Insightful and alarming, *CONVICT'S CANDY* is definitely a reality check for women, and a wake-up call for all worldwide."
—Mika Miller, Author of *And God Created Woman*

"Damon "Amin" Meadows and Jason Poole's *CONVICT'S CANDY* will shock the world with this controversial novel!"
—Dru Noble, Author of *Sonz of Darkness*

"*CONVICT'S CANDY* is sweet drama at its best! Entertaining, yet informative; the brutal truth of life and times in prison."
—Sha, Author of *Harder*

"*CONVICT'S CANDY* is intense and enlightening! Cleverly written to educate the masses of a serious social issue."
—Tony Collins, Author of *Games Women Play*

"A compelling novel. *CONVICT'S CANDY* is intriguing, insightful and deliciously crafted."
—Emlyn DeGannes, Publisher of *The Lies Hustlers Never Tell*

"The sistas were waiting to be put on to 'what's really good' behind the prison walls. *CONVICT'S CANDY* gave it to us raw!"
—Wahida Clark, Author of *Thug Matrimony*

ghettoheat®

This novel has been written by Damon "Amin" Meadows and Jason Poole, and was edited by HICKSON, CEO of GHETTOHEAT®.

CONVICT'S CANDY is based on a true story, yet was written purposely in a fictitious manner to protect the guilty....

GHETTOHEAT® PRODUCTIONS

GHETTOHEAT®
HARDER
AND GOD CREATED WOMAN
SONZ OF DARKNESS
LONDON REIGN
GAMES WOMEN PLAY
GHOST TOWN HUSTLERS
BOY-TOY
SKATE ON!
SOME SEXY, ORGASM 1
SOME SEXY, ORGASM 2

A GHETTOHEAT® PRODUCTION

CONVICT'S CANDY

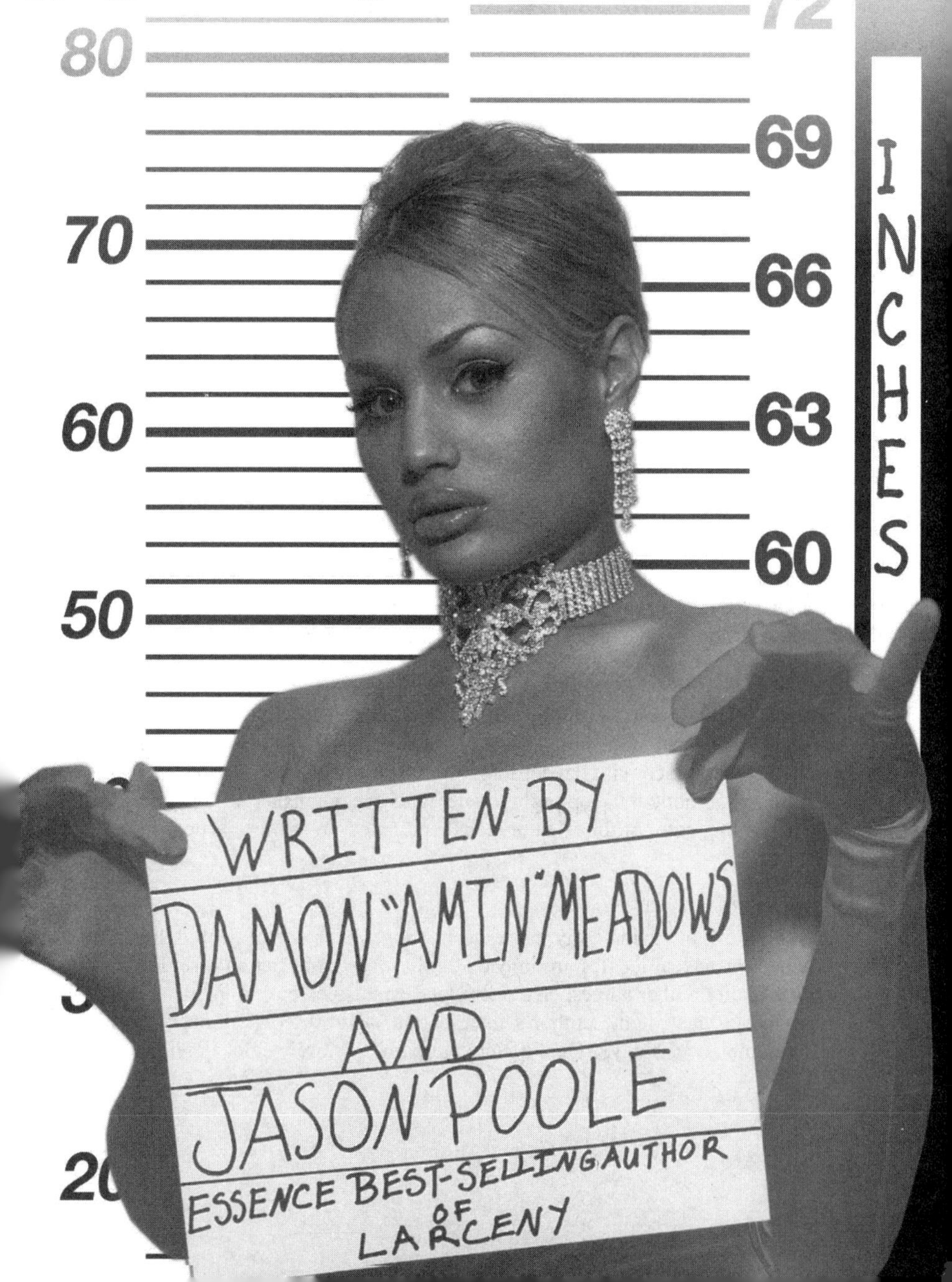

Excerpts from:
BOY-TOY © 2007 by DAMON "AMIN" MEADOWS
GHETTOHEAT® © 2007 by HICKSON
HARDER © 2006 by SHA
SONZ OF DARKNESS © 2007 by DRU NOBLE
AND GOD CREATED WOMAN © 2007 by MIKA MILLER
GHOST TOWN HUSTLERS © 2007 by CARTEL: CASTILLO
GAMES WOMEN PLAY © 2007 by TONY COLLINS
LONDON REIGN © 2007 by A. C. BRITT
SKATE ON! © 2007 by HICKSON
LADY SPEAKS THE TRUTH, VOLUME 1 © 2007 by SHA
SOME SEXY, ORGASM 1 © 2007 by DRU NOBLE
SOME SEXY, ORGASM 2 © 2007 by MIKA MILLER

Published by GHETTOHEAT®, LLC
P.O. BOX 2746, NEW YORK, NY 10027, USA

Library of Congress Control Number: 2005934883

ISBN: 0-9742982-2-0

Printed in the USA. Second Edition, May 2007

PUBLISHER'S NOTE
This is a work of fiction. Any names to historical events, real people, living and dead, or to real locales are intended only to give the fiction a setting in historic reality. Other names, characters, places, businesses and incidents are either the product of the author's imagination or are used fictitiously, and their resemblance, if any, to real life counterparts is entirely coincidental.

DAMON "AMIN" MEADOWS' ACKNOWLEDGMENTS

Carol "Lou-Lover" Meadows, my mom, I could never thank you enough, and I'm sorry for any hurt I've ever caused you. I love you, "Lou-Lover"! To my beautiful daughters, Ronette and Sumiya. Ronette, I still have the yellow slip from when you sent me your allowance of $1, saying you wanted to make sure your daddy had something to eat! I love you! Sumiya, my twin, it seems like yesterday that I was encouraging your mom on the phone to push, so you could come into this world; now my baby is a young lady. I love you! Grandma Lille, I love you. My sister, Dawn "Waffiyyah" Meadows, I know a sister can't fly on one wing. I'll be there shortly (if Allah wills). To my brothers, Donny "Dee'z" Meadows, Tony "Amir" Riley and Kameelah: congratulations. My nieces, Tiara-"Tee-Lover", Tianna-"Yanna-Boo" and Tunisia-"Fathead". My nephews, Lil' Amin and Lil' Thomeen. My cousin/sister, Chaurita "Nadiyyah" Roberts, Zarifah-"Zizy", Kenya-"Khadijah", "Rhonda Babe", Kismet, Abdul Rahman and Traci-"Zaimah, Natasha "Somalia" Hill of Harmony Salon/Day Spa, Cheo Erving and Shannon, Madiyah Watkins, Zulema Golston, Kenya Yarbrough, Bone, Rashan-"Rock", Shelly-"Najiyah", my cousin, Raheem, Omar Teagle of Teagle Group/Versatile Music, Jay Erving III of Coalition, Malik Abdullah, Cheryl-"Murdock", Six, Tamika Morales, Ms. Eva Harral, Turquoise Erving, Abdul Mudee, Zuri Edwards, Chrispus Taylor, Rhonda-"Lover", Joann-"Jo-Jo", Taaibah-"Sonia", Jim Youngman, April Moore, ALFAMEGA, Riddick "Big Daddy" Bowe a.k.a. Abu Julius and Jim Feldman.

To the love ones I've lost: my dad, Donny "Raheem" Meadows, Grandma Dot, Aunt Gwenda-"Gravna", Aunt Edie, Grandpop Charlie, Ms. Evelyn King (Sam's mom), Daily Mike, Derek Jr.-"Scooter", HICKSON, my publisher, thanks for your belief in me and my projects. Jason Poole, my co-author, it's been an honor working with you. Thanks for sharing your expertise and polishing up my writing skills. Peace to the entire GHETTOHEAT® family.

To my fam behind the walls, Qadir-"Pone", Kabir-"Kadi-Ka", Hamza, Qudus, Poppa Smurf, Quadir-"B.Fields", Umar-"Grip", Tariq-"Sputt", Muhammad and M. "Shiesty World". Also, to the transgender we've interviewed: Laquetta, Lashonda, Sasha, Papi, Jr. and Yalonda. Paris Gotti, thanks for gracing the cover.

JASON POOLE'S ACKNOWLEDGMENTS

I'd first like to thank God for giving me the talent to express myself literally. My mother, Yvonne E. Holtz, whom I love eternally. There's a million ways for a man to be destroyed, but only one way to be produced. Thanks you for being that Executive Producer. My son, Lil' Jason, I love you. My sisters, Mia and Tammara. My brother, Eric. My father, Samuel "Winkle" Poole, thank you for giving me life. Surely I'm proud to be the splitting image of you. My stepfather, Stanley Griffin, your lectures of morals and principles still rings in my heads daily.

Vickie Stringer, CEO of Triple Crown Publications, thank you for giving me a jumpstart in the book game by publishing my first novel. I'll always be grateful for that. To my new publisher, HICKSON, CEO of GHETTOHEAT®, thank you for giving me the opportunity to create great works, such as this ground-breaking novel, as well as giving me complete insight of the literary world. For sure, GHETTOHEAT® is going to take the world by storm. To my co-author, Damon "Amin" Meadows, finally, the process is over. You predicted that this novel would be a huge success; this is only the beginning. Surely this novel will help save many lives. I guess you could call us humanitarians.

To my dear friends and family: Aunt Joyce, Suzzi, Peggy, James, Ishmael, Anthony "Short Dogg" Tatum, Shelinda "Pooh" Spieght and the whole Never Give-Up Productions family. Mrs. Diane Richardson in Philly, Latifah Leonard of G.P. Entertainment and my many fans. Thank you for believing in me. Lastly, to my companion in life, Ms. Lisa Duvall, I love you. Smile for me, boo. Now the whole world knows.

To my fellow authors and supporters: Eyonne Williams of Fastlanepub.com, Victor Martin, Marcus Spears, Rodney Wilson of Etched In Stone Publishing, Susan Hampstead of Hampstead Publishing and Don Diva Magazine. Tina Ison of Sexyprisoners.com, Hoodstories.com, Cover-2-Cover Book Club, Essence, Sister-2-Sister, Felon and Smooth Magazine, Oprah Winfrey, Wendy Williams and lastly, to the national best-selling author, Terry McMillan. One bad apple doesn't spoil the whole bunch. Never Give-Up!

Dedicated to my mother, Carol "Lou-Lover" Meadows, my two daughters, Ronette and Sumiya, and to African-American women.
—DAMON "AMIN" MEADOWS

Dedicated to my mother, Yvonne E. Holtz, and to the rest of our African-American queens.
—JASON POOLE

CONVICT'S CANDY

JUDGEMENT DAY
chapter 1

April 1, 2005

"Your Honor, I ask that my client's motion be granted on the sole issues therefore that have been raised during this evidentiary hearing," said the young, handsome attorney who was representing the strikingly beautiful "damsel" in distress.

There she was, looking good as ever. The brightness of her smile shone like the luminous sun after the shower of April's rain. Candy Sweets, a tall, shapely, gorgeous, young femme fatale with features so unique, that one wouldn't, or couldn't imagine that this lovely vixen would be standing in front of a judge, pleading for her freedom. In fact, Candy's appearance alone looked as if she was running late for a magazine shoot for Vibe.

Candy had the beauty and figure to be America's Next Top Model, but from the evil stares that lurked behind the glasses of Judge Alan Kozinkski, it didn't seem as if she'd be auditioning for Tyra Banks' new television show this season—or the next.

As the judge leaned over his desk, studying the motion, Candy impatiently waited for his decision. She knew that she was fighting a hard battle, yet Candy had faith in her lawyer. Well, not exactly her lawyer, but, Candy had faith in Tom. It was he who had his old law school buddy, Patrick Nelson return a favor by representing her, although Tom felt that if he was there, he could've represented Candy to the fullest.

But the fact of the matter is, Tom couldn't. His license to practice law was revoked eighteen months ago, for aiding and abetting a high-profile politician figure in a big embezzlement case out in Philadelphia, Pennsylvania.

"What's he waiting for?" Candy asked, as she whispered to Patrick, who seemed to be just as impatient.

"I don't know, but that's a good sign. The longer he takes, the better," answered the attorney.

At that moment, the judge took off his glasses, placed the motion down onto his desk, leaned back in his seat, took a deep breath and immediately delivered his ruling. As Judge Kozinkski expressed his words, the whole courtroom scene became surreal to Candy.

"In the instant matter of Candy Sweets, Case number 008-01-04, I hereby deny the motion, pursuant to Rule 60(b), because of the fact that this issue should've been brought before the court on the previous 2255 Motion. I also agree with the government, that the Rule 60(b) is just another attempt at filing a Habeas Corpus in disguise. For the reasons set forth, motion denied!"

"WHAT?" Candy yelled shockingly, as she looked at Patrick with hatred and scornfulness. "Motherfucker, you told me that I was getting out! What the fuck is this shit?"

"Calm down, Ms. Sweets. I never guaranteed you that we'd win. I just told you I'd come in here and do my best. Now, whatever you and Tom discussed, that's between the both of you. I'm just doing an old friend a favor."

"A FAVOR? MOTHERFUCKER, HOW ARE YOU DOING ME A FAVOR? BITCH, YOU SOLD ME OUT!" Candy spat, as she reached for the young attorney who now appeared to be frightened. As Candy lunged at Patrick, he fell back and lost his balance before landing onto the floor. She then attempted to strike him, but was interrupted by the chokehold from the U.S. Marshal, who now was restraining Candy in handcuffs.

"FUCK YOU, YOU NO-GOOD ASS MOTHERFUCKER! YOU'RE A LYING, WHITE JEW-BITCH; I HOPE YOU ROT IN HELL!" Candy shouted while being led out of the courtroom in handcuffs and into the small holding cell.

She was going through a lot of stress lately, mostly because of the medication Candy was taking. The pills she'd habitually taken sometimes had a strange effect on her, in which Candy's actions were strongly dictated by her emotions. After being placed in the holding cell, the marshal agreed to take off the handcuffs, only if she calmed down.

"Now, you sure you ain't gonna act up?" asked the marshal, as he removed the handcuffs from Candy.

"Yes, I'm sure," Candy answered embarrassingly. She became ashamed of the way that she acted out of anger. It was rare for Candy to display this type of behavior, for she always carried and conducted herself like a true diva. If Ray were around, Candy wouldn't have been acting out of character. Thoughts of him now made her heart skip a beat, as Candy hadn't heard from Ray in over a week.

"Shit, Ray's probably somewhere shacked up with his dumb-ass baby's mama. Fat bitch doesn't even know what's up with her man," Candy murmured as she fixed her clothes.

She also thought about Trigger, the new rap sensation who had just been nominated at the B.E.T. Awards for "Best New Solo Artist."

Damn, I've done called this *nigga* for about a week straight, and Trigger *still* hasn't done what I've asked him to do. I think it's time for me to go into "silly hoe" mode and *extort* his ass, Candy thought to herself.

As she sat down and thought about the men she'd dealt with in her life, Candy began to smile. Some she'd loved, some Candy cared for, and others—she'd simply played with, just to pass the time.

Soon after, Candy got up, looked around, and walked over to the mirror alongside the sink. She gazed long and hard at the blurred reflection that stared back at her. Candy then smiled and cried simultaneously.

Even though she loved herself immensely, Candy still loved and missed little Andy—always did, always will. Her mind drifted back to the past, thinking of Andy, and the vicious hand that life had dealt him.

CANDY GIRL
chapter 2

1997

"CANDY GIRL, YOU ARE MY WORLD."

Ralph Tresvant's high-pitched voice had filled the entire room, as the young girls danced to the classic *New Edition* song that played on *Hot 97.*

Andy sat on the couch, as he'd watched and admired the way his cousins moved their feet and shook their hips to the beat of the song. He'd always liked how his cousins, Tammy and Lisa danced, but deep inside, Andy had known that he danced better than the two, mostly because he'd practiced dancing behind closed doors, dancing in private; Andy saved himself from the embarrassment of his relatives.

As he'd studied his two cousins, Andy wanted so badly to inform them that they weren't moving their hips from side-to-side in rhythm. In a way, Andy had become a little jealous and envious of them, not being able to express himself as his cousins had.

"C'mon, Andy, get up and dance with us," Tammy had requested, as she noticed the change in his demeanor once the song had come on. She'd known that Andy loved the song, and that it bothered him not being able to dance to it. Not because of any physical injury or anything like that, Andy had been in great shape and in the best of health.

At ten years old, Andy had wide, light-brown eyes, and skin that was smooth as butter. His hair was black, having a thick and silky, curly texture, in which Andy had inherited from his father.

Unfortunately, his father, in which Andy had never met, was a pimp, and was killed in front of the whore house that he'd ran in the Bronx; by an angry father of one of his prostitutes. Andy's father had turned the sixteen-year-old girl on to heroin and immediately placed her in his brothel. He'd sold the young girl to countless degenerate pedophiles that were three times her age.

"Andy!" Lisa yelled, as Andy had shaken his head and smirked, as he watched his cousin, Tammy dance.

"What, girl?"

15

"Get up and dance with us; this your song, right?" Lisa then asked, as she'd snapped her fingers and swayed her hips to the music.

"Yeah, Andy, c'mon. Teach me that step you was doin' last night," Tammy had insisted, as she rocked her shoulders to the song.

Andy frantically looked around the room to make sure that the coast was clear. Although he'd become scared and nervous of being caught by his aunt, Joyce, Andy couldn't resist the urge to dance. He had to, it's what made Andy happy, and he was great at it.

Being a talented dancer was a gift he'd received, one that Andy had hidden. As a child, he'd always felt the need to hide his sexuality, as Andy battled with his true identity. Yet, it was time for the fancy dancer to "come out".

"Alright, move over then, girl," Andy replied as he'd pushed Tammy to the side. "And bring your boney, little butt over here," Andy then continued, as he'd placed Lisa next to him. Critically, Andy instructed the girls on how to groove to the beat.

As Tammy turned up the volume on the radio, Andy coordinated his first dance step, as he'd moved smoothly, natural; Tammy instantly had become jealous. The more Andy danced to the song, the more he'd outshone the two girls.

Lisa smiled, being extremely proud of how well Andy had danced. He'd been not only her cousin, but Lisa's best friend, also. During their early childhood, Andy comforted Lisa and confided in her, as he'd told Lisa his "secret".

While on the other hand, Tammy secretly hated Andy. He'd posed a threat to her, as Tammy felt that Andy had always stole her thunder, getting all of the attention that she wanted. Andy entered into Tammy's territory where she'd felt that he hadn't belonged.

As Andy performed his dance routine in sync, being caught up in the music, he'd begun to let himself go freely. The more the song played, the harder Andy had danced to it.

The lyrics had taken Andy into his secret comfort zone, as *Ralph Tresvant* continued to sing: *"YOU LOOK SO SWEET, YOU'RE A SPECIAL TREAT."*

Tammy then felt that this was her opportunity to capitalize on executing one of her devilish deeds, as she'd reached over and turned the volume up higher. Andy hadn't realized what Tammy had done, being entranced by the music. He'd been so into the song, by the time Lisa attempted to turn the music down, it was too late.

The loud music had awakened his aunt, Joyce. She'd frenziedly forced her three-hundred-pound, obese body through the house, as Joyce allowed her ears to lead her to where the music had blasted from. When she'd reached the living room, Joyce noticed that it had been transformed into a dance theatre for the three kids.

She hadn't become angry at the piercing music that suddenly interrupted her sleep; Joyce had become extremely furious at finding her only nephew in the middle of the floor, as Andy had shaken his hips and poked his behind out effeminately.

WHAP! WHAP! WHAP!

Andy hadn't known what hit him, as he felt the sharp pain that crashed down on the back of his head. His Aunt Joyce had repeatedly pounded onto him.

"What the *hell* is wrong wit' you, boy? What I *tell* you 'bout that *fuckin'* faggot-ass shit?" *WHAP!* "You *ain't* no girl, so stop *dancin'* like one!" Aunt Joyce had retorted, as shameful tears gushed from her eyes. She was hurt to see her sister's only son, only child, act effeminately; Aunt Joyce assumed that Andy had been gay.

"OKAY, AUNT JOYCE; I'M SORRY, I'M SORRY!" Andy then pleaded, as he'd crawled into a corner for cover and balled up his body into a knot. Andy quickly held his arms over his head, as he'd tried his best to avoid the excruciating pain of his aunt's powerful punches. Aunt Joyce's blows were sharp and hard as a rock; she'd wailed a few more hands.

WHAP! WHAP! WHAP!

"Didn't I *tell* ya *ass* before I better not catch you *dancin'* like that in my house again?" *WHAP!*

"OUCH, YES! OH, I'M *S-O-R-R-Y,* AUNT JOYCE, PLEASE STOP—I'M *S-O-R-R-Y!*" Andy whined, as he'd desperately pleaded. Fear then filled his eyes, as Andy carefully lifted up his head; he'd looked to see where the next blow would land.

Andy soon noticed the tears that streamed down Lisa's face, as she'd nervously stood behind his aunt. Lisa felt bad for her cousin, as she'd known that she couldn't help him at that moment. Lisa had become upset that Andy was being punished for who he was, as she always understood and accepted Andy's ways.

"Boy, I swear fo' God, if I *ever* catch ya *ass* in here dancin' and actin' like a little, *fuckin'* faggot again...I swear fo' the life of me, I'ma *kill* ya ass... And if I don't, I damn sure gonna try—you hear me?" His Aunt Joyce blurted out, as she'd gasped for air in between sentences.

"Yes, Aunt Joyce, it won't happen again," Andy had squealed, as he hoped that she would stop attacking him. As Andy continued holding his arms over his head, protecting himself from his aunt's agonizing strikes, Andy's watery doe-shaped eyes peeked through the cracks of his human shield, as he'd found his cousin, Tammy standing behind her mother; sneering sneakily. She'd grinned—Tammy felt the joys of succeeding in her evil act.

Immediately, Andy had known that he'd been deceived by Tammy. She'd always found some awful way to harm him. Tammy hated that her friends loved playing with Andy. Even as a young girl growing up, Tammy had always resented Andy for his girlish ways, and for getting the most attention.

* * * * *

Candy came back to reality after the marshal tapped on the bars of the prison cell with his keys, instantly getting her attention.

"Sweets, yo, Sweets," said the marshal, as he noticed the tall, shapely individual standing there dazed; looking in the mirror in a deep trance. The tailored, cream-colored *Roberto Cavalli* pantsuit fitted Candy well, revealing her well-toned body. The marshal couldn't believe his sights, as he literally had to hold back the lust he began to have for Candy.

"Oh, I'm sorry, what is it, marshal?" Candy asked, as she quickly turned around, wiping her big, beautiful, brown eyes.

"Just came back to let you know that the wagon's gonna be running late, so make yourself as comfortable as you can. Here, this is the best I can do for you while you

18

wait," he said, as the marshal handed her two brown bag lunches through the cell bars.

"What's this?" Candy inquired, as she opened the bag and stuck her face inside, smelling the awful odor of old bologna and cheese sandwiches.

"That's what we officers call 'comfort food'," he answered with a sarcastic grin on his face. Candy sat down on the bench without any emotion as the marshal stood there, hoping that she caught on to his joke. "You wanna know why it's called that?"

"No!" Candy snapped.

"Well I'ma go on and tell you *anyway,* since I'm in the mood for a lil' joke," the correctional officer continued with his grin. "Well, we all figured that once you take a bite of that ol' government bologna and cheese, when you finally get released from jail, you'll always want another one, so what do you do? You come on back to jail to get some more comfort. Now, you've just learned your first lesson: Prison Comfort Food 101, but don't tell anyone that you got it from me; okay, doll baby?" the marshal replied, as he walked off laughing.

Dumb motherfucker, Candy thought, as she looked around the holding cell, reading the names scribbled on the walls; despising the filth that encircled her. *How the fuck am I going to get my ass out of this mess? Damn...I'm calling Dewayne the first chance I get. I know he can try and pull some strings...I have to call Dr. Peters to let her know that I won't be making it to my appointment any time soon. Fuck, she probably thinks that I'm bullshitting. Shit, it's not like I don't have the money, or that I'm afraid. I need her services more than Dr. Peters could imagine.* Candy rationalized.

After she finished thinking about her tasks, Candy sat back, being completely surrounded by silence, reflecting back to the past; thinking about young Andy. Candy thought hard about his lifestyle, and the turmoil that had led Andy into a different direction from which he started.

I WAS BORN THIS WAY
chapter 3

At age fourteen, Andy hung around with so many girls, that it had become accustom for him to hear people calling him obscenities.

"Get the *fuck* outta my way, you lil' *faggot!*" Brian, a teenaged bully had retorted, as he aggressively pushed Andy to the side. The tyrant then dashed out of the back door exit of the school building, as he'd skipped his class.

"Forget you, Brian; you make me sick," Andy whispered, as Brian had run off with his friends.

"I can't *stand* Brian either," Shanna, Andy's best friend had replied. Shanna, other than his cousin, Lisa, had been the only person that Andy confided in. In fact, it was Lisa who had introduced the two.

Shanna treated Andy as if he'd been one of her girlfriends; she'd totally accepted Andy for who he was. Shanna understood his feelings, and empathized with how others had ridiculed and perceived Andy; he'd acted in a girlish manner.

Mostly, Andy found refuge at Shanna's house where her family embraced him; they'd treated Andy with love, opposed to him living with his evil aunt, Joyce—who had despised Andy for what she'd "foreseen" him into becoming.

Yet, Andy truly believed early on that it was meant for him to be that way. He'd reasoned to others: *"I was born this way; this is how God made me."* Many felt that his comment had been an insult to God, but, the few who loved him had considered his statement to be true.

"I know, he's *always* picking on me," Andy had replied, annoyed with Brian's verbal abuse.

"Brian is cute though," Lisa then chimed in as she'd looked at the two; Lisa wanted to know if Shanna and Andy had approved. Shanna then agreed, but Andy blushed uncontrollably— Brian being the first boy he had a secret crush on.

"Why are you blushing so much, Andy?" Lisa asked as she'd smiled; Lisa had known Andy's true feelings for the bully.

"Please, I am *not* blushing!" Andy had responded defensively.

"Yes you are; tell the truth, you like him, don't you?" Lisa then asked.

"NO!"

"Yes you do," Shanna had interjected as she tickled Andy. She'd made him feel embarrassed, as Andy's face turned red.

"No, I don't! Now, can you two stop asking me stupid questions?" Andy then retorted jokingly.

"C'mon, y'all, let's play some Double Dutch!" Lisa had cheered.

"How we gonna play Double Dutch without a jump rope?" Shanna had replied condescendingly in a teasing manner.

"We'll play with my sister, Tammy; she'll let us jump with her friends," Lisa then answered while pointing at Tammy. As Andy, Shanna and Lisa walked towards Tammy and her friends, Shanna quickly noticed Tammy had whispered into one of her friends' ear.

"Hey, can we jump rope with y'all?" Shanna had asked.

"NO!" Tammy had answered nastily.

"Why you acting all funny?" Lisa then joined in.

"'Cause I want to. This *my* rope and *I* say who can jump with me or not!" Tammy had snapped, as she then rolled her eyes while making her remark.

"Why you treat your own sister like that?" Shanna had asked, having a frown upon her face.

"You mind your business, Shanna. Why don't y'all go somewhere else and jump rope?" Tammy then retorted rudely. "And Andy, why don't *you* go play football or something with some boys?" Tammy bitterly replied, hoping that she'd embarrassed Andy.

After Tammy had spoken, everyone stopped what they'd been doing, and diverted their attention to Andy; they'd all known that Tammy, in a sarcastic way, had reminded Andy that he wasn't a girl, nor would she have ever accepted him acting as one.

"*Fuck* you, Tammy!" Andy then shot back harshly, as he'd cut his eyes at her; Andy then stood in place with his hands on his hips, posing girlishly. Tammy then looked at him with disgust, before she'd responded back to Andy.

"Look at you, just like a *bitch*—I hate your *faggot* ass! I'm ashamed to even call you my cousin," Tammy then lashed out, as she'd intentionally tried to hurt Andy's feelings.

"Yeah, well I'm ashamed to say that I know a piece of *trash* like you. I don't want to jump rope with your *ass* anyway. Look at you, all pigeon-toed—you can't even jump right," Andy had retorted.

Everyone laughed at Andy's comment, knowing that he'd told the truth. Immediately, Tammy's friends had begged her to allow Andy to join them in a game of jump rope, as they'd admired his humor; also knowing that Andy was considered the best Double Dutch jumper in the entire school. Tammy then quickly thrown down her jump rope, and had stormed off the schoolyard.

"C'mon y'all, let's jump!" Shanna had suggested, as she picked up the rope and handed the other end to Lisa.

"You jump first, Andy," Lisa then instructed, as she and Shanna had excitedly turned the rope. Tammy's friends all stood around in amazement, as they'd marveled over how Andy jumped up-and-down, back-and-forth and from side-to-side; like a pro. They'd cheered him on: "GO ANDY, IT'S YA BIRTHDAY! GO ANDY, IT'S YA BIRTHDAY!"

Tammy, once again, had felt like an outcast, and overshadowed by her cousin. Tammy hated feeling this way, just as much as she'd hated Andy. Tammy then vowed on her life to pay Andy back one day, for always being the center of attention; he'd won over her friends effortlessly.

*　*　*　*　*

Candy smiled widely, remembering the look on Tammy's face as her friends chose Andy over her. She always wondered why Tammy couldn't accept Andy for who he was. *What was all the hate about? Why?* Although Andy couldn't understand the reason, Candy did.

It wasn't until recently that the truth about Tammy's animosity towards Andy had unfolded. Candy sighed as she continued drifting off in her thoughts, going back in time.

22

GOOD-BYE ANDY: HELLO CANDY!
chapter 4

RING! RING! RING!

Shanna quickly dried the ends of her wet hair with a towel before she'd answered her phone, which rung continuously, as Shanna was taking a hot shower.

"Hello," she'd answered hastily.

"Shanna, I *need* you right now," Andy had stated, as he muffled his cries.

"What's wrong, Andy?" Shanna then asked curiously, as she'd sensed the tremble in her best friend's voice.

"My aunt, Joyce is putting me out the house," Andy had answered, "I can't *stand* her! ...My whole life, I *prayed* for my mama to come home from jail to *save* me from her and this *hell!*"

His aunt, Joyce, from the age of nine, had raised Andy up until this point—him being sixteen at that time. Even though Andy was her only sister's child, his aunt had intentionally put him out onto the streets. She'd had enough of her nephew's "prissy ways". His aunt, Joyce couldn't, nor wouldn't accept Andy for being soft.

Shanna then heard the rawness of his aunt, Joyce's voice in the background, while Andy sniffled as he'd cried.

"*FUCKIN' FAGGOT!*" his aunt, Joyce then yelled. "If you gonna live in *my* house, you live as a boy! You *dress* like a boy, you *act* like a boy! My sister *ain't* raise no *fuckin'* faggot!"

"I'm *not* a faggot," Andy had responded in a sassy manner. At this point, Andy was tired of being mistreated in life, he wasn't backing down anymore, and Andy had begun to rebel.

"Yes, you *are* a *fuckin'* faggot, and if you gonna continue to live your life like this, Andy, you gotta get the *fuck* outta here!" his aunt, Joyce then retorted, as his cousin, Lisa had come to his defense.

"No, mama, how you gonna put him out? He's our family," Lisa had begun to cry.

"He *ain't* any family of mine; acting like a sissy! Andy, why you think I never brought you to see your mama? Here it is, my sister doin' life in prison Upstate for murder, and her *fuckin'* son is a damn *faggot.*"

"I AM *NOT* A FAGGOT!" Andy screamed at the top of his lungs, as he'd held the phone receiver and packed his belongings simultaneously.

"Oh, yeah, then *what* are you? And what's this?" his aunt, Joyce then asked, as she'd held up his personal diary—which Andy had kept secured in a secret location in his room. The only person that had known where Andy hid his diary was his most trusted cousin, Lisa.

Andy then automatically assumed that it had been Lisa's fault as to why he was being ousted from the house. Never in a million years would Andy have ever imagined Lisa selling him out.

After reading portions of Andy's diary, his aunt, Joyce couldn't believe the things that he'd experienced at such a young age. She'd become so disgusted with Andy's admiration and thoughts of being a female, that his aunt couldn't finish reading his entries. As soon as Andy had walked through the front door, his aunt, Joyce demanded that he immediately pack his bags and leave.

"Well, Andy, what are you gonna do?" Shanna had asked concernedly.

"I don't know," Andy then whined, as he'd buried his head in his hand. "I don't know; please, God, help me."

"Fuck it, Andy, just pack *your* shit and come over to my house. You can stay with me."

"How are you going to make that decision? Shanna, you know you have to ask your mother first."

"Andy, my mama *loves* you as if you were her own. Ain't no way in the *world* she'd have you out on the streets."

"Thanks, Shanna, I love you."

"I love you, too. Now hurry your butt up before your aunt, Joyce get to actin' crazy."

"Hmmph, I'm sixteen-years-old now. There's *no* way I'm going to let her *fat* ass put her hands on me—I *wish* she would!" Andy had answered defiantly, as he wiped his tears. He then replaced them with a smile—Andy had known that he could count on Shanna. She had been his only true friend, since he now felt that Lisa had violated his trust. For now on, Shanna would be the only person to ever know Andy's business.

* * * * *

24

Within the first three weeks of living with Shanna, Andy instantly had become a part of her family. This was the family he'd always desired: a loving family who *totally* accepted him. Also, Andy had converted into the "sister" that Shanna always had dreamed of having. Now that it was four people that occupied the three-bedroom apartment in *Crown Heights, Brooklyn,* Shanna had shared her bedroom with Andy—her mother and her brother, Terry had their own.

Shanna's mother had given Andy the freedom that he always wanted and needed, and with that, Andy had begun becoming the "female" that he always desired. He'd started with wearing some of Shanna's clothes, as Andy also put perms in his hair, and had it styled like a female.

Andy always had naturally long and curly hair, so after having his hair processed, he'd flaunted his beautiful mane flamboyantly; Andy made girls with shorter coifs jealous. Also, Andy had begun to develop feminine features.

At age sixteen, Andy was on Estrogen. Addicted to the pills, he'd taken the hormone medication religiously. Often times, Andy also had gone through withdrawal if he hadn't been able to obtain the pills.

As the hormone medication had taken affect, Andy then developed ample-sized breasts, and a large, plump behind, but his true desire to become a woman had tore him down inside. Still being equipped with a large, flaccid ten-inch penis that Andy had seen every time he removed his clothing, left Andy devastated.

He'd hated the mere sight of his sex organs. Andy despised them so much, that he'd closed his eyes whenever he changed his outfits or taken a shower. In addition, the medication had heightened Andy's depression, bipolar mood swings often had made him glum; which caused Andy to exclude himself from the rest of the world.

At this point, Andy had found himself digging deep into the transgender community, as he sought pertinent information from publications such as *Out, Transgender Tapestry* and *Blade*— magazines being geared towards individuals with, or ones who considered having alternative lifestyles.

With *Out* being his favorite, Andy had often buried his head into the magazine, in which certain articles helped him work towards coming out of the closet. Those articles had given Andy the courage and strength to explore life as a female without fear and rejection.

Real life stories from others had helped Andy to deal with the hurt and disappointment, knowing that their family members had also disowned them for having an alternative lifestyle. This made Andy understand different point of views that related to his personal life—especially on how to deal with rejecting relatives like Aunt Joyce.

As Andy continued to read the many articles and case studies, he'd educated himself on sexuality, and had become knowledgeable about who he was; as well as what direction Andy was heading to—in regards to living his life as a female.

The articles also explained to Andy the reasons why he'd had various sporadic mood swings shortly after taking the hormone pills, in which Andy had become extremely dependent upon.

Although the Estrogen worked well, the time factor had become a stressful process—Andy needed the pills to work faster. He'd become so obsessed with becoming a woman, that Andy had become frustrated that his body hadn't taken on female traits instantly.

Andy had desired fast results: take the hormone pills, go to sleep and wake up a full-blown woman overnight. But the reality was that it had taken at six months for him to see real developments in body change.

Yet, the medication had eliminated Andy's erection, which was a relief. Although his penis and testicles was still attached, the suppression of Andy's erections temporarily comforted him for the time being. He'd wanted no parts of being a male—not in this life, nor the next.

In addition to learning about the medication, the side effects and its long-term goals, Andy had learned that, by taking the hormones along with applying cosmetic make-up to emulate a female, that he'd been categorized as a pre-op transsexual. Even though Andy desired being considered as a woman, he'd felt better being called a "transsexual", or referred to as a transgender, opposed to being referred to as a man; being called a "fag" or a "homo".

Andy's classification as a pre-op transsexual was due to him going through the sexual transition of becoming a woman, not having had the sex-change operation. He definitely wasn't a homosexual, in which Andy hadn't considered himself a male, nor had any desires to have man-to-man sex.

One year later...

    As Andy's hormone medication had taken full effect, it had become harder for him to see himself as a male. For that matter, Andy, back then, had been expelled from school for not answering to his given birth name. Being at the turning point in his life, Andy now had only acknowledged people whom addressed him as a female; he'd ignored everyone whom addressed him otherwise.

    While Shanna had gone to school, and as her mother was at work, Andy, due to the suspension from school, had been left in the house with Terry, Shanna's brother; who was four years older than her. Terry couldn't believe the transition Andy had gone through, as he'd drastically changed; right before Terry's eyes.

    In just one year, Andy had blossomed into a fully developed "woman", looking prettier than most females Terry had encountered. Andy had become so beautiful, that he could've modeled the runways for *Victoria's Secret*. Andy's facial features and physique were similar to model/actress, *Tyra Banks,* except that in Andy's case, *Tyra* was a natural woman.

    Yet, Andy's large, light-brown eyes, deep caramel complexion, perfectly rounded, 32-C breasts and hourglass figure, had given him the tools to walk into any room and turn heads in all directions.

    One early afternoon, Andy had been home lounging on the living room couch, wearing nothing but a red *La Perla* negligee on, as he read his *Out* magazine. Andy circled the numbers and addresses of the top plastic surgeons, as he'd sought out one that would best assist him with the transformation. Andy had deeply contemplated on having his sex changed.

    At this point, He'd had his named changed officially to "Candy" with the *Library of Congress*, and now felt that it was time to get rid of the attached penis and testicles, in which "she'd" detested. This was Candy's ultimate dream, for which she'd planned to soon make a reality.

As Candy searched through the magazine, what had stood out the most was the article on Dr, Helen Peters—the best plastic surgeon in *South Beach, Miami.* Her resume included that she'd performed over three thousand successful sex changes, and that the doctor was highly recommended within the transgender community.

While doing research, Candy then discovered that the surgery was very costly, and also required a six-month psychological evaluation course. The purpose for this assessment was to give consultation, and analyze those who'd contemplated having the sex-change operation.

The doctors needed to make sure that the patients really wanted the surgery, and to see if they'd been mentally ready for the transformation; they'd critically instilled the fact that once the permanent transition had been done, it was final.

The course had been intense and vital, due to the psychological effect of the operation being stressful. In previous cases, some had taken their own lives, committing suicide before completion of the course.

"Damn!" Candy blurted out, as she'd looked at the price of the surgery, yet continued circling the addresses and information. *Twenty-five thousand dollars is a lot of money.* "How the *hell* am I going to get that type of money?" Candy then whispered.

She'd wanted so badly to get the surgery immediately, but Candy had known that she couldn't get it—for the simple the fact that one must be eighteen-years-old of age, in order to obtain the sex-change operation. Candy had just turned seventeen, this alone caused tears to gush from her eyes—Candy had desperately wanted to be a female.

As Terry walked through the living room, on his way into the kitchen to get something to eat, he'd noticed that Candy was silently sobbing; tears had fallen from her eyes, as Candy sat Indian-style on the couch.

"What's wrong, you aiiight?" Terry had asked.

"Yeah, Terry, I'm cool," Candy had answered in her soft, feminine voice, sounding exactly like a woman, as she'd wiped her tears.

Terry couldn't believe what he'd heard and seen. Recently, Candy's chest was flat, but at that time, Terry noticed that she'd had full and perky breasts; with erect nipples that protruded through the silkiness of her negligee.

"Damn, Andy! How your chest get like that?" Terry then asked in amazement.

"Boy, shut up. You're so crazy," Candy responded as she'd smiled and blushed; happy that someone finally had noticed her blossoming bosom. "And stop calling me 'Andy'," Candy then insisted, as she'd got up from the couch and walked out of the room. Candy's breasts bounced as she'd switched her ass.

Instantly, everything Terry had known about Andy was quickly being forgotten, as he'd no longer saw a male, as Terry looked hard at Candy. Immediately, he'd realized how beautiful Candy was, as Terry's eyes slowly perused all over her body from head-to-toe.

Terry, being confused and mesmerized, had become intrigued with Candy's new body developments; curiosity had lead Terry into wanting to explore further.

He'd secretly followed behind Candy, as she entered the bedroom that she'd shared with Shanna. Terry now quietly stood in the doorway, as he'd watched Candy, who'd seductively sprawled across the bed on her side.

As Candy laid across the queen-sized bed, half of her butt cheeks had been exposed through the red lace panties that she'd worn under her negligee; negligee sliding to the side when Candy had repositioned her legs.

The sight of seeing this made Terry excited instantly; Terry had tried his hardest to maintain his composure. Curiosity peaked within Terry, his fascination with Candy was now revealed. He'd entered her bedroom to get a closer look.

"Well, since you don't want me to call you 'Andy' no more, then what's your new name?" Terry had asked curiously.

"Terry, you know my name. I'm sure Shanna has told you it."

"Nah, ain't nobody tell me nothin'. I been gone for a while and now that I'm back home from jail, the person I knew as 'Andy', no longer exist. Now, I don't know if it was the jail food they was feeding me, or either I'm hallucinating, but, Andy, you look better than most of the *bitches* I use to *fuck* wit'."

The biggest smile had come across Candy's face, as she'd girlishly giggled and batted her eyes. The words that Terry said were like music to Candy's ears. She'd longed for this moment to be considered feminine, a natural woman, ever since the first day Candy had taken hormones.

"Thanks for the compliment, Terry, but from now on, please don't call me 'Andy'. He doesn't exist. Call me 'Candy'."

"Candy?" Terry had responded excitedly. "Why you chose that name?"

"Isn't it *obvious* fool? Because I'm *sweet*-like-candy."

"How you know that? I *thought* you were a virgin," Terry then implied.

"I *am* a virgin, and how'd you know that?" Candy had asked inquisitively.

"C'mon, Andy, I mean, Candy. You and my sister are best friends, I hear you two talkin' at night sometimes. You always askin' her how it feels to have sex, and that you wished you had a boyfriend who could see past what you *really* are."

Candy then jumped off the bed in an attempt to get Terry out of the doorway of her bedroom, as she'd politely closed the door, now embarrassed by the truth of his words.

"Get out of my room, Terry. You shouldn't be eavesdropping on us," Candy had stated.

"Eavesdroppin'? How can I be eavesdroppin' when y'all talk so *fuckin'* loud? I can hear you two through the walls."

"Okay, Terry, can you please leave my room now?"

Again, Candy had attempted to move Terry aside and close the door, but he wouldn't get out of the doorway. Terry's eyes had been fixed on her jiggling breasts, as she'd gotten closer to him; Candy tried hard to get him out of the doorway.

"Excuse me, Terry, can you *please* move out the way?" Candy had pleaded low and softly, which turned Terry on even more.

Great curiosity mixed with sexual desire forced Terry to move in closer towards Candy, as he'd stood directly in front of her. Being face-to-face, Candy's wide, light-brown eyes pierced through the windows of Terry's soul, as he'd begun to be under a lustful spell—Candy's presence had caused him to become intensely erect.

For the first time, Terry had fully captured Candy's beauty, as he looked deep into her eyes; Terry now had seen Candy for who she was. Terry had come to the conclusion that regardless of who "Candy" use to be, it could never amount to what "she" had become. In Terry's eyes, Candy was a lovely young lady who longed for a masculine man's touch.

As Terry cupped Candy's face in his hands, he'd gently wiped her tears of fear and excitement, before Terry placed his full lips on her soft skin; he'd kissed her salty tears that flowed. The romance and passion had begun to make Candy fall in "love" with Terry.

"No, Terry, stop," Candy had pleaded, as she gently removed her face from his lips. "We can't do this," Candy then whispered.

"Why we can't?" Terry had responded emotionally. "This is between us. Just as long as you *don't* tell no one—we cool. Now, come here, give me a kiss." Terry then gently, but domineeringly, pulled Candy closer towards him; he'd softly planted a passionate kiss on her luscious lips.

Candy couldn't believe the desire she'd felt, as their tongues intertwined; Candy held Terry tightly and lovingly kissed him back. Although the hormone medication had caused Candy to no longer receive erections, her nipples had become highly sensitive, feeling intense sensations when Terry had gently tweaked them with his fingertips.

Candy had whimpered in excitement, as Terry caressed her breasts. He then placed his lips around her perky nipples before sucking on them hungrily. The moans that escaped Candy's mouth were more seductive than any woman that Terry had ever romanced.

Sudden impulse had caused Candy to drop down to her knees and perform oral sex for the very first time in her life. Shanna often had taught Candy her skills by practicing with bananas and ice pops, yet, Candy had learned other techniques by watching the infamous, *Super Head* perform oral sex on porn star, *Mr. Marcus,* observing the porno DVD, *Mr. Marcus' Neighborhood* on Shanna's TV screen.

Candy had completely pleased Terry like the young, female professional had serviced her male sex partner on the DVD; she'd eagerly devoured Terry's large penis in her mouth. After the extensive oral session had ended, Terry anxiously laid her down onto the bed, and proceeded to penetrate Candy inside of her rectum.

"Hold up, Terry," Candy had interrupted, as she quickly moved away.

"What? What's wrong?" Terry had questioned with a disturbed look upon his face.

"I don't know, Terry; I'm just scared," Candy then answered softly; her eyes had watered.

"Scared of what? Come on, you know you want it just as bad as I do."

"I do, but, what about AIDS, Terry? Have you ever thought about getting AIDS? I read stories everyday how people are exposed to AIDS because of unprotected sex."

"Well, shit, hold up!" Terry interjected, as he'd quickly dashed off into his bedroom, naked. He'd immediately returned: "Now what?" Terry then asked sarcastically as he smiled, holding up a *Magnum* ribbed, non-lubricated condom.

Yet, by Candy's facial expression, Terry had become concerned that something else was wrong. He then sat down on the bed beside her and rubbed Candy's shoulders to comfort her.

"Candy, what's wrong?"

"Terry, I never—"

Before Candy could finish her sentence, Terry had interrupted Candy by placing a soft, gentle kiss upon her lips.

"I know this is your first time, it's gonna be aiiight. I'ma take my time—I'll be easy, baby."

With that being said, along with the affectionate touch of Terry's big, strong hands on her breasts, and with him licking on her sensitive erect nipples, Candy had easily given in, as she'd seductively turned over on her stomach and exposed her large, plump ass.

Terry then quickly ripped the condom wrapper open with his front teeth before forcefully rolling it over his eleven-inch dick; followed by lubricating himself with a thick glob of *Vaseline*. Terry had held on to Candy's hands after he slowly entered inside of her. He'd gone as deep as he could through Candy's rectum, lying on top of her, as Terry slowly gyrated in circles.

Trying to soothe Candy as she'd screamed loudly, not being used to the pressure and thickness of Terry's huge penis that anxiously throbbed inside of her, he'd gently kissed the back of Candy's elongated neck. Her body had become extremely tense, especially when Terry first had inserted the wide head of his meat inside her virgin anus.

After he'd become overly excited from whining on top of Candy's behind, as Terry deeply rotated inside of her, he'd increased the speed of his motion—Terry pulsated his penis inside of Candy's tight tunnel, as she'd moaned and screamed; being in pain and bliss altogether.

Sexual stimulation had caused Terry to unintentionally force himself through Candy's rectum, as he'd ripped and tore the lining of her walls. Nothing in the world could've fully described the excruciating pain that Candy had felt.

But with time, Candy would grow accustomed to it, as the soreness would eventually become pleasurable to her. She'd hoped that the feeling would be even more gratifying inside of the "vagina" Candy longed to have, as she'd desperately wanted her sex-change operation; waiting patiently for that day to come.

YOU CAN BE MY CANDYMAN
chapter 6

Candy was smiling uncontrollably, thinking about the first time she had sex. Terry was her first love, and Candy felt that he was the only person that ever understood her. Back then, Terry, in all ways, was her life and soul mate.

Tears instantly rolled down Candy's flawless cheeks, as she thought about him, the things they went through, and how her relationship with Terry caused a lot of heartache and pain.

"Wipe your tears, sweetheart. Everything's gonna be alright; it ain't so bad," the marshal said, while passing the holding cell as he walked; seeing tears fall from Candy's face.

He still was baffled by her beauty, even with working in the courthouse for the past twenty years; seeing all kinds of people from all walks of life. Yet, he still couldn't fathom Candy being born a male. No matter how much the marshal knew the truth—he still couldn't believe his eyes.

"Hey, tell me somethin'," the marshal said, having light conversation with Candy.

"Yes," Candy answered, as she wiped her tears.

"How could a person as *pretty* as you, be what you are?" he asked. "I mean, hey, you're prettier than most women I know."

"I *AM* A WOMAN!" Candy snapped angrily. She became upset and self-conscious by the fact that, regardless of how beautiful she was, and with having her name legally changed, Candy still was considered a man within the system; now apparently also to those who worked for the system.

The marshal burst into laughter at Candy's comment: "Ha, ha, yeah, right. You're a woman, huh? I guess you were just born with the wrong organ, right?"

"FUCK YOU!" Candy spat in anger.

"I would take that as an invitation if I didn't know any better," he replied while walking away, as laughter filled the room.

Motherfuckers always have something smart and sarcastic to say. I bet if he didn't know I was born with this fucking thing between my legs, he'd be trying to fuck me, Candy thought. *Damn, why the fuck these bastards had to get in my business. I was almost at the finish line.*

Overwhelmed by emotions, due to thoughts of a troubled past, and now, her recent misfortune of incarceration, Candy became livid and puzzled simultaneously; upset and confused as to why her life had taken a turn for the worst—being behind bars.

She then looked around at the bars of the holding cell, wondering if animals felt the same way she did at this moment: caged in, trapped, unable to get away. Candy then realized why wildlife attacked their prey every chance they had.

The more Candy thought about her life, how she'd been mistreated in the past, as well as now being held in a cell against her will, Candy's heart now hardened and became cold—cold as ice. No longer had she felt a need to be a compassionate person.

Soon after, Candy arose from the bench, readjusted her tailored pantsuit, and began pacing the holding cell; walking up-and-down as if she was modeling the catwalk of a runway fashion show. While doing so, Candy's mind raced back to her life, thinking of a time when it wasn't full of turmoil. She did have some great times, especially when Candy had spent time with her boyfriend, Terry.

* * * * *

Over the next six months, Candy and Terry had become secret lovers. Their bond was much like any other romantic relationship, as they loved, respected and trusted one another. Entrusting each other so much, that Candy and Terry had stopped using condoms.

Terry now had thought of Candy as a natural woman. Yet and still, he wanted a *complete* woman, in which the two had set out to make that dream come true.

Again while Shanna was in school and her mother had gone to work, Candy and Terry's love affair swiftly escalated. After a long, steamy session of sensuous sex, the two laid together in Candy's bed, as her fingers traveled slowly around Terry's protruding, muscular chest. They'd talked and planned out their future.

"Terry, I love you. You're the *only* person in this world that makes my life complete."

"Same goes for me, too, Candy. I wouldn't give a *fuck* what nobody says."

"Oh, yes you do. If you didn't care, then why is it that we're doing *everything* so discreetly? It's been six months now, and we've never even went to the movies together. What, are you *ashamed* of me? I don't look like I can pass for a woman?"

"Nah, Candy, it's not that. You already know you look better than all of your female friends."

"Terry, you know that I only have but one friend—Shanna, your sister. But to be honest, she's been acting real funny lately."

"Funny how?"

"I don't know exactly, but Shanna's been dating this older dude; I think she said he's a detective. For some reason, she's never brought him home to introduce him to me, in which Shanna *always* introduced me to her boyfriends. I mean, I've never even seen a picture of the guy."

"Damn, Shanna actin' like that? What would make her act that way with you?"

"I don't know. Maybe she's afraid of her boyfriend becoming attracted to me—like the last guy she was dating."

"Did you tell her?"

"Of course. I told her that the guy had flirted with me."

"And what did she say?"

"Shanna said that I was lonely and crazy. That I needed to stop trying to destroy peoples lives by tricking them into thinking I'm a female," Candy had answered back sadly.

Terry sensed the hurt in Candy's voice, as she'd come to the reality that her own best friend, Shanna, hadn't fully accepted her as a female. Terry then held Candy closer to him, and had planted a kiss on her forehead.

"Don't trip, baby, you *are* a woman—*my* woman," Terry indicated as he'd consoled her.

"Thank you," Candy said, as she'd snuggled under him and held Terry tighter.

"So, how much that operation cost?"

"Too much, Terry. Why you ask?"

"'Cause, maybe together, we can raise the money for you to get it."

Candy had risen from the bed, looked into Terry's eyes for assurance and said, "You really mean that, baby?"

"Candy, I'll do *whatever* it takes for you to have that operation."

"I love you so much," Candy then stated, as she'd held Terry close; tears flowed from Candy's eyes.

"C'mon wit' all that cryin', Candy. Now, are you gonna tell me how much it cost or what?"

"Twenty-five thousand."

"Well, that's twenty more thousand we have to go, 'cause I already got five," Terry had indicated with a big smile upon his face. "Now, how do we go about this?"

"Well, first of all, for the last two years, I've been following up on the best surgeon. Her name is Helen N. Peters; she's always featured in *Transgender Tapestry*, which is a very informative publication for those of my category. Anyway, her office is in *South Beach, Florida*, right on the strip—*Ocean Drive*. All I need is a Tracheal Shave and G.R.S."

"What the *fuck* is that?" Terry had asked, unaware of the terms Candy was using.

"You're so silly, Terry," Candy then laughed, before she'd explained to him what the terms meant. "Well, baby, a Tracheal Shave is the surgical term for an Adams Apple reduction. I really need that—it only costs eight-hundred and fifty dollars."

"No, you don't. You don't have a big Adams Apple," Terry interjected, as he'd rubbed his fingers against the small lump in Candy's throat.

"I know, baby. It's not that big, but *it's* there—I want to be a *complete* woman. It's not *supposed* to be there, Terry. I was born with the wrong organs, and they *have* to go. There are only two things that have to be removed—the Adams Apple, and you know what else.

"Terry, why do you think that every time I go outside, I wrap my neck with a scarf or find some way to distract a person from looking at my throat?"

Terry sensed her sincerity, as he'd observed that Candy had become depressed; by the weary look in her eyes. He'd seen a "woman" who was desperate to make "her" life complete. Candy wouldn't be totally happy, unless she'd made the necessary changes.

"Okay, Candy, I understand," Terry reassured before he'd kissed her lips. "Now, what does the G.R.S. stand for?"

"Gender Reassignment Surgery, and you *know* how bad we *need* to get that done."

"Candy, it looks like we gotta find a hustle and head on out to Florida. Now, how long is this operation gonna take?"

"Terry, that's the hard part. It's a one-year process."

"WHAT? A whole year?"

"Yeah, baby. First of all, you have to be eighteen or older, in order to have the surgery done. Before that's even considered, you go through a six-month psychological evaluation."

"Damn, you gotta go through *all* that stuff?"

"Yeah, baby, I have to—I mean, *we* have to go to psychotherapy class, support groups, individual group sessions for gender issues and, physical trauma counseling. We have to do *all* of that together, in order to continue to make our relationship work."

"Shit, Candy, I don't *need* no counseling for that."

Candy had looked into her lover's eyes with adoration, ecstatic to see that Terry had supported her in making her dream come true.

"I know, Terry, but those are the professional requirements of post-operative surgery. A year will go pass quickly, plus, we need time to figure out how we're going to make enough money for everything. We *can't* just get up and leave together. If Shanna and your mother find out about us, they'll go crazy. They would *never* accept us being together."

"I know. That would break my mama's heart. Shanna also would *hate* you."

"I can't even picture my best friend hating me for being in love," Candy had answered back miserably.

"Yeah, but look *who* you're in love with. I'm her older brother," Terry had replied.

"Yes, I know. But we'll work something out," Candy confirmed confidently, as she'd eased off of Terry's chest. Candy then kissed him softly and proceeded down to his crotch. She'd begun to give Terry the oral pleasure that he'd loved, as *98.7 KISS FM* played *Secret Lovers* by Atlantic Starr; which blasted through Shanna's speakers.

Shanna couldn't make out the strange noises that had come from her bedroom, as she entered the apartment; Shanna had cut school, and opted to have a nice, romantic lunch with her new boyfriend—an FBI agent.

As she'd walked through the apartment, the loud music that blasted from her room had increased Shanna's curiosity of what was going on. Shanna had known that Candy would be home, and that Terry was suppose to be out job hunting. Terry had to find a legitimate job, in order to dispel his probation officer's suspicion of him selling drugs on *Nostrand Avenue;* he'd caught Terry on an active, drug-infested block one day while doing a random visit to Terry's apartment.

As Candy's moans had become louder, Shanna smiled to herself, as she'd thought about Candy having sex for the very first time. She then also wondered what type of guy would have sex with Candy, having known she'd been born a male. *Maybe Candy never told him she was really a man and was just suckin' his dick.*

"Nah, can't be, she moanin' too loud. This *bitch* is gettin' *fucked,*" Shanna whispered, as she'd lightly tiptoed to the cracked bedroom door. Shanna almost fainted at what she'd witnessed; Shanna had shaken her head quickly to make sure that she hadn't been dreaming.

As Candy then continued to loudly moan while getting penetrated, Shanna would never forget the sight of the man who powerfully pumped in-and-out of Candy, as Candy's tiny feet were tightly wrapped around his neck.

Being totally engrossed in their lovemaking, neither Candy nor Terry hadn't heard Shanna come inside of the apartment—until it was too late. There was *no* way that the two could ever explain otherwise—Shanna had seen it all!

"*BITCH!* WHAT THE *FUCK* Y'ALL DOIN'?" Shanna screeched, as she'd then pounded all over on Candy's body; Shanna had beaten her as if Candy had been a true enemy. "I'MA *KILL* YOU, YOU *NASTY*-ASS *BITCH!* YOU FAGGOT! YOU

TRICKED MY BROTHER INTO *FUCKIN'* YOUR FAGGOT-ASS! YOU TRIFLIN' *MOTHERFUCKER,* GET OUTTA MY HOUSE, NOW! I'MA TELL MAMA!"

"Hold up, Shanna! No, let me explain!" Candy had pleaded.

"EXPLAIN? WHAT THE *FUCK* YOU GOTTA EXPLAIN? GET YOUR *NASTY,* FREAK-FAGGOT-ASS OUTTA MY HOUSE BEFORE I *KILL* YOU!" Shanna had spat. She'd become so disgusted with Candy, that Shanna couldn't even address her own brother; her eyes had been filled with hatred.

As Shanna then looked at Candy with contempt, she'd felt pain. Everything the two had built together during their childhood, at that point, was thrown away from the heinous act that Shanna witnessed. She'd felt that Candy violated their wonderful friendship, just to satisfy a selfish desire.

"I swear to God, I don't give a *fuck* where you go, who you live with, or what you do. But, you no longer exist in my life at all. And Terry," Shanna then looked in his direction, as he'd quickly struggled putting his clothes on. "I don't know how mama gonna take it when I tell her she got a *faggot* for a son," Shanna had retorted, as tears streamed from her eyes.

Terry had known from that moment on that he'd never be able to step foot in his mother's house again. He wouldn't know how to face her, yet, Terry still was madly in love with Candy; he couldn't change that. Even though Terry's life would be filled with the pain of disappointing his family, he'd been ready for that sacrifice.

"Man, yo, *fuck* that shit! Candy, *pack* your shit, now! We goin' to Florida!" Terry instructed, as he'd known that there was no turning back at this point.

"WHAT? FLORIDA?" Shanna had retorted. "You ain't goin' *nowhere* together. Terry, this is a *fuckin'* man, a *fuckin'* faggot! You can't live your life with a *fag!* How could you explain that to your loved ones? C'mon, Terry, you *can't* do this to your family," Shanna then pleaded.

"Shanna, we're in love," Candy had whined. "I *thought* you were my friend. I'd *never* imagine you'd say or think that way about me. Our whole life, you treated me as a girl, but when I—"

Instantly, Shanna had cut Candy off, "Yeah, *bitch,* until I came in here and caught my own *goddamn* brother, *fuckin'* you in the ass! *Fuck* you, Candy, you *ain't* no woman—you're a *faggot! Faggots* catch AIDS and die!"

The harsh words had sliced into Candy's ears, and then pierced through her heart, as she'd hysterically cried in pain. All of her life, Candy had loved Shanna and trusted her with everything. She'd cared for Shanna more than Candy cared for her own relatives.

To date, this had been the second time in Candy's life that she'd witnessed someone crossing her. First, it was Lisa, and at that time, Shanna.

Before Candy and Terry quickly had headed out of the apartment, Shanna had attempted to stop them one last time.

"Terry, *please* don't do this! You gonna *crush* mama's heart! Terry, just stay home and I won't tell her!"

"What about Candy?" Terry had asked suspiciously.

"Candy? I don't *know* anybody by that name. Candy doesn't exist to me...anymore."

"Then-I'm-gone," Terry answered, as he'd walked out the front door with Candy.

"CANDY, I SWEAR TO GOD ON MY LIFE I'MA GET YOUR ASS! ONE DAY, *BITCH,* TRUST ME, I'MA *GET* YOUR ASS! I HOPE THE BOTH OF YOU *FAGGOT*-ASS *BITCHES* DIE OF AIDS!"

"Candy, are you certain that this is what you want?"

"I'm *more* than certain," Candy answered confidently, as she'd looked directly into the eyes of Dr. Helen N. Peters. This was Candy's fourth psychological evaluation for a sex-change operation, having had three intense sessions since she and Terry first moved to *South Beach, Florida,* over a month ago.

Today, Candy had come to her session alone. Usually Terry would come along with her, but, after the first three sessions, Terry was convinced that he could spend the rest of his life with a transsexual—such as Candy.

Terry's only problem was back home in *Brooklyn.* He constantly thought about how he'd let his mother down, as well as disappointing and hurting his sister, Shanna; all by falling in love with Candy. Terry couldn't stand the fact that he'd devastated his mother for leaving home to be with Candy; Terry had automatically assumed that she'd disowned him as her son.

The stress alone sent Terry into a depressive rage. Most times, he'd found refuge in the nightlife, frequenting the party scene in *South Beach.* Terry and Candy loved the clubs on *Ocean Drive,* where the two had partied hard; they'd visited every nightclub on the strip from 1st to 16th Street.

There was always an exciting, celebrity-filled party happening; some had gone on for twenty-four hours. Terry also enjoyed the clubs on *Washington Avenue,* but the one he'd favored the most was *Club Bed,* filled with comfortable beds throughout the club; theme of the club being "anything goes".

"Okay, now, Candy, this is one of the most important questions I'm about to ask you," Dr. Peters had stated. Her question to Candy hadn't required a verbal answer, as Dr. Peters was more concerned with her body language. By the way Candy had reacted to the question, would've immediately alerted Dr. Peters on how Candy determined her own physical nature and mental connection to having male sex organs.

"So what's your question, Dr. Peters?" Candy had asked, eager to give her answer and end their session. She'd become frustrated with the extensive line of questioning, in which Candy had wanted to get the sessions over with. She'd wanted badly to be on an operating table having the surgery done.

Candy was totally convinced with her decision to have the sex-change operation, yet she'd tolerated the doctor's questions; Candy cooperated with Dr. Peters each time.

Dr. Peters' instincts had indicated that Candy was sure of becoming a woman, yet she had to do her job as a doctor and follow protocol. Dr. Peters had spent long hours with Candy, having her patient discuss her life: past, present and future.

Yet, Candy had realized that the interrogation was just a small sacrifice she had to make before taking a huge step—before Candy had completely transformed herself into a female.

"Candy, look at me face-to-face," Dr. Peters then mildly instructed, as Candy instantly looked her doctor dead in her eyes. "What if the sex-change operation went wrong, how would that affect you?" The doctor asked calmly, as she'd studied Candy's eyes; Dr. Peters had checked to see if Candy would divert her attention to her crotch area and become emotional.

In most cases when patients are asked the question pertaining to having botched operations, usually they stare at their sex organs, showing that they're still physically and emotionally attached to them. Yet, in Candy's case, she'd showed no signs of emotion, or ever looked down between her legs. Candy was totally unfazed, and unaffected.

Candy could care less if her surgery had gone bad or not, as she hadn't considered the penis and testicles a part of "her" body. Regardless of the outcome, Candy hadn't wanted the sex organs.

"Dr. Peters, to be totally honest with you, I wouldn't even care if it went bad. I'd give my *life* to have them removed," Candy had confirmed with conviction, as she'd stared into her doctor's eyes. From the verbal answer given, and the body language that was displayed, Dr. Peters now had been convinced that Candy no longer needed therapy, yet Candy was required to undergo the rest of her session.

Also, Candy hadn't become eighteen yet, but in the next five months, she'd be of age, and would be scheduled to lie on Dr. Peters' surgical table to have the sex organs removed.

"Candy, I'm going to schedule you for your Tracheal Shave first. In the following month, after your throat properly heals, I'm going to conduct your G.R.S.—so are you excited or what?" Dr. Peters asked as she'd grinned.

"OH MY GOD, YES! YES-YES-YES!" Candy shouted, as she'd jumped up-and-down hysterically. "Thank you so much, Dr. Peters," Candy then said before she grabbed the surgeon; Candy had hugged Dr. Peters as if she'd known her all of her life. "You're the *best* doctor in the entire world!"

Dr. Peters then chuckled, "No, I may not be the best doctor in the world, but one thing's for sure, I'm the best damn surgeon in *South Beach, Miami.* Some of the high-fashion models you see walking the runway shows are my former patients."

Candy's eyes had lit up at her doctor's comment.

"Dr. Peters, you're kidding me, right?" Candy had asked curiously, now intrigued as to who were her doctor's clients.

"Not at all, darling. It's all true, and if they didn't sign this confidentiality form, in which I'm about to give you, I would be able to tell you who were my patients in the modeling world." With that being said, Dr. Peters then pushed the confidential form in Candy's face and held up an ink pen. "I think you should sign this immediately. Who knows, one day I may see you on TV," Dr. Peters replied slyly.

Candy had taken the pen, read the confidentiality form and signed it. She'd liked her relationship with Dr. Peters. Their rapport often reminded her of the actors who'd played on her new, favorite television show, *Nip Tuck*, which also was featured in *South Beach.*

But this hadn't been a television series, this was real life, and Dr. Peters was considered the best in her profession. It was then when Candy had fully understood as to why the alternative lifestyle magazines featured the hard-working surgeon.

Five months later…

"What's the matter?" Candy asked Terry, as she'd pranced around like a princess inside the penthouse suite of *Casa Casuarina*—the newly-converted, five-star hotel that had cost them two-thousand dollars a night; formerly being the prestigious and lavish mansion of the late *Gianni Versace.*

This was one of *South Beach's* most valuable and sentimental assets on *Ocean Drive.* Mostly because the building had attracted the attention of many, immediately after the death of the slain fashion designer; killed on the front steps of his extravagant mansion.

Terry, who'd sat on the king-sized bed, lifted his spinning head slowly before he'd looked at Candy's face.

"You've been *fucking* with that shit again. See, Terry, you need to lay off those drugs. That stuff isn't any good for you. Look at you, Terry, you look like a hot mess; even your skin has broken out. Haven't you ever heard of the saying: never get high on your own supply?" Candy stated, as she'd referred to the heavy amounts of Ecstasy and Oxycontin that Terry had recently taken; these were his new drugs of choice.

Shortly after Terry and Candy moved to South Beach, they'd seemed to have become more in conflict with each other. Candy never had sensed that Terry had a problem, but he had become miserable; Terry had abused pills to escape his depression.

Wondering about how his mother viewed him had kept Terry in a slump. Thoughts of her disowning him had lowered his self-esteem; Terry now felt as if he'd been raped of his dignity, robbed of his manhood—all by falling in love with a beautiful transsexual.

Within the first five months of living in Florida, it had seemed as though money was constantly flowing through like a river. After getting settled in, the underground connections in the transgender world had become more available to Candy, as she reaped the benefits of all the scams she'd executed; Candy had become apart of a risky and scandalous subculture.

She'd met many trifling transsexuals that had all kinds of money-making schemes. Candy's favorite was doing credit card scams. Candy used fake ID within twenty-four hour intervals; she'd obtained credit cards by applying for them with others personal information.

Candy then used the cards to shop for expensive jewelry, in which she had Terry sell the goods on the street. This had been their part-time hustle, aside from Terry selling large quantities of Ecstasy and Oxycontin, in which he'd planned to finance Candy's operation with the profits.

Terry felt that the credit card scheme was cool, but he'd also known that Candy couldn't use the same card past the twenty-four hour limit. Extending past that time frame would've put Candy at risk from being caught by the authorities.

Yet, due to Terry's new drug habit, wild partying and outrageous spending pattern, money had dwindled quickly. Terry, at this point, had used the money he'd saved towards Candy's surgery to buy more drugs, but for his personal use. Candy was scheduled for surgery the next month, as she'd counted down the days in excitement—Terry counted down by getting high.

"Look at you, Terry—look at yourself. You *need* to stop getting high," Candy had suggested, upset to see Terry in the altered state that he'd been in.

"BITCH, WHY THE *FUCK* YOU KEEP NAGGIN' AT ME FOR?" Terry then yelled, angry that Candy had ruined his high. The mood-altering Ecstasy had heightened his anger, in which Terry's depression had manifested into rage. Now that Candy had unintentionally instigated his temper, the "E" pills had taken full effect. At this point, it had sent Terry over the brink.

Terry then picked himself up from the bed, balled up his fist, and had proceeded to beat Candy down; this was Terry's first time displaying violence towards her. He'd never acted in this manner, yet, Terry's mind being in a drug-induced state hadn't made the situation any better. His true feelings at that moment had been exposed and enhanced by the Ecstasy.

"*Bitch,* you ain't *nothin'* but a curse! You the *fuckin'* devil in disguise—you alien-ass *bitch!* I lost my family 'cause of you. I lost my morals and principles 'cause of you. Most of all, *bitch,* I lost my dignity and manhood."

As Candy had looked into Terry's eyes, shocked and amazed, she couldn't believe the awful things that he'd said. The more Terry verbally abused Candy, the less of a person she'd felt; Terry had affected her self-esteem. It was then when Candy had thought that no one would ever understand her true nature, except those who were just like her.

Regardless of how much people had said that they'd loved Candy, in due time, they all shown otherwise. Starting from Aunt Joyce, her cousins, Lisa and Tammy, Candy's best friend, Shanna and now, the only person that she'd thought who really loved Candy for who she was, had torn Candy's heart apart, ripped her pride, and stomped on Candy's identity.

"Terry, if that's the way you *really* feel about me, then you can go back to *New York* or do whatever. If it ever came down to someone asking about our relationship, don't worry, I'll deny it; since all of a sudden, you're *ashamed* of who I am," Candy retorted, as she'd tried desperately to fight back the stream of tears that had flowed down her right cheek.

It then appeared as though fire had burned in his eyes, as Terry had furiously walked over to Candy, grabbed her by the throat with his left hand and strongly pinned her to the wall. With his right fist cocked back, Terry then pounded a forceful right-hand punch that had flown pass Candy's head and entered into the wall. He'd punched it with so much force, that Terry had to pry his broken hand out of the hole.

"*Bitch,* you can't *possibly* understand or know what the *fuck* you did to me," Terry retorted, as he'd pushed her to the floor, and grabbed the keys to the new *Ferrari 360 Modena* sports car, one that Candy had rented from *Dream Exotic Rentals;* at the expense of one of her unknown victims. Terry then dashed out the door.

"Whatever was done, Terry, you've done it to yourself," Candy had replied before the door closed. Moments later, she'd wiped her tears and watched from the hotel room window, the love of her life jump into the yellow *Ferrari,* in which Terry had sped off like a crazed maniac.

Soon after, Candy had lounged on the soft Italian leather recliner from *Maurice Villency,* and retrieved her favorite magazine from her brand-new, acid-green leather *Balenciaga* handbag, the same publication Candy had read whenever she needed understanding of the cruel world that she lived in: *Out.* The magazine had been informative and comforting to Candy, it's where she'd escaped—finding a "world in which she'd called her home: a world of complete acceptance.

Candy then grinned with intriguing curiosity, as she'd grabbed the new issue and discovered that the person on the cover was former wrestling superstar/actor, *The Rock.* He'd been featured within the magazine, highlighting the actor's controversial role as a homosexual in the comedy film, *Be Cool.* The only thing that had been on Candy's mind at that time was: *is The Rock gay?* She'd then come to her senses immediately. Candy had realized that he'd probably agreed to pose for the cover and do the article to fully capitalize on gaining or increasing a gay fan base. She'd then flipped through the pages and eagerly tried to find the article on the handsome superstar.

*   *   *   *   *

While Candy was back at the swanky hotel being sucked into her own world, Terry had been dangerously speeding on the freeway, thinking of *Brooklyn.* His anger and depression had now combined; Terry had become overwhelmed with severe emotion.

He then popped another Oxycontin and "E" pill with his throbbing, broken hand, and had chased the drugs down with a fresh bottle of orange juice mixed with *Seagram's* gin.

As Terry recklessly had driven the speeding sports car, loud lyrics of he and Candy's favorite *Luther Vandross* duet with *Cheryl Lynn, "If This World Were Mine",* had sunken deep into his ears. The song had sent Terry into a galaxy of Milky Ways. The freeway had no longer become visible, and the lights weren't needed, as his intended destination of the night had turned into outer space, and the fire-yellow *Ferrari 360 Modena* automobile, now had transformed into a spaceship; due to the mixture of gin, Oxycontin and Ecstasy pills.

Terry's foot had mashed down on the gas at the breakdown point of the song, until there wasn't any more space between the pedal and the floor. He'd closed his eyes as the music had begun—Terry then had planned to set his soul at ease.

The last thing known to him was the words of *Luther Vandross and Cheryl Lynn: "THE WORLD WOULD BE YOURS, YOURS, YOURS, YOURS—Y-O-U-R-S!"* Terry was so much into a daze that he hadn't felt the Ferrari burst through the guard rail that sent the car over the top of the freeway. Terry then landed on the next passageway before he'd flipped over a total of ten times.

Terry had died instantly, before the sports car became a giant ball of flames.

*　*　*　*　*

As Candy had patiently waited for Terry to cool down and return back to the hotel, she'd told herself that no matter how depressed he'd been—that Candy would always love Terry, and do *whatever* to make him understand her.

Candy couldn't wait to have her surgery done. The following month, she'd planned to attend the *RAGS-TO-RICHES* weekend event: the biggest transgender convention ever—which had been held in *Chicago*.

The highlight of the annual affair was the *RAGS-TO-RICHES* ball, which was like merging the *Miss America Pageant* and *American Idol* contest into one huge, spectacular gala for the transgender community; hosted by the famous female impersonator, *Harmonica Sunbeam*.

This would be Candy's first time participating in the *RAGS-TO-RICHES* weekend, now being held during *Black Gay Pride*. She'd prepared for this occasion two months ago, shopping at the many exclusive boutiques at the *Bal Harbour Mall*.

Candy had been able to do so by going to *Twist,* one of her favorite gay clubs, where she'd acquired a new, fake ID card; to go along with the new *Platinum Visa* Candy had gotten from Laquetta, her new transgender friend.

Candy had planned for her trip to *Chicago* to be one of the best weekends of her life. She'd wished so badly that she could've had her operation beforehand, but it had been scheduled exactly one week after the event. Dr. Peters was planned to be there, also—delivering a speech, in addition to accepting an award from *Out* magazine.

Damn, Terry, come back to me, baby; I love you, Candy had thought, as she'd constantly peeped out of the plush, velvet window curtains, and looked into the night. Candy had hoped that Terry would soon pull up in the yellow *Ferrari.* She'd then figured that he'd needed more time to himself to think things out.

Candy had somewhat felt Terry's pain—she understood his point. But Candy had also known that Terry would come to his senses, and face the reality that what they'd had was real love— which hadn't any boundaries. She'd then hissed, as Candy walked away from the huge sliding window, turned on the TV and sat down patiently—as she'd waited for her "world" to return.

* * * * *

Thirty minutes later…

Flames had constantly burned through the car, which instantly turned everything into crisp debris; all but the frame of the car and Terry's teeth had become ashes. It would take almost a week before investigators would be able to identify Terry's remains.

But it only had taken seconds for Candy, as she'd watched *B.E.T. News*, discovering the fire-yellow *Ferrari,* and that the driver of the car was Terry.

Tears then rolled down Candy's face like waterfalls as she'd looked on, as the fire marshals diligently had tried to put out the flames. Candy then had fallen to her knees in great pain, devastated by what was displayed across the wide, high-definition plasma screen TV.

Once again, Candy felt that life had treated her horribly. Back then, Candy's world had crashed down hard on her shoulders.

ARRESTED DEVELOPMENT
chapter 10

CLINK! CLINK! CLINK!

The clanging sound of shackles being sorted out for the incoming inmates startled Candy, taking her out of her trance, as she was reminiscing on her past.

"Is it time to go?" Candy asked politely, who was desperately trying to get back to *Cumberland's Federal Correctional Institute,* wanting to jump back into the swing of things, and take care of her of business.

For one, Candy needed to call her friend, Dewayne. She also needed a favor from her rapper friend, who, all of a sudden, acted as if he'd forgotten about her.

"Well, yes and no. Right now the wagon is downstairs, but we're waiting on five more inmates after the court session is over with," the marshal answered.

"How much *longer* will that be?" Candy inquired impatiently, showing a sign of anxiousness. The marshal lightly laughed and looked at his watch.

"Why? You got somewhere to be?"

"FUCK YOU!" Candy replied nastily before she coughed uncontrollably; irritated by the dry, scratchy cough, and became angry with the marshal for being sarcastic.

"You see, now there you go again with the sexual advances. You keep it up, I just *might* have to charge you for solicitation," the marshal said, as he burst into laughter, and walked off to get the other inmates.

"Crazy-ass motherfucker," Candy said to herself while sticking her middle finger at him. The marshal's comments were beginning to annoy her. At that moment, Candy closed her eyes and thought back to her friend, Shanna; thinking of the last time she'd seen her—a year-and-a-half ago.

NOTHING'S SWEETER THAN CANDY
chapter 11

Although it only had been three weeks since the tragic death of Terry, and that Candy was forbidden to attend her own lover's funeral, due to Terry's family not accepting Candy at the service, somehow she'd still found the strength to enjoy one of the greatest moments of her life.

It seemed as if a festive transgender party had occurred right inside the lobby area of the *Holiday Inn Hotel* at *O'Hare International Convention Center* in *Chicago*, when Candy checked in. The room had been filled with a slew of exotic transsexuals, ones who'd traveled from different states to participate in the *RAGS-TO-RICHES* convention.

The reception area was alive with out-of-towners who'd networked with each other. Many caught up with friends that hadn't seen each other in a while, as they'd taken pictures while gossiping; others simply told jokes and shared pleasantries.

Candy was thrilled to see other beautiful transsexuals, and had been enthralled with the enchantment of the atmosphere—this being the first time Candy had partaken in the fun-filled extravaganza.

During the three-day weekend, Candy had planned to attend several barbecues, pool parties and the transgender expo, where she would meet and talk with other passable transsexuals, such as herself. There, Candy would have the opportunity to consult with others whom already had successful operations, and bond with many pre-ops who'd been in the same position as her.

Candy had looked forward to attending the seminars at the expo, hearing different discussions from the best surgeons within the United States—Dr. Helen N. Peters had been booked as the keynote speaker.

The *RAGS-TO-RICHES* ball was the last of the entertainment planned by the organizers, in which the event had included a runway show that attracted top designers and models from the fashion industry. Various magazine journalists had been scheduled to cover the event, and fashion editors planned to review the runway show; they'd hoped to gain inspiration for their upcoming fashion magazine layouts.

But for Candy, the *RAGS-TO-RICHES* weekend was the kick-off to her pre-celebratory party she'd planned to have after the ball. Candy intended to rejoice her upcoming operation that had been scheduled for the following week, which would ultimately place Candy into "womanhood".

Having coordinated a fantasy-filled fiesta, Candy had rented the exclusive, posh ballroom on the top floor of the hotel, thanks to her new transgender friend, Yolanda, who'd granted Candy with a "Black" card from *American Express*; their most prestigious credit card. Candy even had coded key cards to the elevator for her guests, which had given them access to the express elevator that led directly to the ballroom.

Candy placed several key cards inside the envelopes of the party invitations she'd given out over the weekend. Although many had viewed the young transsexual's affair as an after-party for the *RAGS-TO-RICHES* extravaganza, Candy had intended it to be her pre-celebration of going through the "rites of passage" of becoming a female.

At the ball, Candy grinned wickedly as she'd begun to watch the fashion show. Candy intensely observed *Paris Gotti* open the show as the first runway model; she'd sensuously strutted down the extensive catwalk in a black lace, hand-beaded gown from *Valentino*—his spring 2005 couture collection.

The music that blared from the speakers had immediately made Candy smile widely, as the DJ played *Candy* by *Cameo*. Seated audience members at their tables had nodded their heads and moved to the rhythm of the beat.

The tune was an instant crowd pleaser, yet it had been Candy's ultimate theme song that night, as she'd sashayed around the venue, and passed out the last of her invitations for the after-party from her brand-new, shimmering *Swarovski* crystal clutch.

"Oh, wow, hey, Candy!" Dr. Peters greeted, as she'd hugged her client. "How long have you been here?"

"Dr. Peters, I've been here all weekend long. I went to *all* of the functions. I even came to your seminar. You said you were speaking, but I didn't know you were the keynote speaker."

"Yes, well you know how much the transgender community loves me," Dr. Peters jokingly answered as she'd blushed.

"You go, girl," Candy then cheered.

"And look at you. Are you in the fashion show? And who made this beautiful dress? Candy you're fabulous!" Dr. Peters had stated, as she couldn't resist complimenting Candy on how beautiful she'd look.

Candy had worn a stunning, red satin *Yves St. Laurent* evening gown with matching gloves, a pair of red satin *Jimmy Choo* high-heeled stiletto sandals, sparkling five-carat diamond chandelier earrings, a choker and a matching diamond bracelet; all from *Harry Winston*. She'd been waiting months to finally get into the dress, and from the way that people had stopped and stared at Candy, giving positive comments, it was well worth the wait.

Candy then leaned over and had whispered into Dr. Peters' ear: "It's *not* the dress, Dr. Peters, it's the woman in it that *makes* it so lovely." She then placed an invitation for her party in her surgeon's hand and had briskly walked away. Candy then moved her wide hips in a saunter so smoothly, that no one but her parents would've ever believed that Candy was a transgender.

Dr. Peters smiled as she'd studied the party invitation. The doctor had always felt that Candy had finesse and style. On the front of the invitation was a picture of a cherry lollypop with a tongue licking on it. It read: Nothing's Sweeter Than Candy! On the back: Come join CANDY SWEETS, as she hosts the most elegant rooftop after-party immediately after the *RAGS-TO-RICHES* ball.

While Candy continued to pass out the remaining invitations to the many new friends she'd met at the convention, along with the few she'd known back from *South Beach,* Candy couldn't figure out why this one particular young lady had repeatedly smiled and stared hard at her. She'd looked somewhat familiar to Candy, but Candy believed that she hadn't known the female.

The pretty young lady then walked up to Candy as she'd continued to smile. She looked Candy up-and-down before she'd spoken; the young lady admired how pretty Candy had been—she'd wished to have Candy's hourglass figure.

Although the female was in great shape, Candy's cousin, Tammy, back then, had become a bit jealous, as she'd seen how beautiful Candy had transformed. Tammy then had taken a deep breath before she'd addressed her cousin.

"Well, Candy, aren't you gonna invite me to your party?" Tammy asked inquisitively as she'd smirked. Candy, wondering how the female had known her name, momentarily had taken a long look at her cousin, whom she hadn't recognized; due to Tammy's plastic surgery—which she'd had over the years. After careful observation, Candy still hadn't been able to place her cousin's face.

"I'm sorry, you do look a little familiar. I'm sure we've met before, but I don't recall where or what's your name," Candy answered, as she'd handed Tammy an invitation.

"I guess you wouldn't want to remember me after all of the things I've put you through over the years. I can imagine you *probably* even hate me," Tammy replied coyly, as she'd quickly snatched the invitation out of Candy's hand.

Candy eyes had squinted; she'd tried her hardest to make out who the female was: "Excuse me, miss, but *who* are you?" Candy then asked curiously.

"Mmmph, mmmph, mmmph—*look* at you. You can't *even* recognize your *own* family when you see them. It's me, your cousin, Tammy, fool!" Tammy had joked.

Although Tammy had caused Candy an abundance of pain while growing up, Candy couldn't ignore the fact that this was her family, and over the years, her old wounds would heal with time.

Candy then smiled, as she'd hugged her cousin joyously, but with a strong sense of confused curiosity. *Why would Tammy come to Chicago, all the way from New York City to attend a transgender convention?*

"Oh my goodness! Tammy, I'm sorry, I didn't even recognize you. Look at yourself," Candy had replied. She'd taken a step back to get a good look at her cousin. Candy was astonished by how much Tammy had changed.

The once chubby little girl, who couldn't jump Double Dutch, had become a shapely, gorgeous-looking woman with an angular face. Tammy, at that time had chiseled bone structure.

"Damn, look at you! Tammy, you look great! But it's one thing that's puzzling me—what are you *doing* here? This is a transgender ball, and the last time I remembered, you *despised* me for my alternative lifestyle."

"Yeah, well like they say, change comes with time," Tammy answered as she'd smiled at her cousin. "And looking at you, I can see change *really* has come with time. Are those real?" Tammy then inquired, as she'd pointed at Candy's breasts. Candy couldn't resist her laughter.

"Yes, silly, they're real. So is this," Candy boasted, as she'd turned around in a circle and showed off her perfectly round behind.

"Mmmph, mmmph, mmmph, some things *never* do change. I see you *still* got your confident attitude. And for your information, I'm *not* anti-homo, or hate people who have alternative lifestyles. I'm actually here supporting a great friend of mine.

"You have a gay friend?" Candy asked, as she'd had a puzzled expression on her face.

"No, silly, he's not gay. Believe me, he's a *real* man, and if you didn't notice, everybody in here isn't gay or a lesbian. Or shall I say quote, unquote, transgender," Tammy then snapped, as she'd held up her fingers to make quotation marks.

At that moment, Candy immediately sensed that Tammy's sarcastic comment had been aimed indirectly at her, but Candy hadn't reacted to it, as she'd brushed it off and played along with Tammy.

"Well, it was good to see you, Tammy. I have to finish giving out the last of these invitations. Are you coming to my party?"

"Oh, yeah. I'm *coming* alright," Tammy had replied, now irritated.

"Great. Bring your friend with you; I'd *love* to meet him."

"Oh, you're *gonna* meet him. I'm sure once you do, he'll leave such an impression on you, that you'll *never* forget him."

"O-O-O-O-O-O-H, like that, huh?" Candy had replied coyly.

"All that and then some," Tammy answered, as she'd studied Candy's pretty invitation.

"Okay, then I'll see you after the show—bye-bye."

Candy ended her conversation before she'd departed. Candy then walked seductively, as she'd sauntered her sexiest strut; Candy had hoped to enrage Tammy with envy.

She then thought that something strange had occurred, running into Tammy in *Chicago* the way she had. Candy had wondered, *Out of all the men in the world Tammy could've been with, why was she with one now at a transgender convention?* Candy had felt that Tammy was up to something, and she was determined to find out what it was.

A few hours later...

The regal ballroom on the hotel's top floor had been flooded with upscale partygoers from all over. The high-profiled guests danced and mingled, as Candy had gone throughout the party and played hostess to the many whom attended her soiree. This was a dream come true, but, only one thing had been missing this evening that would've made it complete: Terry.

"Damn, baby, I *wish* you were here to celebrate with me," Candy whispered softly, as she'd looked up to the sky. Candy then quickly grabbed a glass flute of *Cristal* champagne and had sipped its contents; she hadn't allowed the reality of Terry's absence ruin her lovely evening.

"Hey girl," Laquetta had greeted; one of Candy's friends whom she'd met in *South Beach.* In fact, Candy and Laquetta had both been patients of Dr. Peters, and hooked up together after one of their evaluation classes. It was Laquetta who'd turned Candy on to the credit card scam.

"Oh, hey Laquetta," Candy then replied, as she'd hugged her friend. "Damn, you look good; where'd you get that dress?"

"C'mon girl, you know me. I came out to this *motherfucker* with three credit cards and four ID's! You know a *bitch* went crazy down at the boutique on *Lake Shore Drive—* turned the *motherfucker* out!"

"I *know* that's right!" Candy had responded. "Shit, I rented this ballroom for ten-thousand tonight."

"W-H-A-T?" Laquetta had said, as her eyes widened. "Candy, it's *over* for you!" Laquetta then replied excitingly.

"Yes girl. Tonight is *my* night! My last and final days as a male are almost gone. I'm scheduled to lie on Dr. Peters' table next week. I'm trying to get that *diamond* like you have between your legs; from what I hear, it's perfect," Candy stated, as she'd referred to the successful sex-change operation that Laquetta recently had a few months ago.

All around *South Beach,* everyone in the transgender community had talked about the results of Laquetta's operation, as she'd even gone so far as to show people her new slit. It was also rumored that Laquetta, at this point, "allegedly" had dated a famous R&B singer on a regular basis, who'd "allegedly" proposed to Laquetta and placed her in a condo in *Chicago;* where he'd financed all of her expenses.

"Yeah, Candy, I'm happy for you. Now we *really* gonna do our thang once you get your surgery. You think these *bitches* can't take you now, wait 'til you get your diamond next week," Laquetta then said before sipping her glass of *Cristal.*

"Girl, you just don't know how anxious I am. I've been waiting for this all my life. I—"

"Hold on, Candy," Laquetta interjected, as she'd observed a handsome man who stood a few feet away. As he'd noticed that Laquetta looked in his direction, the man winked his eye at her. "Bingo! Candy, I *just* hit the jackpot! Hold that thought—I'll be back," Laquetta then instructed, as she'd quickly stepped off, and walked towards the man whom she'd made eye contact with.

"Be good," Candy replied, as she'd laughed at her flirtatious friend. Soon after, Candy placed her drink down and had decided to head up to the rooftop deck. She'd wanted to mingle, as Candy then overlooked the view of the windy city— *Chicago.*

While Candy had stood alone on the rooftop deck, Tammy walked up behind her, and whispered something so familiar into Candy's ear, that tears had run down her cheek instantly.

"Candy girl, you are my world. You look so sweet, you're a special treat."

Candy then smiled with fond memories of her favorite song, as Tammy had softly sung it in her ear.

"That was your signature song, remember?" Tammy then asked.

Before she'd turned around to face her cousin, Candy quickly wiped her tears. "Yeah, that was the song, wasn't it?" Candy had answered.

At that moment, Candy noticed that Tammy was alone. Instantly, Candy had been on guard. Although they'd been grown at that time, the tricks that Tammy had played on her in the past would never be forgotten. Candy had seriously sensed that Tammy was up to something. Immediately, she'd addressed Tammy.

"Okay, Tammy, *cut* the *bullshit*. What the *fuck* are you doing here?" Tammy then looked into her cousin's face, appearing to have a sincere expression upon her face.

"Candy, I came here to make right what was wrong."

"What the *fuck* are you talking about, Tammy?"

"You, Candy; your life. What you are, and what you've become."

"Tammy, I'm a *grown* woman now. There's *nothing* about *my* life that should be of *your* concern," Candy had retorted, as she'd folded her arms and looked her cousin straight in the eye.

"Well, there are some things I want to tell you, just so you can know," Tammy then replied.

"Oh, yeah, like what?"

"Well, first and foremost, I've been jealous of you all my life, since I was a little girl. You *always* out did me in everything, and you *constantly* took my friends away from me. Everybody liked you. You *even* took my own sister away from me. I mean...Lisa actually loved you *more* than she loved me."

"Oh, yeah, I can't tell. After what Lisa did to me, I'm *not* so sure. She betrayed my trust and love. She gave your mother my diary, which got me kicked out of the house. Then I had to move in with Shanna, and next thing you know...Shit! I can't even stand to talk about this," Candy then stated, as she'd been on the verge of breaking down. Candy then thought about Terry, how she'd violated his mother's home and ruined her friendship with Shanna in the process.

"I know, Candy, I know. But, like I said, I'm here to make it right."

"How are you going to do that?"

"I have a confession."

"Are you *sure* you want to confess to me?" Candy then asked with a surprised look upon her face. She'd never seen Tammy act this humble before, and from her actions, Candy had begun to relax and hear Tammy out.

"Yes, Candy. Well, anyway, I just wanted to tell you that it wasn't Lisa who turned your diary over to my mother—it was me."

Candy had stood in shock, as Tammy continued with her confession.

"Lisa never showed me where it was—I eavesdropped on you two one day, and found out where your secret stash place was.

I'm so sorry, Candy. After all these years, I've been trying to find you to tell you this. Just so you'll know, I was wrong. But, that was the only way I could get you *outta* my life, and get my sister back. I was hoping that I'd run into you at Terry's funeral, but you weren't there. Why didn't you come?"

"Come on with that *bullshit,* Tammy! You know why I didn't come—I COULDN'T!" Candy had yelled furiously, as tears rolled down her face, and had smudged her mascara. "I can't *believe* you can be that evil, Tammy. Why?"

The fact that Candy had literally hated the only person in this world who'd genuinely loved and accepted her for years, and now knowing that Lisa hadn't been responsible for her being ousted from her home, made Candy hate Tammy even more.

Candy couldn't see the smirk on Tammy's face, as Candy had buried her face into her hands. Once again, Tammy had been up to her old tricks.

"I just wanted you to know, Candy. All my life I hated you, and to be honest, from looking at you now, I'm even more *jealous* of you," Tammy then stated, as she'd tried hard to conceal her cynical smirk. Candy had quickly raised her head, and looked Tammy face-to-face.

"*Bitch,* you could *never* amount to the woman I am. Not then, not now—not ever. You *fucking* ruined my life. You made me hate my own cousin, just so you can restore your relationship with Lisa. Where's Lisa? Where is she at now?" Candy had asked emotionally. "*Bitch,* I want you to call her right now and *apologize* for what you did to us," Candy then demanded, as more tears flowed from her eyes.

"You *might* wanna do that yourself—perhaps even write her a letter," Tammy retorted before she'd grinned. Just then, a tall, brown-skinned man who was neatly dressed had appeared on the rooftop deck; he'd joined the two cousins.

"Oh, there you are, Tammy. I've been looking for you all night," the man had said in a deep masculine tone, as he'd stood beside Tammy. "And who's this fine, lovely young lady?"

"Kevin, this is my cousin. Um, what do you want me to call you? Tammy had asked Candy sarcastically.

"You *know* my name!" Candy had answered back angrily.

"Okay then. Candy, this is one of the people I came here with. Kevin, this is Candy. Candy, Kevin."

"One of the people? You didn't tell me that you came with anyone else," Candy then responded.

"There are a lot of things I didn't tell you—now you know!" Tammy had retorted sarcastically. Candy then rolled her eyes and hissed at Tammy, before she'd extended her hand to Kevin.

"Hello Kevin. Nice to meet you. I'm Candy Sweets, the hostess who's throwing this *wonderful* party. Are you enjoying yourself?"

Kevin smiled, as he'd kissed the back of her hand before he'd held on to it tightly. As Candy felt the pressure of his masculine touch, she'd tried to pull back her hand, but Kevin's grip was too tight.

"Not as much as you are," Kevin then answered, as he'd slapped a pair of handcuffs on her tiny wrist; Kevin then quickly twisted Candy's other arm around to fasten the other handcuff.

Candy looked on in disbelief, as she'd been handcuffed in a matter of three seconds. It was so surreal; Candy's head had spun dizzily in confusion. She'd then looked at Tammy with extreme hatred, as Kevin had read Candy her rights and charges.

"Candy Sweets, you are under arrest in the following states: *Miami, Florida,* and *Chicago, Illinois* for bank fraud, credit card fraud and identity theft. You have the right to remain silent. Anything you say, can and will be used against you..."

As Candy continued to look at Tammy with disgust, her tears had immediately been replaced with daggers; she'd darted Tammy with evil stares. After Kevin had read Candy her rights, she'd noticed that Tammy mischievously grinned. Candy then addressed her: "Why, Tammy? What did I *do* to you?"

"What didn't you do, *bitch!* Now your *ass* is goin' to jail with men—where your *ass* belongs. I hope that you now discover that, no matter how hard you try, you could *never* be a woman."

CLAP! CLAP! CLAP! CLAP! CLAP!

"A hell of a performance, hell of a performance; I must say so myself!" said the young lady who'd appeared from the shadows of the rooftop deck. She'd smiled from ear-to-ear as she applauded; the female had quickly clapped her hands together. The young lady then laughed wickedly, as she'd slowly revealed herself to Candy; the young lady then looked at Candy's shocked expression.

Shanna had appeared, and Candy couldn't believe it; she'd become stunned. Candy then realized that Shanna was in on Tammy's trick. Shanna then stood and watched with enjoyment, as her boyfriend, Kevin, the FBI agent, had handcuffed Candy.

Shanna had gone out of her way to find something on Candy. After the death of her brother, Terry, Kevin had decided to help solve his death. He'd found evidence of credit card fraud, linking the rented *Ferrari* sports car to Candy.

After further investigation, Kevin then connected Candy to several other frauds, which had included credit card charges for renting the ritzy hotel suite in *South Beach,* renting the hotel's ballroom in *Chicago* for her lavish party, in which she'd been arrested at; in addition to many purchases of expensive jewelry from *Harry Winston* and clothing—in addition to the exquisite handbags, and the one-of a-kind couture gown, Candy had worn to the ball.

"*BITCH,* DIDN'T I *TELL* YOU I'D FIND A WAY TO *GET* YOUR ASS?" Shanna snapped, as she'd looked hard into Candy's eyes. "Bye, *bitch!* I hope you rot and *die* in prison—you killed my *fuckin'* brother!"

"Shanna, how can you blame *me* for Terry's death? I loved him so much," Candy had pleaded.

"If you loved him, you wouldn't have let him leave with you and *abandon* his family!" Shanna had replied mercilessly. "Like I said, bye, *bitch!* I hope you rot and *die* in prison!"

Five months later...

Candy had been sentenced to five-and-a-half years in a federal prison, and was designated to *Cumberland's Federal Correctional Institution*, located in the *Appalachian Mountains* of *Maryland*.

Candy pinched herself in disbelief, hoping that she'd awaken to what she'd thought was a horrible nightmare....

*   *   *   *   *

"Lift your armpits...open your mouth...move tongue up-and-down...lift nut sack...turn around...bend over...turn around, squat and cough one time."

Candy felt humiliated, as she'd complied with the correctional officer's instructions. Her first day in prison was unforgettable. Candy couldn't stop her legs from shaking; she'd been a nervous wreck. Candy's stomach had been twisted up into knots, and she was very worried when the guard had called out her name.

"CANDY SWEETS!" the correctional officer had yelled out in the crowd of new inmates who'd tried to make small talk with Candy. Even though this had been their first day in prison, some tried desperately and indirectly to get Candy's attention; while others acted as if they'd despised her.

"Right here," Candy replied awkwardly, as she'd eased her way pass the crowd of convicts. As she'd walked by, Candy felt a hand run quickly across her behind. Unnoticed, Candy hadn't known whom to blame. In fact, she wasn't mad at whoever had groped her, Candy had been so scared and nervous, all she'd thought about was being physically attacked, and sexual assaulted.

Candy held on tight to her thoughts, as she'd moved faster in the guard's direction. At that point, Candy had become concerned about getting out of the holding cell. As her mind had focused on that, Candy hadn't notice that she accidentally brushed pass one of the prisoners, who, by the look that was on his face, had despised Candy for whom she was.

"*Motherfucker,* the *fuck* is wrong wit' you?" the convict named, Trigger had yelled, as he forcefully pushed Candy. "Yo, you *faggot*-ass *punk,* you *ever* touch me again, I'll *smash* you, son. That's on the real, yo!"

"I'm sorry; excuse me. I didn't realize I'd touched you," Candy had replied, voice being shaky and uneasy.

The correctional officer who'd called Candy's name had become amused by what happened. He could've stopped the minor conflict, but instead, the guard had wanted to see how Candy handled herself in a scuffle.

From the looks of it, the correctional officer then realized that Candy hadn't been ready for prison, and that this must've been her first experience in jail. In most cases, when a homosexual is tested like this in prison, he would've defended himself against those who'd challenged him; he'd let the antagonists know that he still had been a man, regardless of his sexual desire.

Yet, in Candy's case, the guard had noticed that she'd not only looked and acted like a female, mentally, Candy had considered herself to be one. For that cause alone, required the correctional officer to place her in "the hole": Segregated Housing Unit, on Protective Custody. He'd felt that the federal government couldn't risk another lawsuit from a rape victim.

After Candy was placed in a cell, she'd been given a bedroll, a comb, toilet tissue, a tablet and a pencil. Candy then looked around the small but clean cell, which to her surprise, had been equipped with an individual shower unit. Although the cell had bunk beds, Candy was the only occupant.

While the guard had written Candy's federal ID number, name and the term "Protective Custody" on the front of her cell door, she'd begun to ask a series of questions that had come to mind.

"Excuse me, C.O., is there someone else coming in here?"

"No, you're on P.C. until the captain and warden review your status."

"Why is that?"

"Well, let's just say, you don't look like the average inmate, and for your own protection, until further notice, you'll be in here."

"How long will that be for?"

"The captain should be up to see you later on. Right now he's busy."

"Well, can I at *least* get a phone call?" Candy had pleaded.

"Nope, you gotta wait 'til your captain comes—plus you *just* got here. Chill out and *lay* it down," the guard instructed as he'd walked off.

Damn, these motherfucking *C.O.s don't have any feelings for anyone. ...I can't* believe *Tammy and Shanna tricked me like this. I swear, when I get out, I'm going to let them* bitches *have it!*

As Candy was alone in her cell and conjured the revenge that she'd planned against the two women, a light, silky voice had emerged from the hollow hallway, and into the cracks of Candy's cell door.

"Candy! Hey Candy!" the girlish sounding transgender had yelled. Candy was deep in thought when the transsexual had called out to her. "Candy, get up and come to the window!" the transsexual then instructed. Candy then jumped in front of the window of her cell, and had pierced her eyes up-and-down the empty cellblock.

"Who's that calling me?"

"Me, girl—Yalonda!"

"Yalonda? Yalonda from *Ohio?*" Candy had asked; puzzled. Yalonda had been Candy's new friend whom she'd met down in *South Beach* at *Club Score*; one of the hottest gay clubs in *Florida*. In fact, it was Yalonda who'd supplied Terry with the large quantities of Ecstasy and Oxycontin to sell.

For a second, the thought of Terry, and the mere fact that the pills Yalonda had sold him caused such conflict in their relationship, immediately, had made Candy upset. She was on the verge of blaming Yalonda for his death, but Candy then quickly had come to her senses; she'd known that Yalonda had nothing to do with Terry's drug addiction.

Yalonda was also a top-notch transsexual who'd passed for a natural woman. But the difference between her and Candy: Yalonda loved being in the "Land of Dicksville, USA"—the gay term for jail. Yalonda had known that from her body alone would bring fortunes, and get her a lot of attention and fame, amongst the corrupted convicts.

"Yeah, *bitch,* it's me!" Yalonda had joked.

Candy then smiled at her friend's sassy humor. Candy was happy to know that she'd been jailed with someone she'd known.

"Where are you, Yalonda?"

"I'm down the hall on the same side of the tier as you."

"How did you know I was here?"

"Chile, I saw you from my window when they were bringing you in with the new load!"

"Why didn't you say anything?" Candy had asked, curious as to why Yalonda had waited so long to call out her name.

"'Cause I had a mouth full of *dick* at the time, g-u-r-l!" Yalonda then joked. The entire tier instantly had become alive with laughter after they'd all heard Yalonda's comment; humorous sounds had come from other inmates in their cells who'd eavesdropped on the two prison queens' conversation.

Candy had laughed at her friend's honesty and openness about the lewd sex act.

"Yalonda, your ass is *so* crazy!"

"You know me! A *bitch* ain't got *no* cut card with what I do. I'ma *fierce* ole queen out here in this *motherfucker,* but as you can see, they done boxed a *bitch* up!" Yalonda had loudly replied, upset that she had been placed in solitary confinement. "Candy, why you in here anyway? Last time I saw you, you were pushin' a cherry-red *Porsche* down *Ocean Drive* with the top down; hair blowin' all in the wind."

Candy then smiled, as Yalonda's reference had taken her back to that day in *South Beach.*

"Yes, girl, I was working it. I was living *lovely* in the *Sunshine State.* But, unfortunately, what goes around comes around, and my days of scams are now over. Yolanda, the judge gave me five-and-a-half years for credit card fraud, bank fraud and identity theft."

"Damn, *bitch,* you were rollin' in the dough, huh?" Yalonda had asked curiously; she'd hoped that Candy would elaborate on the lavish gifts and events that had led up to her arrest. While inmates had grown of boredom, being in the Segregated Housing Unit, it had always amused and interested them to hear other prisoners' adventurous stories of their past lifestyle.

It was entertaining, since there hadn't been any TVs for the convicts to look at. Although there had been a few great books by various authors on *GHETTOHEAT*® that floated throughout the prison, inmates had preferred to hear stories from a person from the streets who'd recently been incarcerated.

"Mm-hmm, Yalonda, guess what?" Candy had said.

"What, *bitch?*"

"My own cousin and former best friend are the ones who set me up to get caught."

"S-T-O-P! GET THE *FUCK* OUT OF HERE!" Yalonda had responded; shocked.

"Yalonda, check this shit out..." Candy then stated, as she'd run down in detail, every moment that led up to her getting tricked and arrested. The entire tier had come to a complete silence, as each prisoner sat back and listened; they'd eavesdropped, as the convicts visualized Candy's story.

After Candy had told her story, almost every convict's face on the tier had been pressed against their cell windows. They'd tried getting a glimpse of this transsexual who'd claimed to be so passable, that the jurors had been dumbfounded when they'd discovered that Candy was born a male.

"Candy, you was *doin'* the damn thang! Mmmph, you better work, *bitch!*" Yalonda had said before she chuckled. "So, you was just about to get your diamond, huh, g-u-r-l?"

"Yalonda, I had everything set up. Now, I'm stuck here in this *motherfucking* cell. They won't even let me out on the compound. Why the *hell* they have me on lock like this?" Candy then whined.

"'Cause, Candy, you's a *b-a-d* bitch! They know them *niggas* gonna be at your *ass*, as *soon* as you get on the compound! They tryna avoid a rape case, and have you *suin'* their asses and the government for some money," Yolanda had hissed.

"RAPED?" Candy had blurted nervously; she'd then tried hard to block out the thoughts her mind had voluntarily entertained again. Candy had thought about being abused from the very first day the FBI agent had placed handcuffs around her tiny wrists.

Other than being murdered, getting raped in prison was the most horrific scenario that Candy had imagined, especially after she'd recently lost her virginity to her deceased boyfriend, Terry. Candy had become mortified; she'd then realized that she could've easily fallen victim to the possibility.

Yalonda then laughed at the crackle in Candy's unsteady voice; Yolanda had sensed her fear. She'd figured that Candy would be afraid, this being Candy's first time in prison. To ease her anxiety, Yalonda then decided to give her some firsthand advice on how to adjust within the facility.

"Miss Thing, don't you *e-v-e-n* worry 'bout that. You been watchin' too much of that *OZ* shit on *HBO!* Prison ain't *nothin'* like that. Well, federal prison ain't, anyway. It's *too* many open and closeted homosexuals in prison nowadays. There's *no* need tryna rape somebody when these *horny* queens are more than willin' to give a dude in here some ass!

"Yeah, now in the late eighties, a *bitch* mighta had some problems, but, Candy, we in the new millennium. A *nigga* will buy you everything in the *fuckin'* commissary, just for some head, let alone a piece of ass!" Yalonda had ranted.

"No, that's okay, Yalonda. I'm *not* interested in turning tricks," Candy had dryly indicated.

"G-u-r-l, I ain't sayin' you have to sell some ass, but you're gonna run into some major playas in here wit' a lot of paper. Remember, we in the feds, ain't nothin' but *niggas* wit' bank floatin' all over this *motherfucker!*"

"I'm not trying to have sex with anybody in here. I just want to do my time, and go back home," Candy had replied. "And besides, how are you going to have sex without condoms? It's not like they pass out condoms in prison—or do they?" Candy then asked inquisitively. Again, Yalonda had laughed at Candy's ignorance about life in prison.

"Miss Honey, *don't* be silly! No, chile, they don't *give* out condoms. We use the fingers from the latex rubber gloves. Just make sure the *nigga* got it on nice and tight, 'cause once it burst, you might be cursed! Next thing you know, your *ass* be ridin' in the back of a hearse," Yalonda then warned, as she'd referred to the high rate of HIV transmissions in prison. "And how you think your ass is gonna do five-and-a-years without catchin' feelings for somebody in here? *Puh-l-e-a-s-e...* Shit, ain't *nothin'* like a nice piece of *dick,* and I know your ass *ain't* no virgin no more!"

"Shut up, Yalonda," Candy retorted, embarrassed, as she'd blushed at Yalonda's comment.

"Look, Candy, since I was fightin' wit' some *nigga* who tried to play me out-of-pocket, I have to stay back here in the hole for a few months. But I know how you can get on the compound."

"Okay, how so?"

"Listen, in the mornin' when the captain comes through, ask for a BP-8, let him know that according to your Civil Constitutional and Human Rights, you've been discriminated against; because of your sexual orientation and preference. Tell him that according to *Supreme Court Law,* no prisoner is to be deprived of his or her rights to General Population, because of their sexual preference. Candy, that's the law, and once they see that you know the law, and that you're threatin' to *sue* their asses, they gonna let you outta the hole to go into General Population."

"So you're telling me if they hold me back here because of what I am, that I can file a lawsuit?"

"Uh-huh!"

"And if I go into General Population, and something happens to me, I can *still* file a law suit?" Candy had asked curiously; she'd been ignorant to the law.

"Yeah, *bitch,* that's *one* of the great benefits of being a queen!" Yalonda had proudly answered; she'd felt great that she was able to properly educate Candy.

"I *HATE* YOU *FUCKIN'* FAGGOTS!" an irate inmate had yelled at the top of his lungs. He'd become irritated and angry, as the disgruntled inmate overheard the two queens' conversation. The convict had had enough of hearing the two naturally-born males acting as women. "IT'S *MOTHERFUCKERS* LIKE Y'ALL WHO HAS THE WORLD SO *FUCKED* UP; SICK-ASS *BASTARDS!* THEY NEED TO LINE ALL OF YOU *FREAKS* UP AGAINST THE WALL AND *STONE* Y'ALL TO DEATH— *BITCH*-ASS *MOTHERFUCKERS!* STONE Y'ALL JUST LIKE THEY USE TO DO IN THE BIBLICAL DAYS," the infuriated convict then retorted.

The bitter tone of his voice alone had sent chills of fear down Candy's spine, while Yalonda, on the other hand, had eased her tension. She'd displayed courage, as Yalonda stood up to the prisoner.

"*Nigga,* what your ass *need* to do is mind your *own* business and stop ear-hustlin'! Tryna get up *all* in *our* business, listenin' so hard to our conversation! You make a *motherfucker* wonder what you *really* in jail for!" Yalonda had hissed, as she insinuated that he'd been a snitch.

"I SWEAR TO GOD, WHEN I SEE YOUR *FAGGOT*-ASS, I'MA *SLAM* YOU—FUCKIN' *BITCH!* YOU MIGHT THINK YOUR *ASS* IS A WOMAN, BUT I'MA SHOW YOU

HOW MUCH A MAN YOU ARE!" the angry convict had shot, as he'd become heated from the false accusation.

In prison, there are three major things that one must have proof of, before accusing or insinuating someone of being: a snitch, a homosexual or a thief. According to the prison rules amongst inmates, these three things are punishable to the fullest, depending on the person who's protecting himself from those accusations.

In most cases, if a person is guilty, he won't show any physical action, opposed to one who isn't; who most likely will defend himself and his reputation, by brutally beating or severely stabbing the accuser.

"Nigga, *fuck* you! You *ain't* gonna do *shit* but sit here and bar-fight! You ain't *nothin'* but a cell-gangsta; I'm hip to your *bitch*-ass. You in P.C. 'cause them DC cats *checked* your *punk*-ass in. You can't *even* come on the compound without gettin' your *ass* beat down, so shut your fuckin' *bitch*-ass up!" Yalonda had snapped back at the hostile convict. "Candy, I'ma go 'head and lay down. I'll talk to you tomorrow, okay? This poo-putt *nigga* done pissed me the *fuck* off!"

After Yolanda had exposed and humiliated the angry inmate, the rest of the convicts yelled and cursed at him, as they'd screamed obscenities. The whole tier had been in an uproar, as Candy had shaken her head and laid on her bunk. Candy then had sunken into the reality of her first day in prison.

"Sweets... Sweets, wake up!" the marshal said forcefully, as he tapped his keys on the cell bars; interrupting Candy's daydream. Candy became annoyed by him for disturbing her, as she was reminiscing back to a year-and-a-half ago, when she first entered the federal prison system.

"O-o-h, what's up, Marshal?" Candy responded sleepily.

"Get yourself ready. The wagon is gassed up and ready to go. As soon as my partner bring in these fools from upstairs, we gonna be ready to cuff up and move out."

Candy then took a deep breath before dousing her face with cold water, hoping that the splashes of water would keep her awake for the long ride back to *Cumberland's Federal Correctional Institution.*

Never have I been so anxious to get back to prison, Candy thought, as she eagerly waited to be patted down and cuffed from the ankles up.

Soon after, the second marshal brought in five other inmates who were detained and sentenced today. Candy smiled to herself, thinking that each individual reminded her of the men of her past; the past in which Candy was unable to put behind her—one that continuously haunts her.

Damn, he looks like Ray, Candy thought to herself, as she admired the tall, handsome-looking man who had strong facial features. *I wonder if he can play basketball like Ray... Mmmph, mmmph, mmmph—damn, I miss Ray.*

After the marshals cuffed and shackled each inmate, they led the convicts into the back of the transport van that had dark tinted windows. Once inside, Candy again observed each inmate one-by-one.

Even though it was now obvious to the other prisoners that Candy was naturally born a male, and that she was being transported and housed in the same prison with them, it definitely didn't deny the fact that Candy was bewitchingly beautiful. During the ride, the inmates couldn't help but to sneak glimpses of her, constantly stealing looks when Candy was oblivious to them examining her.

Candy lightly smiled, as she knew from her recent past experience in prison that, each one of these men had their own individual issues, and if Candy had to speculate, she would assume that, out of the five men, at least one of them had some sort of involvement, or experience sexually with a person who has an alternative lifestyle; whether inside or outside of a jail facility.

The first of the five guys who were chained together, made eye contact with Candy. He was the man who reminded her of her ex, Ray.

"How you doin'?" he mouthed to Candy.

Candy inhaled a deep breath, and exhaled before she whispered back: "I'm doing fine."

From him locking eyes with Candy, she instantly knew that he was "trade": a masculine man, usually appearing as straight, who discreetly indulges in a person with an alternative lifestyle. Candy smiled as she laid her head back, closed her eyes, and thought back to Ray—her prime example of true trade.

WHAT'S THE TEA?
chapter 15

"Sweets, pack your *shit,* you going on the compound. The captain is letting you out," the guard instructed, as he'd made his rounds to each cell.

Two weeks after Candy had filed the necessary paperwork that her friend, Yalonda had advised her to, the captain and the warden immediately decided to take her off Protective Custody, and had released Candy to General Population.

"Hey Yalonda!" Candy yelled out to her friend, as she'd awakened Yalonda at seven o'clock AM. After two weeks in the Segregated Housing Unit, Candy was taught so much about prison life by Yalonda, that she'd become eager to hit the compound and find out what it was like for herself.

"Yeah, what's the tea, diva?" Yalonda's groggy-sounding voice echoed throughout the hallway, as she'd asked Candy what had happened.

"They're about to let me out on the compound, Yalonda."

"When? Right now?"

"Yes, the C.O. just told me to pack my things," Candy had said nervously.

"Did he tell you which unit you're going to?"

"Unit A-1?"

There had been silence for a brief moment, as Yalonda had thought as to whom was in that cellblock.

"...Aye, Candy!"

"Yes, Yalonda?"

"Look, it's a few good trades down in Unit A-1!"

"Yalonda, I thought I told you that I'm *not* looking to get involved with anybody in here."

"Yeah, whatever, g-u-r-l—you'll see! Oh, yeah, I almost forgot to tell you. When you get out there, it's a queen in Unit B-2 named, Ke-Ke. Stay *away* from that *bitch,* and stay far, far away from that chile's trades!"

"Yolanda, what's the tea on Ke-Ke?"

"G-u-r-l, that butch-queen ain't *nothin'* but trouble! Mmmph, just shady boots! He's cool when he wants to be, but chile, don't get too personal, 'cause *that* one is many things! Ke-Ke be doin' shows! A *bitch* keeps money, but I hear that Ke-Ke has a *big* ole 'House In Virginia'!"

Candy had become silent for a moment, as she'd taken a deep breath and sighed; fixed on the reality that Yalonda had warned her about. "House In Virginia"—a slang term used within the gay community for HIV, and whenever a person adds the word "big" to it, that means a person has full-blown AIDS.

"Damn...a *big* one you say?" Candy then asked; she'd wanted full confirmation.

"Yeah, so-keep-it-cute, Miss Honey. Do you, but *watch* your back, and *keep* your eyes and ears open at all times. Oh, yeah, there's an undercover queen-in-training in Unit A-1, also. He's real cool people. I ain't tryna scream his name out on the tier, but believe me, he's gonna holla at you. When he do, tell him that I said it's time for 'her' to come out the closet and be 'herself'."

"Okay, Yalonda, the C.O.s are at my door now; thanks for everything!" Candy had yelled to Yalonda, happy to finally get out of Protective Custody while being in "the hole". She was sad to leave her friend behind, as Yalonda had become her mentor in prison—Candy had seen her as a lifesaver.

Before Yalonda had informed her of the people, the structure, daily operations, and the interactions of the inmates and officers, Candy always had the stereotypical thought about life behind bars, which hadn't been fully portrayed on TV series and in movies; which desperately instilled fear in its viewers.

But to her surprise, prison wasn't exactly like that at all. Candy had also learned that certain convicts had maintained "romantic relationships" within the jail. Yet, the code of silence was fully understood and respected: *"WHAT HAPPENS IN PRISON STAYS IN PRISON...."*

THE JUMP-OFF
chapter 16

Unit A-1 had become completely silent when Candy entered the cellblock with her bedroll, and had placed her belongings on the floor. Card games ended, chess matches had paused, and conversations instantaneously halted, as the inmates looked in awe at the lovely transsexual, whose looks were stunningly mesmerizing. They couldn't believe what they'd seen.

Candy was the most passable transgender that any convict in the facility had ever seen. Although there had been a few who was pretty, like Yalonda, none had come close to Candy. Much to their surprise, none also had ever strutted on the compound at *Cumberland's Federal Correctional Institution* like Candy.

All eyes had been glued on her, as Candy sashayed to the correctional officer's desk, and had inquired about her living quarters.

"Damn, slim, check this *shit* out," J-Rock said smoothly, as he'd pointed at Candy. "I can't *believe* this *shit*."

"Stop playin'! That's a man? Damn, he looks *just* like a woman," Riddick had responded.

"Fam, that's crazy! What is this world coming to?" Amin then stated.

The three convicts stood on the top tier of the unit and had looked down at Candy, totally shocked at what they'd witnessed. They'd been surprised at how Candy resembled a real woman, baffled by her beautiful looks.

Although none of the three men had, or would ever consider dealing with a homosexual, more-or-less a transsexual, they couldn't deny the fact that Candy looked like a natural woman. The three were extremely confident with their manhood; voicing their opinion on Candy's appearance had meant nothing to Riddick, Amin and J-Rock.

On the other hand, some inmates on the compound had reacted differently, and expressed disparaging words of hatred. Conflicted with their own sexuality, these boisterous men had actually been real trades who were considered "on the low";

78

who'd secretly lurked in the darkness of their prison cells, as they'd pierced their eyes through Candy in admiration.

Also, there had been others who boldly courted homosexuals within the prison, yet discreetly. Privately, these trades had maintained relationships with gay men, as they had with their female counterparts.

These same men were the type who'd get released from prison to come home to their family, girlfriends, and wives—continuing to deceive them all as they'd portrayed the role of masculine, heterosexual men; ones who hadn't ever been involved with a homosexual. They'd strongly adhered to the code of silence: *"WHAT HAPPENS IN PRISON STAYS IN PRISON...."*

Case in point, Trigger, a young, strong, masculine brother, had been inside the TV room within the prison when Candy arrived to the unit. He'd venomously expressed his hatred for her, in which Riddick, Amin and J-Rock had looked on in disappointment. Mainly because the three had been incarcerated long enough to see right through Trigger's fakeness; they'd assumed what the thug had done behind closed doors.

"Yo, what the *fuck* is everybody lookin' at that *faggot* for? Niggas is *sick* for even payin' that *gump* any mind. Shit, he probably got the "package" wit' him," Trigger said with anger, as he'd referred to Candy as a homosexual who perhaps had HIV/AIDS—as Trigger pretended to be tougher than he'd been.

"Aye, Trigger, you don't have no cellie, they might put him in your room," J-Rock then teased.

"S-h-i-i-i-t, they put that alien in my cell, I'd *never* get to go home. I'd catch a murder case in the first five minutes."

"Damn, Trigger. So you're saying you'd rather risk going home next year just because they put a *punk* in your cell with you?" Amin questioned, as he'd purposely asked the question to prove to his two friends how stupid and insecure Trigger had been.

"*Fuck* yeah, dun! I'd straight *smash* him, kid," Trigger had retorted.

"Damn, young nigga, you mean to tell me that you'd risk doing life in prison for killin' a *homo* that the C.O.'s put in your cell, oppose to just movin' out of the cell into another one?" Riddick had questioned.

All three convicts had interrogated Trigger, just to hear the dumb youngster's response. Amin, Riddick and J-Rock had shaken their heads in disappointment at the lack of intelligence

Trigger displayed. The three had hoped that Trigger would one day become conscious of his wrongdoings, take off his mask of aggression, and truly be himself.

Although prison had been considered to some as the "House of Ignorance", each of the three convicts, particularly Amin and J-Rock, who'd done time for over a decade, viewed prison as a university, and their major was the principles of life— socially, philosophically, religiously, morally, culturally, as well as economically.

The three men had taken complete advantage of the few opportunities prison had to offer, as they'd capitalized on their business tactics.

J-Rock, better known as the "jailhouse lawyer" for his expertise in law, was highly respected amongst his fellow inmates, as well as in his hometown, *Washington, DC.*

A man of great wisdom, J-Rock had a medium build, black wavy hair, wore a dark Caesar haircut, brown eyes, and a light complexion with smooth skin.

A talented author who'd penned his first novel, *Larceny* while having been incarcerated in federal prison, J-Rock had been honored and highly admired by his fellow convicts and fans nationally, for having his novel, based on street-life in *Washington, DC,* placed on *Essence* magazine bestsellers list.

Then there was Amin from *South Philadelphia,* the Imam of the Sunni Muslims within the prison facility, who was directly linked to *Atlanta's* new rap artist, *ALFAMEGA.*

Amin "allegedly" also had been known for once being romantically involved with a well-known female author/publisher, whose ground-breaking, *Philadelphia*-based, street tale was highly inspired by him—the two being engaged to be married back then, had separated shortly, after Amin realized she'd no longer been "true to the game"....

Amin had a short, muscular build, a light-brown skin tone, almond shaped brown eyes, wore a low Caesar haircut, and a thick, yet, neatly groomed, full facial beard—his signature of symbolizing the religion of Al-Islam; in which he'd faithfully practiced.

Last, but not least, there was Riddick "Big Daddy" Bowe, the former heavyweight championship boxer. Unlike Amin and J-Rock, who'd served lengthy sentences due to harsh drug charges, Riddick, at the time, had served a short sentence of a year-and-a-half—an alleged domestic abuse dispute between he and his wife; yet had served time in federal prison, due to being a high-profile figure.

After Trigger had walked away, Riddick expressed his disappointment: "Man, it's messed up to see a dude around here fakin' like that," he'd said in his deep, masculine voice.

"Yeah, I know. Hopefully he finds himself something positive to get into, before he ends up like your homie, Ray, J-Rock," Amin had stated, referring to a man from J-Rock's hometown.

Ray was a federal prison's nightmare, who'd stood at 6'2"and weighed 240 pounds—his body frame had been similar to Riddick's. He was very handsome, having a light-brown complexion and hazel-colored eyes; also known for being an abusive womanizer.

Ray, at that time, had been in his late thirties, but appeared to be youthful; others had mistaken him for being in his twenties. Although he'd been a bona fide dope fiend, the drug hadn't destroyed Ray; at least not externally.

Unfortunately, he was very violent and had an extensive criminal record—Ray, pegged as a relentless sex predator that had often preyed on vulnerable victims within the jail.

In addition to viciously raping male inmates, Ray had played mind games on his prey, psychologically outwitting the convicts; forcing inmates into bad situations unbeknownst to them, in which these prisoners back then, would ultimately need Ray for a favor.

"Nah, Amin, shorty ain't *nothin'* like Ray—they're different. That nigga, Ray just don't give a *fuck* about anything or anybody," J-Rock had interjected. "Now, Trigger on the other hand, see, he's the type of *nigga* that hides and do shit. He'd never let a *nigga* see his true colors. But Ray, that fool will walk the compound wit' a gump, and dare a *nigga* to say somethin'."

At that statement, Amin, Riddick and J-Rock all had burst into laughter. As they laughed, Ray had walked down the tier with his eyes locked on Candy, as he'd stared at her with intense lust.

"Speaking of the Devil, there he go right there, *stalkin'* his next prey," Riddick had said.

"Hey, J-Rock, your homie is a vicious man. He don't have no cut card, naw mean?" Amin then replied in his *Philly* accent.

"Yeah, but he's from *DC*. Even though the nigga's sick in the head, Ray is still a good soldier when needed—plus he respected real men at all cost," J-Rock had answered.

Internally, J-Rock had been enraged by Ray's actions, but he didn't want to display it amongst his peers back then. Regardless of how poorly Ray had carried himself, he still was a native of *DC*. J-Rock had only expressed his anger towards Ray privately, face-to-face. Ray had listened to him attentively each time—he'd highly respected J-Rock's street reputation.

Yet, no matter of the countless conversations the two had had in the past, unfortunately, Ray hadn't changed his ways—with no intentions of ever doing so. Most straight convicts had labeled Ray as being mentally ill for desiring gay men, while the imprisoned homosexuals had considered him to be a good piece of trade.

As Riddick, Amin and J-Rock had been engaged in conversation, they observed Ray's actions. The three of them had seen Ray devise a plan along with his two crooked friends. It was apparent that he and his two associates had been up to something. Recognizing that he'd been obvious, Ray and his two partners in crime had quickly ended their conversation and parted ways.

"Man, I'm gone. I got this new novel I'm working on," J-Rock had proudly stated, wiping off his *Armani* glasses.

"That's what's up, J-Rock. I gotta finish up my new joint, too," Amin had interjected.

What's the jump-off called?" Riddick Bowe had asked Amin curiously.

" *'Boy-Toy'*."

" *'Boy-Toy'?*" Riddick Bowe had responded suspiciously.

"Yeah, *'Boy-Toy'*. It's another *GHETTOHEAT®* production, you know how we do!" Amin then bragged with pride. "It's the hotness in the streets!!!™."

"Slim, I'll get at you later," J-Rock had stated.

"Do your thang, baby boy. It's about that time for me to offer my Salat," Amin replied, as he'd looked at his watch.

"I'ma catch this flick in the TV room," Riddick had joined in.

"Aiiight, champ!" Amin then retorted sarcastically, as he'd joked with the boxer as Riddick walked away.

"As-Salaamu-Alaikum," J-Rock had said to Amin, as he'd known that his statement would immediately irritate Amin.

"Aye, man, what I *tell* you 'bout that? Don't play with the Deen, J-Rock," Amin had retorted. He'd reacted the way J-Rock had known he would.

Amin always had been bothered when J-Rock said or did anything in an Islamic manner, mainly because he'd felt that J-Rock would've been a good Muslim. Whenever Amin had the chance, he'd always tried to convince J-Rock into converting into one.

"You need to come on up to Jumu'ah," Amin had indicated.

"Nah, Ahk, can't do that. I'm down wit' *Noble Drew Ali.* I'll holla though—As-Salaamu-Alaikum!" J-Rock then yelled out, as he'd quickly departed. He'd left Amin standing alone.

"Wa'laikum," Amin answered back, as he'd laughed to himself at J-Rock's silly antics.

"Sweets, you're in cell 1325; upper bunk," the correctional officer indicated, as he'd instructed Candy on which cell to report to. When she'd heard "upper bunk", Candy wondered who'd be occupying the cell with her. As Candy grabbed her bedroll and headed towards the cell, located near the far end of the tier, and away from the officer's desk and sight, butterflies had grown deep inside of her stomach; as Candy had become overwhelmed with nervousness. She'd tried hard to camouflage her fear.

This was Candy's first time in prison and she'd been frightened, forcefully trapped in terror against her will. Candy had become extremely horrified, especially when her eyes met directly with Trigger's, the young, hostile thug she'd accidentally bumped into; as Candy had been placed inside the holding cell. Trigger rudely shoved Candy when she'd first arrived to the facility.

"THE *FUCK* YOU LOOKIN' AT, *HOMO?*" Trigger had spat; embarrassed that Candy had looked at him. Trigger immediately wondered if she'd been able to detect that something was different about him and his masculinity. Trigger had hoped that Candy hadn't gotten any ideas that he might've been attracted to her, since Candy had caught Trigger staring hard at her.

Candy then quickly turned her face in the opposite direction, she'd wanted desperately not to provoke Trigger, as the thought of getting beat down by him, instantly had come to Candy's mind.

She couldn't exactly figure out the young thug, although Candy thought she might've had a clue as to why Trigger had displayed so much anger and hatred towards her. Yet, this hadn't been the time to come to any conclusions, as Candy was more concerned with whom she'd be sharing the cell with.

When Candy reached cell 1325, she'd glanced twice at the number printed above on the door, and made sure that she was at the right cell before Candy had entered. She'd then peeped inside the window to see if anyone was there. Seeing that it was empty,

Candy had stepped inside of the cell that would serve as her new home for the next five-and-a-half years.

Candy was overwhelmed with joy when she'd found the cell had been perfectly neat and clean, and for a moment, Candy sensed that it had a woman's touch. The room had smelled like sweet perfume, instead of the strong musk oil that was sold on commissary.

Right away, Candy dropped her bedroll and had raced towards the picture board that hung on the wall. She'd analyzed every photo; Candy had become curious, wanting to know who occupied the cell, and how they'd lived. She'd believed that a photo was like a thousand words—Candy felt that people told a lot about themselves by the way they'd posed in photographs, including how they'd displayed them.

Candy then smiled, as her eyes had perused over photos of gorgeous models, both male and female, and had become happy when she found the huge portrait of her new cellmate. Judging by his long, jet-black wavy hair, facial features and large green eyes, Candy had assumed that he was Hispanic.

Now that she'd known the identity of her cellmate, Candy had decided that it would be best to go find him and introduce herself; Candy had hoped that he'd fully accept her into the room.

As Candy then turned around and headed out the door, she'd abruptly been stopped by a hard, powerful, right-handed fist to her chiseled jaw, followed by the tight grip of a person's left hand hooking around her throat; Candy's vocal cords were being crushed, so she couldn't scream.

Candy haphazardly had fallen back into a corner and hit the back of her head against the wall, before she'd become unconscious momentarily. Within the first five seconds of gaining back her conscious, Candy had pondered who'd bashed her so hard in her face.

The first person that had come to mind was Trigger. Secondly, Candy also had thought it might've been her new cellmate, who obviously hadn't wanted Candy in his cell. She'd assumed this by the blow that was taken to her flawless face.

Struggling her way back from darkness, Candy's eyes had widened wide, at that point, being terribly frightened, as she was face-to-face with two unknown convicts who'd worn white pillow cases over their heads; mean eyes peeked from the two holes that had been cut out from the cloth. The two attackers had resembled members of the *Ku Klux Klan* bandits, as they'd hid their faces; both had been armed with sharp, ten-inch knives.

Overcome with panic, there had been no doubt in Candy's mind that she was going to be brutally raped, as there was no way out. Candy then quickly prayed to herself, and had hoped that they wouldn't take her life as well. Yet, being raped no longer was an important factor to Candy, as they could've had their way with her. All Candy had been concerned with at that moment was continuing to live.

The sight of the two inmates holding her at knifepoint had forced Candy to flash back to Yalonda. At that very moment, she'd developed extreme hatred for her: *That bitch, Yalonda lied to me!*

Yalonda told Candy that she'd never have to worry about getting raped, but Candy, at this point, had been balled up in the corner of her cell, trapped—as she'd watched her attackers worked in unison; as if they'd raped victims together for years.

"Put the sign up, shorty," the inmate had instructed to his friend to cover the cell door's window with the *"DO NOT DISTURB"* cardboard sign, as he'd stood over Candy's body. While his partner had blocked the view to keep other convicts from looking into the cell, he'd begun to unbutton his khaki pants.

"P-l-e-a-s-e, just don't *kill* me," Candy had desperately pleaded with fear and tears in her eyes. Candy had been so terrified, she'd begun to shake uncontrollably.

"Shut up, *bitch,*" the other attacker growled, as he'd kicked Candy in the head. She'd hit her head again against the wall, as the attacker had followed up with a hard slap in the mouth, which caused Candy's lip to split.

Tears had run from her eyes, which dripped from the bottom of Candy's chin, as she'd cried and prayed to God simultaneously.

Candy then had seen one of her attackers rip long strips from her bed sheet, as he'd proceeded to fasten Candy up in a hog tie. Before she could scream for help, Candy had been introduced to the sharp point of a knife, pressed hard against her neck.

"You scream, and I'll *drive* this knife right through your jugular vein, *bitch*—do you *understand* me?" the attacker warned after he'd tied her up. Candy had shaken her head in compliance.

"Now take this *shit* off!" the other attacker demanded, as he'd stripped Candy's underwear off of her before he'd rolled

86

Candy over on her stomach, while on the ground; the attacker had exposed her behind. There wasn't anything in the world that could've described Candy's fear, as she'd looked back in horror at one of her attackers; he'd begun to forcefully take her sexually.

Candy had noticed that he had a huge penis, and that the attacker hadn't any protection—instantly, she'd worried about being infected with AIDS. Candy then relentlessly clenched her anus as tight as she could.

"N-o-o-o-o-o-o, p-l-e-a-s-e don't do this," Candy had begged.

"*Bitch,* you make another sound, I swear I'ma *kill* your ass," the attacker holding the blade to her neck had threatened. He'd then pressed a little harder against her neck, alerting Candy that he'd been serious. The pressure from the knife had kept her in complete silence.

After quickly moistening Candy's anal area with his bare fingers, and lubricating himself up with *Vaseline*, the rapist then parted Candy's butt cheeks to reveal her tight hole; he'd anxiously proceeded to enter her. He'd put the head of his meat against Candy's tightened anus, and had prepared to insert his erect, ten-inch penis up her rectum, as Candy had clenched her hole tighter and squirmed.

Instantaneously, Ray busted into the cell and had caused a commotion, as both attackers then nervously jumped; he'd caught the two men off-guard.

Ray had towered over the two attackers with his massive muscular body; chest solid and protruding, big, bulging biceps had flexed through his fitted "wife beater" tank top. Ray was ready to take action, as he'd balled up both of his fists.

"Get up!" Ray had instructed Candy, who was puzzled at what had occurred.

"What the *fuck* you think you doin', Ray?" the rapist then asked, upset that Ray had intercepted him from penetrating Candy.

"Man, mind your business," his partner ordered Ray, before he'd turned back to Candy with his weapon drawn; he'd proceeded to lightly puncture her skin. "*Bitch,* you get up, I'll *slaughter* you in here."

"Not before I slaughter your ass!" Ray stated, as he'd pounded a sharp right hook across the attacker's temple, which had instantly knocked him down. Ray then grabbed the other attacker by the wrist and twisted it, which had caused him to drop the knife to the floor.

"Pick it up!" Ray then ordered, as Candy had retrieved the knife. Candy quickly snatched it up before she'd untied herself, and immediately gotten dressed. Ray disarmed the other attacker before he'd gained his conscious.

"Take the masks off!" Ray then demanded, as he'd held both attackers at knifepoint.

"Aw, come on wit' that *shit,* Ray. You know who we are," one attacker had whined.

"Yeah, *I* know who the *fuck* you are—but *he* don't!" Ray answered, as he'd nodded his chin in Candy's direction.

Candy was elated that Ray had saved her life, but was crushed that he'd referred to her as a man. Ray had known what he'd done, as it was all an act—a game that he'd played all too well. Ray had conned Candy into thinking that he'd really rescued her—Ray deceived Candy into believing that he'd been her savior.

Ray would later express his feelings for Candy, making her vulnerable to open up to him. Ray also would pretend that it would be his first experience—being attracted to a transsexual. Little had Candy known that Ray was a big con artist, and had pulled stunts like this for the last fifteen years in prison.

Even though he would be released next year, and had a girlfriend, Ray wanted Candy badly; he'd found her to be simply irresistible. When Ray first laid eyes on Candy when she'd arrived on the cellblock, Ray had known that he had to quickly devise his plan before anyone else had. It was Ray's only opportunity, in having first dibs of making Candy his "prison-bitch".

"*Motherfucker,* like I said, take the *fuckin'* masks off," Ray had responded.

Candy then looked long and hard at the attackers who'd attempted to rape her, as they'd removed their masks; the two then exposed their faces in shame. She'd immediately understood why Unibomber, the first attacker, had tried to sexually assault her, he being gruesome and hideous. Any woman would've been repulsed to be seen with him, let alone have sex with Unibomber.

Yet, Candy couldn't fathom why his partner, Ty, a young, handsome-looking brother with smooth, light-brown skin, who had long braids that had gone to the back of his head, had attempted to rape her; considering he didn't have to—judging by his looks. Candy had even sworn that she'd seen him in the *Source* magazine before.

Candy had shaken her head, as she'd thought about the countless women out in society that would've been more than willing to have had sex with Ty, just based on his great looks and well-toned body. Yet, he'd attempted to rape Candy without a condom, even with having a scheduled six-month release date from prison.

"Take a good look at these two *punk*-ass *niggas*," Ray demanded, as he'd stared at Candy. "If you ever see these *niggas*, or *think* they tryna get at you, then you come and get me, okay?"

"Okay," Candy then responded lowly.

Ray had known just from Candy's answer that they would soon have a relationship together. Ray and Candy then gazed into each other's eyes, infatuated, as they'd both stared into the windows of each other's soul.

In Ray's eyes was a reflection of Candy, a gorgeous transsexual who'd been born a male—one still equipped with a ten-inch dick. And in Candy's, she'd seen a "real" man—a brave, handsome, strapping man; one who'd reminded her of her ex-boyfriend, Terry.

From the rehearsed act of courage Ray had displayed, Candy had fallen deep into his web of trickery, as she'd then managed to crack a faint smile at her hero—even with having a bruised, busted lip.

"Aiiight, now get the *fuck* outta here before I *punish* you niggas!" Ray had instructed his two foolish friends; his act had been well-performed. Ray then slipped an eyewink at Ty and Unibomber, as they'd exited the cell; Ray had reassured them with his gesture that they'd done a great job—the two rapists would soon be rewarded for their deception.

Candy then looked at Ray curiously; she'd wondered why he'd gone out of his way to save her from the two attackers—especially knowing that they hadn't met before. Candy also had assumed that Ray would want a sexual favor in return, but much to her surprise, he'd pretended as if he hadn't been interested in Candy.

"Check it, my name is Ray, and I didn't come in here looking to save you from them two fools. I came in here for your cellie, Jose. It just so happens that I stumbled through when all that *shit* was 'bout to go down."

"I understand, but I want to thank you for looking out for me," Candy responded humbly, as she'd scurried about, grabbing for her things. Candy had immediately prepared to leave the cell.

Ray then watched in amazement, as he'd lusted over the vulnerable, voluptuous victim. Ray had become spellbound by Candy's beauty; his mind then raced with wild sexual fantasies. Ray couldn't wait for the day to have an intimate moment with sweet Candy.

"Where you goin'?" Ray had asked suspiciously.

"I've got to get the *hell* out of here! I'm going back to the hole on Protective Custody! There's *no* way I can stay on the compound! I've only been out here for twenty minutes, and almost gotten raped and killed!" Candy then replied with resentment.

Hatred towards everyone had begun to build inside of Candy, as she'd thought about how everyone in her life had betrayed her in some form or fashion. Candy had no longer trusted anyone.

"Hold up. Put your things back down," Ray had ordered. Candy then looked at him with uncertainty, before she'd taken heed. It was something about Ray's eyes that had falsely told Candy that she could've trusted him. Candy had felt a sense of security in Ray, being that he'd "saved" her life.

She'd also become attracted to him, mainly because Ray had acted as if he hadn't wanted her or Candy's friendship—at least that's what she'd thought. Little had Candy known that Ray really was trade.

Standing still with a blank expression upon her face, Candy then put her bedroll and belongings down: "Now what?" she'd asked Ray, as Candy shrugged her shoulders. Ray then smirked slightly, as he'd opened Candy's cellmate's locker; Ray being familiar with the room.

As he'd sorted through the locker to retrieve a new washcloth and some antibiotic ointment, Candy then looked on with suspicion.

"Here, take this and dampen it with warm water—place it over the cut and wipe softly," Ray then instructed. Candy had been in a romantic daze, as Ray exposed his aggressive, but smooth character—he'd given Candy no choice but to follow his orders. "Let me see that," Ray ordered, as he'd retrieved the washcloth, and gently wiped Candy's open wound; Ray had taken full care of her. He then squeezed a dab of antibiotic ointment on his finger and proceeded to cautiously rub it upon her cut.

Unsure of Ray's intentions, Candy jerked back as he'd attempted to place the ointment on her lip. She'd looked at Ray inquisitively.

"What's that?"

"This is antibiotic ointment—it'll be good for you," Ray had answered. "It helps prevent open wound infections. Now come here and let me put this on your lip," Ray had insisted charmingly.

Candy then leaned forward as if she was about to kiss Ray, as Candy had looked deep into his eyes. Ray then lightly rubbed the ointment onto the cut which was on the side of her bottom lip, before he'd inserted the remaining portion into his pants pocket.

"Look, your cellmate's name is Jose Lopez. He's from *Puerto Rico*. He works in the hospital, that's why he has all this *shit* up in here. Jose's mad cool, you won't have to worry 'bout nothin'. I'm sure you two are gonna get along."

"How do you know for sure?"

"Because Jose's—"

Before Ray had finished his sentence, Jose had entered the cell, being extremely tired from working a long, hard day in the prison's infirmary. Jose then looked at Ray and lightly rolled his eyes, before he'd diverted his attention to Candy; Jose then extended his hand to her.

"Hi, you must be Sweets. The C.O. informed me that I had a new cellie."

"Yes, that's me. But please, call me 'Candy'," Candy suggested, as she'd reached for Jose's hand. From the faint sound of Jose's gentle voice, the softness of his weak handshake, along with the sweet-smelling scent of tuberose, that had surrounded the cell, Candy had immediately figured out that Jose was the "queen-in-training" that Yalonda had mentioned.

"Well, Candy, I see you've met Ray," Jose then replied condescendingly, as he'd looked at Ray with much suspicion. He'd then discovered the gash on Candy's lip, and immediately wondered if Ray had attacked her.

As Jose sharply pierced his eyes into Ray's for an answer, Ray then had quickly left the cell, darting out before Jose had exposed his game to Candy.

While Candy and Jose had become acquainted in their cell together, Ray was downstairs in Lil' Will's cell—a prison buddy of his, whom for the last fifteen years, Ray had often gotten high with.

Over the years, the two had maintained a love/hate relationship—feelings often had been determined upon how much heroin and cocaine one had had for the other; or if one had informed the other of whom within the prison, had the best drug supply.

"Aye, I heard your homie, Ice Man across the hall in A-2 got that raw diggity," Ray had mentioned, referring to the heroin they'd both craved for. While Lil' Will had been a true dope fiend who'd been open about his drug habit, shooting up in front of others in the past, Ray, on the other hand, had been a closet fiend, who'd discreetly mainlined dope on the down low.

Ray's physical make-up and handsome features had always been well kept, due to the fact that prison helped preserve his body, and the toiletries sold at the commissary had enhanced his skin; in addition that Ray had good eating habits.

No one had ever known that Ray snorted cocaine and spiked needles in his veins, unless they'd paid close attention to his irrational mood swings; or to the small but perfectly healed needle marks that Ray had on his inner forearm.

This was one of the main reasons why he'd gone into Jose's locker and retrieved the antibiotic ointment. It had really been for himself, not necessarily for Candy's sake.

"Nah, Ice Man *ain't* got that dog food, he woulda came over and gave me a sample by now," Lil' Will lazily replied, as he'd scratched his arms and talked in his *Baltimore* accent.

"*Nigga,* I'm *tellin'* you he *got* that *shit*—I know what the *fuck* I'm *talkin'* 'bout! He *just* sold some to the dude, Fats down in D-2!" Ray shot back aggressively, as he'd tried to persuade Lil' Will. Ray had badly wanted to find a way to get him to ask his friend for a hit. Ray had known that by doing so, his cover wouldn't be blown; Ray had kept other inmates out of his business.

"Aiiight, yo. On the next yard re-call, I'ma go 'cross the hall and holla at him. You got some books?" Lil' Will then asked curiously, as he'd inquired about postage; Lil' Will then stuck out his skinny hand. Postage substituted for money within the federal prison, where inmates had purchased goods from other inmates with stamps.

"*Nigga,* what happened to those fifteen books I gave you yesterday?" Ray had asked with his eyebrows furled.

"C'mon, Ray, you know *damn* well we both got high wit' those books yesterday," Lil' Will answered as he'd raised his eyebrow. Lil' Will's facial expression had alerted Ray to knowing that he'd been keen to Ray's trifling antics.

Ray then cracked a smile at his frail, fiendish friend, before he'd handed Lil' Will eight books of stamps. "Here, *nigga.* Get us a fifty." Lil' Will looked at the stamps before he'd diverted his attention back to Ray, indicating that Ray had forgotten something. "What's wrong now?"

"Ray, you *only* gave me eight books of stamps. *Nigga,* how the *fuck* am I gonna get a fifty wit' *only* eight books?"

"*Motherfucker,* if you don't get your dope fiend-ass outta my face wit' that weak-ass game, I'ma *crack* your rib cage!"

"*Fuck* you, yo!" Lil' Will retorted, as he'd left the cell to get the drugs. As Lil' Will had exited, Ty and Unibomber then entered.

"Aye, man, you ain't have to punch a *nigga* all hard and *shit!*" Unibomber complained, as he'd displayed the big lump on the side of his head.

Ray then chuckled, "*Nigga,* you'll be aiiight. I had to make it look real. Seriously though, I was doin' everything in my power not to laugh. And you," Ray stated as he'd pointed at Ty, "what the *fuck* you think *you* was doin', greasin' up and shit?"

"S-h-i-i-i-t, *nigga,* I wasn't bullshittin'. After I saw how pretty that *motherfucker* looked, and when I pulled off that *bitch-*ass *nigga's* clothes and saw how fat and round the *ass* was, I wasn't stagin' a rape scene. If you woulda came in just a minute later, you woulda caught me wit' my whole *dick* in that *ass!*" Ty replied, as he'd grabbed his penis through his pants.

"Yo, it's like this, *nigga*—that's *my* bitch now! If *anybody* try to holla at her, I'm puttin' my *knife* in they *ass!* I don't give a *fuck* who it is!" Ray said sternly with a mean expression upon his face, as he'd let the two know that he'd meant business. Unibomber and Ty had understood by Ray's eyes that he wasn't joking.

"Aiiight, man—whatever! Just give us what you owe us," Ty then retorted as he'd extended his hand outward.

"Damn, y'all some lil' greedy-ass *niggas*. Here, this all I got right now, until Kim brings her fat *ass* up here and hit me off," Ray answered, as he'd then handed them a bag of marijuana.

Ray's fiancée, Kim had been highly reliable, and always had stood by his side through all of Ray's adversities; he'd often referred to her as his "ride-or-die" chick. For the past fifteen years, Kim had visited Ray every time he'd requested her to; she'd done anything that Ray told Kim to do.

Mainly because he'd given Kim what other men hadn't—attention. Also, Ray was the only man that had ever shown Kim any form of love—at least that's what she'd thought it to be.

Kim, being dangerously overweight, had known in her heart that she'd never get a man like Ray out in society—the two had met years ago, as they'd been pen pals. She was pretty, but had weighed 265 pounds; Kim stood at 5'2". Her breasts had also been huge, with Kim's bra size being a 36 double D.

Ray and Kim had met face-to-face at *Lorton Prison Facility* fifteen years ago, before Ray had been sent to federal prison. There, the two had their first sexual encounter during a fair.

That one experience had led to Kim becoming pregnant with their daughter, Raye-Raye; Kim had two other kids by two different men other than Ray. When she'd brought their daughter to see Ray during prison visits, Kim often smuggled balloons of marijuana in Raye-Raye's diapers; just to satisfy what she'd thought was Ray's weed habit.

Ray really hadn't been into marijuana, he'd sold the weed to make money to finance his heroin habit. Ray occasionally had asked Kim to bring him heroin, but rarely requested her to; Ray hadn't wanted Kim knowing that he'd been shooting up, and that dope was his real drug of choice.

Being very cautious about swallowing the balloons of heroin, Ray had known that if one had burst inside his stomach that he'd instantly die. Instead, Ray had paid Lil' Will to be his mule, in which he'd smuggled in Ray's drugs regularly. Plus, Lil'

Will had a connection with a drug supplier in *Baltimore* who'd had the best heroin, which made it easier for Ray to get higher profits for purer dope.

"Hold up, Ray! You said you was gonna give us *five* Js and *five* books. This here is only *three* Js!" Unibomber had said angrily.

"*Nigga,* if you don't get your rotten, ugly-ass face outta here, I'ma take back the *shit* I just gave you!" Ray had retorted cruelly.

"Aiiight, man, we gone. I'll holla at you later," Ty had interjected, as he and Unibomber both had noticed the change in Ray's demeanor. Ray hadn't been mad at the two, his mood swings had overwhelmed him; in addition, Ray had become ill— he'd needed a blast of dope.

Lil' Will had taken a long time in getting his fix, as Ray had begun to feel extremely weak; Ray suffered from fatigue and often had vomited. Ray had brushed his sickness off as a sign of him going through withdrawal.

Three weeks later…

"Begin ten-minute move," the correctional officer yelled over the loudspeaker, as he'd alerted the inmates of their time limit to get to their next destination. In federal prison, this was called "controlled movement", which had been regulated hourly. Had an inmate not made his destination before the end of the move, he'd been considered "out-of-bounds", which caused minor infractions.

"Damn, look how these *fools* scurry around like roaches once the move is announced," Candy said while she and Jose had looked outside onto the compound from their cell window.

"Yeah, I see. O-o-h, Candy, look at Abdul's fine ass," Jose responded in a sensual manner, as he'd lustfully laid eyes on the Muslim heading towards the gym.

"I thought you warned me that Muslims were off limits," Candy had stated, referring to the one-on-one prison rules amongst the inmates Jose had schooled her on three weeks ago.

"They're *definitely* off limits, but that doesn't mean we can't look and fantasize," Jose answered softly, as he'd sounded like a woman.

After the first week of rooming together, Candy and Jose had quickly become best friends. The two found out that they'd had a lot in common, although they were different.

Unlike Candy, who'd obviously been an openly transsexual at the facility, Jose was considered a confused, undercover gay male with latent female tendencies; being closeted, and scared to reveal his sexuality. Yet, Jose was fully unaware that he was heading into the direction of becoming a transgender, being very soft and extremely effeminate.

Although Jose had desperately wanted to come out of the closet, he was scared to proudly display his sexuality, afraid that he'd have problems with other vicious, openly gay men that courted "down low" men. Jose had feared that the homosexuals would be intimidated by his good looks—ultimately physically attacking Jose if he'd stole away their attention from the trades.

Jose was considered a "pretty boy" who had perfectly smooth, cream-colored skin, wavy shoulder-length hair, and long eyelashes; ones he'd batted like a woman, whenever Jose had cut his large, green eyes. Jose never had to shave, only having a few small hairs that had grown under his chin, in which Jose had plucked out with his tweezers.

Outside the cell, Jose had carried himself like a true gentleman, yet, behind his cell door with Candy, he'd frolicked about like a hot, flaming queen; Jose had traipsed around in homemade thongs, cropped T-shits, cut-off shorts and shower slippers.

Other than Yalonda, Candy and Ray, who'd easily spotted a man with gay tendencies by the way he'd walked, talked, and by other body gestures and mannerisms, no other inmates on the compound had known of Jose's secret; yet, one officer, by accident, had discovered that Jose was gay.

Officer Mummy, a discreet, undercover trade, had stumbled across Jose's bundle of gay magazines and homemade female clothing, as he'd searched Jose's cell one day during a routine shake down. Since then, the officer had become his secret admirer. Often he'd left bottles of *Thierry Mugler's "Angel"* perfume under Jose's pillow, while Jose was at work at the infirmary.

Then there was Ray, who Jose had shared his first sexual experience with; Jose had become obsessed with giving Ray oral sex since their initial meeting. Frequently, Ray had met Jose at his job, where he'd secretly given Ray oral pleasure inside of a broom closet; repeatedly, he'd hungrily engulfed Ray's rock-hard penis.

Unbeknownst to Ray, Jose had fallen madly in love with him, yet, he wasn't effeminate enough for Ray. Jose, not fully coming out of the closet before Candy had appeared, had put a damper on him courting Ray; Candy's exquisiteness and feminine charm continued to cause a ruckus amongst the men throughout the entire jail. All of the masculine, "down low" trades, especially Ray, had wanted a piece of Candy.

Being totally discreet, Jose had never informed Candy of him and Ray's companionship. Jose had seen how much Candy had admired Ray—being head-over-heels for the trifling trade. Jose also had been aware of Ray being secretly attracted to Candy, yet Ray hadn't made a move on her, which had made Jose puzzled as to why.

Ray had been cleverly plotting and scheming, playing his cards strategically across the board. He'd plan to set Candy up at the right time, and take full advantage of the golden opportunity; which would later become "wide open".

"Well, I guess you're right," Candy had replied. "There's no crime in looking."

"Yes, but don't *ever* let them catch you looking," Jose had answered with a serious look on his face.

"I know what you mean. I made the mistake of glancing at that guy named, Trigger, and his little *crazy* ass went *off* on me."

"Trigger *isn't* as tough as he seems," Jose hissed as he'd rolled his eyes.

"I know...it's something about Trigger...but, anyway, I don't want to talk about him right now."

"So let's talk about you being the 'Queen Bitch' of *South Beach*—tell me a-l-l the stories, Candy!" Jose had requested, enthralled by Candy's life experiences.

"What do you want to know?" Candy then asked, as she'd giggled naughtily.

"Well, tell me this before we go into your adventures. Why did you get so upset at me last night when I joked and referred to you as a 'homo'?"

Candy had always despised it when someone had used the term "homo" or "faggot" to describe her sexual orientation, which had always left a sour taste in her mouth in the past—and at this very moment. All of her life, Candy had struggled explaining the difference in her alternative lifestyle, which had left her once again, forced to educate Jose.

"Jose, I'm *not* a homo, and I don't think you're one either."

"How can you be so quick to say what I am, Candy?"

"Because, Jose, I've come across many types of men who were either gay, bisexual, 'on the low', and ones who were intrigued with being with, or becoming a transsexual. I'm usually good at detecting them all. Being though you haven't come across many within the prison, you don't know of the different categories. So honestly, you don't even know what category you're in. Now, I'll school you on the different types, but it's up to you to decide on what role to take."

"Well, go ahead; teach me," Jose squealed as he'd begged, before immediately putting up the cardboard sign in the cell door's window for privacy.

"Okay, Jose, now I know you weren't *intentionally* putting me in the same class as a 'homo', mostly because I knew that you simply didn't know the real difference. So, no, I wasn't upset at you for calling me that. It's just that the term has been used to ridicule me all my life; and I *hate* it!

"Now, Jose, there are different types of transgender. The most common of the three are transsexuals, in which I'm giving you a *fierce* description of now; inside and out," Candy jokingly bragged, as she'd got up from the bunk and twirled around in a complete circle; Candy emulated a model at a fashion show.

"Okay, *bitch,* I get the point; you're a transvestite," Jose said as he'd giggled lightly.

"No, Jose, I'm a transsexual, *not* a transvestite, which is a cross-dresser. Cross-dressers differ from transsexuals, where they have no desire, or aren't preoccupied with removing their sex organs, or their primary and secondary sex characteristics—being that transvestites take on both sex roles. Dressing up like the opposite sex sexually arouses them, in which some like to give, and receive when having sex." Candy then had explained.

"Damn, that sounds like Ke-Ke's *freaky* ass. I heard that he goes down in the D-Block and *'flips'* young boys. Yolanda told me that Ke-Ke goes there and sucks on them young *niggas* dicks, then slips his finger in their asshole. If the dude continues in letting Ke-Ke finger him, Ke-Ke then turns back into 'Keith'; in which he proceeds to fuck the boy," Jose said, as he'd gasp and cringed; shocked of Ke-Ke's sex acts.

"Well, I heard something like that myself. I'd also heard some other *fucked* up *shit* about Ke-Ke. I—"

"Okay, okay, enough about that *cum*-guzzling whore! Candy, tell me more about the different types of transgender," Jose had pleaded, eager to learn.

"Alright, calm down. The third is a hermaphrodite. True hermaphrodites are rare and characterized by being born with both male and female organs; at birth, having the equal amount of male and female chromosomes."

"Damn, what are you some sort of doctor or something?" Jose had asked surprisingly, amazed at how knowledgeable Candy had been of the terms.

"No, I'm not a doctor, silly," Candy smirked before she'd continued. "So those are the different types of transgender. Now, let's discuss the different types of gay men. Lately, there's been this hype about homosexual men who are 'on the low', or considered 'down low' men. These men are usually afraid, or ashamed to come out of the closet for various reasons; many reasons. Even here in prison, you have a lot of masculine men running around here who *love* to suck dick and take it in the ass—some you wouldn't *even* imagine," Candy then replied, as she'd turned up her nose.

"Again, like I said earlier, sounds like you're talking about Ke-Ke's *beastly*-looking ass, or rather should I say, 'Keith'," Jose retorted, as if he'd had a problem with Ke-Ke.

"No, Jose, I'm talking more like—" Candy then had stopped herself, she'd opted not to give her opinion on the guy she'd become suspicious of, not having full confirmation on the inmate's sexual preference. "...well, let's just say there are a lot of men, masculine men, who have *gay* sex discreetly with other men, while protecting their identity.

"Then, there are bisexual men who have sex with both men and women. In some cases, these men don't favor one sex over the other, being satisfied by both. Yet, others prefer to be with a man, but will continue to have sex with women because of denial, confusion, or for not wanting anyone to know about their *true* preference. Sometimes, these types of men would even try to court me, due to the fact that I'm close to being a natural woman than an effeminate man; such as yourself at the moment," Candy then had stated to Jose, after teaching him a lesson about transgender and gay men categories.

"What? What are you *trying* to say, Candy?" Jose asked, as he'd snapped; being defensive.

"Jose," Candy had begun, "honestly, and please don't get upset and take this personal but, I feel that you're *very* effeminate—look at you," Candy stated, as she'd pulled Jose towards the mirror that hung over the sink, and positioned him in front of it; as they'd both seen each other's reflection.

"You're so pretty and soft, just like me...there's a woman inside of you that's just *dying* to come out. But there's *something* that's keeping 'her' in. Now, I personally don't know exactly why you're so scared to release 'her' and face reality, but, Jose, one day you're going to have to look in the mirror and decide, who it is you're *really* meant to be," Candy had sincerely said to Jose, as the two stared long and hard at each other through the mirror.

Immediately, tears had fallen silently from Jose's wide green eyes, as his newfound reality had set in.

Over the following months, Candy had become very familiar with the inmates and operations of the federal prison. She'd figured out the undercover homosexuals from the openly gay men, some even had pointed out the trades to Candy often.

Candy had also taken heed to what Yalonda had said about Ke-Ke's men, and made sure that she'd known every last one of them. Although Candy hadn't contemplated on getting involved with any "down low" men, she'd made sure that she knew who they were anyway.

Yet, thoughts of Ray had imposed upon Candy's mind, she'd thought about how well he'd treated her. As time had flown by, Ray and Candy's courtship had grown deeper.

Anything Candy had wanted or needed, Ray had provided it for her. From conversations to food items, sweat suits and sneakers, whatever she'd requested from commissary.

Candy and Ray had often walked the prison yard together, as the two talked regularly—they'd gotten to know each other. Ray and Candy had learned each other's likes and dislikes, their outlook on life, and how they'd perceived the world.

Candy and Ray hadn't had sex at the time yet, but the whole compound assumed that the couple had been in love. Some inmates had even flashed fake smiles as the two walked by; others had just nastily talked behind the pair's backs.

Regardless of how others within the prison had viewed them, the reality back then was: Candy and Ray had been considered to be "married", with Ray doing anything, and everything to protect Candy; his "woman"—even if it had meant risking his own life.

On occasion, other manly, hardcore convicts had become Candy's secret admirers, and had even gone to her new job at the infirmary—they'd left love letters. The discreet inmates had hoped that Candy would give into their poetic charm. But no matter how enticing the other prisoners' words had been, no one had occupied Candy's mind but Ray.

As Candy and Ray both had walked the yard together, as the couple held hands, Candy then proceeded with a series of questions.

"Hey, Ray, can I ask you something?"

"Yeah, what's up, boo?"

"Do you love Kim?"

"Hmmm...good question...before I answer, I wanna know why you wanna know."

"Because, Ray, your answer will determine what I *really* want to ask you," Candy replied, as she'd stopped walking abruptly to face Ray.

"Aiiight then, my answer is yes and no."

"Excuse me?"

"The reason why I said yes is, because she does anything I *tell* her to do. And no because she's not easy on my eyes."

"Mmmph, mmmph, mmmph, so I guess *I'm* easy on your eyes? Candy then asked, as she'd flashed her brilliant smile. Ray then had smiled back.

Instantly, Ray had known that his plan worked. Candy hadn't only fallen in love with Ray, but she'd also fallen in love with his mind. Ray then laughed to himself, as he'd begun lying to Candy.

"Now, Candy, you know I ain't *never* had sex with a—"

Before Ray had finished his sentence, Candy had cut him off.

"Ray, I'm a *woman*, please don't *ever* refer to me as a man!"

"Candy, then you have to *prove* to me that you're a woman," Ray replied, as he'd looked deep into her eyes. Candy had known from that statement alone, that Ray was ready for what she'd been willing to give him—ever since the first day Candy had laid eyes on Ray.

"Alright then, Ray. Meet me in my cell tonight at nine o'clock,"

"How you gonna pull that off? What about your cellie?" Ray had asked curiously; he hadn't wanted to get busted by Jose by meeting with Candy.

"Don't worry about Jose; he already knows how I feel about you. I'll just ask him to go to the TV room or something."

"You told Jose how you *felt* about me?" Ray had asked suspiciously. He'd wondered if Jose had exposed to Candy that he was trade. If so, Ray would be sure to beat Jose's ass, first chance he'd gotten.

"Yes, I told him, I hope you're not upset. We talk about things like that all the time. You didn't know that Jose was gay?"

"Hell nah, I ain't know," Ray had lied with a straight face. He'd become relieved to know that Candy had still been in the dark about him and Jose's "friendship".

"So you coming by or what?" Candy then asked seductively.

"Yeah, I'll be there—nine o'clock, right?"

"Nine o'clock. I'm going to show you something *really* nice," Candy said tauntingly, as she'd walked away abruptly. Candy then had switched her large behind to make Ray aroused.

"What time is it?" Ray asked before he'd snorted his last hit of cocaine.

"It's ten minutes to nine. Why, *nigga,* you got somewhere to be?" Lil' Will had answered suspiciously. "And why the *fuck* you smelling all good for? You *only* wear that *shit* on visits," he then replied, as Lil' Will had observed Ray; Lil' Will had noticed a change in him.

"*Nigga,* this *my* cologne. I put it on whenever the *fuck* I want to—get you some business, yo!" Ray had retorted.

"Aye, I already know what you up to. You tryna *fuck* that C.O. bitch, Ms. Adams, huh?"

Ray then had smiled to himself, as Lil' Will thought he'd been on to Ray, not having a clue that it had been Candy whom he'd had a date with.

"Yeah, I'm tryna *fuck* that fat *bitch.* You know she be reading my mail. I be sending Kim them freak letters, and whenever I drop 'em off at the box, Ms. Adams always reads my *shit* first. Now, either that *bitch* just nosy-as-*fuck,* or she a freak tryna get *fucked,*" Ray answered slyly, as he'd thrown Lil' Will way off course.

"Yeah, kid, that *bitch* tryna get *fucked.* C'mon, look at the fat *bitch,* you know ain't nobody *fuckin'* her fat *ass* out in them streets. The *bitch* only took this job to get some *dick* from the inmates. Why you think she's here? That fat *bitch* is lonely out there in society."

"Yeah, Lil' Will, I know—and I'ma find out. Lay back, shorty, I'm gone," Ray replied, as he'd easily slipped out of his cell, and quickly had walked down the tier, unnoticed.

When Ray had arrived to Candy's room, he'd noticed that the "DO NOT DISTURB" cardboard sign had been in the cell door's window, indicating that she'd wanted privacy. Ray had figured that Candy had it up to keep away other convicts, or either she'd had someone else in there. Ray then opted to tap on the cell door before he'd entered.

KNOCK-KNOCK-KNOCK!

"Who is it?" Candy had answered in her soft, feminine voice.

"It's Ray, baby."

"Come in."

When Ray had opened the door, he couldn't believe his eyes. Candy had made the cell room cozy; she'd rearranged it to look like a hotel room. Ray blushed as he'd closed the door behind himself.

He'd slowly nodded his head to the soft melody of Sade's "Sweetest Taboo", as the smoothness of her voice had come from the speakers of Candy's Walkman. Ray then smiled at the homemade candles that had burned: "I like those," he'd stated, as Ray had become pleased with the candles.

"Thanks. They're nice, right?" Candy had answered back sweetly. As she'd talked, Ray had fixed his eyes on the prettiest person he'd ever seen. Candy instantly hypnotized him, as she'd displayed her soft, pretty thighs through the homemade dress that was once a shower curtain.

In prison, cross-dressers, queens and transsexuals, always had a way to supplement the essentials that they'd needed, in order to appear as feminine as possible.

Candy's luscious lips had been done up with bright red coloring, which she'd made from the cherry-flavored Kool-Aid packets. Also, the eyeliner that had enhanced her wide, startling, light-brown eyes was created from a Number 2 pencil, in which Candy had melted the tip with matches.

Her nails had been glossed with floor wax to give a buffed, clear shine. As a substitute for mascara, Candy had used a mixture of Murray's hair pomade and ink from a black magic marker, applying it to her long eyelashes; Candy had also used a portion to outline her perfectly arched eyebrows.

As Ray had reasoned, Candy hadn't needed any of the homemade make-up enhancements; she'd already been naturally pretty. Candy had passed as a real woman without any cosmetics, yet, the little application of make-up had enhanced her natural beauty, which made Candy look like a Cover Girl model.

"Damn, you look good," Ray had whispered lowly, unable to take his eyes off of Candy.

"Ray, you asked me to prove to you that I'm a woman. So for starters, I want to show you these," Candy stated, as she'd

106

opened the top part of her homemade dress; Candy had exposed her erect nipples and round breasts.

Ray's eyes then widened, as he'd zoomed in on her big breasts. Candy then turned her back to him, and had dropped her dress to reveal her plump, perfectly round and soft butt cheeks. Candy's behind had protruded through the homemade thong that she'd made from a silk T-shirt.

Ray had become fully stimulated by the sight of Candy. He hadn't needed any more persuasion, as Ray was convinced that Candy was indeed a "woman"; in his eyes—equipped with the wrong organ. Ray had wanted her badly at that point, more than before.

Candy then bent over slowly and eased her thong off from her smooth, round ass. Ray's dick then had swelled to its highest peak, as Candy had gingerly rolled her thong down to her ankles. She'd then seductively parted her butt cheeks and exposed her love tunnel to Ray, in which no one, other than her former lover, Terry, had traveled through.

Throughout the striptease, Ray had never seen Candy's big penis, which made him harder, more aroused; the illusion had seemed "real" to Ray.

"Ray, close your eyes, baby," Candy had instructed lightly, as he'd immediately obliged. When Candy had turned back around to face Ray, at that moment, completely naked, he'd still had his eyes closed. In Ray's mind, there was no way in the world, after he'd witnessed all of this, that Ray would ever believe that Candy was born a male.

"Okay, baby, you can open your eyes now. I promise, you *won't* be disappointed."

When Ray opened his eyes, he'd soon gone into a complete state-of-shock. Candy's large, limp penis was tucked away so neatly, that it had become invisible, as Ray then stared down hard at the perfectly trimmed bush of public hair that had given the "illusion" of a vagina.

"So, now do you accept me as a woman?" Candy then asked; eyes being watery. She'd prayed that Ray would approve of her; it was all Candy had wanted—all she'd needed. The two had discovered that they'd been compatible to each other, other than being physical. At that point, Candy had needed to know if they'd been fully compatible; she'd intensely desired Ray sexually.

Even though Ray was trade, and had had sex with many effeminate homosexuals, he'd felt that no matter how feminine they'd acted, at the end of the day, they still were men. All except Candy. She'd "made" Ray a believer.

Ray then grabbed Candy and pulled her close, as he'd kissed her passionately.

"Yeah, Candy, you proved your point. From here on now, you're *my* woman."

"Make me know it," Candy responded, as she had a devilish grin upon her face.

Ray then laid her down and gently caressed her body as if she'd been a woman. He'd kissed and sucked on her nipples, as Candy had moaned sensuously.

Candy then had become overheated by the passion Ray had given. What had taken her to ecstasy was when Ray turned Candy around, and had lovingly licked around her anus slowly with his long, warm tongue; Ray had licked her hole as if it was a vagina. The sheer pleasure alone had made Candy fall deeper in love with a man, whose past was much fiercer than her own.

*   *   *   *   *

When Candy came back from her daydream, thinking of her first sexual experience with Ray, she found herself face-to-face with a convict that resembled him. He was smiling from ear-to-ear when Candy opened her eyes.

"So, what's your name?" asked the convict who tried to make small talk during the long ride.

Candy laughed to herself, as she looked at him with pity. Transsexuals, like Candy, had never respected trades, mostly because of how they secretly operated.

To Candy, trade was just a male on the "down low" who didn't mind having sex with another homosexual; so in return, he's just as gay as the next homosexual.

Candy blew air out of mouth, as she sighed in disgust, hoping that the guy would get the hint that he was annoying her.

"So you ain't tryna talk, huh?" asked the prisoner.

"No, not right now. I'm *not* in the mood for conversation; in fact, I'm rather tired," Candy retorted, as she began to close her eyes.

When Candy closed her eyes completely, she thought about the quiet brother whom she caught a glimpse of, as he sat next to the convict who Candy considered to be trade. Candy smiled delightfully, as she began to reminisce her past.

Eight months later...

"Code Red! We need staff and medical assistance in Unit A-1!" the guard nervously shouted over his radio as he'd requested backup; hysterical shocked. He'd opened the cell door for a routine shakedown, and found Lil' Will on the floor unconscious with a needle stuck in his arm.

This had been the correctional officer's first week on duty in the unit, and judging from his nervous reaction, it was the first time the guard had seen a true dope fiend, die from an overdose of raw heroin. Convicts had looked on, as staff members and nurses pulled Lil' Will out on a stretcher. Some laughed while others had looked in disappointment.

"Aye, yo. That *nigga* musta had some of that good *shit*—knocked his lil' ass straight out, huh?" Trigger replied jokingly, as he and a few youngsters had looked on and laughed at the helpless drug addict.

"Damn, his lil' cruddy ass finally stumbled upon some *shit* he couldn't handle," Ty joined in, as he'd cracked his joke.

"Man, that *shit* ain't funny, y'all. He could be *dead* on that stretcher, and y'all up here laughing—making jokes and *shit,*" Unibomber stated, as he'd felt sympathy for his fellow inmate's tragedy.

"Man, *fuck* that *nigga!* He never gave a *fuck* about you! *Fuck* you worried about his dope fiend-ass for anyway? The same *nigga* you having sympathy for, is the same *nigga* who would rob and kill your *ass* in a heartbeat; just for a bag of that *shit!*" Ty blurted out, as the younger inmates all then agreed with him.

"Yo, dun, he's tellin' the truth. I done seen niggas get their whole *fuckin'* wig split over a bag of that 'dookie'," Trigger had replied in his *New York City* accent.

"Yeah, you right," Unibomber had answered sullenly.

"What the *fuck* we sittin' here talkin' 'bout him for? Aye, Trigger, spit some rap lyrics 'bout his *junkie*-ass," Ty instructed, as he'd pounded on his chest to make a beat.

Trigger had been the prisoner's best "rap sensation". Everywhere he'd gone throughout the jail, inmates always pulled him aside, and often had begged him to rap a few verses. In the past, convicts immediately had halted in their actions, just to hear Trigger rhyme. The entire prison had been amazed by Trigger's rap skills. Even a few guards had come over to eavesdrop, just to hear him feverishly flow amongst his peers.

While Trigger had entertained his peers with freestyle lyrics about Lil' Will's tragedy, Candy had run out of the TV room, as she frantically looked for Ray. She'd known that Ray and Lil' Will were close buddies, and that he'd recently gone on a visit to transport some balloons of cocaine and heroin for Ray.

When Candy had seen the hospital response team bring Lil' Will out on a stretcher, instantly, she'd thought about Ray. As the guard had made the ten-minute move announcement over the loudspeaker, Candy raced out of the dorm to inform Ray of what had happened.

"Damn, she runnin' fast-as-*shit!*" Unibomber said, as he'd interrupted Trigger's flow.

"*Fuck* yeah. Look at her titties bouncin' up-and-down," Ty stated, as he'd grabbed his crotch while examining her breasts.

Trigger immediately had stopped rapping and looked at both inmates with disgust: "Be easy, son. Don't disrespect me like that no *fuckin'* more. That's a *damn* man you two corny *niggas* is lustin' over! Yo, what the *fuck* is wrong wit' you *niggas?*"

"S-h-i-i-i-t, that's a woman trapped in what *used* to be, a man's body. *Nigga,* that punk look just like a *bitch,*" Ty interjected, as he'd quickly justified his actions.

"For real, Trigger, that *bitch* look better than most of the hoes I ever *fucked* wit'," Unibomber had replied.

"*Nigga,* she looks better than *every* bitch you ever *fucked* wit'—you ugly *motherfucker.* You know *damn* well you ain't *never* had a hoe that looked like Candy," Ty joked, as he'd made fun of Unibomber's gruesome looks.

"*Fuck* you, Ty—pretty *motherfucker!*" Unibomber then chuckled.

"Yo, you *niggas* is really trippin'. The *fuck* goin' on in your head, dun?" Trigger spat, as he'd looked at Unibomber. "You just referred to *him* as a *she.* And you," Trigger had begun as he pointed at Ty, "you should be *ashamed* of yourself. *Nigga,* look at you. Them *bitches* out there in the world would do whatever to get

111

wit' your pretty *ass*. Yet, son, you up in here *fuckin'* wit' them boys. Plus you 'bout to go home soon and—"

"Man, you can kill all that *bullshit* you talkin' 'cause, for real, nigga, you know if your *ass* was somewhere alone wit' that punk in a quiet place when nobody's around, you'd probably try to get wit' Candy, too," Ty interrupted Trigger, as he'd insinuated that Trigger had been a hypocrite.

"Yo, dun, you got the 'Trigger' *fucked* up! Ain't no way in the world I'd ever be in here *fuckin'* a *fag!* I got my rich *bitch,* Susan playin' wit' that *pussy* while we be on the phone, son. I'd rather beat my *dick,* I wouldn't care how much time I got! *Nigga,* I could have a life bid, and I'll *never* fuck wit' a gump! Son, I'm *all* man. I represent the *N.Y.C.*—the city that's so nice, they had to spell it twice!"

"Yeah, well, I'm the 'Unibomber', and I represent the D.I.C.K., and if that *bitch,* Candy tryna give me some of that bomb-diggity, then I'ma give her some of this monster," Unibomber had answered, holding his penis through his pants as he and Ty then laughed.

"Yo, I'm out, kid. You two *niggas* is sick, just like that *nigga,* Ray," Trigger retorted, as he'd hurried off the tier; Trigger hadn't given the two a chance to respond.

While the three youngsters were on one side of the tier, there had been a few convicts who'd come out of their cells on the opposite side. They'd observed the paramedics who desperately tried to bring Lil' Will back to life.

"Who's that on the stretcher?" J-Rock curiously asked, as he'd joined Chris and Pooh on the tier. Pooh, Chris and J-Rock weren't only fellow convicts, they'd been more like cousins—the three childhood friends had grown up together since second grade in elementary school.

Although they'd done everything together and had a lot in common, when it had come to religion, they had different viewpoints and beliefs. Their debates often had become heated—at least between Chris and J-Rock.

Most times, Pooh had sat back and laughed, as they'd argued with each other daily. Chris was a Sunni Muslim, while J-Rock had been a member of the *Moorish Science Temple.*

"That's Lil' Will. Looks like he OD'd," Pooh answered as he'd shaken his head.

"Damn, look at that *shit. Nigga* locked up but still gettin' high," Chris had stated, as he looked on at his humorous friend. Chris had liked how Lil' Will joked around, as he'd made everyone laugh every chance he'd gotten.

"Where's Ray?" J-Rock then asked; he'd known that Ray would've been the only person seriously affected by Lil' Will's overdose.

"I don't know, but I'm 'bout to offer Salat wit' the brothers," Chris had replied, as he then nodded at Amin and Abdul; they'd headed in the Chris' and J-Rock's direction.

"As-Salaamu-Alaikum," Amin and Abdul had both greeted Chris in the Arabic language.

"Wa'laikum-Salaam," Chris had replied.

"Who's that they have on the stretcher?" Amin asked as he'd looked on.

"That's 'Ill Will'," Pooh had answered, referring to Lil' Will by his jailhouse nickname.

"Yeah, he sure does look ill," Amin then answered, as he'd continued to look at the helpless dope fiend.

"Where's his boy, Ray?" Abdul had asked.

"Here he comes now," J-Rock responded, as they'd noticed that Ray had entered into the unit with a weary look upon his face. Ray immediately had begun to grieve, as he'd looked at his friend's lifeless body—the paramedics had covered Lil' Will's head with a sheet; after countless efforts of trying to bring him back to life. Lil' Will had died instantly.

Most had speculated from an overdose. Ray had assumed that one of the balloons filled with drugs, had burst inside his body, and caused Lil' Will's heart to stop. Others simply hadn't cared.

The reality back then: no one, with the exception of those who'd performed his autopsy, would've ever known the real reason why Lil' Will had died; not even his next of kin. For Lil' Will had no family members who'd cared. His only family had been those who watched him die—his fellow convicts.

"From Allah, we come, and to Allah, we shall return! C'mon, Ahk, you ready to offer Salat?" Amin then asked Chris after he'd made his statement.

Even though the inmates at that time, had witnessed death in its purest form, a true convict believed that life still had to go

on; what a prisoner had witnessed in prison, was an everyday learning experience.

"Yeah, I'm ready," Chris answered back, as he'd then thrown his prayer rug over his shoulder and proceeded down the tier. J-Rock, once again, had taken the opportunity to joke with Amin.

"Aye, Amin, why you didn't ask *me* to offer Salat with you?" J-Rock asked jokingly as he'd smiled.

"Aye, man, what I tell you 'bout that, Ahk? Stop *playin'* with the Deen. You gonna make me go to your body," Amin had replied.

"Jason, you better stop playin'. Allah's gonna *punish* you if you keep jokin' wit' the Deen," Chris interjected, as he'd become irritated by J-Rock's humor. Chris was heated. This had been the only time and person, to ever call J-Rock by his birth name. Whenever Chris had, you'd known that he'd been angry.

Pooh immediately burst into laughter, as he'd laughed loudly to instigate a heated debate.

"Aiiight, then. I see y'all getting emotional—As-Salaamu-Alaikum," J-Rock said, as he'd quickly departed before anyone could respond.

Amin and Chris then looked at each other and had shaken their heads, as they'd smiled. They couldn't resist J-Rock's good spirit.

"Wa'laikum," they'd both retorted, before the two walked off.

THE PLAYERS' CLUB
chapter 23

One week after Lil' Will was pronounced dead amongst his peers, the biggest championship basketball game had been held inside the indoor gym at seven o'clock PM.

The game had been the talk on the compound amongst the inmates, in which it featured two of the best teams; not only the best basketball players at *Cumberland's Federal Correctional Institution*, but some of the best ball players within the federal prison system.

The game had been so anticipated, that gambling bookies had placed bets on their tickets. That night was the event that every convict had waited all year long for—in which 1,500 prisoners had attended the game.

Inmates had put on new outfits, as some prepared to take pictures. Others had packed cold sodas and honey buns to sell to spectators who'd sat in the bleachers.

Flamboyant drag queens also had dressed as feminine as possible without being harassed by guards; they'd hoped to be able to pull as many tricks underneath the bleachers.

"HEY, CANDY, YOU GOIN' TO THE GAME?" Ke-Ke yelled, as he'd hollered loudly across the walkway; Candy had headed to the unit.

"Of course I'm going; my *husband* is playing," Candy replied girlishly, as she'd referred to Ray.

Ke-Ke Overness, infamous ringleader of the well-known gay gang called the House of Overness, based in *New York City,* was a masculine transvestite who'd been considered a blatant drag queen; being very burly and non-passable as a woman. He was tall, dark-skinned and very muscular, standing at 6' 3" with big biceps. Ke-Ke looked like the professional bodybuilders within *Muscle & Fitness* magazine.

Even though he'd worn homemade women's clothing, Ke-Ke's genetic make-up still had made him look very manly. Yet, he'd tried his best to look like a female, but couldn't, even with applying cosmetics; yet hadn't any problems getting trades.

Although Ke-Ke dressed in homemade miniskirts, cutting his pants, his mission had been to turn trades out. Often times, Ke-Ke had aggressively penetrated them—he'd known all along that the masculine trades had been closeted homosexuals.

"Oh, so I *guess* you gonna be his own personal cheerleader, huh, *bitch?*" Ke-Ke had said sarcastically. He'd become extremely jealous of Candy's feminine features, but Ke-Ke had never outwardly revealed this to her.

"A girl gots to support her man," Candy then replied coyly, excited to see Ray play basketball. Not only had she been eager to see Ray play, but the whole compound had anticipated seeing the one-time, *NBA* draft pick prospect, who unfortunately, couldn't stay out of jail, and off of drugs.

Ray had been considered, play-by-play, the second best ball player within the prison system, next to Daryell C.; a bright, young man whose conspiracy charge in *Richmond, Virginia,* disabled him from going to the *NBA.*

When the clock had struck seven o'clock that evening, and the ten-minute move was called over the loudspeaker, the compound had been filled with many inmates in transit towards the gym, that the warden called in extra correctional officers; standing in to avoid any bad situations.

Officers had known that any sport that required close contact, would provoke a fight, having different types of inmates with egos who'd played aggressively. Also, there had been bullies who tried to manhandle the game, who'd definitely needed to be watched as well.

The gym was packed with individual crews, in which some inmates had come equipped with weapons, as others simply had come to enjoy the event and support their friends on the team.

In Candy's case, she'd come to support her man, better yet, her "husband". She'd sat on the opposite side of the gym along with the rest of the homosexuals, transgender, and other non-respectable convicts, who hadn't been allowed to sit with other inmates who'd been convicted for hardcore crimes; the gym had been purposely segregated.

"Damn, why every time we come inside this gym, we *have* to sit in this designated area?" Candy had hissed frustratingly; irritated.

"'Cause, *bitch,* we the outcast, remember? Even though I probably can whip half them niggas asses over there, we still got

116

rules in prison that we *must* follow. Queens sit wit' other queens or either their man, and in your case, your man is playin' ball; so your ass have the privilege to sit wit' us hoes!" Ke-Ke had answered while Jose lightly smirked.

"C'mon, Candy, your ass has been on the compound too long now. You mean to tell me you're *still* acting like you don't know the rules?" Jose had replied sarcastically in a soft, feminine tone.

"No, Jose, it's just that I'm getting *tired* of *motherfuckers* treating us like we're not human. Some of them *same* fools over there are undercover trades, just *waiting* for the day to get with us," Candy then replied furiously.

"Yeah, whatever, Candy. You can voice your opinion all day long, but at the end of the day, queens *must* stay where the *fuck* they belong. I'll be braiding some *nigga's* hair, and your *ass* will still be here, sitting on *this* side of the gym with me," Jose had snapped.

As the three had engaged in conversation, Candy, Jose and Ke-Ke sat back and had observed the prisoners who'd entered the gym; Candy had labeled some according to their body language and mannerism, and by the level of respect other convicts had given each other.

For instance, although Ty and Unibomber had been undercover trades, and from the constant glimpses that Trigger had taken of Candy, she'd felt that these inmates didn't belong on the opposite side of the gym with the other respectable convicts. Yet, once again, they all blended in well...

"THE *FUCK* YOU LOOKIN' AT?" Trigger nastily yelled, as he'd caught Candy looking back at him. Candy then sucked her teeth and blew hot air out of her mouth, as she'd exhaled; Candy had ignored Trigger's fake, rugged demeanor. She'd come to the conclusion that: Trigger had either been an undercover trade, a male filled with sexual curiosity, or a damn fool to risk his life by harassing her.

Everyone on the compound had known that Candy had been Ray's girl, and if he'd found out that Trigger had ever disrespected her in anyway, Ray surely would've gone to war with the young, thug-wannabe convict; most likely killing him, as Ray had done to others before—being a skilled knifeman and a prized fighter.

"Boy, take your *crazy* ass on somewhere! Ain't *nobody* lookin' at you, fool!" Ke-Ke shouted, as he'd changed his fake, feminine voice to his deep, manly speech; Ke-Ke had shown Trigger that he could be just as dangerous.

"*FUCK* YOU, YOU *FAGGOT*-ASS *NIGGA!*" Trigger had spat before Ty pulled him away.

"C'mon, man, leave them punks alone," Ty had instructed.

As the men had departed, Jose's eyes widened and sparked when he'd observed Abdul walk into the gym. He'd headed towards the secluded group of Muslims, who seemed to have had their own section within the gym.

"Ooh, y'all, there goes Abdul's *sexy* ass," Jose had said in an extremely low whisper.

"Look, but turn away quickly, 'cause, *bitch,* if anyone of them Muslims see your *ass* gawkin', they gonna *stab* first and ask questions later," Ke-Ke warned cautiously, as he'd reminded Jose of their prison rules.

Although Candy had been madly in love with Ray, she still couldn't deny the fact that Abdul was fine. Yet, Candy had felt that she, or her two friends, who'd sat on the bleaches with her, wouldn't ever have the privilege to be with him.

Candy's illusion of Abdul quickly faded away, as she'd noticed that Ray had come onto the basketball court in his uniform; he'd worn his brand-new white, *"Air Force-1" Nike* high-top sneakers.

"There goes my baby right there," Candy had said excitedly in a girlish voice.

"Oh God, this *bitch* is really in love," Ke-Ke then replied facetiously, as jealousy had begun to eat at him.

Ray had arrived on the basketball court like a true sportsman, as he'd shaken each team member's hands on the opposing team, all but C-Low's.

C-Low was a heavyset gang-banger from *South Central Los Angeles,* whose intimidating presence had scared many half-to-death. Yet, C-Low had been a coward at heart who'd constantly worn his mask of aggression.

So much, that when Ray was aware of this, he'd begun to despise C-Low. In addition, Candy had told Ray about the love letters that she'd received at her job one day, in which Candy believed that C-Low had secretly delivered them to her. Candy discovered the letters, immediately as she'd arrived for duty, and as C-Low had exited the infirmary.

Knowing this, Ray had become highly upset, and often wished that Jose had never gotten Candy the job at the hospital, where she'd been exposed to countless trades; who'd constantly flirted with her.

Making matters worse, tension was in the air within the *Bureau of Prisons,* because of the war that had occurred—*DC* vs. *California.* It had been rumored that in the *USP Florence Facility* in *Colorado,* allegedly, a guy from *DC* had smashed a *Californian* in the head with a 45-pound dead weight, and in return, the *DC* and *California* beef had turned into a full-scale war—especially within the institutions around the *West Coast.*

Ray had looked into C-Low's mean eyes with hatred, fully believing that he was a coward. He'd then stared hard at C-Low and waited for him to bow his head, and divert his eyes towards the ground, giving Ray the satisfaction of knowing that he'd mentally dominated C-Low.

C-Low then forced himself not to budge, as he'd tightened his jaws and gritted his teeth, as C-Low then looked back at Ray. No one within the gym had known why the tension between the two power forwards was so thick, yet the audience sat back and had observed the intense energy; convicts then hoped that the hostility would be applied to the game. Bets had begun to be placed.

"I got twenty books on Ray and 'em," Pooh indicated, as he'd sat with his comrades.

"I don't know 'bout that one, Pooh," Chris had interjected, "Ray like that, but you know that *nigga,* C-Low done stepped up his game."

"Who's on Ray's team?" J-Rock had joined in.

"Man, you got Lil' Pig from *DC,* Charlie Hurt from *B-More,* Charlie Webb from *DC* and Danny Boy from *St. Louis.* Now, you know that *nigga,* Danny Boy can jump straight out the gym," Pooh had replied, as his peers immediately agreed.

"Yeah, he might can jump, but look who they're playing against," Chris had answered back. "You got two of the best ballers in the whole *Bureau of Prisons* playing on the same team. Look at the starting line-up: C-Low, Daryell C. from *V.A.,* Carlos from *Simple City*, 88-Yo from *B-More* and Big Ahk from *Connecticut,"* Chris had ranted on. "Yeah, Pooh, Big Ahk like that. Plus, he's my Muslim brother. I think I'ma go wit' C-Low and 'em."

"There you go with that Muslim stuff. Tell you what, put twenty books on your Muslim brother; do that, *nigga!* Put your money on your man, Big Ahk!" Pooh replied, as he'd tried to provoke Chris.

"BET THEN, *NIGGA.* YOU AIN'T SAID *SHIT!*" Chris had yelled.

"DOUBLE THAT, FAM, SINCE YOU'RE TALKIN' SHIT ABOUT OUR BROTHER, BIG AHK!" Jamil from Philly had screamed.

"Here, Chris, put this twenty books with yours, 'cause I'm going over there with the brothers. You know if Amin sees me over here with Pooh, he'll know that I'm gambling," Abdul had replied discreetly.

They'd all burst out and laughed, as Abdul then snuck off when the game had started. Carlos immediately had made the first three-point shot.

"BLACK AND MILD! BLACK AND MILD! COLD SODAS AND HONEY BUNS!" yelled the jailhouse vendor, as he'd walked up-and-down the gym and sold items.

It was only five minutes left in the last quarter, as Ray and his team had been down by six points.

"Aye, Oogie, let me get an ice-cold soda for my man here, so he can cool down," Chris replied slyly, as he'd indirectly tried to irritate Pooh; Pooh's team had been losing.

J-Rock and Chris couldn't hold back the laughter, as they'd seen the reaction on Pooh's face when C-Low had dunked the ball on Ray. The entire gym had been silent before they'd all cheered in a loud outburst: "O-O-O-O-O-O-O-O-O-H!"

Ray had tried his best to instill fear into C-Low, as they'd both played defensively, facing one another; as the two waited for the ball to be passed.

"*Nigga,* you ain't do *shit,*" Ray had stated to C-Low; annoyed.

"Oh, yeah. Your girl, Candy *seemed* to like it," C-Low had replied shadily; he'd known that this distracting comment would've knocked Ray out of his game.

It was the last basket of the game, and both teams had tied in scores, in which C-Low's team had checked the ball. Ray had been so heated by C-Low's comment—he couldn't fathom Candy being impressed with his opponent's game.

Jealousy had quickly eaten at Ray, as his mind stayed affixed on C-Low's remark. He'd then diverted his attention to Candy; Ray had made sure that she hadn't looked at C-Low. At that point, Ray had been insecure, and with that, he and his team had paid greatly.

As Ray monitored Candy, 88-Yo had drilled a hard pass to C-Low, which had given him the open shot to drive pass Ray. C-Low then knocked Ray down, and had gone up to the basket to score; ending the game with the smoothest reverse-dunk move, ever to be seen at *Cumberland's Federal Correctional Institute.*

C-Low's game play was so vicious, that convict's had jumped out of the bleachers, and screamed uncontrollably when the game had ended. His well-executed dunk shot hadn't been the only highlight of the game that evening—it was the start of a beef that would later erupt.

"Go down the unit and get my *shit*—meet me on the walk," Ray had demanded to Candy. She'd seen the look in Ray's eyes, and immediately had known that he'd meant business, as Ray had instructed Candy to go secure his knife.

Candy had known that, not just from the game, but that it had been an accumulation of things that had caused Ray to act so irrational. Also, he'd still grieved Lil' Will's death, which had caused him to be very upset.

"C'mon, Ray, it's just a game," Candy then stated, as she'd tried to comfort him; her large, doe-shaped, light-brown eyes had begun to water. Candy couldn't imagine doing the rest of her time without Ray. She'd needed him; Ray had been her all. Candy had no family, no friends—no nothing. "Look, baby, *please* don't do this. It's not worth it," Candy had cried nervously.

Ray had known that Candy had been right, but he had to take his frustration out on somebody, and figured: what better person to take it out on than C-Low. Ray, at that moment, felt that he had justifiable reasons to punish C-Low.

"*BITCH,* DO WHAT THE *FUCK* I SAID!" Ray then shouted, as anger had built deeper within him. Candy had quickly jumped and hurried out of the gym; she'd hoped that he wouldn't embarrass her in front of Jose and Ke-Ke. Candy also had known that when Ray had become heated like this, to stay far away; he'd transformed into an angry maniac in the past.

When the ten-minute move announcement had been made over the loudspeaker, Candy was the first person to rush out of the gym and head down the unit; she'd secured Ray's knife. Candy felt that she had to play her position and help her man, at *all* cost; even if it had meant risking her *own* life. For Candy had believed deep in her heart, that Ray would've done the same.

As the prisoners had quickly left the gym and raced to their units, Ray had lagged behind to follow C-Low. He'd then shaken everyone's hand inside the gym. The crowd had become smaller, having a few convicts present in the gym who'd gathered their things.

As Ray rapidly changed out of his uniform, he'd spotted C-Low heading his way. Ray had been tying his shoes when C-Low had approached him. C-Low then held out his hand for a fair sportsman's shake.

"Good game, Ray. Maybe next year you'll get me back," C-Low had stated with his hand extended.

"Nah, more like right now," Ray then answered back angrily, as he'd leaped up, and delivered a powerful uppercut to C-Low's chin, followed by a quick right hook to the eye; Ray had instantly gashed C-low's flesh over his eyebrow. The cut was so deep, that C-Low's blood had streamed down his face like a waterfall.

C-Low immediately regrouped, and had tried to fight back, but he hadn't been fast enough, or strong enough to defend himself, as Ray had caught him in the mouth with a hard punch.

Ray then screamed in agony, as C-Low's tooth had cut into his fist from the punch. But his anger had overrode the pain, as Ray then continued to beat C-Low's face; C-Low had looked as if he was going to bleed to death.

"Aiiight, Ray, that's enough!" J-Rock had said forcefully, as he'd felt the need not only to save C-Low's life, but to also save Ray from catching a case. When Ray had heard J-Rock's voice, he'd known that it was time to stop attacking.

When Ray had stopped beating into C-Low's face, his hands had been covered with so much blood, that he'd taken off his shirt and had wrapped it around his cut.

After leaving the gym, Ray then walked to the unit, immediately, he'd smiled with pleasure when he'd seen Candy at the top of the walkway waiting for him. Ray then felt that he had a "girl" who had been down for him, one who'd followed his every instruction.

"You okay, Ray?" Candy had cautiously asked with concern, as she'd looked at his hand wrapped in the bloodied T-shirt.

"Yeah, I'm cool. Look, I ain't gonna need the knife, so go back and meet me in my room," Ray had instructed Candy. "Bring some of that antibiotic shit, some peroxide, and a needle and thread."

Candy quickly had done what she'd been told, in fact, it then had turned her on: having a man with such confidence and aggression.

After Ray had washed and stitched up his own open wound, Candy then immediately calmed Ray's nerves, as she'd given him intensified, nerve-tingling, body-jerking oral sex. Ray later had ejaculated uncontrollably in her warm mouth, as Candy then voluntarily swallowed all of his semen; she hadn't missed a drop.

"I love you, Ray," Candy whispered, as she'd wiped a few droplets of sperm from her lips and licked her fingers.

"I love you, too, Candy," Ray answered as he'd looked into her eyes, as Candy had knelt on the floor.

"How much?"

"Enough to do *anything* for you, Candy"

"And vice-versa, baby."

*   *   *   *   *

When the prison van hit the bump, Candy's thoughts of the past were interrupted: "What, are we here yet?" she asked indirectly to the other inmates.

"Nah, not yet. The dumb-ass driver just ran over a few bumps," said the strikingly handsome brother with the full-facial beard. His face alone resembled Abdul—the Muslim brother Jose lusted over. Candy shook her head in shame, as she thought about Jose's fantasy man.

"Poor Abdul," Candy said in a low whisper, while slowly drifting off to sleep.

124

CASH RULES EVERYTHING AROUND ME
chapter 25

"Look, Candy, baby, I'm *tellin'* you—you can do it, boo," Ray had said, as he'd eagerly tried to persuade Candy into smuggling drugs in for him from a visit; Ray had wanted her to be his new mule.

"I don't know, Ray...I mean, I've never done anything like this before."

"There's a first time for everything. Now look, we *gotta* do this, baby if we wanna continue to survive. We don't have *nobody* out here doin' *shit* for us. We *all* we got, Candy; we *gotta* make a way for ourselves.

"Now, I know you need a lawyer to do your appeal, and the *only* way we gonna do that is if we got money. Candy, baby, the White guy named, Tom who works in the Law Library, is a *real* fuckin' lawyer. All we gotta do is pay him, and the *only* way we gonna be able to pay him is if we get the blow," Ray had explained.

"Well, what about your homie, J-Rock? Why can't he help us with my appeal? Isn't he some type of lawyer, too?" Candy asked, as she'd referred to the jailhouse rumors about J-Rock's legal skills.

"Candy, now you *must've* bumped your head against some cell bars if you *think* J-Rock's gonna help *you* get outta jail. I mean, that's my homie and all, but he won't have *nothin'* to do wit' *you,* or *your* case. J-Rock only helps the people who mean the most to him. He may look over it if I ask him too, just to give his opinion, but for real, Tom is the *real* lawyer—that's who we *really* need. And besides, J-Rock's on some ole other shit right now, talkin' 'bout bein' down wit' *GHETTOHEAT®,* writin' novels and screenplays. He ain't even *thinkin'* 'bout no law work.

"You really think this guy, Tom can get me out?" Candy had asked excitedly, being curious.

"Candy, you must not be hearin' me well. Didn't I say that Tom is a *real* lawyer? Baby, Tom had his own *fuckin'* office out there in the real world. Matter fact, he and his co-defendant are both here together. Remember the scandal in Philly, *'Pay-2-Play',* where the feds bugged the mayor's office, and the city council and government officials got caught up in that big money launderin' embezzlement case?"

"Yes, I remember reading that in the *Philadelphia Daily Newspaper* you got from the Muslim guy, um, what's his name? ...Amin?"

"Yeah, Amin. He be givin' me those papers. Well, anyway, baby, the lawyer and city council that got caught up in that case is Tom, and his co-defendant Dewayne, the Christian brother who be at the chapel all the time."

"Damn, I didn't even know that. So when are you going to talk to him?" Candy had asked anxiously.

Once again, Ray's plan had worked, as he'd then tricked Candy into being his next mule for the drugs. Ever since Lil' Will had died, Ray had needed another person to bring in the dope. He'd eagerly needed to feed his habit, as well as keep Candy's, and his locker filled with commissary.

"I'ma talk to him as soon as we get the first package. After we make about a good four thousand, I'ma give him twenty-five hundred to do your appeal, and re-up with the rest. After that, we'll keep payin' him in installments until he gets you back in court. Then, baby, we gonna live like a king and queen," Ray then said and smiled; he'd enticed Candy to smuggle the drugs in for him even more.

The large amount of money that Ray had talked about to Candy almost seemed impossible to make, as she'd been ignorant as to how much money could be made in prison.

"Damn, Ray, I wish you would've told me how much money could've been made a long time ago. I would've been up in the 'VIP' toting those drugs back then. Now, tell me what I have to do, because, baby, I *need* a lawyer badly," Candy had replied, as she'd committed herself.

Ray had begun to explain in detail, as he'd told Candy that she would go out on a visit with Kim's cousin, Reecey, retrieve the package, then slide it into her anus; which back then, had been stretched wide open—from the continuous sex they'd had on a daily basis.

Most importantly, Ray had gone over the technique and strategy that Candy had to do, in order to get by the guard whom had been on duty. Candy then listened carefully back then, as Ray repeatedly had run down instructions to her everyday that week.

Often times, he'd drilled and practiced in her cell. This, including Ray stretching out Candy's anus with his massive dick, continued up until the day before the visit.

* * * * *

"So you got it all down?" Ray asked, as he'd made sure that Candy had understood the plan.

"Yes, Ray; I *got* it! Stop worrying!" Candy then replied; irritated. Ray's instructing her on how to bring in the package had gotten on Candy's nerves. From the way he'd acted, she'd almost thought that Ray had been the one using drugs, instead of selling it.

"Aiiight, I'm just makin' sure, 'cause you know our big day is tomorrow," Ray had stated. Candy then blown hot air out of her mouth, as she'd sighed; indirectly Candy had let Ray know that he'd annoyed her.

"Yes, Ray, I know; how *can* I forget? You've been *telling* me this *everyday* for the last past week!"

Ray then had sensed that Candy had become irrational, somewhat like a real woman who'd been experiencing P.M.S. Before he'd allowed the situation to get out of hand, avoiding a big argument with Candy, Ray had decided that it was best to go to the barbershop and get his haircut.

Making sure that he'd always looked good, every time he'd set foot in the visiting hall, in which the convict's named it the "VIP" room, Ray had kept himself well-groomed. So good, that Ray had often noticed other convict's female visitors looking at him.

Ray's main reason for being so immaculate had been to keep his fiancée, Kim intrigued with him, in hopes that she'd eventually marry Ray; which would cause Kim to be available to him at Ray's convenience. She'd already been madly in love with Ray. Also, Kim unfortunately had believed everything that Ray had said—even when Kim had felt that he'd lied to her.

"Aiiight, then. I see you 'bout to catch a lil' attitude. I'ma head on down to the barbershop to get my haircut."

"Okay, I'll see you later," Candy had answered in a much softer tone, one that quickly eased the tension between Candy and her lover.

"Oh, yeah, and *don't* even *try* to show off when you see me and Kim together."

Instantly, Candy had become angry again: "Bye, Ray! Go and get your haircut—I'll see you some *other* time!" she'd snapped; Candy had tried to push him out of her cell.

Candy was hurt, she'd believed deep inside that Ray had "loved" her, but Candy also had known that regardless of that fact, Kim would always have something that she hadn't—a *real* vagina; something that Candy would *die* for—and Ray had known it.

"I'm not going to *fuck* up your little relationship with that fat *bitch!* Anyway, you're about to go home next year. I *hope* you two live happily ever after," Candy then spat facetiously with resentment; she'd had hurt feelings.

"Come here!" Ray then demanded, as he'd grabbed her. Ray then held Candy tight in his arms. He'd planted a long, passionate kiss on her lips, a kiss so intense, that it had instantly turned Candy's volatile anger into erotic pleasure.

"Aye, this ain't 'bout no *goddamn* Kim—this is 'bout me and you. My mission is to get that package, sell it, and get you a lawyer; so we'll *both* be home together. Then, we can go to *California,* and live our lives together. Candy, you *my* bitch for life—believe that, baby!"

"I know, Ray. It's just that, every time you say Kim's name, I get so frustrated. I'm sorry, daddy," Candy had answered back seductively, as she'd tried to get Ray aroused.

"Candy, tell you what, go get yourself together. I'ma go get my haircut, and when I come back, I'ma *tap* that ass r-e-a-l good," Ray then stated, as he'd smiled.

"O-O-O-O-O-O-H, hurry up and get that haircut!" Candy had replied, as she pushed him out the cell. They'd both laughed....

CUT!
chapter 26

"WHO'S NEXT?" Ray asked loudly as he'd busted inside the barbershop; just moments after Riddick Bowe had exited from getting his shape-up.

When Ray entered, everyone had looked at him with disgust, mainly for what he'd done to C-Low. Highly respected convicts at that time, had considered Ray not only to be mentally unstable, but also felt that he'd lacked heavily in morals and principles.

Ray had almost killed C-Low over a transsexual. That was definitely forbidden, according to the inmates' prison rules. Certain inmates at the time had shunned Ray.

"Check it, son, you gonna have to let Nook cut your hair—I got a long line," Yusuf replied in his *New York City* accent, as he'd proceeded to give his customer a haircut. Yusuf was a chubby, light-skinned Dominican with long braided hair, and a neatly, groomed beard; in which inmates considered a Sunnah—one of Muslim's distinguishing looks.

He'd been considered the best barber on the entire compound, in which everyone favored him; Yusuf was preferred for his grooming skills. Some had even called him the "Shape-Up King"; Yusuf being known for his trademark razor-sharp hairlines.

"Damn, I ain't *tryna* let that *nigga,* Nook cut my *shit!*" Ray had answered angrily.

"Well, Ray, I don't know what to tell you, son. But like I *said,* I got the brothers today," Yusuf then retorted, as he'd referred to the Muslims: Amin, Corleone, Jamil and Abdul.

As Ray then quickly stomped out of the shop angrily, everyone had burst into laughter.

"Aye, Yusuf, why you ain't cut the homie head?" Pooh asked as he'd snickered.

"C'mon, Pooh, you know I ain't *never* cutting Ray's hair. Son, that *nigga* be on some ole *other* shit—for real! Son, I don't *want* my clippers on his head, for the simple fact that I'm scared I might nick him by mistake, and draw some blood," Yusuf then explained.

"Damn, you clean your clippers, don't you?" Corleone had asked in his deep Philly accent.

"Yeah, I soak 'em with *Barbicide* and disinfect 'em after every cut. But yo, that shit *ain't* no guarantee that the blade is completely clean, son."

"Hold up, hold up, Yusuf. Now, you know *Barbicide* is the most effective disinfectant you can use. It's specifically says right here on the bottle that *'it prevents all germs, even HIV',*" Nook had joined in, holding up the can of disinfectant, as he'd continued to cut Unibomber's hair.

"C'mon, Nook, *fuck* that *Barbicide* shit and finish my head! I don't pay you to talk while cuttin' my *shit!*" Unibomber replied as he'd looked at Ty, who anxiously had wanted to leave.

Unibomber and Ty both had observed the barbershop, and had known that from the convicts who'd been there, that they hadn't been welcomed. The other respectable, heterosexual men in the barbershop hadn't accepted Ty and Unibomber.

To the left stood Amin, Corleone, Jamil and Abdul; and to the right: Chris, Pooh and J-Rock. Ty and Trigger had stood over in the corner, as they'd waited for Unibomber.

"Aye, Yusuf, so you sayin' you bias, huh?" Ty had asked.

"Biased about *what,* Ty?"

"You know, you ain't gonna cut a *nigga's* head 'cause he *fuck* wit' boys," Ty had answered.

Instantly, Yusuf had become defensive, as he stood firm on what he'd believed.

"You *motherfuckin'* right! If I know a nigga's *fuckin'* wit' them punks, he *can't* sit nowhere *near* my chair. I don't give a *fuck* who you are or *suppose* to be. I fear *none* but Allah," Yusuf had stated, as he had a serious expression upon his face.

At Yusuf's statement, Amin had seen that the topic was at the verge of getting out of hand, yet, he'd wanted Ty to get a complete message. Amin, at that moment, had taken over the conversation.

"Yusuf, you can give him the Haqq without using foul language—Insha-Allah. And Ty, if your uncle were still here in prison, you wouldn't even *be* around a guy like Ray, let alone standing here trying to defend him. You need to come to Jumu'ah and ask Allah to forgive you for what you've been doing in prison, because you're not only ruining yourself, you're going to ruin your community!" Amin had stated, as he moved his hands while he'd talked.

"My community? How am *I* ruinin' *my* community? What that got to do wit' me hittin' up a boy? What I do in prison *stays* in prison. My community don't know *nothin'*," Ty had answered nonchalantly.

Ty's comment had made most of the prisoners in the barbershop livid, as they'd begun badgering him with a series of questions.

"Aye, Ty, what he's saying is that, since your community don't know, what happens if you catch a disease, and got out there and gave it to one of them fine sistas who be writing you all the time? Then in turn, she cheats on you, gives it to another person, or worse, gets pregnant and gives it to your child. Man, AIDS ain't *nothing* to be played wit'," J-Rock had stated, desperately, he'd tried to reach out to the young, uneducated brother.

"Man, *fuck* that! I ain't *catchin'* no AIDS, I straps up every time I hit," Ty had retorted with a dumb expression upon his face.

"*Fuck* strappin' up, Ty, what about your morals as a man? How the *fuck* can you actually have *sex* with another man as if he was a woman? Where's your dignity and respect as a man? What about your family, your woman at home? Where's your respect for them, if not for yourself?" Corleone then joined in, as he too had become frustrated at the youngster's ignorance.

"Yo, *fuck* home. The whole time I been down, ain't nobody do *shit* for me, not even my uncle. My so-called girl rolled out in the first six months of my bid, and now, seven years later, all of a sudden she tryna get back in a *nigga's* life; 'cause she know I'm 'bout to shine in a couple months.

"Man, *fuck* that *bitch!* Look at all the *shit* I done for her when I was out there. I risked my *life* everyday standin' on the corner, hustlin', just to take care of that *bitch!* I paid for her college tuition and all that!

"Now, the *bitch* gotta job at a law firm, and she can't even help a *nigga* out, let alone send me a *punk-ass* one-hundred dollars. They *act* like they don't know we really need money to survive in this joint. *Shit,* we gotta pay to wash our *own* clothes here in prison," Ty spat, as he'd gone off on a tangent.

Ty's statement alone had everyone in the barbershop quiet. With the exception of dealing with homosexuals, each inmate had dealt with the same issues that Ty had been dealing with. Some had conquered their pain, some hadn't, but most of all, none of these convicts had let their reality turn them away from their manhood; except Ty.

"Yeah, Ty, I'm sure we all can agree wit' you on that issue, but that still don't mean you gotta turn to another man for comfort," J-Rock had interjected.

"Aye, I respect every last one of you *niggas* in here, but regardless of what y'all say, I'm *still* gonna do me! Ty gonna be Ty! I ain't *come* to jail like this…it's the people in the world who crossed me that made my heart harden. So like I said, *fuck* 'em!" Ty had shouted.

After his statement, no one had spoken to Ty. They'd been finished with trying to school the ignorant youngster. Ty had showed them all that it was useless in trying to talk sense into him.

"Aiiight, that's ten stamps," Nook stated, as he'd held his hand out to Unibomber after Nook had cut his hair. When Unibomber got out of the chair, laughter had erupted throughout the barbershop. Nook had completely sabotaged Unibomber's head; he'd cut out deep patches, and left Unibomber's fade unblended.

"I see why Ray rolled out," Corleone had joked, as everyone else then joined in.

"Damn, Nook, man, you gotta fix that," Trigger had said, as he and Ty had looked at each other; they'd tried to hold in their laughter.

"S-h-i-i-i-t, fix what? I'm good," Unibomber then replied, as he'd looked into the mirror. Unibomber then patted his head—he hadn't known that he had a bald spot in the back.

"Aiiight then, son, if you like it, then pay the man so we can go. I gots to get my flow ready for the talent show," Trigger retorted, as he'd reminded everyone indirectly that he'd be rapping in the upcoming talent show.

After Trigger, Ty and Unibomber had departed, everyone had gone back to having their usually barbershop conversation, discussing sports, religion, books, court cases, and girls.

The next day…

"ATTENTION ON THE YARD AND HOUSING UNITS, INMATE SWEETS, 48301-004, AND INMATE SMITH, 05412-061, REPORT TO THE VISITING ROOM!" the correctional officer had loudly instructed over the PA system.

It's now or never, Candy had thought, as she nervously headed towards the door of the visiting dress-out room. Candy then took a deep breath before she'd pushed the button—Candy alarmed the guards that she'd been at the door, and had waited for a visit.

Candy then looked over her shoulder and noticed that Abdul had come for his visit as well. She'd looked at Abdul in the past and noticed how handsome he'd been, but never had acted upon her feelings, due to being in love with Ray; Candy also had known that Jose had been his secret admirer.

But this had been the closest Candy had ever been next to Abdul, as she'd looked at him lustfully out the corner of her eyes. For the very first time, Candy had found him to be more attractive than ever before.

"Mmmph, mmmph, mmmph," Candy murmured lightly, as she'd quickly put her hand over her mouth. Candy tried hard not to expose her shameless reaction; she'd hoped that Abdul hadn't heard her.

As Abdul looked in the opposite direction, not paying any attention to Candy, she'd smiled, as Candy had glanced down at the big print that bulged in his pants.

Damn! Abdul is packing; for real! Candy had peeked at the forbidden fruit. Silence filled the air, and Candy's desire had halted, as Abdul then turned towards her and had asked: "Did you hit the button?"

"Yes," Candy had replied, as she slightly blushed.

This had been the first time that Abdul had spoken to her, let alone acknowledged Candy's presence. Due to strict rules in the Muslim community, any homosexual act, or encounter with another person with an alternative lifestyle is considered Haram in Islamic Law.

Candy had tried desperately to hide her attraction to Abdul, but couldn't. Mostly because the more she'd looked at him, the more Abdul had reminded Candy of Terry; Abdul had resembled her ex-boyfriend—more so than Ray had. Abdul hadn't only resembled Terry in looks, but also possessed the same confidence and boldness in his walk as Terry had.

"Who's first?" Officer Mummy asked, as he'd opened the strip room door. As soon as the guard had seen Abdul, instantly, he'd put a frown upon his face, and shown true signs of hatred. Officer Mummy had disliked all Muslims for the mere fact that, he'd just come back into the *United States* from serving two years in *Iraq*.

That experience alone had made the guard bias to those who'd practiced Islam. So in return, Officer Mummy had made it his business to harass all Muslims whenever he had the chance to. At that moment, Officer Mummy had smiled to himself, being that the perfect opportunity had presented itself.

"He can go first if he wants to," Candy had replied, as she'd shown Abdul respect, while she quickly studied Officer Mummy's face. Candy tried to embed his face into her memory, as she'd also tried to remember the color of Ray's cousin's blouse— Candy anxiously had wanted to know who Reecey was.

"I'll take you both," Officer Mummy had answered with a sneaky grin upon his face. Instantly, Abdul had contested.

"C'mon, Mummy, you *know* I can't undress in front of *him*," Abdul had said as he pointed towards Candy.

As Officer Mummy had realized his plan had worked, he'd kept at it: "Either I check you now or you *don't* get your visit!" Officer Mummy had replied harshly, as he'd pointed his nicotine-stained finger in Abdul's face.

Abdul then balled up his fists tightly, as he'd eagerly contemplated hitting him, but then reality had set in. Abdul immediately thought about his wife and child who'd been sitting out in the visiting hall, anxiously awaiting him to come out. "Where's the L.T.?" Abdul had managed to ask about the lieutenant through tightened lips.

"Listen, I'm *giving* you a *direct* order! You either come in this strip room now, or I'm *taking* it as you're refusing your visit!"

Seizing the opportunity to defend Abdul, Candy had interjected: "Let him go first, you know you want me *all* to yourself," she'd playfully teased Officer Mummy, as Candy then swung her long hair back flirtatiously.

Officer Mummy had always made sexual advances towards Candy when he'd worked the unit, but today, his mind had been set on making Abdul's day a living hell.

"Interfere in my duties again as an officer, and you *won't* get a visit *either!*" Officer Mummy had retorted roughly.

Candy quickly had shut her mouth. She'd known that she couldn't foil the mission; Ray would've beaten Candy's ass. Plus, she'd needed money. The money was intended to go towards Candy's legal defense. She'd stayed focused; Candy then re-grouped, so everything would go as smoothly as Ray had planned.

Ray had Kim bring his cousin, Reecey, to see Candy during the visit. Reecey had intended to pass Candy the package that had contained two ounces of marijuana, and a half-ounce of heroin.

Candy had hoped that they'd packed the package correctly; she'd also wished that it would easily fit inside of her rectum. To make sure of this, Ray had fucked Candy, long and deep, twenty minutes before the visits had been announced.

Abdul had become furious, as he'd taken long breaths and exhaled. He then lightly brushed passed Officer Mummy inside of the strip room. Candy paused briefly before she'd followed behind Abdul. Officer Mummy then instructed them both to stand side-by-side each other; he'd had only a chair in between the two for them to rest their clothing on—as Abdul and Candy had reluctantly gotten undressed.

Candy hadn't moved until she'd seen Abdul take off his freshly-ironed shirt, out from the corner of her eye. She'd then unbuttoned her khaki shirt, which had been altered at the sides; Candy hand-sewing the shirt, she'd tailored it down two sizes smaller to give emphasis to her breasts.

"Do they sell those blouses on commissary?" Officer Mummy had asked sarcastically. Candy ignored the officer and had laid her clothes neatly onto the chair. Abdul had done the same, having his eyes focused straight ahead in Officer Mummy's direction. Candy and Abdul then stood next to each other, stark naked, as they'd waited for the officer's strip room instructions.

135

Officer Mummy had become more vindictive, as he'd made them both wait, as Candy and Abdul awkwardly stood in the nude. The guard purposely had stalled as he reviewed the visitor's clipboard. To avoid the tension, Candy had looked down at her feet, and admired how good the two coats of floor wax she'd applied, made her toe nails shine.

"Hold your arms out straight," Office Mummy ordered, as he'd instructed Abdul first. Abdul had taken a deep breath and complied. "Let me see both sides of your hands...Now take that *thing* off your head, and run your fingers through your hair!" As Officer Mummy had disrespected his headdress, referring to Abdul's kufi as a "thing", Abdul had become more frustrated. "...Run your fingers through your beard."

Abdul's piercing eyes had shot straight into Officer Mummy's, as he'd let the guard know indirectly that, no matter how hard he'd tried to provoke him, that Abdul wouldn't be broken.

"Turn to the left and bend you left ear...Now turn to the right and bend your right ear."

Abdul's hatred towards Officer Mummy had grown deep—Abdul quickly had thought about how he'd harm the guard if Abdul had seen Officer Mummy in the outside world. Abdul had been upset because he'd known that, once he'd turned to the right, Abdul would be forced to see Candy naked.

Candy impulsively had covered the one thing on her body that she'd detested all of her life—her penis, and had turned her head, so Abdul wouldn't observe the shame on her face. Abdul then quickly followed Officer Mummy's instructions, and had avoided Candy standing nakedly beside him, as Abdul rapidly turned back to the left.

"I *didn't* see you bend your ear, *turn* your head around again!" Officer Mummy demanded, as he'd noticed Abdul's awkwardness.

Abdul had let out the air he held deep within his lungs, and had quietly asked Allah in his mind to, *quickly get the search over with,* so he could enjoy the visit with his lovely wife and child. Abdul then closed his eyes as he'd turned his head again, only to be opened by the harsh sound of Officer Mummy's voice.

"HOLD IT *RIGHT* THERE! WHAT'S THAT?" Officer Mummy had asked. When Abdul's eyes had opened, he appreciated the respect that Candy had displayed by covering up herself, yet Abdul had been totally disgusted by the guard's tactics.

"There isn't *anything* behind my ear," Abdul then retorted. Unwillingly, he'd then taken a good look at Candy. Unable to deny her beauty, Abdul had quickly sought refuge in Allah, as he'd felt the shame of sin. Pleased with the execution of his mischievous plan, Officer Mummy had further instructed Abdul.

"Now, lift your nut sack…Turn around…Now bend over and *spread* 'em!" Officer Mummy had sarcastically ordered. Abdul had never felt so humiliated in his life, as he parted his buttocks. "COUGH!" Officer Mummy then continued with his orders.

Abdul had prayed fast and hard to Allah, he'd asked Him to punish the non-believer as He'd seen fit. Abdul then thought about his son, and had prayed that he would never have to know, or encounter the experience, of having to be stripped of his manhood.

Relieved that the strip search was over, Abdul had turned around and grabbed his underwear from the chair, and immediately gotten dressed.

"HOLD UP, HOLD UP!" Officer Mummy had begun to yell, "DID I *TELL* YOU TO GET DRESSED? I HAVEN'T CHECKED YOUR CLOTHES YET!"

Abdul had had enough, he couldn't take it anymore: "This is *bullshit,* Mummy! You know *damn* well I'm not *carrying* any weapons on my visit.

"I'm just doing my job, Smith. Now, let me check, Sweets, so you both can get dressed and enjoy your visits," Officer Mummy had answered, as he had a silly grin upon his face.

Seeing Officer Mummy for the true coward he'd been, Abdul had become angry; he'd intensely stared at the guard. Candy then was given her instructions, as her search had begun.

"Hold your arms out straight," Officer Mummy requested, as he'd looked at Candy's firm breasts and erect nipples. She'd glanced over at Abdul, and had noticed that he wasn't looking.

Candy had known that if she hadn't completed her mission, she could be faced with twenty years in prison. Candy then looked at Officer Mummy seductively with her wide, sparkling, light-brown eyes, and had slightly wiggled her breasts. Candy had noticed that the guard's eyes never had left her breasts, convinced at this point that Ray's instructions had worked.

"Now turn around...bend over and *spread* 'em, Sweets," Officer Mummy had gladly demanded, as he winked his left eye. Candy then bent over, and had run her long fingernails over her soft, plump buttocks, yet she hadn't parted her butt cheeks. Candy had distracted Officer Mummy, as she then jiggled her rear end.

Looking back as she'd bent over, seeing the guard lick his chapped lips, had given Candy confidence that everything had gone smoothly.

"Okay, you both can get dressed. Enjoy your visits," Officer Mummy stated as he'd checked the clipboard. Abdul then snatched his boxers quickly to cover himself; he'd hoped that Candy hadn't seen his privates.

Although Abdul had retrieved his underwear swiftly, his sudden movement had made Candy glance in his direction. She couldn't resist the urge, as Candy had glimpsed at his twelve-inch dick—she'd noticed how big, black and beautiful it was.

Before Abdul had noticed her violation, Candy immediately focused back on getting dressed, and what had been waiting for her on the other side of the door.

Officer Mummy then handed both of them their ID cards and opened the door. Abdul had walked out first, as he'd immediately fixed his kufi upon his head. Abdul had regrouped, yet, still had been frustrated by Officer Mummy's foolishness.

"ABU! ABU!" Abdul's son, Umar had yelled the Arabic word for father. Abdul had heard his son, but hadn't seen him until he'd felt the small hands that wrapped around his leg, like Umar used to do back at home.

"As-Salaamu-Alaikum, Umar," Abdul had greeted his son.

"Wa'laikum-Salaam."

"Where's your mother?"

"Mommy's in the restroom."

Abdul then picked up his son and had looked into his eyes. Instantly, the love for his son had made him forget all the humiliation he'd just gone through with Officer Mummy.

"Hey, daddy, girls go to this school, too?" Umar asked curiously, as the young boy had referred to Candy, as she'd slowly sauntered into the visiting room. Candy had lightly blushed at hearing little Umar's question, but had become curious as to know what Abdul's answer would be. Candy then eavesdropped as she'd walked pass the two.

"Look, there's mommy. Let's go see if she wants something out of the vending machine," Abdul replied, as he'd distracted his son. Abdul hadn't been ready to explain to Umar, at such a tender age, that Candy had been born a male.

When Candy had fixed her eyes on Ray, as he'd sat with his fiancée, Kim; the couple locked eyes until Ray had spotted Candy. He then nodded his chin, and had given his cousin, Reecey the signal from across the room. Catching on, Reecey then stood up to call her over, and acted as if she'd been Candy's friend.

"Candy, over here, girl!" Reecey cheered as she'd waved her hand. As Candy approached her, they'd hugged before they sat side-by-side each other.

"Weren't you suppose to wear a red blouse?" Candy had asked curiously.

"Them correctional *bitches* made me change my blouse, talkin' 'bout it was too revealin'," Reecey spat, before she'd sucked her teeth with disgust. She then observed Candy from head-to-toe, amazed at how beautifully she'd looked; baffled that Candy was a transsexual.

As Reecey and Candy had become somewhat acquainted, Kim and Ray had been in the process of discussing the drug-filled package.

"Baby girl, is the *gift* neatly wrapped?" Ray suspiciously asked, as he'd inquired how the drugs had been packaged.

"Um, *don't* I handle business *every* time?" Kim then replied, as she'd sloppily licked the tomato sauce off of her fingers from the pizza she'd quickly gobbled down.

"Yeah, boo, always. I just hope this *faggot*-ass *motherfucker* don't freeze up on me," Ray answered, as he'd acted like he and Candy had only done business together.

"I don't know why you *switched* up anyway. If it ain't broke, why fix it?"

"Yeah, Kim, but you know Lil' Will died—the only mule that was willing to go was this punk. Plus, this *motherfucker* can tote a lot of *shit*—so he says. So when we hit 'em hard like this, I won't have to worry 'bout my queen toting every week no more. Plus, I ain't *tryna* have that *shit* bustin' in my stomach like it did with Lil' Will."

"Yeah, I feel you, daddy," Kim had replied, being easily persuaded by Ray's false act of concern.

As Abdul had walked towards Amin, who'd sat with his visitors, he'd made it his business to greet the Imam, and had introduced his son to Amin.

"As-Salaamu-Alaikum, Brother Amin,"

"Wa'laikum-Salaam," Amin had answered. "Abdul, who's this young brother right here?"

"This is Brother Umar, my son," Abdul had answered. "Greet the Imam, son," Abdul immediately suggested, as he'd shown Amin respect. Umar then flashed a bright smile and had reached out his hand, before he'd greeted Amin in the Arabic language. Amin then followed with a gracious greeting before the two had shaken hands.

"Oh, Abdul, I want you to meet my family and business partners," Amin said to Abdul, as he'd introduced him to *Omar Teagle* of *Versatile Music*, *Jay Erving* of *Coalition* and *Zuri Edwards* of *Edwards Entertainment Group*.

Abdul always had known that Amin was well-connected in the entertainment industry, but never had figured that Amin

140

would be on a visit with such affluent Black people who'd been known public figures.

Abdul also had greeted Amin's guests in Arabic, as they'd all returned the greeting back to him.

"What took you so long? You know your wife's been out here waiting for some time now," Amin had stated, being concerned.

"You know how these kufars are, always trying to keep their foot on a brother's neck," Abdul had indicated, as he'd run down the list of events he'd experienced in the strip room with Officer Mummy.

While doing so, Abdul had unwillingly thought about Candy's naked, beautiful body, as he talked with Amin, but quickly had removed the image from his head.

"Hey, Amin, I'm going to see what's up with my wife. I'll see you later—As-Salaamu-Alaikum."

"Wa'laikum-Salaam."

After a few hours of getting to know each other, Reecey and Candy had become friends.

"Ain't he a boxer or somethin'?" Reecey asked Candy, as she'd subtly nodded her head to her left.

"Who?"

"The muscular guy over there wit' the *bitch* wearin' the fly-ass mink," Reecey retorted, as she'd tapped Candy's leg with the back of her hand.

"Girl, you don't know who that is? That's Riddick Bowe, the former heavyweight champion of the world."

"Ooh, Candy, for r-e-a-l? C-h-i-l-e, what he *doin'* here in jail?" Reecey had asked suspiciously, being shady in her questioning, as Reecey had used stereotypical Black people's dialect in her speech.

"Allegedly, he's here on domestic abuse charges," Candy answered, as she'd smiled at her newfound friend, until Candy had become extremely jealous over the sight of Ray and Kim, engaged in conversation.

"What's up, J-Rock?" Ray had greeted J-Rock, who'd walked towards Ray and Kim, as he'd headed towards the vending machine."

"Ain't nothing, slim," J-Rock had answered, not breaking his stride.

"Aye, Kim, that's my homie from *DC* I was tellin' you 'bout, the one whose book, *Larceny* made *Essence* magazine bestseller's list."

"Oh, okay. Yeah, I'm not surprised though, all of my girlfriends and co-workers brought that book; I hear it's hot," Kim replied, as she'd tried to catch her breath. Kim had stuffed her mouth with her second slice of pizza, and had talked at the same time.

"J-Rock and the brother, Amin, suppose to be writin' a book together. I know it's gonna blow. You know I asked them to put me in that joint."

"I *know* that's right!" Kim responded; as she'd eaten the melted mozzarella cheese that had fallen from her pizza, off from her plate. "Who's that sittin' at J-Rock's table?"

"Oh, that's *Anthony "Short Dogg" Tatum* and *Shelinda Spieght* of *Never Give-Up Productions.*

"How's everything at home, baby?" Abdul asked his wife, Kareema, as he'd lifted her face veil to kiss her.

"All praises due to Allah. We're fine, husband. It just seems that, since you're getting closer to your release date, the days are slower and the nights are longer," Kareema then answered, as she'd stroked the palm of Abdul's hand; Abdul's wife had longed for his touch.

It's okay, Kareema. We're at the door right now, and I'll *never* leave you or Umar ever again. Insha-Allah," Abdul replied, as he'd bounced his son on his lap.

Meanwhile, on the other side of the room, Reecey had been plotting to give Candy the drugs that Candy was to smuggle in for Ray.

"Candy, I brought you a bag of *Doritos,*" Reecey indicated, as she'd placed the small bag of chips onto the table.

"Oh no, Reecey, I don't eat *Doritos,* they make your breath stink, girl." Candy replied, as she'd shaken her head.

"Candy, I said the *chips* are for you. Sweetie, *don't* get it twisted on why I'm here—*take* the *Doritos,*" Reecey instructed as she'd widened her eyes; Reecey had given Candy indication, as she then handed Candy the package of drugs.

"Oh, oh, I got you," Candy then responded, as she'd looked around nervously.

"And why you keep *lookin'* over there at my cousin, Ray? You know we gotta play this *shit* off smooth."

"I'm not looking at Ray. I'm checking out who that piece of trade is out here with," Candy lied, as she'd tried to convince Reecey that she hadn't observed Ray; who at that point, had kissed Kim, as Candy had cleverly watched from her table.

TASTE LIKE CANDY! Candy had immediately thought, as she'd reflected back on how wonderful it had felt, when Ray attentively, and tenderly, licked her anus, just before he'd come on his visit with Kim; Ray hadn't brushed his teeth before he'd tongue-kissed her. The thought had made Candy smirk wickedly.

"What the *fuck* is a piece of trade?" Reecey had asked curiously.

"A trade is a masculine guy pretending to be straight, but deals with gay men and femme-queens, such as myself," Candy had snapped.

"WHAT? I know *d-a-m-n* well that *fine-ass* nigga *ain't* no homo-thug?" Reecey had asked nosily, as she looked suspiciously at the tall, handsome man, who'd sat with the cute, young lady.

"Girl, you'd be surprised...Actually, a queen I know named, Yalonda just cut him off, because he told her that he was interested in becoming a queen himself. So she put him on to Ke-Ke, a transvestite who *fucks* men, because like myself, Yalonda loves to catch, not pitch. Ke-Ke has eleven inches, and Reecey, Ke-Ke said that that dude there took *a-l-l* of it, with no problem."

"S-T-O-P! You are lying, Candy!"

"Nope. Ke-Ke also told me that the homo-thug tossed Ke-Ke's salad real good."

"Duh, like I know what the *fuck* is a tossed salad," Reecey had joked, still in disbelief and shocked of the news Candy had given her, about the young, handsome guy who'd been a closeted homosexual, living on the "down low".

"That's when someone licks your asshole," Candy had said as she grinned. Candy then thought about how great Ray always had performed the sex act on her, the same treat he'd just given her, moments before Ray had kissed his fiancée, Kim. Candy then cleverly glanced at Ray again without Reecey noticing; Candy had seen Ray leave his table.

"Hey, baby girl, I gotta go to the restroom—I'll be right back," Ray had said before he kissed Kim on the lips and departed. Discreetly observing the scene, Candy then thought that this had been a good opportunity to indirectly let Kim know, who she *really* was to Ray.

"Reecey, I'm going to heat up my hot wings, you want me to put yours in the microwave?" Candy had politely asked.

"Nah, I'm cool," Reecey had answered back nonchalantly. As Candy walked towards the microwave, she'd approached Kim at Ray's table, and had interrupted Kim's thoughts of Ray.

"Excuse me, but I just had to compliment you on your khaki outfit—it's *Prada,* right?" Candy had asked coyly.

"Yeah, it is; thank you. It's my fiancé's—"

"Favorite color? …Yes, I know. Ray likes me in *my* khaki outfit, too," Candy had slyly interjected, before she walked off to heat up her hot wings.

Kim instantly had become upset, but had known that she couldn't afford to create a scene. Instead, Kim had remained cool, as she sat back and folded her arms. Kim then looked on, as Candy walked away; Candy had switched her behind.

This faggot-ass bitch is fuckin' wit' the right one now! Kim had thought, as she'd waited for Ray to return from the bathroom. When he'd arrived back to the table, Ray then noticed the angry expression upon Kim's face.

"What's wrong?" Ray had asked; perplexed.

"You *fuckin'* wit' that faggot?" Kim had asked distrustfully, as she then looked into his eyes with anger and disgust.

"Huh? …The *fuck* is you talkin' 'bout? And calm the *fuck* down, you out here trippin'," Ray had expressed, being totally embarrassed, yet he'd played it off.

"That fuckin' *thing* just came over here talkin' 'bout *he* likes my outfit, and how *you* like me, and *him*, in the *same* color, too," Kim had gritted through her teeth, as she still had been bothered by Candy's comment.

"Look, don't be out here makin' a scene. You know *goddamn* well that I don't *fuck* wit' no *fags*. It's strictly business and business only. The *fag* is smugglin' in the drugs for me, that's all, baby. Now, we talk a lil' sometime, and I showed him some pictures of you, explaining to him that I love you in khaki outfits; you bein' my queen."

With that said, Kim had instantly blushed at being called his "queen", and Ray was satisfied; his secret still had been safe.

"Baby, I'ma check that *faggot*-ass *nigga* for even sayin' somethin' to you," Ray responded, as he'd immediately patronized Kim.

"You *better* keep that fuckin' *thing* in his place. And look at Reecey over there, all laughin' and *shit;* bein' a *fuckin'* fag-hag," Kim retorted, as she'd noticed that Candy had sat back with Reecey, and had engaged in humorous conversation. Ray and Kim both then laughed, as they'd looked at Reecey talk with Candy.

As Candy had eaten her chicken wings, she'd begun to give a show to the many eyes that focused on her, as Candy then licked the hot sauce off of her fingertips—she'd pretended as if she had been giving oral sex.

"You a *fuckin'* trip," Reecey chimed in, as she'd observed Candy.

"They want to look and whisper, then I'll *give* them something to go home and talk about!" Candy had snapped, before she'd licked even more seductively. Candy then stopped, and had begun to show respect to the older woman who'd come to visit Trigger, as Candy had noticed that she'd looked at her with disgust.

For the woman to be in her early fifties, she still had been very youthful and attractive. Candy had adored the pink and peach-colored *St. John* knit twin set and black slacks that the woman had worn. Her pink stilettos with peach piping, and the jewelry she'd worn, had all been by *Chanel*; the woman also had been adorned with diamond *Chanel* earrings with the signature interlocking "Cs".

Candy had wondered if she was Trigger's mother or perhaps an elderly aunt. But the thought had quickly gone away when Trigger arisen from the table, and had tongue-kissed the older, regal woman, immediately after the correctional officer had yelled that visiting hours had been over.

"Damn," Candy replied, as she'd witnessed Trigger putting his playboy charm onto the older woman. Candy then removed herself from the table and had hugged Reecey good-bye; Candy had proceeded to let Reecey know that she'd appreciated the visit.

"Don't forget your *Doritos,* girl," Reecey reminded Candy, as she'd indirectly instilled into Candy that it hadn't been a friendly visit; but a business meeting.

"I know, I won't," Candy answered back firmly to Reecey, as she'd pumped herself up in the process. Candy had known that this had been her true test—getting the drugs over into General Population.

Candy then pulled her shirt out of her pants, as she'd waited in line to be strip-searched. Ray, at that time, had eased up behind Candy and whispered into her ear: "*Bitch,* you was out-of-order."

146

It was then when Candy had realized that it hadn't been a good idea approaching Kim. Candy had allowed her feelings to dictate her actions.

Although Ray had planned to chastise Candy, he'd decided to wait until later; Ray had known that at that exact moment, wasn't the time—not wanting Candy to be distracted and mess up the plan. He'd then spotted his fellow convict, Corleone.

"Hey, Corleone, from the looks of how you had that young, pretty thang that just left, I guess you ain't lost your touch, huh?" Ray had stated jokingly to the guy from *Philadelphia*.

"Ain't *nothin'* change but my address, and since I'm gettin' short, I *might* start sendin' her up here to see you; naw mean?" he'd stated, as Corleone pretended as if he'd be willing to pass the girl on to Ray, since his release date was near.

Corleone and Ray then laughed, as a few other inmates that had waited in line joined in. Ray had known that he needed to make a diversion, so Candy could easily execute her move. He'd continued making loud jokes and had laughed wholeheartedly; Ray then purposely brought attention to himself, as the guard, at this point, had focused hard on him.

When he'd looked in Ray's direction, quickly, Candy cunningly had taken the long, fat balloon that resembled a dildo, out of the *Doritos* bag, spat saliva in the palm of her hand, and had turned her back towards the wall.

Candy had swiftly lubricated herself with her own saliva, before she'd inserted the drug missile smoothly, but deep; sticking it inside of her opened anus. Candy then contracted her muscles, she'd squeezed and tightened her hole; Candy made sure that the balloon had gone in deeper…the same way she'd done earlier that day with Ray….

"Sweets, you're first. C'mon, I *don't* have all day!" Officer Mummy replied, as he'd had lust in his eyes. Candy made direct eye contact with the guard before her eyes had traveled down towards the bulge in his pants. Instantly, Candy had made Officer Mummy follow her inside the strip room.

When Candy entered the strip room, she'd taunted him, as Candy sensually had licked her lips with her tongue; she'd gotten Officer Mummy intensely aroused. Candy had known that if she kept teasing him, she'd pass through with the drugs much easier than Ray had planned.

"This is my *favorite* part of the day," Officer Mummy stated, as the guard had closed the strip room door behind himself before he'd locked it.

Candy hadn't faced him. She'd immediately begun taking off her shirt, and had placed it over the chair. Candy then glanced over her left shoulder, and had found Officer Mummy, sitting in a chair with his legs sprawled apart. Candy then turned around in the guard's direction with her arms folded, and had covered her ample breasts with her hands.

"Officer Mummy, I have to hold my arms out, right?" Candy had asked coyly.

"You know what you *have* to do," he'd replied, as Officer Mummy lightly tapped his foot on the floor. Slowly, Candy then held out her arms to reveal her perfectly round, perky breasts. Candy then opened her mouth wide, stuck her tongue out and wrapped it repeatedly around her index finger, like she'd had with the bulbous head of Ray's penis.

"I wish I had something *else* in my mouth instead," Candy said seductively, as she'd continued teasing Officer Mummy with her finger.

"Turn around and *drop* 'em," he'd demanded, as Officer Mummy tried hard to contain his erection.

I have to do something to get his mind off from looking in my asshole. Candy had taken off her pants, as she'd continued to squeeze her anus tightly.

Candy then devised a plan. She'd schemed on emulating the scandalous dance moves the video girls had performed in *Nelly's* controversial *"Tip Drill"* video—which had gotten the multi-platinum rapper into a lot of trouble at the prestigious *Spelman College.*

Wiggling her butt cheeks, as she'd begun to seduce Officer Mummy with the erotic, dance routine, Candy had jiggled her ass from left-to-right, bouncing her large behind in the guard's dumbfounded face. As Candy cleverly clinched her hole, she'd simultaneously made a rippling effect with her rear.

Candy continued to make her ass jump, as she'd mesmerized Officer Mummy with her undulation; Candy then poked her behind outward, as it made a light, clapping sound. Flinging her head around, as she'd tossed her long hair, Candy then seduced him with her hypnotizing eyes, as she'd given Officer Mummy a naughty look; Candy had pretended as if she'd wanted to be fucked.

"S-h-h-h-s-h, chill, Sweets. They'll hear you out there," Officer Mummy had whispered nervously. At that moment, Candy had quickly tucked her limp penis between her legs, and had turned around to face him, as she'd bounced her breasts.

"You like that, *don't* you?" Candy had asked Officer Mummy wickedly.

KNOCK-KNOCK-KNOCK!

"YO, I GOTTA GO TO THE BATHROOM AND TAKE A LEAK!" Ray yelled, as he'd pounded on the strip room door. Ray had worried about Candy, and felt that he had to do something, to ensure that she'd gotten over to the other side of the prison. Ray then figured that, if she'd gotten caught with the drug-filled balloon, by him knocking on the door would distract Officer Mummy, giving Candy enough time to flush the drugs down the toilet.

"BANG ON MY *FUCKIN'* DOOR AGAIN, AND I'LL MAKE *SURE* YOU PISS IN YOUR PANTS!" Officer Mummy then shouted, as he'd signaled Candy to get dressed; angry that Ray had interrupted his anticipated lap dance session.

"Sweets, I'll be workin' your block this weekend, we can pick up where we left off," Officer Mummy whispered, as he'd opened the door that led to the other end of the compound; the guard then granted Candy access.

"I hope you bring your handcuffs with you," Candy had said in a low, soft whisper, before she dashed towards the compound, happy that she'd been successful in completing her mission.

On Candy's way to the unit, the only thing that had been on her mind was hiring Tom as her lawyer; so he can help her with getting an appeal. Candy had longed for her freedom, so much, that she could actually taste it.

Later that day, Candy had thought about heading back to *South Beach,* but the large envelope she'd received during mail call from her new friend, *Paris Gotti* in *New York City,* quickly changed her mind. Candy had eagerly desired going back to her hometown, but this time, as a new and improved queen—now that she'd fully plotted on having her sex-change operation. Candy then thought that she could be just as fabulous in *Manhattan* as *Paris Gotti.*

Paris Gotti was an up-and-coming transsexual who'd quickly taken the busy streets of *New York City* by storm, having the lovely face and a body of a full-fledged female. Being part Jamaican and Hispanic, "she" was just as beautiful as Candy, having smooth, butterscotch-colored skin, luscious lips and dreamy, light-brown eyes.

Paris Gotti's naturally long, dark hair cascaded past her shoulders, which back then, had been colored blond. She'd had the physique of a model—long lean legs, the neck of a swan and a short torso, standing at 5'8".

Candy, along with many others within the gay, lesbian and transgender community, had considered *Paris Gotti* to be a top-notch transsexual. She was so passable that, not only had successful, platinum rappers, actors and athletes tried courting her, but also closeted, bisexual women had made several advances at *Paris Gotti;* often times, they'd thought that she'd been born a female.

Candy quickly had heard of *Paris Gotti,* and how she'd always won trophies and cash prizes whenever *Paris Gotti* had participated in balls and pageants, winning in the "face" and "femme-queen realness in designer labels" categories; but had the pleasure of meeting *Paris Gotti* briefly at the *RAGS-TO-RICHES* ball in *Chicago.*

The two had talked and exchanged numbers, but unfortunately, Candy hadn't been able to call her new friend; Candy having had her personal items confiscated, shortly after she'd been arrested.

Paris Gotti had gotten word of Candy's incarceration, in which she'd then logged onto *Bop.gov*, entered Candy's full name, and successfully found out her whereabouts in prison. She'd then sent Candy a package that contained information on the *MONSTER BALL* in *New York City,* which was held at *Escuelita*; hosted by *Harmonica Sunbeam.*

The invitational press kit package was so intriguing, and had been neatly put together, that it actually had made Candy cried, mainly because she couldn't attend. It had always been her dream to fully become a female, and one day, be featured as a celebrity guest at such a prestigious ball as this.

For Candy had known in her heart that there hadn't been any other passable transsexuals, with the exception of *Paris Gotti,* who could compete with her; in which Candy back then, had plans to come for *Paris Gotti.* Candy had intended to knock her off of her throne, while snatching *Paris Gotti's* crown. Candy had been certain that she could become the most famous transsexual ever, yet, only the skills of a great attorney like Tom would decide that fate.

Two weeks later...

"Ray, did you talk to the lawyer, Tom yet?" Candy had asked impatiently. Ever since Ray had gotten the package of drugs, everything between the two changed rapidly. Ray no longer had been nice to Candy, or had catered to her every need anymore.

In fact, Ray, at that point, had often avoided Candy as much as he could, only seeing her whenever he'd become horny. Habitually, Ray would just request oral sex or a quickie, as he back then, only had preferred entering Candy from behind, in order not to face her.

Their sessions of deep, passionate lovemaking had stopped, which immediately manifested in Ray refusing to perform his most desired oral sex act on Candy; Ray had been obsessed with sensually sucking her anus in the past.

Candy had become confused, and somewhat frustrated with Ray, who'd back then, shown his true colors, as Ray had acted selfishly with the proceeds from the drugs.

"*Look,* Candy, I *told* you I *hollered* at the guy! Tom said he was gonna be a lil' busy doing some other cases. After he's finished, *then* he'll talk to you! *Damn!* I wish you stop *buggin'* me 'bout this *shit!*"

Ray had been irritated, but in all actuality, it hadn't been Candy that bothered him. At that moment, Ray had been experiencing migraine headaches; dehydration—and had been short-winded in breath. Ray felt that the drugs had caught up to him, and that he needed to shake his habit. Ray was due for parole in a few months back then. There was no way in the world that he would survive out in society with the drug habit Ray had had.

"Alright then, Ray, whatever. But for real, you're starting to change. I don't know *what* it is, but I'm starting to see a difference in you. Maybe you changed your mind about *us* when you were out there all *lovey-dovey* with that fat *bitch,* Kim!"

"Candy your *ass* is trippin' again. Ever since the warden has stopped them from giving you those hormone pills, what's it called?"

"ESTROGEN!" Candy had snapped.

"See, that's what I'm *talkin'* 'bout. Ever since they took you off that *shit,* you've been actin' up," Ray explained, as he'd used reverse psychology, in order for Candy to feel guilty.

Candy felt that Ray had told the truth, so she'd assumed. Back then, Candy had been going through various mood swings, due to the prison had stopped providing her with hormone treatments. Yet, in Candy's case, she'd been awaiting the *Supreme Court's* decision, which had raised that issue.

Depending upon the outcome of their choice, if in favor of those who'd previously taken hormones before they'd entered the prison, Candy would be amongst those to sue the government for a large sum of money.

"I know, Ray, I'm sorry, baby. It's just that I *need* my pills. Look at me, my breasts have shrunken, I'm starting to get peach fuzz on my face. Last week I had to pluck some hairs from underneath my chin with tweezers," Candy had whined.

She'd really gone through a hormonal transition, but the thing that was the most troubling had been Candy's penile erections. The Estrogen pills had prevented her from getting erections, yet, Candy had become paranoid and self-conscious about her body; and with having sex.

During that time, when she'd had impersonal sex with Ray, Candy hadn't cared so much as she'd done in the past, when Ray had suggested putting her in the "doggy style" position. After their sex session, Candy would lie on her stomach purposely—not getting up until her erection had gone down.

"Candy, come here. Everything's gonna work out, okay?" Ray had replied, as he pulled Candy close to him, and had planted a soft kiss on her full lips. "I'ma flip the rest of this *shit,* then we gonna pay Tom, and the rest will be history. I go up for parole in a few months, hopefully I'll make it. If not, then I only have a lil' bit of time left to serve anyway. We'll be out in the real world together, baby…You said you wanna head back to *New York City* to give *Paris Gotti* a run for her money, right?"

Candy then blushed lightly, "Yes, Ray, I do. But she's so lovely—that *cunt* is *not* to be *fucked* with! You know, *Paris Gotti's* becoming famous in the real world. I was informed that she recently did a photo shoot to be on the cover of a novel, which is causing quite a scandal in the publishing industry. The story is off the hook I hear. I'm happy for Paris, because out of all of the queens that I've met, she was the *only* one who really looked out for me. I owe her for that."

"Well, right now I think you *owe* me somethin', don't you?" Ray had asked sneakily.

"I sure do, daddy," Candy answered, as she'd immediately dropped to her knees, and engulfed Ray's nine-and-a-half-inch dick down the back of her throat; just the way he'd loved it.

* * * * *

"Cut the TV down," Pooh had instructed, as everyone in the TV room had become quiet; they'd listened to Trigger's newest rhyme he'd made up within the last half hour. Trigger's flow was poetic like *Tupac's*, hardcore like *Scarface's*, with a bit of *Nas'* brilliant wordplay and wisdom.

Trigger's rhyming skills had been like no others within the prison. There was no doubt in anybody's mind that whenever he'd been released to go home, Trigger would be the next multi-platinum selling artist in the rap game.

"Damn, Trigger can flow," J-Rock had said quietly to Amin, after Trigger had left the TV room.

"Yeah, he's aiiight, but my man, *ALFAMEGA,* yo, he'd get in his business," Amin had boasted.

"Yeah, but that's two different styles you're talking about," J-Rock answered back, as he'd rationalized the two individuals rapping skills.

"Yeah, you're right, but what counts are those record sales."

"Yeah, I know. I wish I knew how to rap, I'd be a rapping-ass *nigga* for the type of money they're making in the rap industry!" J-Rock had replied enthusiastically.

Amin had lightly laughed, "Nah, Ahk, stick to the novels and scripts. Your big break will come one day soon—Insha-Allah.

"Oh, so what you're saying—I can't flow?" J-Rock responded as he'd laughed.

"Nah, fam, it's not that. All I'm saying is that your flow isn't like Trigger's," Amin had replied jokingly.

"Yeah, right," J-Rock had retorted. "Oh, speaking of Trigger, did you see that broad he was in the VIP room with recently? Older broad, real classy—sexy, too; but she's just a little too old for the young boy."

Amin then sat up and looked at J-Rock, "Man, J-Rock, c'mon! You mean to *tell* me you don't *know* who that lady was?" Amin had said surprisingly, shocked that J-Rock had been unaware of whom the woman was.

"Nah, how I'm suppose to know her? I've never seen that lady before a day in my life."

"Hold on, I'll be right back," Amin replied, as he'd briefly left the TV room. Amin then quickly returned with a *Sister-2-Sister* magazine in his hand. He'd opened it to an article, and playfully shoved it into J-Rock's face. "Look at that!"

J-Rock couldn't believe what he'd seen and read, as the article had featured a story on the woman he'd seen Trigger kissing; kissing the older woman as if she'd been a young teenager in heat.

"Damn, it says here that she's Susan Stone, Vice President of *Dope Jam Records,* who earned over forty million dollars in revenue last year alone. DAMN!" J-Rock had yelled, as he couldn't believe what he'd read. "How the *fuck* a knucklehead-ass *nigga* like *Trigger,* end up with a broad like that?" J-Rock had questioned in amazement.

J-Rock hadn't discredited Trigger, he'd actually been happy for him, yet baffled by the connection of the two.

"Man, you know Trigger been on one of those prison pen pal internet sites since he's been locked up," Amin had answered.

"Yeah, I remember him saying something about that a while ago."

"Well, the lady suppose to be married, but she met Trigger online and started corresponding with him. Then Trigger told her that he could rap. Next thing you know, Susan Stone's up here coming to see him. From what I hear, they say she has a million-dollar rap deal waiting for Trigger when he comes home.

"But the sad part about it is that, he actually has to be her *'boy-toy'* on call. Man, you *know* how it is. She's probably been married for thirty years, hubby can't get it up, so she found a young stud like Trigger who would sell his soul for a few dollars; without destroying her marriage," Amin had explained.

"Damn, so that's how his young *ass* keeps spending up to the limit when he goes to commissary. He has money to blow, huh?"

"I can imagine so, J-Rock."

"Well, I hope he does something with his career when he gets out there in the world. When is he suppose to leave anyway?"

"Trigger says he got a few months left. You know he was trying to get me to holla at my peoples in the music industry for him. I told Trigger I had other deals to close first!" Amin had bragged.

"Aiiight, Amin, stop practicing your business talk on me," J-Rock had replied jokingly. "You know you really should get into marketing," J-Rock then advised his friend.

"I am, soon as we finish our book we're working on. I'm going take this thing to another level. Man, we gonna be on *Oprah!* Insha-Allah. Watch what I tell you, J-Rock!" Amin then answered convincingly.

"Yeah, well, we need to hurry up and fully outline the concept then."

"That's what I'm *trying* to tell you!" Amin had said to J-Rock, as the two then burst into laughter.

As Candy and Ray had lounged inside of Ray's cell, playing a game of checkers, the guard had come in and interrupted their quality time.

"Hey, White, you need to grab your ID and report to the lieutenant's office."

Right away, Candy and Ray had become nervous; they'd known that it must've been a serious matter for Ray to be called into the lieutenant's office.

"I'm going with you," Candy responded, as she'd begun putting on her shoes.

"Nah, Sweets, that *won't* be necessary. The lieutenant called for White, *not* you," the correctional officer replied, as he'd become repulsed while looking at the couple. He'd then left the cell to open the unit door for Ray, as the correctional officer had given Ray and Candy enough time to say good-bye to each other.

"Damn, Ray, what the *fuck* is going on?" Candy had asked hysterically.

"I don't know, baby, but if I go in the hole, I better not hear a *fuckin'* word about you *fuckin'* wit' none of these *niggas!* If I do, when I come out, I'ma *kill* you and them *niggas!*"

"What makes you think you're going to the hole?" Candy had questioned, as tears welled in her eyes.

"I don't know, but just in case I do, I thought I'd put that out there; just so you'll know that I'll *kill* for you."

Although Ray had told Candy he hadn't known what was going on, Ray had known in advance that he was going to "the hole" for using drugs. A week prior, when asked for a urine sample for drug testing, Ray had failed; he'd had heroin flooded in his system.

* * * * *

It had been two weeks since Ray had gone to "the hole", sent there for sixty days for not passing his drug testing. While there, Candy had cried everyday, hour-after-hour.

"Damn, Candy, he's *only* gone for sixty days, you *act* like he has a murder charge or something," Jose stated, as he'd become annoyed with her; he felt that Candy had overreacted. Candy's crying had affected Jose, as he'd secretly loved Ray, just as much as Candy had.

"Jose, you don't understand, I love Ray...he's *all* I got," Candy had replied in between sobs.

"*FUCK* THAT! Look, your stupid *ass* need to wake up and smell the *fucking* coffee! You think Ray loves your *ass?* You're nothing to him but a jump-off! Ray doesn't give a *fuck* about you or nobody else!"

The sharp remarks Jose had made, cut into Candy like a sword. She'd never seen Jose act so irate before. There had to be some truth to his words, for Candy had known from the look in Jose's eyes. Candy had continued to listen to Jose, as the river of tears flowed nonstop from her eyes.

"Candy, Ray is a *fucking* trade; always was, always will be! He *tricked* you! The rape scenario with Ty and Unibomber was a-l-l a hoax! You being the first *queen* he'd ever *fucked* was false! Everything was a big...*fucking*...lie—a *fucking* scam, Candy! Ray paying the lawyer with the profits from that drug package you smuggled in, Candy please—Ray's lying! He doesn't *care* about you, Candy. I'm the *only* one in here who cares about you!" Jose answered emotionally, as he'd gone off into a tangent.

"Jose, if you *care* about me so much, then why you wait so long to tell me this? Why wait until Ray went to the hole?" Candy cried, as she'd become overwhelmed with hatred.

"Because, Candy, you know *damn* well Ray would've killed me! My life is worth *more* than our friendship. I'm just being straight up with you!"

At that moment, Candy had developed a deep hatred for every inmate she'd encountered. Candy then decided that she had to change; it was *her* turn to show the world how cruel a *bitch* can get! Candy, at that point, had plans for revenge, but with finesse.

Candy had been ready to reincarnate herself into the Devil, and walk the Earth to-and-fro, seeking whomever she could devour. No one would ever know the evil that had lurked behind her big, bright, brown eyes. Candy's mission at that time had been to seek and destroy, as she'd wiped her tears, and set her plan in motion.

* * * * *

158

Candy awakened again from her past, this time, by a convict who was loudly rapping intensely; being skillful in his delivery. She swore it was Trigger, but in fact, the inmate rhymed to Trigger's new song, which made the number one position on *Bill Board's* chart.

"Oh, my bad, did I wake you?" asked the young prisoner, after Candy listened to him rhyme.

"No, you didn't wake me. I actually like that song—can you finish it, please?" Candy requested.

The youngster looked out of the window of the transit van and continued to rap, as Candy closed her eyes once again, sinking back into her past.

Within the few weeks of Ray being in "the hole", it had seemed as if almost every snake that had lurked in dark shadows, had come out from its hiding space, trying to get a hold of Candy. Back then, she'd been considered "free meat" while Ray had been in "the hole". Every trade on the compound had taken direct and indirect shots at the vulnerable queen.

Candy hissed and exhaled when she'd entered her cell and found a letter from a secret admirer; that had rested on top of her pillow. *"For Candy's Eyes Only"* had been handwritten on the envelope, in which a drawing of two doe eyes substituted the word "eyes".

Candy had laughed to herself, being disgusted by the discreet, closeted homosexual. Whoever he was, he'd been too scared to show his face. Actually, Candy had received five of those invitational letters with the same handwriting, so she'd known it had been definitely from the same person.

Although Candy had somewhat of an idea of who it had been, she hadn't known his identity for sure. Candy then had shaken her head before she opened the letter. It read:

Dear Candy,

Yo, this my 5ᵗʰ letter I wrote u, ma! So I think u already know who I am and u definitely know what I want. I want u bad, Candy. I got a big fuckin' dick and I wanna stick this hard pipe in that phat ass of yours and fuck u like u suppose 2 b fucked. If u gonna take me up on my offer, meet me down in the back shower stall at five o'clock tonight. Go in first and wait for me 'til I cum. I promise u won't b disappointed. I want that sweet ass, Candy!

Your Secret Admirer

Candy smirked as she'd balled up the letter and thrown it in the trash, but had retrieved it soon after and filed it with the rest of her personal belongings. Candy then thought that perhaps she could use it as evidence in the near future.

She'd quickly devised a plan, scheming hard, as Candy had desperately tried to figure out who the closeted admirer could've been. Candy also had thought that maybe she could've bribed the admirer, and get money from him. Candy then had planned to put the cash towards her retainer fee, so Tom could help Candy with her appeal.

It was 4:45 PM when Candy glanced at the clock. She'd had only fifteen minutes to freshen up and go to the shower stall. Candy quickly had grabbed her empty lotion bottle, and had filled it up with warm water and a drop of *Herbal Essence* shampoo. She'd shaken it up, and slowly inserted the bottle into her anus.

Candy then squeezed the mixture up into her rectum, as she'd used the plastic container as an enema. Candy hadn't wanted any fecal matter on the admirer, if he'd to have sex with her. Candy had prepared to "take" this man, for all he'd been worth….

* * * * *

While Candy had changed into her robe and shower shoes, Ty had been in the TV room, embracing his fellow convicts as he'd been in the process to be released into society.

"Aiiight, y'all, you *niggas* be easy and keep ya heads up," Ty stated, as he'd entered the TV room to say his final good-byes. Most of the inmates in the room really hadn't cared for the youngster, but still had cared for the rest of the world. They'd tried to educate Ty about his sexual behavior patterns for the last time, the prisoners had hoped he'd listen.

"Ty, listen up. Whatever you do out there, know that it comes with consequences, and that you create your own situations," Pooh had replied.

"Yeah, thanks, Pooh. I'ma try my hardest when I get out there."

"So who's coming to pick you up, Ty?" Corleone had joined in.

"Oh, man, you know I go my young, hot *bitch* comin' to get me! She should be out front."

"So I guess you goin' to the nearest hotel you can find, huh?" Nook had asked.

"And you know it, my *nigga!* I'ma beat that *pussy* up like I never had none before."

Everyone had laughed at Ty's statement.

"*Nigga,* yo *ass* can't even wait 'til five o'clock, huh? Chris had questioned.

"Nah, not really. I only got a few more minutes left, so I'ma holla at you *niggas.* Yo, I know some of y'all don't *fuck* wit' me because I be on some down low *shit,* but for real, I still hope you *niggas* be safe—one! C'mon, Unibomber, let's go find Trigger," Ty replied before he and Unibomber had departed the TV room.

"Damn, I hope that young *nigga* don't hit that girl raw," Chris stated, as he'd shaken his head. Chris had known that Ty had had unprotected sex with homosexuals in prison in the past.

"Man, Ty don't give a *fuck* about nobody if he's *fuckin'* wit' punks. He's already thrown away his manhood. Ain't no turning back from that *shit!* Ty doesn't respect *nothin',* because he doesn't respect himself. You know *damn* well that *nigga* gonna *fuck* his girl without a condom, and any other broad he meets after her," Nook had replied angrily.

"You see, that's what messes me up 'bout them *type* of dudes. It's dudes like that who will go home and meet your daughter, sister, cousin, aunt, niece, etc., and charm her with his good looks, knowing that he has a deadly disease. Man, if I *ever* see dude in the street tryna holla at a sista, I'm goin' to yell: 'YO, THAT *NIGGA,* TY WAS *FUCKIN'* FAGS IN JAIL!'" Corleone had replied.

As everyone had voiced their opinions about young Ty, Amin and J-Rock had sat and observed what had happened around them. The two then looked at each other and had had an epiphany. At that moment, Amin and J-Rock had fully known what their new novel was going to be based on. They'd felt that it had been their duty to educate the world—on what goes down behind the prison walls….

* * * * *

Candy had sat quietly in the last shower stall, as she waited for her secret admirer to arrive. Candy had grown impatient, as she looked at her watch and a saw that it had been seven minutes after five. *Damn, whoever this trade is must be too scared to meet me.*

She'd become tired of waiting. Candy then figured that either he'd been nervous about revealing himself, or had changed his mind.

Candy then gathered her things and had begun to leave the shower stall. As she'd reached for the doorknob, Trigger had eased himself in.

"Oh, excuse me, Trigger, I was just leaving out; the shower's all yours," Candy had politely replied.

"*Fuck* you *leavin'* for? You got my last letter, right? Ain't that's why you here?" Trigger had said slyly, as he looked deep into Candy's eyes. Immediately, Trigger had moved in closer to her—face-to-face. Candy's mouth then dropped, she'd been in shock; Candy couldn't believe what she'd heard and seen. At that moment, every event Candy had encountered with Trigger had quickly flashed back to her.

Trigger had been an undercover trade who'd been clever at disguising his sexuality, and had desired Candy from the first time he'd laid eyes on her.

Instantly, Candy then started scheming. Right away, Candy had known that she'd hit the jackpot, mainly because Trigger would've given *anything*, not to be exposed. This had been Candy's chance to show that she'd meant business. At this point, Candy then revealed how cruel and ruthless she would be on the compound. From that day forth, Candy no longer would be the victim—she would become the "Queen Bitch".

"Alright then, Trigger, it's going down like this, *nigga.* I'll *suck* your *dick* until the skin falls off, and let you *fuck* me anyway you want. You can cum in my mouth, eat my ass, suck *a-l-l* on my titties—all that good *shit.* You can have as much as you want until you leave this joint, but there's *one* thing you have to give me.

"What's that?" Trigger anxiously asked, as he'd groped his hard and erect, nine-inch penis through his pants; Trigger had become overly aroused by Candy's proposition. She then looked straight into his eyes.

"*Motherfucker,* I want one-thousand dollars sent to my account, *first* thing tomorrow morning, and don't even *think* about telling me you don't have it, because I know about everything!

"I know you have that old, rich *bitch* from off the internet, the one who's featured in this month's *Sister-2-Sister* magazine—Susan Stone; the one who makes over forty-million dollars a year. I'm also aware about the million-dollar contract you were offered, and about to receive once you get home, in about *six* months; right, Trigger?" Candy had asked wickedly. Trigger then stood there baffled, surprised that Candy had known of his resources, and at that point, had tried to extort him.

"*Nigga,* I can make your l-a-s-t six months be the most *pleasurable* six months of your life."

"WHAT? Yo, you lost your *fuckin'* mind, *bitch!* What the *fuck* I look like givin' *you* a thousand dollars?" Trigger had spat angrily.

For a moment, Candy then thought that she'd lost control of the situation, so Candy had begun to quickly distract Trigger, as she'd continued devising her plan.

"Trigger, you're in a *no-win* situation. You mean to *tell* me, you wouldn't pay for this? Look," Candy said as she'd opened her robe, slow and seductively; Candy had exposed her perfectly round breasts.

Immediately, Trigger's curved dick had swelled even more at the sight of Candy's breasts, yet, he hadn't given in easy.

"Look, I'll smash you off wit' somethin' from commissary, but I *ain't* givin' your *ass* no *fuckin'* G—you done lost your *rabbit-ass* mind."

"Trigger, you *don't* have a choice. Now, either you *give* up the thousand dollars, or I'll run out of this shower room *right* now, butt-ass naked and scream rape!" Candy then retorted. The coldness in her eyes had warned Trigger that Candy hadn't been playing. Yet, Trigger couldn't imagine her having the courage to actually try to extort him.

Candy had known that from what she'd said that Candy had taken a huge step, and had risked her life. Yet, Candy then thought about all she'd been through: the trickery and treachery in her life. Instantly, Candy had become heartless; Trigger had lost his cool.

"You bitch—"

"QUEEN BITCH!" Candy had sharply interjected.

"I'll break your *fuckin'* neck and *kill* you in here!" Trigger retorted, as he'd looked Candy in the eye with hatred—mixed in with lust and sexual tension altogether.

"Whatever, *nigga.* You probably *would* try to kill me, but you know the C.O.'s desk is *right* down the tier. All he has to do is hear me scream, and then he's coming; along with backup! Then you'll be out there in the open where the *whole* unit can see.

"Now, you and I know that you have that *'gangster'* image to protect, plus you're about to be a *'big'* rap star in six months—I *know* you don't want to *fuck* that up with a scandal like this. And besides, if you harm me physically, you'll go to the hole. Guess who's in the whole right now? Ray! Trigger, you know *damn* well if I tell Ray you tried to rape me that he'll *kill* you. So, *nigga,* like I said before, you *have* no choice!" Candy had ranted.

At that point, Trigger was in disbelief of what had happened to him.

"Now here, Trigger, take this," Candy instructed, as she'd handed him a piece a paper.

"What the *fuck* is this?"

"It's my full name and ID number. When I check my account tomorrow morning, it *better* be a thousand dollars in there, hopefully more. Because after this, I'm *sure* you're going to tip me well," Candy had replied, as she then grabbed Trigger's meat through his pants.

Candy had unbuttoned Trigger pants and pulled his trousers down, fast and hard to his ankles. Candy then assumed the position on her knees, as she'd begun to give Trigger a "special" treat.

Candy had glided her mouth up-and-down Trigger's large, rock-hard penis, as if it had been an oversized, tasty, chocolate lollypop. As she'd received him deep inside her throat repeatedly, Candy had glanced up at Trigger's face, and noticed that his eyes had rolled in the back of his head; Trigger had experienced tremendous pleasure.

Taking him to a state of bliss, Candy then put the head of Trigger's dick in her mouth and had sucked on it. It was then when she'd known that he couldn't handle Candy's oral skills. By Trigger's low and deep grunts, and by the way his body had jerked, Candy immediately had sensed that Trigger's balls had tightened, and that he'd been ready to ejaculate.

Knowing this, Candy then engulfed Trigger totally down her deep throat, and had swallowed him down to the base of Trigger's shaft; she'd taken all of his throbbing meat. Candy had relaxed her throat even more, she'd made it easier to take Trigger all the way in, as his warm, thick, milky semen shot straight down the back of her throat.

Candy then moaned and smiled to herself, as she'd looked up to terribly-trifling, treacherous Trigger—the new piece of trade Candy had triumphantly turned out.

TRIGGER FINGERS
chapter 34

The next morning…

RING-RING-RING!

"Hello," Susan answered her cell phone that she'd specifically bought to only receive Trigger's calls from.

"Yo, what up, ma?" Trigger had greeted her in his New York City accent. Susan had loved the way Trigger talked. It had been his youthfulness that brought life to the fifty-three-year-old millionaire, who'd been married to her husband for thirty years— ten of those years unhappily.

"Hey, baby, why are you calling so early? You must've been thinking about me, huh?" Susan said, as she'd smiled from ear-to-ear. Trigger's voice alone had sent chills up Susan's spine, and wetness between her legs.

"You know it, ma. A *nigga's* dick is rock-hard thinkin' 'bout you. Yo, I swear, I can't *wait* to put this good *dick* up in your gut and *smash* you off lovely."

"*O-o-o-o-o-o-h,* Trigger, you know I get so *wet* when you talk like that. Damn, my *pussy* is throbbing."

"Well, you know what to do, ma. Let me hear you play wit' that *pussy; my* pussy. Go 'head, ma, stick my fingers in that *pussy* and cum for me," Trigger had demanded over the phone; he'd also known that Susan loved it when he'd talked dirty to her.

This had been the most excitement she'd had in the last ten years. Even though Susan had enough money to pay for sex from any other young guy, she'd found something else in Trigger other than just sex.

Susan had found the next "rap sensation", and had done whatever she had to, just to get Trigger home to sign the contract; before the opposing labels had gotten to him.

"Okay, baby, *o-o-o-h*…I got your fingers all up in my *pussy* now, daddy. *O-o-o-h,* this is *yours,* Trigger. Oh yes, *fuck* me, Trigger. *Fuck* me harder, Trigger."

As Susan had masturbated, getting amazing pleasure from Trigger's phone sex, he'd been on the other end snickering.

Trigger had chuckled lightly, grinning at how he had such a hold on the fifty-three-year-old, wealthy woman, who would've done anything for Trigger.

After Susan had reached her second orgasm that morning, Trigger had popped the question: "Hey, ma, can you do me a favor?"

"Okay, what is it, baby?"

"Yo, I need you to send a thousand dollars to a friend of mine."

"For what? Didn't I *just* send you two-thousand dollars last month?"

"Yeah, but you know a *nigga* ain't gonna ask if I don't need it. Now, this here is my man I grew up with from the hood. He's a lil' *fucked* up, and he need some paper, so he can pay this jailhouse lawyer to do his appeal. He asked me for my help. Now, like I said, this here is my homie, we came up together from pre-school. I *can't* turn my back on him now," Trigger said, as he'd tried to sound convincing.

"Okay, yeah, I understand. You know, that's one of the reasons why I love you, Trigger. You have a big heart. Hold up, let me get a pen. Now, what's his name?"

Trigger had shaken his head and smiled wickedly, as he'd pulled out the piece of paper Candy had given him yesterday with her name and ID number on it.

"The name is C. Sweets."

"The letter 'C' with a period, last name 'Sweets'?"

"Yeah, ma, and the ID number is 48301-004. Send him that as quickly as possible, aiiight?"

"Yeah, baby, I'll send it out by *Western Union* right now from my computer."

"Okay, ma. Look, get that *pussy* nice and wet for me, 'cause after you send it, I wanna hear you *cum* again."

"Okay, daddy," Susan had replied, as she couldn't resist the urge the young thug, Trigger had given her.

* * * * *

The next month...

After receiving the first payment of a thousand dollars Trigger had Susan send to Candy, Candy had known that she'd had a lucky streak. As long as Trigger kept Susan in check, Candy

168

also had known that she'd be able to extort him, whenever Trigger had made it big.

To Candy, having sex with him, giving it to Trigger whenever and however he'd wanted it, had been considered a short-term investment. Candy had figured that, from that point on, all of her sexual favors would be for Candy's benefit and her benefit alone.

Candy had sat inside of her cell, and prepared for her usual sex session with Trigger—five o'clock PM in the shower. As Candy had gathered her things, Jose then stormed into the room; anger had ridden his face.

"What's wrong, Jose?"

"I just looked at the call-out sheet for tomorrow—guess what I saw?" Jose said as he'd pouted.

"What?" Candy had asked inquisitively, curious as to why Jose had become so upset about a "call-out sheet"—the document that had contained the daily operations within the federal prison system.

"Candy, these *motherfuckers* changed my job to *Unicor.*"

"Well, isn't that what you wanted?"

"Yeah, that's what I wanted. But I only applied for that factory job, just to get close to Abdul."

Candy then burst into laughter, "C'mon, Jose, you know *damn* well Abdul isn't *fucking* with a queen. And besides, what are you so mad for? You got what you wished for. Doesn't Abdul work in *Unicor?*"

Jose's whole demeanor then changed from angry to sad, as he'd sat down on the bed next to Candy with his head down. Jose then looked up at Candy with watery eyes.

"Candy, Abdul's name's on the call-out, also. They've switched our jobs. Starting tomorrow, Abdul will be working in the hospital…with you.

At that, Candy had felt Jose's pain, and for a quick moment, she'd held Jose in her arms, and had attempted to console him. But within a millisecond, Candy's thoughts had been interrupted—with flashbacks of all the bad things others had done to her in her lifetime.

Candy then thought back to how Jose had allowed Ray to lie to her, and how Ray had tricked Candy into loving him. She'd then thought about how Ke-Ke told her that Jose had still been giving Ray oral sex, every chance he'd gotten behind Candy's back.

Thoughts of her aunt, Joyce kicking her out had come to mind, and how Tammy and Shanna had deceivingly tricked her; as well as everything else that had caused Candy's heart to become cold as ice. From her past experience, Candy, at that point, had officially become ruthless, even when it had come down to her friend, Jose.

Candy had smiled inwardly, as she'd skillfully thought about whom her next "victim" would be....

The next day...

"Excuse me, Sweets," the head doctor had called out to Candy in the back office of the prison's infirmary.

"Yes, Ms. Chase?" Candy had answered, ready to perform any duty her boss had asked. Candy had loved her job at the hospital, it was quiet, clean, and most of all, Candy's position at the hospital had paid well.

She'd been hired as an orderly, after Jose had begged Ms. Chase for several months to hire Candy. Ten months later, Jose had been transferred to *Unicor*, and Candy had been promoted as head orderly.

"Sweets, we have a new orderly that's starting this morning—his name is Smith. Do you know him?" Ms. Chase had asked.

"No," Candy answered, as she'd lied. Yet, Candy hadn't been officially introduced to Abdul, so technically, she hadn't known him. Also, flashing back to the visiting strip room, Candy had remembered that Abdul had been hung like a horse, having the biggest penis she'd ever laid her eyes on. The thought of sucking on it had made Candy's mouth water.

"Well, he's about to come in. When Smith arrives, I need you to show him around the hospital and give him his job description. Sweets, have him clean out the nurses' station and the employees' restrooms."

"Okay, Ms. Chase. Is there anything else?"

"No, that will be all. Oh, Sweets, you need to change the garbage bag in the staff's bathroom. I think it's some *trash* at the bottom," Ms. Chase replied, as she'd smiled and winked her eye at Candy, knowing that she'd planted a tube of *Mac "Lip Glass"* lip gloss for Candy; before Ms. Chase had gone into an office with a patient—one who'd been stabbed in his chest with a knife.

When Abdul had entered the infirmary, Candy had been out front to greet him. Inside, she'd felt giddy, yet Candy hadn't revealed it. She'd abided by the convict's prison rules of never looking at a heterosexual man, especially a Muslim, in the eyes.

Candy then quickly turned her face from his and nervously asked: "Are you Smith?"

Momentarily, Abdul had looked around to see if she'd been addressing someone else. He couldn't believe that a transsexual had the courage to attempt to speak to him, but in the back of Abdul's mind, he'd reflected back to that time in the visiting strip room. Abdul had thought about how Candy resembled a real woman, and how pretty she'd looked; Candy had distracted Abdul back then with her with curvaceous body—one in which he'd tried his best to avoid looking at.

Abdul then observed the room to make sure no one else had seen him, as Abdul had spoken to Candy for the second time, since she'd been on the compound.

"Yeah, I'm Smith," Abdul had answered back smoothly, with his distinguished, gentlemanly mannerism. He'd reminded Candy of Terry so much that, she had to catch herself; as Candy had almost called Abdul by Terry's name.

"Okay, Ter…oops, I mean, Smith. Sorry about that…It's just that, you really remind me of an old friend."

Again, Abdul had looked around frantically, as he'd become extremely nervous; Abdul had hoped that no one had caught him talking to Candy.

The more Abdul had looked at her face, the more he couldn't resist thinking about their first encounter, back then in the visiting strip room. Thoughts of how hard Abdul had to ignore the Devil's "whispering" in his ears had come to mind. Abdul, at that moment, had become lustfully aroused, as he'd talked to Candy.

"C'mon, Smith—follow me," Candy instructed, as she'd taken Abdul on a tour of the hospital, while giving him is job description.

As Candy led Abdul through the hospital, his dick had swelled to the fullest through his pants, as Abdul had fixed his beady brown eyes on her round, fat ass—that protruded through Candy's khaki uniform.

Every word had gone into Abdul's ear, and out of the other, as Candy had talked; Abdul had been caught up in a sexual daze. He also couldn't understand why the administration had allowed a transsexual into General Population, one who looked *exactly* like a woman.

Abdul then believed that the government purposely had designed prisons like this, to keep a psychological affect on convicts; keeping a level of ruckus and disorder that had ultimately caused disputes between the inmates. *There had to be some sort of plot behind it all that was higher than the warden's instructions,* Abdul had thought.

When Candy had stopped at the mop closet, turning around to face Abdul, she'd completely taken him out of his stupor.

"This is the mop closet and supply room. You have to come here every morning to get the cleaning products. Most of the time, you really won't have to do much, just make sure that the restrooms are tidy, and that the hallway is spotless. Other than that, no one would ever know that you're here. All they want is for the place to be neat and disinfected," Candy explained as she'd avoided eye contact with Abdul.

Again, before Abdul had addressed Candy, he'd quickly perused the room to see if anyone had been watching them.

"So, you said that I *remind* you of somebody? Who?" Abdul had curiously asked. Candy then blushed; she'd been taken aback while being in a state-of-shock, seeing that Abdul had the courage to engage in conversation with her.

At first, Candy had hesitated to respond, as she'd lifted her head and looked into his face; Candy had lightly batted her wide, doe-shaped, light-brown eyes.

"You…you remind me of my ex…my first love," Candy had responded genuinely, as she'd shown Abdul her vulnerable side. Although Candy had secretly adored him, she wasn't going to make the first move.

"Can I ask you something?" Abdul then said as he'd looked over his shoulders.

"Yes, you can ask me anything."

"Do they check-up on the orderlies?"

Candy then laughed, "Oh, you must be lazy," she'd joked. "No, like I said earlier, as long as the place is kept clean, they don't sweat you. And if you really want to hide, just come back here in the closet and sit and relax. When you hear keys jiggling, that means someone's coming, and to be alert," Candy had warned Abdul.

"So you're saying that, we can chill back here all day, and *nobody's* going to say anything?" Abdul had asked curiously.

"I've been working here for ten months now, and I've *never* got in trouble for hanging out," Candy said softly, as she'd quickly glanced down at the big bulge that stirred in Abdul's pants. Candy then had boldly looked directly into his eyes. It was then when she'd realized that Abdul had been curious, and highly stimulated.

Candy then decided to indirectly proposition him. She'd stared in Abdul's eyes, as Candy purposely had asked him a question that could've been interpreted two different ways. If Abdul had become offended by Candy's question, she could've always used the excuse of not meaning it the way that he'd deciphered it. And if not, then Candy would've known she had a chance with Abdul.

Resting the knuckles of her fists upon her wide hips, Candy then poked out her ample-sized breasts and had asked softly: "So, what's up?"

Abdul then perused the entire room again, and within an instant, he'd shoved Candy inside of the mop closet, closed the door, and had begun kissing her passionately; kissing Candy as if she'd been a woman. Abdul's erotic impulse had made him forget that Candy hadn't been a female.

Candy couldn't believe what had occurred, but she hadn't fought back the pleasure. This had been a sexual fantasy brought to life—something in Candy's wildest of dreams that she'd never thought would happen.

Low moans of passion had slipped out of her mouth, as Candy cried. Romantically, she'd kissed Abdul, as Candy thought of her ex-boyfriend, Terry simultaneously.

Abdul then pulled back before he'd quickly unbuttoned Candy's shirt. Abdul, at that point, had exposed her perfectly round and perky breasts, breasts that his hungry mouth had eagerly anticipated sucking on. After Abdul had caressed and licked on them, he'd immediately unbuckled his pants.

Candy had looked on in heated amazement, as she observed Abdul, seeing that he'd been ready to penetrate her with his long, thick penis; one that Candy had been so curious about. Instantly, she'd wantcd Abdul badly.

"Hold up, Abdul," Candy then said, as she'd quickly reached for the shelf, and pulled down a pair of rubber surgical gloves. Candy had tugged on the index finger of the latex glove, and stretched it out, before she'd gently placed it over Abdul's dick—Candy had jerked him off at the same time.

She'd then handed Abdul a small container of *Vaseline* to lubricate her anus, as Candy had leaned forward in front of him and parted her butt cheeks with her hands. Abdul then excitedly forced himself all the way inside of Candy, he'd filled her hot hole with his throbbing twelve inches, pleasingly penetrating Candy long, deep and hard; as she'd seductively moaned uncontrollably.

"*Y-e-s,* Abdul, that's it, baby. C'mon and *fuck* this *ass,* boo," Candy had groaned while grabbing her ankles, as Abdul had pounded away from behind. "Take this *ass,* Abdul, *take* it!" Candy had responded, as Abdul continued to oblige—until his eruption of warm semen later had exploded inside of the rubber glove.

As Abdul had begun to catch his breath, he immediately had been ridden with guilt; Abdul felt humiliated for what he'd done. As a man, Abdul was shameful, feeling that he'd compromised his manhood. As a Muslim, this *definitely* had been forbidden, and the sin Abdul committed had torn him apart. He'd broke down internally, as Abdul had pleaded to Allah for forgiveness. Abdul then looked into Candy's eyes with extreme hatred and disgust.

"What's wrong?" Candy asked nervously, as she'd analyzed his facial expression; confused as to why Abdul had been hurt. "Abdul, you felt so *good* inside of me—what, you didn't like it? Candy then asked with concern, as she'd realized that something had seriously gone wrong.

"Just *leave* me alone. You *better* not say a *word* about this to *nobody* or else I'll *kill* you—you hear me?" Abdul said harshly, as he'd coldly stared at Candy.

"Yes…I understand, Abdul. What we just did is between you and I—it stays between us. I'll *die* before I tell anyone. I couldn't say anything to anyone anyway. If Ray *ever* gotten word of this, he'll *kill* us both," Candy had stated nervously.

"Just stay the *hell* away from me!" Abdul warned angrily, as he'd quickly darted out of the closet and headed down the hall.

I'LL TAKE YOU TO THE CANDY SHOP
chapter 36

After three weeks of having her way with Trigger and Abdul, Candy was all smiles at the choice of discreet trades she'd picked. Never in this lifetime would Candy have planned to reveal their secret—especially if they'd complied with her rules.

With Trigger, it had been all about the money, but Abdul simply had given Candy the pleasure she'd needed and longed for. Yet, something about Abdul's behavior had bothered Candy. Every time after they'd had sex, immediately, Abdul's demeanor would change from warm and affectionate, to cold and hard.

Nevertheless, from the great sex Candy and Abdul had had, and from how much he'd reminded her of Terry, Candy had been willing to deal with Abdul's weird mood swings. She'd figured he'd give in one day, just like Terry and Ray had—the more they'd made love to Candy, the more feelings had developed, and trust was established back then, which had made Abdul surrender himself to Candy; as their relationship had evolved.

Before giving Abdul the oral satisfaction that he'd needed on a daily basis at the workplace one day, Candy had seen great pain in Abdul's eyes, as she'd also heard the crackling and uneasiness in his voice. Candy then realized that Abdul had been hurting badly.

She couldn't figure out why his disposition had been so sullen, but recognized that Abdul had always reacted differently, *after* he'd penetrated her. Once the thrill was gone, Abdul had routinely become overwhelmed with guilt—the shame of committing a sinful act of taboo had imposed on his conscience.

"What's wrong, baby?" Candy had asked sympathetically.

"Candy, did you look at the call-out sheet this morning?" Abdul had asked lowly.

"No. Why you ask?"

Abdul then lowered his head in shame. What he'd planned to do was going to break his heart, more than it would Candy's.

"Abdul…" Candy had paused, "…what's wrong? Baby, *nobody* knows about us or our relationship—we're safe," Candy then stated, as she'd tried to reassure Abdul, in hopes that he'd express his feelings to her.

"It's not that. I already know you're not *crazy* enough to put us both out there like that,"

"Then what is it, baby? C'mon, Abdul…you're scaring me."

Abdul then examined the room after he'd lifted his head, eyes watery, ashamed that he'd fallen in love with Candy—a vivacious transsexual. Abdul had felt guilty for betraying Allah, yet, his heart allowed Abdul another chance to repent.

"Candy, this *can't* go on any longer between us!" Abdul had said in a serious manner.

"WHAT? No, Abdul, don't *do* this to me, baby. I love you, Abdul—you can't *do* this to me. What's done is done. Face it, Abdul, we can't *change* what's already happened. Abdul, baby, *please,* don't leave me like this," Candy pleaded as she'd cried.

"DIDN'T YOU *HEAR* WHAT I SAID? IT'S OVER!" Abdul had yelled harshly, as he grabbed Candy by her upper arms, and had shaken her momentarily; Abdul had made Candy realize that she'd been fighting a losing battle. At that moment, his Muslim brother and barber, Yusuf had witnessed what had happened, as he'd checked out the scene at a distance.

"Look, *bitch,* you'll be alright. If you'd *checked* the call-out sheet this morning, you would've known that Ray gets out of the hole today. So hey, you still have a chance to *fuck* up another man's life," Abdul replied coldly, as he'd shoved Candy away from him.

The harshness of Abdul's words, and sudden change in his disposition had forced Candy to stop crying, as she'd wiped her tears away. Candy then stared hard at Abdul, as her hatred for him quickly formed internally. Immediately, Candy had darted Abdul the same evil look that he'd shot at her, wanting Abdul to feel all of her agonizing pain.

Candy had also fallen in love with Abdul, but then quickly reminded herself of her new, self-proclaimed title within the jailhouse: "Queen Bitch"; a vixen with a heart so cold, that ice-water had run through her veins.

"*FUCK* YOU THEN, *NIGGA!* PAYBACK'S A *BITCH!*" Candy screamed at the top of her lungs, as she'd quickly headed down the unit. Candy had left to warn Trigger, informing him that their secret love affair would have to slow down, due to Ray being released from "the hole" momentarily.

Yusuf had stood still, puzzled about what he'd seen. He then approached Abdul, needing to know what had transpired.

* * * * *

"Damn. You *act* like you ain't *happy* I'm out the hole," Ray stated to Candy, as he'd looked at the disturbed transsexual. "The *fuck* is wrong wit' you? What, you been *fuckin'* one of those *punk*-ass *niggas* while I was gone?"

"No, Ray!" Candy snapped back, as she'd been in a bad state-of-mind; distraught. Candy had thought about how badly Abdul had crushed her heart just minutes ago back then, and of how she'd wanted to seek revenge upon him—still needing Abdul to feel her grief.

"Then why the *fuck* your *pussy* ain't tight?" Ray asked angrily, as he'd forcefully inserted his middle finger inside of Candy's rectum; Ray had referred to her anus as if it had been a real vagina. He'd become livid, so much that if it had been possible, fire would've shot from Ray's eyes. "*BITCH,* WHO THE *FUCK* HAS BEEN *FUCKIN'* YOU, CANDY!"

"Ray, baby, I *swear,* I haven't been with *anybody* while you were in the hole. I've been waiting for you to come out," Candy quickly had lied, as the fear of getting severely beaten by Ray had settled into her mind. Candy then reflected back to the last time he'd threatened to crucially hurt her, back when Candy had pulled that stunt in the visiting hall, and had sneered at his fiancée, Kim.

"*BITCH,* YOU LYING!" Ray had yelled while looking into Candy's weary, watery eyes. "WHAT? YOU THOUGHT I WAS *BULLSHITTIN'* WHEN I TOLD YOU IF I FOUND OUT YOU WERE *FUCKIN'* WIT' ANOTHER *NIGGA* THAT I WOULD *KILL* YOU, *BITCH?* DID YOU? *HUH?*"

"Ray, you're tripping for no reason. I haven't—"

Before Candy had finished her sentence, Ray then interjected by rudely cutting her off.

"Candy, I *swear* to God, *bitch,* you lie to me just-one-mo'-time, I'ma *smash* your *fuckin'* pretty lil' head into the wall!"

Candy had cautiously thought about Ray's last comment and threat, and had quickly begun to hatch a plan. She'd known that Ray had been more than serious, and wouldn't let up on finding out if Candy had had sex with another man.

At that point, being disappointed with herself, Candy had become upset, being sloppy and careless as she'd had her affair with Abdul. Although Ray had a large penis, Candy had known that Abdul's was longer, and much wider; Abdul having thicker girth. Candy had also been angry for not checking to see when Ray was being released from "the hole". If she'd had, Candy would've been able to give herself a homemade enema with her empty lotion bottle, which had always seemed to tighten the walls of Candy's rectum.

"Seriously, Ray, I—"

WHAP!

Before Candy had a chance to finish her words, Ray had slapped her with the back of his hand. Ray had hit Candy so hard, that whelps immediately had formed on the right side of her innocent-looking face.

"OH MY *GOD*—NO, RAY, *N-O-O-O!*" Candy had yelled and squealed, crying, as she'd fallen to the floor. Candy then balled up her body into the fetal position. Ray had proceeded to grab Candy off the floor by her shirt collar, and had violently slapped Candy across her face with the palm of his hand; busting Candy's lip in the process.

Dazed, Candy had tried to resist the pain that had sharply ridden her face; confused as to if Ray had slapped her, or punched her in the face with his powerful fist.

"*BITCH,* LIE JUST-ONE-MO'-TIME SO I CAN *MURDER* YOUR *ASS* UP IN THIS CELL!" Ray had said forcefully with great conviction, as his eyes then squinted. Ray had stared long and hard at Candy, letting her know that he'd been serious.

Candy had been petrified and stuck, trapped with no way of escaping. There had been no way of fleeing from Ray, or from the infidelity she'd committed—Candy had to come clean. As Ray had lifted his hand to strike her again, Candy had immediately thought of a plan.

Although what she'd told him had been wrong, and a cold-blooded lie, Candy had been afraid for her life.

"Okay, okay, Ray, enough…this is what happened," Candy stated, right before she'd swiftly run to the toilet; relieving herself from the sudden case of diarrhea she'd had. Candy then assumed that the irregular bowel movement had come from having a nervous stomach from all of the stressful commotion with Ray— as well as from the powerful, pleasurable penetration of Abdul's massively wide, twelve-inch dick, she'd willingly and happily received.

Throughout the night, Ray hadn't slept, let alone been able to think straight. He'd been disturbed by what Candy revealed to him the day before. At that point, Ray had known that he'd been in conflict with going home smoothly the following month, and with risking his life for a transsexual; whom Ray had made his own personal prison-bitch.

Ray couldn't live with the fact that a convict had disrespected him in such a way. Not only that, it had been the inmate involved that disturbed Ray the most.

Making his decision as he'd sat back in his cell, Ray, at that point, had been willing to risk his freedom and life over Candy. But before he'd made a foolish move, there was one thing that Ray had to do. He'd played by the penitentiary rules amongst inmates; Ray had to address his situation by convicts' law. He'd needed to consult with a higher authority amongst the inmates— the Imam of the Sunni Muslims.

"Brother Amin, Amin, hold up for a second!" Ray had called out, rushing; as he tried to catch Amin before he'd gone into the unit.

"What's up, Ray?" Amin asked, as he'd sensed the urgency in Ray's voice. Normally, you wouldn't have caught Amin talking to Ray outside of the unit, but from the way Ray had flagged him down, Amin figured that there had to be an issue of some importance.

Ray and Amin had a mutual respect for one another. The two had gone to trial with their individual cases, oppose to letting their lawyers deceive them to take a plea bargain; which was a great sign of weakness amongst inmates.

In the federal system, convicts highly respected those who'd fought to the end and lived by the principles to never give up.

Ray had been a big-time drug dealer in DC, and Amin, being the Imam of the Sunni Muslims, was highly respected in his hometown of Philadelphia. Yet, in federal prison it was rumored that, guys within urban regions of the tri-state area had clashed with one another, due to the similarities and competitiveness these men had with each other.

"Can I holla at you for a minute?" Ray then asked, as he'd stared Amin in his eyes, letting Amin know that he had a serious matter. "Let's step over here so these *niggas* won't be all in our business," Ray had suggested as he looked around.

"Aiiight, what's up, Ray? You have a problem with one of the brothers or something?" Amin had asked with suspicion. He'd figured that whatever Ray had to say, most likely had pertained to one of his Muslim brothers.

Amin had resolved all issues that regarded any Muslim within the prison. People would consult with the Imam before things had gotten out of hand. Muslims had stuck together like real blood brothers. If you had a problem with one Muslim—you had a problem with all....

"Yeah, slim, it's about my *peoples* up in the block," Ray answered, as he'd referred to Candy. Ray had normally addressed Candy as a female to other convicts, but in this case, he hadn't wanted to disrespect Amin. Ray had known that Amin wouldn't approve of him referring to a transgender as a woman.

Amin immediately had known that Ray had been talking about Candy, yet he'd become confused as to why Ray needed to speak to him about a transsexual.

"What do your *peoples* have to do with the Muslims?" Amin had asked Ray with a calm but firm tone; he'd wanted to know exactly where Ray had been coming from.

"Amin, when I was in the hole, one of your Muslim brothers *raped* Candy," Ray spat, as he'd continued to look Amin in his eyes. Ray had known the seriousness of his accusations, and the consequences that followed for both Ray and the accused— depending upon the truth of the matter.

"I'm going to allow you to *rethink* what you just *said* to me, Ray!" Amin stated, as he'd become heated by Ray's comment.

"Man, you known me long enough to know I would *never* come to you about something like this if I wasn't more than sure. Amin, when I came outta the hole, the *bitch* was acting real strange."

"Hold up, hold up, Ray!" Amin said, as he'd held up his hand to stop Ray. "Look, Ray. You're going to have to *watch* how you refer to your peoples!" Amin then stated, as he'd shaken his head.

"Aiiight, slim, excuse my language, but like I was saying, when I came outta the hole, my peoples was crying; acting real strange. So I sensed something was up, like she was hiding something from me. I asked her what was the matter, and she hesitated to answer. So when I put my *pimp-slap* game on her, that's when she came out and told me that your brother, Abdul *raped* her at work!" Ray had explained, as anger had begun to build inside of him; rethinking of what Candy had told him.

"Ray, before I go *any* further, let me first say this. If you *ever* refer to your peoples as a *'she'* to me *ever* again, I'm going to take that as a form of disrespect. Now, I've known you for ten years, I'm aware of what *you* and your *peoples* do, that's your business. But when you address your peoples to me, *never* refer to them as a female!" Amin said sternly, as he'd made sure that Ray had addressed him properly. "Now, are your *peoples* willing to stand on what *he* told you?" Amin then asked, still baffled by the fact that Ray had been willing to go to war, and perhaps, risk his own life over a transsexual.

"Yeah, my peoples will stand strongly on it, that's why I came to you first. I explained about the seriousness of those accusations, and that lives could be taken behind this matter. That *bitch* knows I'll *kill* her if she lied to me," Ray replied convincingly to Amin, as Amin had immediately shot him an evil look.

"My bad, Amin. Slim, you know I'm all *fucked* up in the head; you know we go way back. I ain't referring to my peoples like that on purpose. It's just that I ain't use to switching up the terms," Ray answered, as he'd justified why he'd repeatedly referred to Candy as a female.

At that moment, Amin had figured that Ray must've been either mentally ill or extremely confused over Candy, that he couldn't help himself. He'd immediately disregarded Ray's actions as any signs of disrespect to him. Amin had felt that Ray had been lost and needed help badly.

"Look, Ray you know I can't let anyone slander a good Muslim's character," Amin indicated, as he'd tried defending his Muslim brother, Abdul in his absence. Yet, Amin had known that he, being the Imam—was his own duty to seek the truth.

"Ray, have your peoples at the chapel at six o'clock tonight, and we'll get to the bottom of this foolishness."

"You got that, slim, but Amin, my back's against the wall. So are you gonna *handle* Abdul, or do I *have* to?" Ray had asked with concern; he'd needed to know who would reprimand Abdul, if found guilty of the alleged sex attack.

"The question is: are *you* going to take care of your peoples, or will *we* have the honor? Because you know Muslims handle their own affairs," Amin answered back, as he'd taken heed to Ray's statement. "Six o'clock in the chapel," Amin confirmed, before he'd picked up his bag off of the ground.

"We'll be there," Ray then replied, as they both parted their separate ways. Amin had entered the unit, and had gone straight to his cell. From what he'd been told, Amin had to offer Salat and ask Allah for guidance. The truth had to be made clear about the accusation, mostly because whatever the outcome would've been, it would've come from Amin's judgment.

As the Imam, Amin couldn't be bias in his decision, so it had been an obligatory action for him to hear both sides from Abdul and Candy.

Just as Amin had arisen from the floor, after he'd said his prayers, his cellmate, Yusuf had walked in.

"As-Salaamu-Alaikum, Amin."

"Wa'laikum-Salaam."

"Yo, Amin, I gotta holla at you 'bout somethin' real serious, son," Yusuf had stated.

"What's up, baby boy?"

"Amin, if you peeped somethin' that looked funny, would you holla at somebody or keep it to yourself?"

"All depends on the situation, Ahk. Now, are we talking about a kufar or a Muslim?

"On the real, Amin, I don't want to seem like I'm *shittin'* on the brother, but what I saw yesterday *bugged* me out."

"Then why you wait until today to address it?"

"I ain't want to make any false assumptions, but as I studied the after effects, I just had to say somethin'."

"Well, since it's regarding a Muslim you should let me know, because it might not be what you think," Amin answered, as he'd hoped that it hadn't anything to do with Abdul.

"Yo, check it, Amin. I went up to medical yesterday to get a TB shot, when I went into the waitin' room, I see the brother,

184

Abdul talkin' to that transsexual Ray is messin' with. Then, I noticed that the transsexual was cryin'."

"Why would that bug you out? Brother Abdul was probably giving the punk some truth about Allah; that Allah created him to be a man, *not* a female," Amin indicated, as he'd still tried to protect Abdul from the allegations, until he further investigated.

"Easy, Amin; let me finish. When I was watchin', I saw Abdul grab the *gump,* shakin' the transsexual forcefully with both of his hands. So I walked out the waitin' room to see why Abdul was puttin' his hands on the transsexual. Right before I approached them, the transsexual cursed at Abdul before quickly runnin' way. When I asked Abdul what was up, he downplayed the scene, and told me that everything was cool. But, Abdul had this weird look on his face—like he just lost his best friend or somethin'."

"I see," Amin replied, as he'd listened attentively to Yusuf.

"I was lookin' for you earlier, but the brothers told me you were out front talkin' to that booty bandit, Ray."

Amin had taken a deep breath, as he thought of the two disgraceful stories that he'd heard about Abdul. Yet, he still hadn't heard Abdul's side, so a decision couldn't be made until six o'clock that evening.

"Yusuf, you need to be at the chapel at six o'clock tonight. The brothers on the Majalees will be there, as well as Abdul and the accusers. We'll give Abdul a chance to clean up a few things; Insha-Allah."

"Oh, *I'll* be there, and you best believe I can stand on *everything* I just said," Yusuf had replied.

"Well, you just might have to, Yusuf," Amin stated, as he'd picked up his Quran to read, and hoped that Abdul hadn't been at fault.

"Hey, Yusuf, tell the brother, Abdul I need to speak with him immediately!"

"Aiiight, Amin. Ahk, I'll stop past his cell on my way to the phone."

* * * * *

185

Yusuf had looked into Abdul's cell and seen that he'd been writing. Yusuf then knocked on the door and peeked in, before they'd greeted each other.

"Hey, Abdul, Amin said to come down to his cell; he needs to holla at you right now."

"For what?" Abdul had asked; taken aback.

"I don't know why—you go and see. Man, I gotta go make a phone call. I'll see you at six o'clock," Yusuf answered, as he'd headed towards the phone.

As Abdul made his way to Amin's cell, he'd wondered why Yusuf had made the comment of seeing him at six o'clock. Abdul had been curious as to why Amin had sent for him, instead of just coming to his cell.

Standing in front of Amin's cell door, Abdul had taken a deep breath and proceeded to knock on his door, until Amin had interrupted him: "Abdul, come on in; I've been waiting for you," Amin indicated, as he'd sat back in his chair; arms folded. He then looked directly into Abdul's eyes.

"As-Salaamu-Alaikum."

"Wa'laikum-Salaam. Have a seat, Abdul. Now, Ahk, I'm going to get *straight* to the point. I've heard two very disturbing stories about you today concerning the transsexual, Sweets."

Instantly, Abdul had become defensive: "Like *what*, Ahk? I haven't done *nothin'*. I—"

"Hold up, Abdul, before you start defending yourself," Amin had interjected, "you know we practice the Shariah as sternly as we can in prison, and *never* will I take a nonbeliever's word over a Muslim.

"So we're going to do this the right way. Now, I've set up a Majalees meeting for six o'clock this evening. The Shariefs will bring the accusers, and the Majalees council will hear both sides, then, a decision will be made; Insha-Allah. I *pray* that these accusations are false. So, at six o'clock, be in the chapel, brother. That's all for now—As-Salaam-Alaikum," Amin had instructed.

"Wa'laikum-Salaam," Abdul answered back in a low whisper, as he'd departed the cell. Abdul had been in a state-of-confusion: *There must be some mistake. Candy wouldn't have exposed me; Ray would've killed her. Someone must've seen us in the act together...but that can't be. Every time I fucked Candy, it was in the supply room. UNLESS SHE TOLD SOMEBODY ELSE...JOSE? OH SHIT, KE-KE!*

186

"Damn," Abdul had said, as he'd gone into his cell. Abdul then sat back on his bed, and had stared at the picture with his lovely wife, Kareema and their son, Umar. "What the *hell* have I done?" he'd whispered to himself, as tears then rolled down Abdul's face.

WA'LAIKUM-SALAAM
chapter 38

Six o'clock...

"As-Salaamu-Alaikum, where's the brother?" Amin had asked, referring to Abdul, as he'd noticed that everyone else had been on time for the Majalees meeting; including Ray and Candy, who'd sat patiently in the chapel; the two had waited to tell their story.

"I don't know, Ahk, I stopped pass his cell on my way out. It looked like he was packing his things," Yusuf had replied.

This hadn't been a good sign for Abdul. Usually, right before a meeting such as this, the guilty party had always tried to check into Protective Custody before a sanction had been made. But in this case, the crime that allegedly had been committed was so serious, that Amin had planned beforehand to stop anyone from packing up and fleeing to check-in.

Never had Amin thought that it would be Abdul trying to do so, but from his actions, Abdul had made it very easy to assume that he'd been planning to go into Protective Custody. After twenty minutes had gone by, waiting on Abdul, Chris had reported to the Majalees the developments of the situation. Abdul not being present had begun to look very suspicious.

Amin had Chris keep a watchful eye on Abdul as they'd waited, mainly because he'd seen a sign of guilt in Abdul's actions earlier. So when Chris had arrived to the chapel and told Amin that he'd witnessed Abdul packing his things, Amin had known that Abdul had planned to flee into Protective Custody.

At that point, it had been confirmed to Amin that Abdul was guilty, but before he'd given his decision, Amin had to get the verdict from his most-trusted brothers, who'd sat on the Majalees council. With a head nod from each council member, Abdul's fate would've been decided.

As each council member had nodded their heads in agreement that Abdul had been guilty, Amin then turned to the Shariefs, whom were regarded as the Swords of Islam. With a head gesture, and a tear that had fallen from Amin's face, he'd let them know that the decision had been unanimous, and that action had to be taken swiftly. As painful as it was to make, the decision had been justified.

Amin's decision had been the practice of the Shariah, which is based on the Quran and Sunnah. Never would he have gone against the revealed words of Allah, just to gratify his feelings for a human being. In Islam, such stern punishments are applied, so indecency and corruption won't become widespread.

The two Shariefs, Hamza and Qudus, had moved swiftly from the orders of Amin, as if they'd been trained specifically for this type of mission—Hamza and Qudus had been willing to give up their lives for Allah.

As the two had entered Abdul's cell, Hamza and Qudus had known from the shocked look on Abdul's face, and from his packed bags, that he'd definitely planned to escape to Protective Custody. Abdul would've gotten away freely, if he hadn't come back for his picture of his wife and son.

"As-Salaamu-Alaikum, Brother Abdul; going somewhere?" Hamza had asked. Instantly, Abdul had begun to stutter.

"Uh, uh, uh…nah, man, I was just cleaning up," Abdul had answered nervously.

"Damn, you doing a *whole* lot of cleaning, ain't you?" Qudus replied, as he'd looked into Abdul's empty locker.

"Yeah, Ahk. Look, I left something out on the tier, let me go get it," Abdul then answered, as he'd attempted to exit the cell.

Hamza and Qudus then made eye contact, as Chris had stood in front of Abdul's cell as a lookout guy; Chris had made sure that the coast had been clear. As Abdul then proceeded to head out, Qudus had allowed him to walk pass, while Hamza had stood in front of Abdul; Hamza then blocked him completely.

"Excuse me, Ahk, let me get pass," Abdul had requested.

"Nah, excuse us, Allahu-Akbar," Hamza had responded, as he'd pulled out his nine-inch blade from his waistband. The knife had been so sharp, that it had to be kept in its leather holster, to avoid from being cut from the hacksaw ridges on its side. Abdul had made this same knife while previously working in *Unicor,* never knowing that the knife would've actually been used on him.

Before Abdul could yell, Qudus had grabbed him from behind and put Abdul in a choke-hold, as Qudus had kept Abdul's body steady and still. Abdul's eyes then widened, as he'd begun to witness his own slaughtering.

Hamza had quickly forced the nine-inch knife deep inside of Abdul's stomach, which caused Abdul to go into complete shock; Qudus had continued holding him up. Hamza then grabbed the blade with both hands and had jerked upwards; he'd dug deep into Abdul's flesh, as Hamza sliced through his arteries.

Forcing the knife towards the left kidney and lung area, Hamza then had begun jigging the blade, as if he'd been sawing wood. As he'd continued cutting Abdul's insides, tears had fallen from Hamza's face, as he'd coldly looked into Abdul's eyes.

"May Allah have mercy on your soul," Hamza stated to Abdul, as he'd quickly yanked the knife out from Abdul's stomach before jumping backwards, only to see Abdul's guts immediately fall onto the floor.

No one had ever known how diligently the Muslims had worked, as Hamza and Qudus then cleaned up and covered their tracks. The two had made the murder look like an attack by White supremacists. It had always been known that White hate groups had ongoing gripes against the Muslims.

Soon after, the administration had quickly shutdown the compound, in hopes that there wouldn't be any more bloodshed behind the murdered Muslim, Abdul.

* * * * *

Although the entire compound had been shut down for a month, the administration never found out who'd killed Abdul. Yet, they'd profiled White inmates who'd been known to be gang-related, and those who'd had a history of violent crimes and major beefs with Muslims. The administration immediately reprimanded each White convict whom they'd felt may have been responsible for Abdul's death.

Each member that had been logged into the inmates' monitoring computer system as part of the *Aryan* brotherhood or *"Dirty White Boys"* gang, had been transferred to the *USP Florence* facility in *Colorado,* and to the *Marion Correctional Institution* in *North Carolina*—two maximum-security prisons.

Although no one specifically had been charged with Abdul's murder, they'd all felt the wrath, being confined within the two facilities that required twenty-three hour lockdown, and only one hour of recreation.

The Muslims had been pleased with the outcome, feeling totally vindicated; while on the other hand, the White supremacists had felt slighted for being in the wrong prison at the wrong time.

STRENGTH, COURAGE & WISDOM
chapter 39

During the thirty-day lockdown, both Candy and Jose had cried repeatedly, as they'd grieved hard for the man they loved. In Candy's case, this had been the second man whom she'd driven to his death—all from love. For Jose, Abdul had been the man that he'd *always* wanted to love.

After all prison cells had opened, Ray had swiftly run up the tier and headed to Candy's and Jose's room.

"Aye, Jose, *step* out the cell for a minute," Ray ordered, as he'd looked at Candy for surety; Ray had detected that something had been wrong with her.

Jose had immediately become suspicious, as he'd noticed how peculiar Candy and Ray's eye contact had been when they'd looked at each other. Curiosity also had allowed Jose to courageously linger outside the cell and eavesdrop, while Ray had displayed the cardboard sign in the cell door's window for privacy.

"What the *fuck* is wrong wit' you? Why you lookin' all *fuckin'* sad for?" Ray had questioned, not understanding why Candy had been so upset.

"Because, Ray, my conscience is *fucking* with me. I didn't know they were going to kill Abdul," Candy replied, as tears had welled from her eyes. "Now Abdul's blood is on my hands. He had a wife and a kid, Ray—why kill him?"

"WHAT? The *hell* you mean why? That nigga *raped* you, threatened to *kill* you! Now all of a sudden you wanna feel *sorry* for him? You's a *stupid*-ass *bitch!*" Ray had spat. "*Fuck* that *nigga,* Abdul. Candy, what happened, happened!" Ray had replied, as he'd let Candy know indirectly that there were rules that convicts had lived by.

Candy then lifted her throbbing head, looked Ray in his eyes, as she'd continued to sob: "But why *kill* him, Ray? Why? Abdul *didn't* deserve death."

"*Bitch* you in here trippin'! You better *keep* your mouth shut, 'cause the same thing that happened to him, can happen to

192

your ass, too! Like I said, that's how *shit* is handled here. Face it, Candy, you're in prison, for real! This *ain't* no *fuckin'* game!

"Yeah, it may look like a college campus wit' all the green lawns, TVs, microwaves, and all that other *shit,* but the reality of it all is that, you're in the belly of the beast! The first law of nature is self-preservation: only the strong survives!" Ray then yelled, as he'd tried hard to instill his wisdom to Candy; he'd informed her of the harsh reality of a prisoner.

"Yes, that's *r-e-a-l* easy for you to say. Your time is short; you're going *home* next month. I, on the other hand, Ray have to do four more years. Speaking of which, when are you going to *give* me the money to pay the lawyer guy, Tom?" Candy had asked Ray suspiciously, as she'd immediately focused on herself instead of Abdul.

Ray then quickly thought of a way not to answer Candy's question, as he hadn't any desire at this point, or ever to help her. In fact, the money Ray had made off of the package of heroin that Candy had smuggled inside for him, Ray had planned to use it to purchase a diamond ring for his fiancée, Kim.

Preparing for his future, in addition to leaving jail life behind, Ray had received his parole decision in the mail on this day back then, along with his release date to the halfway house the following month.

"Look, I'ma go down to get my haircut right-quick. You see how I'm wolfin'?" Ray responded, as he'd run his fingers through his curly hair.

"Why can't you *answer* my question?" Candy snapped before Ray had hurried out of the cell.

"Candy, I'ma holla at you later!" Ray then yelled back, not turning around or acknowledging Jose, who'd leaned on the rail of the tier; as he'd listened to Candy and Ray's conversation.

"Yeah, well, *fuck* you, too," Candy then whispered to herself, as Candy at that point, had despised Ray: the man who'd tricked her into loving him. At that very moment, Ray had shown her his true character—exactly one month before his release date.

Jose contained his tears, as he'd thought about Candy and Ray's conversation. Throughout the thirty days of being locked down, Candy had never revealed to Jose, the truth behind Abdul's murder.

For what Candy had done, Jose instantly hated her. He'd known that Abdul would never rape anyone. Jose had quickly suspected that Candy and Abdul had a secret love affair while Ray was in "the hole"; he then assumed that Ray had found out about it.

Jose then had guessed that Candy, fearful of Ray killing her for cheating on him, had lied on Abdul and said that he'd raped her. Jose also had suspected that Candy had become saddened, depressed and extremely guilty, because she hadn't realized that her false accusations would've gotten Abdul killed.

As Ray had left the block and headed towards the barbershop, Jose then entered the cell and had closed the door behind him, before he'd put up the privacy sign.

"Why are you putting the sign up?" Candy asked, as she'd noticed the tears that had poured down Jose's face.

"YOU *SHADY*-ASS *BITCH!* YOU HEARTLESS *PUNK*—PUTA *MARECON!*" Jose yelled angrily, as he'd called Candy a faggot-motherfucker in Spanish.

"What are you *talking* about? And why are you calling me out of my name?" Candy had asked concernedly. She hadn't understood why Jose had cursed and disrespected her in that manner.

"*Bitch,* I heard you and Ray's conversation!" Jose spat, as he'd looked into Candy's eyes for answers. Jose then expected her to lie to him immediately.

"Jose, it wasn't even like that. I—"

Before Candy had defended herself, Jose had stuffed her mouth with a hard right-handed punch, followed by a left uppercut. He then proceeded by grabbing Candy by her neck with both hands, as Jose had attempted to strangle her.

Enraged, Jose then shoved Candy against the wall, and had caused her to bang the back of her head against it, as he'd continued to choke Candy aggressively.

Jose had choked her so hard, that Candy had known that if she hadn't found a way to get his clenched hands off from around her neck, that Candy would've been dead within minutes. She'd prayed that Ray would come bursting into the cell to save her again, but then realized that Ray's intention had *never* been to be her savior—he'd never be there for Candy when her life had really been in danger.

As Ray had told her earlier, *"The first law of nature is self-preservation: only the strong survives!"* As the reality of that message had sunken deep into Candy's mind, as she'd faded for loss of oxygen, suddenly, for the first time in her life, Candy had discovered her true inner-strength.

Candy instantaneously had forced her knee into Jose's testicles, so hard, that he'd immediately released Candy's neck, instantly being in excruciating pain.

Candy then regrouped, and had taken both of her thumbs and dug them deeply into Jose's pretty green eyes. The sharpness of her fingernails had been like razorblades, as they'd cut into Jose's retinas.

"A-U-G-G-G-H! SOMEBODY GET THIS CRAZY *BITCH* OFF OF ME!" Jose had yelled at the top of his lungs as he'd screamed for help. Candy, the feminine transsexual, had continued to fight back tenaciously.

As she'd forcefully attacked Jose, he'd fallen to the floor and had yelled louder for help. Candy then jumped on top of his chest, and had pounded on Jose's face as if he'd been a punching bag.

The sound of many keys jingling had caused Candy to stop and quickly get up, as a group of correctional officers had run down the tier to the cell.

Before the guards had arrived, Candy jumped off of Jose, quickly unbuttoned her shirt to expose her breasts, slumped down into the corner, and had pretended to be the victim instead. She'd then revealed the blood that dripped from her mouth and hollered for help, as the guards then busted into the cell.

Instantly, the guards had forcefully snatched Jose up while giving empathy to Candy, the transgender who'd balled herself up in the corner and appeared helpless; Candy had persuasively made them believe that Jose tried to rape her.

"You okay?" asked Officer Mummy.

"No...I think my jaw is broke," Candy lied as she'd mumbled. Candy pretended that her jaw had been broken, yet, she'd known that the inside of her bottom gums had been cut from the seriously hard uppercut Jose had given Candy.

*   *   *   *   *

After the fight had ended, Candy and Jose both had received thirty days in "the hole", and a separation order had been placed on the two. Because of this, Candy and Jose hadn't been able to remain on the same compound together. Since Jose had been the aggressor in the eyes of the guards, he'd been transferred, which allowed Candy to stay.

During Candy's thirty-day lockdown in the Segregated Housing Unit, she'd cried every night, knowing that Abdul had been killed because of her foolish actions; just as Terry had.

Candy then sat back and thought about her life at that time, reminiscing on how it had turned out thus far. She'd thought of how everyone had crossed her: Tammy, Shanna, Ray, and at that time, Jose.

At that moment, Candy had come to the conclusion that it had been time for her to immediately get out of jail. She'd planned to approach Tom for his help, but Candy only had a thousand dollars. She'd then thought that if Trigger hadn't still been upset with her for abruptly ending their love affair, then perhaps she could've persuaded Trigger into assisting Candy with the legal retainer fee.

One month later…

A week before Candy had been scheduled to be released from "the hole" and allowed back onto the compound, Ray had been released from prison, and sent to a halfway house. This was part of his parole package, to spend six months there for rehabilitation; which would've allowed Ray enough time to secure a reliable job, and attend drug-counseling classes.

Candy had been all smiles as she'd been released out of "the hole", reporting back to General Population. She'd felt rejuvenated, like a "brand-new woman" to be exact: single, sexy and free—somewhat.

The fact that Ray was gone, and Jose, being transferred at that time, had given Candy the true "freedom" within the jailhouse to become the diva she'd always wanted to be. Also, the *Supreme Court* had overturned Candy's ruling of acquiring hormone treatment, giving Candy the ability to continue with her much needed treatments.

The outcome of it all had made Candy ecstatic. Eventually, her breasts would become fuller and perkier again, and the penile erections would be suppressed. Yet, this all wouldn't happen overnight. But, within the following three months, Candy would obtain the perfect body that would make *real* women envious, and men within the prison crave for.

"Candy! Aye, Candy!" Ke-Ke yelled, as he'd run across the compound to help Candy with her bags.

"Hi Ke-Ke," Candy had greeted, as she dropped her bags and had given him a hug; the two had been happy to see each other.

"Ke-Ke, why are you squeezing me so hard? Damn, your ass is strong!" Candy replied before she'd laughed. Although Ke-Ke had been burly, Candy had noticed a difference in him. Ke-Ke had lost a great amount of weight and muscle tone, in which his skin had also appeared to be sallow and dry; Ke-Ke's face had peeled, and his complexion faded.

"Shut up, hoe! Give me them *damn* bags wit' your weak ass," Ke-Ke joked, as he'd grabbed Candy's bags and had effortlessly flung them over his shoulders; all while trying to look feminine in the process.

"Thanks, boo," Candy said to Ke-Ke, as she'd walked ahead while leading the way to her old unit. While walking, Candy had switched her ass seductively from side-to-side, and had showed all of the trades on the compound what they'd missed while she was in "the hole".

"Houg ymug odgug," Ke-Ke had replied, as he'd said "Oh my God" in Pig Latin. Ke-Ke had talked in code so the other convicts wouldn't catch on to what he'd said. "Mmmph, mmmph, mmmph, bitch, what were you doing, a thousand squats a day?" Ke-Ke then responded, as he'd realized how fat and round Candy's behind had become. "You make a queen like me wanna *bump pocketbooks* with you," Ke-Ke had joked, referring to the gay term when two effeminate homosexuals have sex and penetrate each other.

"WHAT? Ke-Ke, you *must've* bumped your *motherfucking* head or something. Matter of fact, *put* my bags down, I'll take it from here. Ke-Ke, you know that I'll *never* have sex with you—I *don't* get down like that," Candy had snapped angrily, feeling disrespected by Ke-Ke's indirect sexual advance. "Don't you *ever* disrespect me like that again!

"Damn, Candy. You act like your *dick* don't get hard," Ke-Ke replied, as he'd implied that Candy had still used her penis to penetrate the men whom she'd had sex with.

"No, *bitch!* Ke-Ke, I'm a l-a-d-y! I don't stick—I get stuck! I'm not with that flip-flop *shit,* fucking men who I want to *fuck* me; unlike your freaky *ass*—goddamn butch-queen!" Candy had snapped. "I'm telling you, Ke-Ke, I would attempt to *fight* your ass right now, but I know better," Candy then retorted, knowing that the only thing that had stopped her from fighting Ke-Ke had been the scandalous rumor that Ke-Ke had AIDS.

"Yeah, you're right about that, because I'll *knock* your *ass* the *fuck* out! Who the *fuck* you think you is, tryna throw shade on a *bitch?* What, you think you all that because you got bigger titties and a fatter *ass* now?

"Mm-hmm—whatever, Ke-Ke! Good-bye. Have a nice day, *bitch!*" Candy had retorted nastily, as she then picked up her bags, and had dragged the heavy load into the unit.

Once Candy had stepped onto the unit, it seemed as if she'd experienced déjà vu. Just like the first day when Candy had arrived to prison, card games had halted, chess games paused, and conversations and whispers had been on the topic of Candy; Candy Sweets.

Not because of what she was, because these convicts had known Candy for over a year now, so it hadn't been shocking for them to see a transsexual transform into a beautiful "woman".

What had become appealing was the fact that Candy's behind at that point, was even plumper and wider, thanks to her new rigorous workout routine—doing many squats a day; along with eating meals regularly and taking her hormone pills religiously.

Although Candy had changed physically, convincingly looking more like a natural woman, there still had been an undercover trade whose attitude hadn't changed, as he again displayed his feign hatred for her.

"Yo, son, why the *fuck* you always starin' at that *fuckin'* *faggot*-ass *freak* for?" Trigger retorted, as he'd walked pass Unibomber. Candy smirked, as she'd tried her hardest not to laugh or to expose Trigger.

Candy then continued to carry her bags, and had proceeded back to her old cell. But this time, Candy had been given the opportunity to live alone. Orders had come down from the warden's office to give her a single cell, based on the fact that Candy hadn't sued the government for the alleged attempted rape scenario; the one that the administration had been totally convinced that Jose had committed.

* * * * *

Later that day...

"*O-o-o-o-o-o-h,* yes, Trigger. *Damn,* I missed how you *eat* my *pussy,*" Candy groaned lightly, as she'd bent over and looked back while Trigger had licked her anus; before he'd playfully poked inside of it with the tip of his tongue. Just one hour after Candy had arrived to the unit, Trigger had been at it again with composing his "anonymous" letters. Trigger had instructed Candy to meet him that evening, with the usual five o'clock appointment inside the shower stall.

Yet, at that time, Trigger had been the one whom waited on Candy. He'd been so excited to finally be able to fuck Candy again, that Trigger had been masturbating, right before she'd entered.

Instantly, Trigger had eagerly taken Candy in his arms, as he'd longed for her touch. Trigger then kissed Candy aggressively, as he'd frantically stripped off her clothes at the same time.

"*O-o-o-o-o-o-h,* yes, Trigger—*m-m-m-m-m-m.* Yes, like that! That's right, baby; *toss* my salad! *Ooh,* Trigger, c'mon baby, I can't *take* it any more; put that big *dick* deep inside of me, now!"

The moans that had escaped Candy's mouth had given Trigger the erotic fulfillment he'd always desired. Trigger had been obsessed with anal sex. Mainly because on the outside world, none of his female companions would ever let him have anal intercourse with them.

The women had complained that Trigger's penis was too big, or they hadn't ever engaged in anal sex; yet, it had *always* been Trigger's fantasy to perform the sex act.

After having watched several porno DVDs before his incarceration, Trigger had often masturbated heavily during the anal sex scenes. Trigger promised himself that, whenever he'd made it big within the rap industry, when groupies showed an interest in Trigger, that it would be *mandatory* for them all to allow him to perform the sex act.

No matter how pretty the fans were, or how great their bodies might've been, if they hadn't been down for Trigger entering inside their rectums, then he'd planned to forcefully dismiss them. But, until that day, Trigger wouldn't let his sexual fantasy take control of his mind, as he'd taken great pleasure in penetrating Candy's rectum, until she'd become sore.

"Damn, Trigger! Why were you so *rough* today? You *fucked* me too hard. Trigger, you know I haven't had any *dick* since I was in the hole," Candy had whined while putting back on her robe. She'd then tried to stand upright, bearing the excruciating pain that had burned intensely inside of her tunnel.

"Yeah, I know, ma, but I couldn't control myself. I ain't had that fat *ass* in a while. A *nigga* like me been jerkin' my *dick* ever since you been gone," Trigger answered, as he'd grinned while grabbing his semi-erect penis.

Candy then blushed at the undercover trade with the promising rap career, as she'd realized that Trigger had fallen in love with her sexual pleasures. Every time Candy had looked into his eyes, she'd instantly seen dollar signs."

"Hey Trigger, I need a favor, boo."

"C'mon wit' that *shit*, Candy! Yo, I'ma get Susan to hit you off wit' that dough in the mornin', aiiight?"

"No, it ain't that," Candy replied sadly, as she'd pretended to look worried.

"Then what is it, ma?"

"Trigger, I need a lawyer badly. The lawyer guy, Tom told Ray that he'd do my case for three-thousand dollars."

"WHAT? Oh, *h-e-l-l-s* nah, yo! You *gots* to be outta your mind if you think I'm givin' *you* three G's!"

"Trigger, I *need* that money, for real. Look, I tell you what, baby, if you do this small favor for me, then I'll *never* charge you for my services again. You can have this fat *ass* whenever, and however you want it; I'll even let you *cum* all over my pretty face. Trigger, I'll swallow you whole until you leave to go home. Baby, you'll *never* have to jerk that big *dick* of yours again," Candy had propositioned. "C'mon, Trigger, *p-l-e-a-s-e*...I really *need* this money; I'm trying to go home, too.

By the looks of sincerity that Candy had shown in her hypnotic eyes, and by the fact that her sex acts would be at Trigger's mercy from here on out, had made him more excited than ever. Trigger had been wide open on Candy, and she'd known so, as Candy had turned him out in no time.

"Aiiight, look. I'ma smash you off with two G's—three thousand is *outta* the question. I'll give you the dough, but *only* under one condition."

"What's that, daddy?" Candy had asked seductively as she rubbed Trigger's chest, feeding into his ego. Even though Candy couldn't get the extra thousand dollars she'd asked for, Candy hadn't a problem with receiving two thousand dollars from Trigger. Along with what she'd already had, Candy would be able to give Tom a twenty-five-hundred-dollar advance, on a one-way ticket to freedom.

Candy could've hired a lawyer from the outside world, but figured that by hiring an imprisoned lawyer to do her appeal, the lawyer would be more sympathetic to her incarceration; in return, the lawyer would work harder to help Candy win her trial.

"Yo, I'ma give you this dough, but you *gotta* continue to be my *bitch* undercover, until I get released. Meaning, you *suck* my *dick* only, and make sure that you give nobody else that," Trigger said, as he'd smacked Candy on her behind. "That's *my* ass. Now that Ray's gone, you ain't gotta worry 'bout *shit*. So if *niggas* tryna holla, you bat that *shit* down for me, ma, aiiight?"

Candy almost had burst into laughter, but she'd held her composure, as Candy couldn't believe what Trigger had said.

"Alright, Trigger, you got that. From now on until you leave, I swear on *everything* that I love, I won't give this *ass* to anybody but you—I'm your property now. No one will know but you and I," Candy had sworn to Trigger.

Candy's words had been so convincing to Trigger, especially with her swearing on *everything* that she'd loved. Unfortunately, Trigger had been blind to the fact that Candy hadn't loved anything at that point; not even herself.

The following week...

As Candy had walked into the prison's Law Library, Ke-Ke had been exiting. The two had ignored each other, and acted as if they'd never met, as Candy and Ke-Ke had passed each other.

Whew, that beastly bitch stinks! Candy had thought as Ke-Ke walked by; Ke-Ke, having a fowl body odor that had lingered throughout the Law Library. *Motherfucker must've shitted on himself—nasty ass!* Candy then frowned up her face, as she'd fanned the air and entered the library.

The Law Library had been extremely quiet, mainly because in the early hours of the day, clerks only had occupied the library, and to Candy's surprise, Tom had been on duty.

"Excuse me, are you Tom?" Candy asked, as she'd hovered over the tiny White man who'd seemed to be deep in thought; as Tom had read his law book at his desk.

Tom then held up his index finger, alerting Candy that he'd only be a moment; Tom hadn't wanted to lose his place within the book. After reading the case, Tom then closed the law book, looked at Candy with a shocked expression and had said: "Yes, I'm Tom. Who might you be?" he'd asked, as Tom slightly smiled.

"Oh, I'm sorry, my name is Candy Sweets. A friend of mine had referred me to you, but he was recently released before being able to fully introduce me to you."

"Okay, and *who* might this friend of yours be?" Tom had asked slyly; he'd already been approached by Ray regarding Candy's case a few months ago. But when Tom had told Ray what the retainer fee would cost, Ray then quickly backed off, leaving Candy no choice but to find her own way to Tom.

"His name is Ray, but look, that's *irrelevant* now. What's important is that I was enhanced two extra years for identification theft, but the element of the crime wasn't even in my indictment. I wasn't charged with it."

"Hmmm," Tom replied, as he'd leaned back in the recliner chair and placed his index finger on his thin lips. Tom had been deep in thought before he'd given his opinion. "Well, that sounds like an Apprendi issue. You know that same case has just been applied again in the *Supreme Court*—Booker decision."

"Booker? Look, Tom, I'm *not* a lawyer, I'm not familiar with law terms and I *damn* sure don't know a Booker! All I know is that I'm in jail serving a sentence illegally. Now, I'm not about to look at *CNN* all day on TV, waiting on the *Supreme Court* to make some *damn* decision that won't even help me out. I need a lawyer, and from what I hear, you're supposed to be the man for the job!" Candy had said aggressively.

Tom then smiled, as he'd realized that most of the prisoners on the compound had recognized his skills, and many had even remembered Tom from his case. Often times, Tom had seen his face, as well as his co-defendant, Dewayne Larkin, on almost every news channel, and in newspapers.

Tom was a young, prestigious, White lawyer, who had a huge attraction to Black women. He'd been a high-power attorney at his firm, who'd gotten caught up with a bunch of wealthy politicians in an embezzlement case out of *Philadelphia.*

The case had been widely spread, mostly because it had involved the mayor, the city council, Lizzy, Tom's ex-fiancée, a Black woman who owned a printing company, and his friend, Dewayne, who owned half of the *"Pizza Cut"* and *"Burger Queen"* franchises. The case had been so big, that prosecutors, as well as the media, had dubbed the case the *"Pay-2-Play"* corruption scandal.

"So, you want me to do your case? Can I ask something, ahhh—"

"Sweets, my name again is Sweets; but you can call me 'Candy'."

Tom then smirked, "Okay then, Candy. Let me ask you this, why me? Why not pay your money to a lawyer out in society?"

Candy then placed both of her hands on her hips, and had sucked her teeth before she'd responded: "Now, look, Tom. I think you *damn* well know why! No lawyer on the outside is going to work as hard you. Plus, I can always come check on you to see if you're *bullshitting* with my case or not!"

Tom had smiled again, "I doubt that last part. When I take on a case, I put my all into it; as if it's my very own."

"Okay then, Tom, so do we have a deal or what? I need my freedom now!" Candy had sharply stated. "So what's it going to cost me?" Candy then asked curiously, as she'd handed Tom her paperwork regarding her case.

"I tell you what, Candy. I'll look over your paperwork this evening, and see what I can make out of your case. Come see me tonight and we'll work it out—deal?" Tom answered, as he'd then reached out his hand to shake Candy's. Tom not only wanted to seal the deal, he'd also been enthralled with Candy; Tom, at that point, had wanted to feel how soft her hands had been.

From the lightness of the Tom's handshake, and from the way he'd looked into Candy's eyes, Candy had smiled to herself; she'd immediately sensed that Tom had been a closet case.

But what Candy hadn't known that, not only had Tom been living on the "down low" as a gay man, but that he'd also desperately wanted to tell someone about his confusion— regarding his sexual identity. Tom had needed a mentor to guide him, someone to help Tom find his way.

Unfortunately, Tom had recently made a huge mistake. Tom had allowed his lustful ways to lead him into the big burly arms of his newfound friend, Ke-Ke; who'd planned to make sure that he'd been the *only* prison-bitch that Tom had trusted with his "buried treasure".

That evening...

"*O-O-O-O-O-O-H*, MY GOSH, *Y-E-S*—FUCK! It hurts so *fuckin'* good! SLOW DOWN, NOT SO HARD! *A-a-a-a-h;* put some more *Vaseline* on!" Tom had yelled loudly at the top of his lungs, in the back of the Law Library, during lunch hour when no one had been around.

No matter how many times Ke-Ke had penetrated Tom, it always had been awfully painful for him. Yet, being into S & M— Tom had loved it. He'd requested Ke-Ke to forcefully shove his large eleven-inch penis, quickly in-and-out of Tom's anus; as Ke-Ke had taken great joy in tearing the tissues of his rectum—as Tom had bled heavily.

After Ke-Ke had exploded his semen inside of Tom, as he'd spanked on Tom's pale, white butt cheeks with his huge hands, Ke-Ke then had turned around, spread eagle, and had positioned himself to give Tom the exact same pleasure. Gay men considered this sex act "flip-flopping": each one taking turns at penetrating his mate.

The two had often joked by saying: *"The pancake ain't done until it's flipped over",* and in Ke-Ke's case, he'd specialized in "flipping" closeted homosexuals. Ke-Ke had many convicts so turned out by his massive penis, that oftentimes, the convicts had seriously contemplated on coming out—and live their lives as openly gay men.

Tom often had wondered if Lizzy would've accepted him for being gay. They had a great friendship, and a very special relationship. So special, that even after Tom had been incarcerated and sentenced to fifteen years in prison, that he hadn't objected when Lizzy told him that she'd, at that time, been engaged to one of his office colleagues, and personal friend, Patrick Nelson.

Lizzy was an independent Black woman, in which Tom had known and respected. Also, he'd believed that Lizzy had loved White men with superiority. Lizzy had felt more comfortable with being with White men than dating within her own race. She'd honestly believed that *all* Black men were no-good, lazy and definitely couldn't be trusted, due to the bad experiences Lizzy had had with the few she'd dated in the past.

Lizzy had received all of her printing contracts from the firm through her relationship with Tom. Before owning her own company, Lizzy had worked for Tom's firm. She'd been there so long, that Lizzy had begun to assimilate; Lizzy had talked and acted as her White counterparts, whom she'd grown to love and admire.

Wishing badly that she'd been born White, Lizzy had become a snooty, high-class Black woman who'd hated her own race—having self-esteem issues. Yet, Tom had loved everything about her.

After Tom and Ke-Ke had finished having sex, they'd straightened up, and Ke-Ke had headed out the door. This had been when Ke-Ke and Candy had crossed paths at the Law Library. Although they hadn't spoken to each other, Ke-Ke had a devilish smile upon his face, in which Candy had thought was odd; she'd known that they hadn't been on good terms. Candy still had been upset at the sexual advance Ke-Ke had made to her.

"That *motherfucker* needs to wash his funky *ass*," Candy whispered as she'd pinched her nose, avoiding Ke-Ke's body odor; as Candy had entered the Law Library. Tom annoyingly had begun spraying his air freshener.

"Thank God you have air spray," Candy had stated. *Mmmph, mmmph, mmmph, smells like shit is oozing out of Ke-Ke's pores!*

Tom hadn't said anything, he'd just smirked and lightly laughed, before Tom had told Candy his opinion about her case.

"Candy, I went over your paperwork carefully. I think I can get you back on a 60(b) Motion. If the judge agrees, then they'll take the two-year enhancement off, maybe more; depending on how strong we argue it," Tom had stated, as he couldn't help admiring Candy's beauty and her sexy physique; as she'd attentively listened to Tom.

Candy had become excited at the great news of the possibility of gaining her freedom back.

"Really, Tom? You think the judge will take off more than the two years?" Candy asked excitedly, as she'd grabbed Tom's arm by impulse. Candy then noticed that Tom hadn't minded her touching him.

"Now, this is the deal. If I get you back in court, I won't be able to represent you, but I can have my friend from the office step in to assist you," Tom indicated, as he'd shamelessly grabbed his crouch while rudely staring at Candy's breasts.

Immediately, Candy had known for sure that Tom had been gay by the way he'd reacted to her, in addition to seeing how Tom couldn't control, or hide his erection; at that moment, Tom being extremely attracted to Candy.

"Now, my friend's appearance in court won't cost you because I know that you don't have much money. But, I'm *willing* to work with you, *if* you're willing to *work* with me," Tom said, as he'd groped himself again while looking hard into Candy's beautiful eyes. Tom then guided her eyes down to the small print in his pants, by the light, jerking motion of his hand.

Candy immediately had understood what Tom had implied. She'd reached down to his pants and had grabbed Tom's small penis.

"Oh, Tom, I'm willing, and am *more* than able to work with you; anytime you want me to. I'll take care of you, baby, just give me a time and place. I'll be there all greased up and ready to go," Candy then replied, as she'd gently grabbed his erect penis while smiling wickedly; Candy had also noticed how small it was. "All I want is to get out of jail, Tom."

"Meet me up here tomorrow morning when no one is around. Come to the Clerks window, and just walk to the back as if you work here. I'll be in the back in between the last aisle of the law books," Tom instructed, as he'd then touched Candy's bodacious ass. Tom realized that her khaki pants hadn't any back pockets, in which he'd then smoothly glided his hand over Candy's behind.

Tom had continued to rub his hand over her rump, as Tom had anticipated their sexual escapade that was soon to come.

NEVER CAN SAY GOOD-BYE
chapter 43

The next morning...

"Aiiight, *niggas.* Y'all take care, and don't forget to hit me up on the horn, yo! I'll be on *106 and Park* in a few months," Trigger stated to his fellow inmates, as he'd said his final good-byes; right before being released from the facility.

Trigger then proceeded to pass Candy's cell, and had walked down the tier and into the TV room. Candy had noticed that Trigger intentionally bypassed her cell, not wanting to acknowledge Candy before he'd left the prison facility.

Oh-no-he-didn't! No this trick-ass nigga don't have the decency to say good-bye to me. This motherfucker rams his dick up in my ass everyday at five o'clock, and he can't even peek in his head to say good-bye? UHN-UHN, I'M NOT HAVING IT! Candy had become upset with Trigger disregarding her.

Candy had quickly put on the new tennis sneakers that Ray had purchased for her from commissary, and had walked down to the TV room to confront Trigger. After all, he'd been in the process of being fully released, and there wasn't anything that Trigger could've done to Candy at that point.

Plus, she hadn't any respect for Trigger during this time, so it really hadn't mattered how Candy had expressed herself to him. Not because Trigger was trade, being on the "down low" about his sexuality, but for being overly discreet about their relationship. Trigger had acted as if he'd been very masculine and rugged; Trigger had put up a big front.

In a furious rage, Candy had entered the TV room. Suddenly, everyone had become quiet, mainly because this room had been reserved only for highly respectable inmates, a place where hardcore convict's had parlayed.

Instantly, Candy had known that she'd been out of place by being there, and quickly had nervously begun apologizing to the inmates. It was then when Candy had broken the jailhouse rules, as she'd entered an area where her "kind" had been prohibited.

209

"Um, excuse me, everybody. I'm sorry if I'm disrespecting any of you in any kind of way. It's just that, I wanted to say good-bye to Trigger before he left."

Everyone in the room had disregarded Candy's comment, and had proceeded to shoot her evil looks, giving Candy indication that she'd crossed the line. They'd also been baffled as to why Candy had wanted to speak to Trigger: a person who'd treated her so badly, ever since Candy had first step foot inside the jail. But before anyone had the chance to address the transsexual, Trigger had jumped into defense mode. Immediately, he'd put Candy in check.

"Yo, son! What the *fuck* you wanna say bye to *me* for? *WHAT?* You tryna *front* on me or somethin'? Yo, I swear, if I wasn't on my way out the door, I'd *smash* your whole *fuckin'* grill! *FAGGOT*-ASS *BITCH!* You *better* get your *gump*-ass outta this *fuckin'* TV room before you get crushed! THAT'S ON THE REAL!" Trigger had retorted with his fists balled up.

Trigger had let Candy know that if she'd attempted to challenge him in front of the other inmates, that he'd break Candy's jaw right on the spot.

Candy then looked into Trigger's eyes and had become appalled. She'd known that Trigger had been serious about the threat he'd made. Although Candy had believed that this had been the perfect opportunity to alert the other convicts about Trigger's sexuality, their relationship, and the sexual escapades they'd had—she'd resisted, Candy had seen the bigger picture.

From his actions, she'd known that Trigger would've done, and given anything, not to be exposed. From the deal that Candy had known Susan Stone had offered him at *Dope Jam Records,* and all of Trigger's future royalties he'd earn, Candy then believed that Trigger would definitely be put in a position to take care of her for the rest of Candy's life. Realizing this, she'd then withdrawn from exposing Trigger—at that very moment, Candy had thought about her future investment.

"You're right, Trigger, I apologize; I must be tripping. I think the meds that I'm on are starting to make me hallucinate. I'm sorry, everyone; I apologize for the intrusion. It won't ever happen again," Candy had softly pleaded before quickly getting one last look at Trigger. Candy then fled out of the TV room as fast as she'd come.

When Candy had departed the room, everyone had laughed loudly at what had occurred between she and Trigger; everyone except J-Rock and Amin. The two had instantly realized by Candy's body language and actions, that her medication hadn't caused Candy to accost Trigger. J-Rock and Amin had both sensed that Trigger and Candy had been seeing each other intimately.

The two then sat back and had looked at each other. At an instance, J-Rock and Amin had thought of the perfect book concept that would take both of their literary skills to the next level.

"You thinking what I'm thinking?" J-Rock had asked Amin.

"No doubt, J-Rock, I got a *better* concept for the book project we're working on," Amin had answered, as a bright smile had come across his face.

"Aiiight, let's see if we're on the same page, slim."

"You peeped what just went down?"

"Didn't I just *ask* were you thinking what I was thinking?" J-Rock had joked sarcastically."

"Aiiight, so we both figured out what's *really* good with Trigger and Candy. Look, we already had the basic format of the book concept; the only thing that was missing was the rawness of the reality of what *really* goes on here in prison."

"So we add what just went down between Candy and Trigger, ask her a few questions and—"

"We work towards having a national best-selling book!" Amin had answered excitedly.

"Man, it's already a best-seller. Did you *forget* who you're writing this book wit'? Jason Poole!" J-Rock teasingly had boasted. "That's right, Amin, the author of *Larceny;* who made the best-sellers' list while in prison, without any advertising or promotion," J-Rock had continued while proudly pounding on his chest with his fist.

Amin then sat back and chuckled, as he'd shaken his head at J-Rock's playful cockiness; he couldn't deny J-Rock's huge accomplishment. This had been the main reason why Amin had asked him to collaborate on their project back then.

"Yeah-yeah-yeah, J-Rock, I know you got skills. But on the real, the book should fully go down like this..." Amin had indicated, before he'd begun whispering the details to J-Rock. The two had gone into business mode—both having serious expressions upon their faces; as Amin and J-Rock discussed the new concept of their novel.

After J-Rock and Amin had plotted the first few scenes of their book, the two men had been so confident with their ideas, that J-Rock and Amin had believed that they could finish writing a book, that would inform the world about the scandalous secrets behind prison walls; in regards to sexuality, how the infidelities of these convicts, who lived their lives on the down low, had devastatingly affected the women in their lives first, and ultimately, everyone else in the world....

"Aye, J-Rock, call *GHETTOHEAT®* and tell HICKSON what we discussed."

"I'm already on it," J-Rock answered, as he'd quickly headed to the phone.

* * * * *

Candy giggled to herself as she'd headed to the Law Library. She'd thought about what had transpired in the TV room. For one, the dumbfounded expression upon Trigger's face had exposed him more than anything to the other prisoners. Secondly, that had been her first time ever going into the TV room, a place where Candy had been forbidden to enter.

Damn, I must've been really bugging, entering the TV room like that. I've never even gone in there when Ray was in prison, Candy had thought, as she'd then realized the danger Candy could've put herself in.

Candy then had shaken her head and quickly entered the Law Library. When she'd arrived, Candy noticed that the Law Library had been quieter than it was, once she'd arrived earlier.

The silence had made Candy feel somewhat eerie, like she'd been the only person there. Yet, Candy had known that she hadn't been—this was the luxury of the Law Library: peaceful, quiet, and out of the eyesight of the guards.

Candy then followed Tom's previous instructions and had gone behind the Clerks' desk, acting as if she'd worked there; before Candy had proceeded down the long aisles of law books. Heading down until she'd reached the last aisle, Candy had discovered Tom sitting there with his small penis in his hand—just as Candy had imagined.

"For a minute, I thought you weren't coming," Tom stated, as he'd gingerly caressed his little pale penis. Candy then looked down at Tom's tiny prick and snickered before she'd responded. Candy then had reached down for it.

"How could I miss out on this pretty, pink, piece of meat," Candy had answered. She'd now eagerly wanted to taste her first sample of a White man. Candy then seductively dropped down to her knees, and easily had placed Tom's penis in her mouth.

Tom's meat was so small, that it hadn't taken Candy any effort to swallow it completely down to the base. She'd opened her mouth as wide as she could, and devoured Tom's penis and testicles simultaneously.

"*M-m-m-m-m-m,* Tom...."

* * * * *

Tom and Candy's sexual excursions had continued for the rest of the month within the Law Library, until Tom one day, had asked her to do something that compromised Candy's bedside manner; which had caused her to become highly insulted in the process.

From that moment on, Candy hadn't any desires of having sex with Tom anymore at that moment, even though she'd desperately needed him to help her with the appeal—Candy had needed to win back her freedom.

Yet, Candy could've cared less; she'd rather suffer in prison and die, then to succumb to Tom's sexual wishes.

CANDY LAND
chapter 44

"Damn, how long is this fucking ride?" asked one of the prisoners on the transit van. His scratchy voice annoyed Candy, as she was reflecting back to her past. She hissed and sucked her teeth at him for breaking her concentration.

When Candy looked up at the young, clean-cut White male, she smiled to herself, seeing that he too, had something to hide. Over the years of dealing with so many men, and their different characteristics, had made it easy for Candy to spot a closeted gay man.

Candy also came to the conclusion that every man that she'd dealt with had something deep inside of them that they tried to suppress. Yet, no matter how much they attempted to hide their sexuality—in a matter of time, it all came out.

Looking out the window to observe her surroundings, Candy wanted to see how far they've gotten, before they actually reached the prison.

"Are we almost there?" the White inmate asked again, still seeking an answer.

"No. We still have ways to go," Candy managed to answer in between a heavy, dry cough. She then laid back and closed her eyes, hoping that no one would disturb her again before they reached the prison.

For some reason, the White convict resembled Tom so much, that when Candy actually closed her eyes, her thoughts were filled with nothing but past memories of Tom, as Candy drifted back in time....

* * * * *

"Yes, Tom, *fuck* me harder; punish this *ass!*" Candy said, as she'd talked dirty to Tom. He'd pounded Candy from the back, and she'd hoped that her naughty words would make Tom ejaculate faster. They'd had one of their private sex sessions in the back of the Law Library, and Candy had been in a rush to get the sex romp over with as fast as she could. Candy had wanted to hurry back to the unit to catch the *"World Premier"* of Trigger's new rap video on *B.E.T.'s Access Granted.*

It had only been a month since his new release had debuted, and Trigger, at that point, already had his second hit single out, *"Many Thugs"*; in which the new video to the song had been featured on television that evening.

Magazine articles had indicated that from the first day Trigger had come home, that Susan Stone had him in the studio. But what the writer of the magazine hadn't known was that, she also had Trigger repeatedly in her bedroom; Susan, at that time, had the young rapper colliding inside of her frequently. Susan had made sure she'd gotten all of her moneys worth from Trigger's million-dollar contract.

Candy had been in awe of the numerous articles that had proclaimed Trigger as America's "most valuable rapper". They'd highlighted his fake thug persona, dwelled on how he'd been shot several times and had recovered, as well as revealed the three-year bid, Trigger had done in federal prison.

Smiling, as she'd shaken her head, Candy had become shameful of how Trigger had tricked the entire world. No one had ever known that the true Trigger, a.k.a. Douglas De'shawn, was more than a fraud in the hip-hop industry, he'd been an undercover homosexual—a trade within the prison facility; and Candy had been the beautiful transsexual, who'd held the key to Trigger's demise.

Candy then bent over to assume the "doggy-style" position, as she'd held both of her butt cheeks with her hands and exposed her stretched anus. By doing so, Candy had allowed Tom to see his tiny penis move in-and-out of her, as Candy had hoped that Tom would explode faster.

Candy then whined her hips in a swift rhythm before she'd bounced her butt like a stripper. Tom had quickly shot his load of semen into the pinky finger of the latex glove that they'd used to substitute as a condom.

"Damn, that was so good," Tom murmured, as he'd easily pulled himself out of Candy's rectum; Tom then looked at her from behind. Since Candy's hormone pills had taken a while to fully kick in, she'd still been in conflict with suppressing the penile erections; Candy had fought hard for her organ to stay limp.

Every time she and Tom had sex, Candy had requested that he enter her from behind; Candy had not wanted Tom to discover her penis being erect. Also, whenever they'd finished, Candy had made sure to get dressed immediately.

As Candy had stood upward with her back still turned towards Tom, he'd walked up from behind and held Candy tight. Tom then caressed her arms, as he'd humped on Candy's butt with his limp dick. He'd begun to gently kiss Candy's neck, and without warning, Tom had reached around and placed his soft hand on the head of Candy's erect penis; Tom then caressed it slowly.

The first stroke had sent an intense jolt of pleasure through Candy's penis, a sensation that she'd never experienced. Yet, the feeling had disturbed Candy mentally, being psychologically fixed on the idea that she'd really been a woman.

From what Tom had done to Candy, and for how long she allowed it to happen, not only had it been ill-mannered, it had also been a painful act mentally; one that had caused Candy to have a mental breakdown.

At that very moment, tears had rushed from Candy's eyes like a river, as Tom had proceeded with his hand job; he'd given her a second stroke. Forcefully, Candy had broken away free from Tom and the unwanted pleasure. Instantly, Candy had despised him for making her discover this newfound, trembling feeling— that had raced swiftly through Candy's large penis.

"GET THE *FUCK* OFF OF ME, YOU MOTHERFUCKER! WHAT THE *HELL* DO YOU THINK YOU'RE DOING?" Candy shouted angrily as she'd balled up her fists. Candy had clenched her fists so tight, that her nails had cut through the flesh of her petite palms.

Tom had gone into a complete shock, as he'd thought for the first few seconds, that Candy actually had enjoyed him stroking her penis with his hand. Whenever Tom had performed the "reach around" on Ke-Ke, he'd immensely enjoyed Tom's hand jobs. Ke-Ke had loved the stroking to the point of uncontrollably squirting his sticky semen onto Tom's bony, pale hands.

"C'mon, Candy, what's the big deal? So what if we both like the same thing? I love cock and I always will. Candy, I'm not your typical, hardcore trade, who walks around in prison acting overly masculine. I'm a conservative, White gay man who *has* to

216

live in the closet, for personal reasons. Now, I like to get *fucked,* also—just as much as you do. I can't help what I feel, and I'm *not* going to fight it. Candy, I know you won't *fuck* me, but…can I please *suck* your cock?" Tom shamefully begged, as he'd wanted to perform oral sex on Candy.

"*WHAT?* ARE YOU *FUCKING* CRAZY?" Candy had spat, taken aback by Tom's request.

"P-l-e-a-s-e, Candy, let me *suck* on your cock—I promise, you'll like it. This is my *ultimate* sexual fantasy, Candy, to *suck* and get *fucked* by a beautiful transsexual; one who's *exactly* like you. I always wanted to know what's it like to feel the supple, softness of breasts of a transsexual on my back, as I'm getting rammed by *her* big tool up my tight, hairy asshole," Tom had honestly explained, as Candy had stood in shock, still naked. She'd looked at Tom as if he'd been deranged, as Tom then continued to speak.

"I've never experienced anything like this before. All of my sexual experiences have been with soft, effeminate gay men, with the exception of Ke-Ke. But you, Candy, you have nice, big tits, a fat ass, and a gorgeous, angelic face—you look *exactly* like a woman. P-l-e-a-s-e, Candy, just this one time, baby; let me *suck* your cock," Tom pleaded, as he'd hoped that his true confession of him being gay, and Tom's openness about his sexual desires, would give Candy an incentive to fulfill his lustful request.

Candy had actually been the first person Tom had revealed and entrusted his true sexual identity to. Although he'd had sex with Ke-Ke, Tom had never talked to him in depth about being gay, or about his fantasies. Although Tom had longed for the day to honestly tell his fiancée, Lizzy that he'd been gay, Tom hadn't been able to muster up the strength to do so; for Tom had felt that she'd be the only person who would fully understand, and accept him for who he was.

"*MOTHERFUCKER,* YOU'VE DONE LOST YOUR MIND! You…*fucking*…freak-ass…pervert, I don't stick or flip-flop! I'm a *woman* you dumb bastard! Don't you ever, *ever* in your life, disrespect me like this again! I swear, Tom, if you do, I'll try my best to *kill* you! And from now on, you *sorry*-ass *motherfucker,* the sexual agreement that we've made is now finished. I'll pay you in cash, *bitch!*" Candy yelled, as she'd quickly put on her clothing and stormed out of the Law Library.

Tom then held his head down low in complete shame, as he'd eagerly wanted someone to be sensitive to his painful secret; one that Tom had kept hidden all of these years. He'd then walked to a table and retrieved a tablet. Immediately, Tom had composed a letter to Lizzy.

Two months later…

After thinking long and hard about the incident she'd had with Tom, Candy then decided to go have a talk with him, after carefully evaluating Tom's sexual desires. She'd felt that it hadn't been disrespectful for him to voice his feelings and openly come out to her. It just had shocked Candy to hear it, having it being her first experience with a man whom Candy thought was a "top"; one who'd had an interest in having Candy insert *"her"* penis into his mouth.

The two had come to the agreement to never be intimate with each other anymore, yet, they'd remained friends; in which Tom had continued to work diligently on Candy's case.

One evening while at the Law Library, researching notes regarding Candy's case, a guard had come to Tom's desk; telling Tom to get prepared for a legal visit.

"Haystack. Inmate Haystack," the correctional officer had called out, as Tom had been buried deep into Candy's appeal. Tom had quickly looked up at the guard in shock, knowing that he hadn't done anything for any guards to ever approach him.

"Yes, sir, can I help you?" Tom asked professionally, as he'd addressed the correctional officer as if he'd been a client whom sought legal advice. He'd smiled at Tom, before informing him that Tom's services would be on hold for thirty minutes.

"Get your things together, you have a legal visit," the guard had stated.

"A legal visit?" Tom had asked with curiosity, surprised; knowing that he hadn't needed a lawyer for anything.

"Yes, a legal visit," the guard had reiterated, as he then assured Tom that it was a lawyer who'd wanted to speak with him, and not The FBI; agents constantly had tried to get Tom to cooperate against his cohorts.

"Okay, just give me a second," Tom stated, as he'd gathered his papers together and proceeded towards the empty visiting hall. Before Tom had entered, the guard on duty had reminded him that he only had thirty minutes to consult with the lawyer. He'd made sure that Tom understood that he had to get everything done in a short matter of time.

As Tom entered the visiting room, he had the brightest smile upon his face, as Tom had noticed Lizzy sitting behind the desk across from his chair. She'd looked prettier than ever, as Tom then thought back to how much he'd loved her in the past; in addition to how much Tom valued their true friendship.

"Wow! How in the *hell* did you pull this off?" Tom asked, as he'd pulled out a chair to sit in. Lizzy then smiled at the man she'd originally fell in love with, yet, back then, held tight to their sacred friendship. The sight of Tom's piercing blue eyes and curly brown hair had aroused Lizzy, as she too, had reflected back to their past.

"S-h-h-h, Tom, someone might hear you," Lizzy warned lowly, as she'd placed her finger on his lips to keep him quiet. Lizzy had hoped that no one would find out that this hadn't been an ordinary legal visit.

"Don't worry, no one's in here but us two. The guard on duty went out to smoke a cigarette. We only have thirty minutes to talk though," Tom reminded her, as he'd thought back to the day he'd written Lizzy. Tom had asked Lizzy to come visit him, in which Tom indicated that he'd needed desperately to share something with her.

Lizzy had told him that she'd come in the following month, but never told Tom that she'd come passing as his lawyer. During that time, Lizzy had passed the Bar exam, and had become a lawyer at the same firm that Tom use to work for; where she'd previously been a printing contractor.

Wanting to surprise Tom with her new achievement, Lizzy had thought that it would be just as much a celebration to get the opportunity to see him on a legal visit, in order for the two of them to sit down and talk face-to-face.

"Tom, before I explain to you how I got in, tell me, what's so urgent that you needed to speak to me right away about?"

At an instance, Tom's heart had raced at high speed, as he'd held out his hands to Lizzy to hold; Tom had sat across the table from her. This had been Tom's final hour, his moment of truth. Tom finally had been filled with the courage he'd needed, to let his true friend know his deepest and darkest secret.

Lizzy then placed both of her hands into Tom's. When he'd squeezed them tightly, it had been an aphrodisiac to Lizzy.

Flashbacks of their passionate lovemaking when they'd been a couple, had made her wetter than *Niagara Falls,* as Tom's touch had turned Lizzy on.

"Tom, before you start, remember that we *only* have thirty minutes," Lizzy warned, as she'd nervously perused the room while holding Tom's hands.

"Yeah, but I really need to—"

Before Tom had been able to finish his sentence, Lizzy had jumped across the table and kissed Tom passionately. She'd known that this had been a once in a lifetime opportunity, to have sex with Tom before marrying his friend and work colleague, Patrick. Also, with Tom having a sentencing of fifteen years, Lizzy had convinced herself that it would be best to give him a piece of her good pussy; she'd wanted to leave Tom with everlasting memories of how great it had felt.

Lizzy had unbuttoned her blouse and immediately stuffed Tom's mouth with her small, but perfectly round breast. He couldn't resist the urge, as Tom's blood had swelled to the head of his penis, which made Tom hard as a rock. Tom then disregarded the *real* reason why he'd wanted Lizzy to visit him.

"Oh, yes, Tom, I've longed for this moment," Lizzy squealed, as she'd whimpered in ecstasy. As Tom had sucked and licked on Lizzy's breasts, he'd then reached down and pulled up her skirt, at that point, pleased that Lizzy still hadn't worn any panties.

During that time, she'd stopped wearing panties, because Lizzy had loved having sex in the office. Since she'd owned her company, Patrick had come by everyday on his lunch hour, and had given Lizzy her daily dose of passion.

Yet it had been Tom's time to have his delicious treat, as Tom had plunged his face into her moist slit; Tom had hungrily licked and sucked on Lizzy's pussy the way she'd always loved him to. Lizzy then pulled down Tom's pants and had straddled his thick penis; Lizzy had gyrated forcefully in between Tom's lap.

The wetness from her tight vagina had flowed so much, that it had become a lubricant for the two. Lizzy had taken full advantage of dominating their sexual romp—she'd then placed Tom's dick slowly into her anus, as Lizzy had bounced ferociously up-and-down on it. She'd then taken Tom's meat out, and had slid it back into her pussy, grinding back-and-forth, as

Lizzy then kissed Tom passionately; both Lizzy and Tom had known that this would definitely be their last time to have sex.

Tom couldn't hold back any longer. The excitement itself had made him explode so much sperm into Lizzy's love canal, that she'd actually felt the warm, thick semen squirt inside of her.

Soon after, the sound of keys jingling had made the two stop in the act. Tom and Lizzy had frantically gotten dressed, as they'd then appeared as if nothing had happened, when the guard had informed them that their visit was over.

With his face being ridden with hurt and disappointment, Tom had looked sadly at Lizzy. Tom had wanted badly to tell her his secret regarding his true sexual identity—the lusty desires Tom had longed for.

"I guess we'll talk another time?" Lizzy stated as she'd smiled. Lizzy then gathered her things before leaving.

There may not ever be another time, Tom had thought. "Yes, dear, at another time," he'd answered, as Tom headed out the door in the opposite direction. As he'd walked down to his unit, tears had streamed down the side of Tom's cheeks, as he once again, had been forced to live a lie.

Meanwhile, as Tom had been out on his visit having the time of his life with Lizzy, Candy had been at mail call, waiting for a response letter from Ray.

Candy had written him a lengthy letter, as she'd sought answers. Candy had needed to know why Ray had tricked her into believing that he'd loved her, especially when knowing that Candy could've risked her freedom by smuggling in the package of heroin and cocaine for him. She'd also needed to know the truth about Ray's relationship with Jose, and why Ray had staged the rape scenario with Ty and Unibomber.

Candy had asked everything in the letter that she'd been afraid to ask Ray in person.

"Sweets!" the guard yelled out during mail call, as he'd held an envelope in his hand for Candy.

"Right here, C.O.," Candy replied, as she'd nervously jumped at the sound of her name. Candy then flashed her brilliant smile as the envelope had been passed down to her. But when Candy had received it, and read the return address printed above, instantly, Candy's heart had skipped a beat.

When she'd seen the name "Lisa A. Sweets" in the upper, left-hand corner, Candy then hurried back to her room to open up the letter from her long lost cousin, whom Candy had thought about everyday.

The anticipation of the contents within the letter had been so overwhelming, that Candy had closed her door, put up the privacy sign and cried—before she'd had a chance to open it. Candy had taken a deep breath before she'd torn into the envelope:

Dear Candy,

Hello cousin. Before I begin, I first want to say that Jesus loves you. He is your Lord and Savior, and I encourage you to go seek Him faithfully.

Now, I know you're wondering how I've found you. I saw Tammy at your mother's funeral. Yes, I'm sorry to inform you that she died of tuberculosis two weeks ago. When I found out, I immediately flew up from Atlanta to console my mother, your aunt, Joyce, as you know that she was your mother's only sister.

During the funeral arrangements, everyone in the family was trying to find your whereabouts. I even had a "missing person" report filed out on you at the precinct for a while, until I found out from Tammy that you'd no longer gone by "Andy", and that you've changed your name. Anyway, to make a long story short, Tammy finally confessed about the awful thing that she and Shanna had done to you.

Candy, always put your trust in the Lord. Things happen for a reason. Now that I've found you, I want our relationship to be like how it once was, as when we were kids. As you already know, I accept you for who you are, and so does Jesus. Candy, if you're not attending church, please do so now. Go and seek Him. My phone number is printed above; call me anytime. I'll be waiting. Love you forever.

Your cousin and true friend,
Lisa

Candy dropped the letter, and had buried her face into her hands, as Candy had uncontrollably cried at the painful news that had been delivered to her. Not only had Candy become extremely hurt by her mother's death, but had always been troubled by her aunt, Joyce for never taking her up to visit her mother in prison; due to "Andy" being extremely effeminate as a young boy in the past. Candy never had a chance to build a true relationship with her mother. Her aunt, Joyce had intentionally deprived both of them of that.

Candy then quickly wiped her tears and re-read the letter again. She'd noticed that Lisa had emphasized on Jesus being her Lord and Savior, and that Candy had to seek Him.

After many times of reading the letter repeatedly, analyzing everything she'd gone through in life, Candy's hardened heart had no longer been cold. She'd immediately had become a more sensitive and compassionate person. In all reality, Candy had known that she'd only put up her defenses to ward off others wrongdoings, and that Candy couldn't endure being as evil as her enemies had been to her.

Pondering on all of her life regrets, Candy had eagerly wanted to repent and be saved. She'd definitely wanted Jesus to "wash" Abdul's blood completely from her hands, and Terry's tragic death from her conscience.

Voluntarily dropping to her knees, Candy had surrendered herself, and immediately had begun praying to her Savior.

Three weeks later…

"HALLELUJAH, in Jesus' name—amen!" the jailhouse preacher recited, as he'd proudly stood behind the podium emulating *Reverend Jesse Jackson.* The preacher had tried his hardest to deliver the sermon as the Civil Rights leader had done so in the past.

Candy had closed her eyes and waved her hands in the air. Candy then thought she'd caught the Holy Ghost, as the reverent preacher had continued. For the past three weeks, Candy had seriously taken her cousin, Lisa's advice and had joined the church, being empowered by the inspirational conversations Candy had with her during that time.

Candy had begun to enjoy the insightful sermons, as well as the harmonious choir that had sung, but what she'd *really* loved the most: the one-on-one conversations Candy had with Dewayne, the church's custodian. He'd given Candy guidance by providing her with spiritual advisement.

After Candy had heard Dewayne's story about how he and Tom had been arrested, and how his young daughter had been sickened with the chronic disease, leukemia, Candy had become sympathetic to Dewayne's crisis and pain; while being overwhelmed with her own as well. Often times, Candy and Dewayne had come to each other for strength and encouragement, as they'd met regularly; more during this time than the two had before.

Cheryl, Dewayne's twelve-year-old daughter, had been battling myeloid leukemia over the past year. She'd first been diagnosed with the disease after having gone to the doctor for severe leg pains—Dewayne then discovered that his daughter's blood cell count had been twenty times higher than a person's normal rate.

After the startling revelation, Cheryl had been quickly placed on the bone marrow donor's list, as Dwayne and his wife had desperately sought out a match for a transplant. Due to Dewayne's incarceration, getting approval from the warden to see if he'd been a match for his daughter had been a long, drawn out process altogether, in which red tape had delayed Dewayne from getting tested in the prison's infirmary.

Being that he'd been a wealthy, fast-food mogul, money hadn't any value towards Dewayne saving his daughter's precious life; in which he would've paid any price to fully rid her of the illness.

Minorities alone have a one out of a twenty-thousandth chance of finding a match outside of their families. Due to lack of knowledge, there aren't enough people in the world, especially those dwelling in urban areas, who knows and understands the importance of donating bone marrow; leaving opportunity of them developing leukemia and other cancerous diseases.

Cheryl had faced an uphill battle, due to being African-American. Out of the 5.5 million potential donors in the *Bone Marrow Registry,* there had been only 420,000 African-Americans listed, which had made the search in finding a match for Dewayne's daughter even more critical.

This had been one of the main reasons why the rapper, *Nelly* had started the *4Sho 4Kids Foundation*, not only for his sister who'd succumbed to the deadly disease, not being able to find a donor in time, but for the rest of the African-American communities. *Nelly* had established awareness by showing Black people the importance of getting signed to the *Bone Marrow Registry* through their doctors.

After church service had ended, everyone then departed the chapel and had gone to their units. Candy had stayed around with Dewayne, and helped him clean up and organize the chapel.

"Thank you, Miss Candy. I really appreciate the help," Dewayne said, as he'd put the church's Bibles inside the Christians' locker cabinet.

"You're welcome, Dewayne. You know, I wanted to stick around and talk to you anyway. There are some things I need to ask you concerning the Word," Candy had stated, referring to the Bible. After they'd tidied up, Dewayne and Candy had sat in chairs opposite each other, like they'd normally done everyday after service. The two had begun to talk.

"What is it that you wish to discuss, Candy?"

"Dewayne, I wanted to talk to you regarding something that's been on my mind. Since I'm now saved, my cousin, Lisa informed me that I must forgive my cousins, Tammy and Shanna;

226

for all of the wrongdoings they've done to me," Candy had replied, as the pain of remembering what had happened in the past, made Candy bow her head in shame.

Dewayne then lifted Candy's head, as he'd raised her chin with his hand. Their eyes then met, as Dewayne had begun to console Candy's pain.

"Candy, Jesus, our Lord and Savior was persecuted and crucified for *our* sins. If He could give His life for us, then it should be an honor for you to forgive them; in His name."

"Yes, Dewayne, that's easy for you to say, but look at what they've done to me. They've ridiculed me for who I am; I've *hated* them for that," Candy replied, as her eyes had begun to water.

"Candy, you're a Christian now, and loving Christians don't hate. We learn to love unconditionally, and to forgive. We learn to turn the other cheek and to pray for our enemies. Don't worry about if someone accepts you or not. Jesus loves you, and *always* accepts you however you are," Dewayne stated, as he'd convinced Candy to change her way of thinking.

"Thank you, Dewayne. You always have such a positive influence on me," Candy replied, as she'd lightly put her hand onto his knee. Candy had innocently done this in the past, in which Dewayne never opposed to the body contact.

In fact, Dewayne had acted as if it hadn't fazed him, but deep down inside, Dewayne struggled hard to fight the "Devil's" temptation; he'd become excited by Candy's subtle touch. Dewayne then held out both of his hands, and had nodded his head for Candy to join him in prayer.

"Let us pray," Dewayne had suggested, as Candy then placed her soft hands onto his. Her gentle touch had driven Dewayne wild, as Dewayne then thought of the last time he'd ever touched a woman.

The mere fact that Dewayne had been in prison, and was a possible match as a donor for their daughter, had made his wife disown him; upset that Dewayne had allowed himself to be in such a situation. His wife had believed that if Dewayne hadn't been in prison, then he could've done more in saving their daughter.

At that time, Dewayne had become approved to finally have his blood checked in the infirmary, wanting to confirm if he'd qualified in being a donor for his daughter. Yet, Dewayne hadn't wanted the results until it had been time for him to be released; which would've been in the following month.

Dewayne's sentence hadn't been as long as Tom's. When they'd first got arrested, Dewayne had known that he and Tom were guilty—immediately, Dewayne had taken the first plea that the government had offered; opting for three years. Opposed to the fifteen Tom had received.

Dewayne had figured that if he hadn't been a match, then there wasn't any chance of ever having a loving relationship with his wife again. But, if Dewayne was a match for his daughter's transplant, not only would he have been able to save his daughter, but also his marriage.

As Dewayne had held Candy's soft hands in his large palms, Dewayne had closed his eyes and begun his prayer. But, before Dewayne had uttered a word, the sensation from Candy's touch had made him think of his wife, along with the sweet scent of the *Bulgari* perfume Candy had worn; which she'd received from her boss, Ms. Chase in the infirmary. Dewayne had become confused of the *real* reason why they'd joined hands.

Candy had sensed great sexual tension between them. The feelings that had surfaced had been like high voltages of electricity—which flowed free and fast through Candy and Dewayne's bodies. Although Candy had known that her emotions had been strong for Dewayne, and that the chapel was a place considered to be sanctified, Candy still couldn't help being overwhelmed by the desire of the gentlemen's touch—more than ever, Candy had longed for Dewayne to make a move.

Normally, Candy had given a trade the first opportunity to approach her, but in this case, she couldn't control her lust; Candy hadn't cared if Dewayne had opposed or not. Candy then closed her eyes and leaned over; she'd placed a soft kiss on Dewayne's full lips.

Noticing that Dewayne hadn't put up a resistance to what Candy had done, had made her even more excited. Candy had kissed him passionately; softly, she'd then placed her hands upon Dewayne's handsome face. The two had begun to open their mouths wider, and had proceeded in tongue kissing; Dewayne and Candy had been totally enraptured in the heated moment.

Not once had Dewayne opened his eyes as he'd kissed Candy; Dewayne had thought long and hard about his wife. After the long, sensual kiss, Candy then boldly placed her tiny hand around the hardness between Dewayne's legs, as she'd gently caressed his thick bulge. Dewayne hadn't resisted the urgency.

"C'mon, Candy, let's go inside the custodian's closet," Dewayne eagerly suggested, as he'd guided Candy by the hand inside of the closet. Once inside, an instant rush of guilt had come over Dewayne, when he'd noticed the stack of Bibles resting in the glass cabinet. Dewayne then quickly closed the cabinet and had immediately tugged at Candy's clothes, acting as if this would be their last opportunity to share intimacy with each other.

"Hold up, Dewayne. We can't have sex, we don't have any protection," Candy interjected, as she'd alerted Dewayne in knowing that she'd practiced safe sex. Dewayne had totally understood and respected her gesture, as he'd also been cautious in practicing safe sex. Dewayne instantly had become impressed with Candy, he seeing that she'd possessed great qualities.

"Alright, Candy, I respect that. So what are we going to do then?" Dewayne had asked; he'd become slightly disappointed.

"Well, I guess I can accommodate you with a little treat for now," Candy answered as she'd unfastened Dewayne's khaki pants. Candy then had dropped down slowly to her knees, and begun performing the best oral sex on Dewayne that he'd ever experienced.

As Candy slowly bobbed up-and-down on Dewayne's ten-inch penis, giving him great pleasure, she'd desperately tried to ignore the minor soreness of the small gash in her bottom gums. The cut had never healed properly from the fight Candy had had with Jose. Between the crunchy corn chips Candy had munched on, and from the way she'd forcefully brushed her teeth, the wound kept re-opening.

"*Oh,* Candy, your mouth is *so* wet and hot…it feels *so,* so good, baby," Dewayne groaned lowly, as he'd closed his eyes and had thought about how great his wife's oral pleasure was, when they'd been together.

As the pleasure had become more intense, and Dewayne couldn't hold back his climax anymore, he'd hysterically grabbed Candy by the back of her head, and had made Candy engulf most of his huge, throbbing penis; as Dewayne had uncontrollably exploded years of built-up semen into her mouth.

Candy then swallowed the warm globs of semen that Dewayne had quickly shot inside of her mouth, as she'd rolled the thick, milky fluid around her gums—before Candy had allowed every drop to fall slowly down her throat.

A month had passed by, and Dewayne and Candy's relationship had formed rapidly. It had come to the point that Candy had attended every church service: Mass, Bible study, Sunday school, and any other function the church had given. Not that she'd gone to get closer to Jesus—Candy had anticipated having more sexual excursions she'd continuously had with Dewayne.

Becoming less interested in church as a whole, Candy's hidden agenda of forming a relationship with Dewayne, and her lustful temptations had overwhelmed Candy to attend the church—only to be sexually intimate with Dewayne. She'd used the chapel as an outlet to be around him as much as possible.

Candy, once again, had foolishly fallen in love. This action had become a constant pattern in her life, as Candy had tried after being with Ray, not to give her heart to anyone else; especially to those within the prison facility.

One Sunday, after church service had ended, Candy and Dewayne had gone at it again. After they'd cleaned up and checked the area, making sure that no one had been around, the two had sneaked into the custodian closet, and had begun having sex.

As Dewayne sat down in the chair with his pants pulled down low at his ankles, Candy had placed the latex glove over his swollen, aching dick, and used it as a homemade condom before she'd bent over. Dewayne, at that time, had the pleasure of moistening Candy's anus with his curious tongue. After Dewayne had happily performed oral sex on her, and spat a bubble of saliva in between her butt cheeks, Candy had taken her middle finger and inserted it into her anus; she'd begun to slowly gyrate.

Needing more lubrication, Candy then applied *Vaseline* around and into her anus, before she'd sat in Dewayne's lap. Candy then allowed his ten-inch penis to slowly slide easily, and deeply into her love tunnel. She'd then moved up-and-down, as Candy had straddled herself onto Dewayne's dick. First, she'd worked in a slow rhythm, feeling his thick, massiveness swell inside of her, before Candy had rode fervently.

As the two had become excited their pace increased, as Candy and Dewayne both moved faster in sync. Pure passionate pleasurable penetration had led Candy to take total control, as she'd bounced up-and-down even harder on Dewayne's erect penis, as he'd eagerly watched Candy flop upon him like a cowgirl who'd rode her frenzied bucking stallion.

Intensity then forced Dewayne to grab her hips with his large, strong hands, as he'd forcefully pulled Candy's ass down onto his stiff dick as hard as he could. Soon after, Dewayne had exploded his large load of his cum inside of Candy's rectum unintentionally.

Having a blissful moment, Dewayne had been deep in thought, thinking that this time around, how the sex had been the best he'd ever had with Candy. The friction had felt so much more stimulating than any other time he'd plowed inside of Candy's tunnel. Dewayne hadn't ever ejaculated so hard before in his life, in which he'd shaken involuntarily for a brief moment, being overwhelmed by the sexual encounter they'd had.

As Dewayne then pondered briefly as to why he and Candy's lovemaking had been so powerful and satisfying, as Dewayne had lightly gyrated inside of Candy, she'd immediately had figured out what the difference had been.

When Candy had felt the wetness of his warm, thick semen shoot inside of her rectum, she'd immediately become nervous, scared that the homemade condom that they'd made from the latex glove had burst; due to the pressure Dewayne applied, as he'd forcefully fucked Candy.

Candy then quickly jumped off of Dewayne's pulsating penis as if she'd sat in a lap full of ignited firecrackers.

"SHIT! FUCK!" Candy had yelled in disgruntlement.

"What? What's wrong?" Dewayne instantly had reacted, confused, unaware of what had happened; still in wonderment of his release inside of Candy.

Dewayne had become so caught up in the pleasure of sex, that he hadn't noticed the ripped, semen-filled glove that had popped off of his meat, which at that point, had haphazardly hung over Dewayne's scrotum sack—glove having droplets of blood on it.

The pressure from Dewayne's vigorous thrusts, as he'd excitedly rammed his swollen dick deep into Candy, as she'd straddled him, had caused Candy's rectum tissues to tear.

"LOOK! THAT'S WHAT'S WRONG!" Candy had shouted at the top of her lungs at Dewayne again, as she'd pointed at the hanging glove. As soon as Dewayne had looked down at the bloodied rubber glove that rested at the base of his semi-erect penis Dewayne had immediately gone limp afterwards, as his mind had gone into a state-of-shock; Dewayne then had regrets.

"Damn," had been the only thing that Dewayne mouthed, as he'd simultaneously gasped like a dying person who'd been on his last breath, when Dewayne had responded. He'd then pitifully looked Candy in her eyes; Dewayne desperately had searched for an answer of surety.

"Don't worry, I don't have anything—do you?" Candy had asked lowly and inquisitively, as she'd quickly wiped her anus with her bare hand; before Candy had scurried to get dressed. Candy then prepared herself to rush back to her unit to shower, and take a homemade enema. *I hope Dewayne wasn't a true trade before he met me!*

"Nah, Candy, I'm straight. I just took a blood test to see if I was a match for my daughter's bone marrow operation that she's about to have. They checked for everything—I'm clean," Dewayne had indicated, making sure Candy had understood that he'd received his results; which had shown Dewayne having a clean bill of health. Dewayne had also reassured Candy that, this had only been his first sexual experience with a person whom was other than a woman.

"Well, I got checked when I first got locked up. I'm not infected with HIV or AIDS. I had a few encounters since I've been here, but I *always* practice safe sex—always!" Candy retorted, as she'd brought to Dewayne's attention that this had never happened to her in the past.

"Whew!" Dewayne responded, as he'd exhaled while wiping the tiny sweat beads from his forehead. Dewayne had felt better—Candy had relieved him with her last comment.

Candy, fully regrouped, said good-bye to Dewayne before she'd raced out of the chapel. Candy then headed to her housing unit just in time, as she'd been on the end of the ten-minute move; hearing the announcement over the loudspeaker.

YOU REMIND ME
chapter 48

"Damn! What the *fuck* you tryna do, kill us?" yelled the young, rowdy thug who resembled Trigger, after the marshal hit a sharp turn while coming around the *Appalachian Mountains*—as he drove towards the prison. Everyone slid to one side of the transit van, falling on top of each other.

"Go ahead and crash so we can get a huge law suit," yelled the clean-cut guy who looked like Tom.

"Can't wait 'til we get these *motherfuckin'* cuffs off; my *fuckin'* wrists are swollen," said the other handsome inmate who favored Ray.

"Lord, have mercy on us. Please get us to our destination safely—amen," the inmate who resembled Dewayne whispered behind her.

Candy was hallucinating, thinking that each guy in the van looked like her ex-lovers. As she watched them closely, Candy realized that they each had something to say, except for the quiet inmate who sat next to her, observing everyone's character as the van sped off.

Candy literally had to turn her head away from him, as the inmate reminded her of Abdul. Every time Candy looked at him, she felt a discomforting cramp in her stomach and a sharp pain in her heart.

"Cachew, cachew—c-o-u-u-u-g-h!" Candy sneezed twice, followed by a dry, heavy hacking cough. Everyone looked at Candy with disgust, being turned off by the nasty coughing sound that she made. It sounded like a dog's bark, which didn't match the image of the beautiful transsexual.

"God bless you," said the quiet, attractive inmate who resembled Abdul.

"Thank you," Candy replied, as she looked straight ahead, not wanting to look the inmate in his face. The similarity of Abdul was so close, that it pained her terribly to acknowledge him up close.

At that moment, Candy realized that she was delusional, thinking that the van was full of the men she'd been intimately involved with, throughout her eighteen months in prison.

"Mail call!" the guard had yelled, as all of the inmates gathered around, and had waited for their names to be called. Most of the time, Candy only had listened out for her name when she'd expected mail. Candy hadn't thought that she'd been receiving mail on that day, because the only person who'd written Candy had been her cousin, Lisa; who'd come to visit Candy that past weekend. Lisa had also brought her two daughters, Tonya and Latoya along to meet Candy.

"Sweets!" the correctional officer yelled, as he'd held up a white envelope in the air. Candy then proceeded to walk towards her cell when she'd thought she heard the guard call out her last name. Candy then stopped in her tracks, and had walked back to the area where the prisoners had gathered to get their mail.

C.O., whose name did you just call?" Candy had asked politely; she'd wanted to make sure that he hadn't made a mistake.

"Yours! Now do you want it or should I throw it back in the bag?" the guard had replied back sarcastically; he'd been cranky, annoyed, and had acted negatively towards Candy.

"Yes-I-want-my-mail! It has my name on it, right?" Candy answered back in a sassy, condescending manner, as she'd then placed her hands on her hips. After Candy received her mail, she'd walked off hastily to her tier and whispered to herself: "Damn, he always *acts* like he doesn't get any pussy at home. *Motherfucking* ass always coming to work with an attitude."

Overhearing Candy's smart remark, the guard had immediately become upset. He'd wanted to reprimand Candy for her sly comment, but hadn't enough on her to make out a write-up. Instead, the guard had plotted to have the other inmates turn on her, by shutting down the mail call. He'd figured that if he'd blamed Candy for the shut down, in return, someone would attack her.

"That's it! No more mail call! You'll get the rest of your mail when my shift ends," the irate correctional officer replied, as he'd angrily stuffed the letters back into the large mail bag.

"Awe, man, how you just gonna stop callin' the mail like that?" Riddick Bowe had asked.

"Bowe, ask Tinkerbell over there with the smart mouth!" the guard answered as he'd pointed at Candy, insinuating that she'd been the reason why he'd stopped delivery the mail. The guard had hoped that the convicts would gang up on Candy instantly.

"Oh, so now you gonna blame it on the punk? So, I guess you want a *nigga* to go beat his ass? Then you put us all in the hole, right? What, you think we all *stupid* in here? Man, we know all the tricks y'all C.O.'s play. C'mon, you coulda came wit' some better *shit* than that," Corleone had stated.

"Yeah, well, *like* I said, get it when the other C.O. comes in, 'cause I ain't passin' out *nothin'* on my shift but incident reports!" the guard shot back, as he'd hinted that he'd soon shake down every room; in hopes of finding contraband.

"MAN, *FUCK* YOU! DO YOUR JOB, *BITCH!*" C-Low and Jamil then shouted from the top tier, as they'd hid out-of-sight.

"Alright, that's it! Lockdown!" the correctional officer yelled, as he'd alerted the convicts that they'd be locked in their cells for the rest of the shift; due to them being unruly.

"*FUCK* YOU, YOU WHITE CRACKER-*BITCH!*"

"I HOPE YOUR MOTHER DIES, *MOTHERFUCKER!*"

"YOUR WIFE'S A *SLUT!*"

"*DICK*-SUCKIN' *FAGGOT!*"

"I HOPE YOU CRASH AND FALL OFF THE BRIDGE COMIN' HOME FROM WORK, *COCKSUCKER!*"

The inmates had shouted obscenities at the guard for locking them up. They'd expressed their true feelings that they had towards him, and other correctional officers who'd treated the prisoners like animals.

"Yeah, yeah, yeah, whatever! The slave master is locking you *all* up in your cells for the rest of the shift," the guard then replied in a low tone, as he had a sneaky expression upon his face; knowing that he'd won the battle between him and the convicts.

Meanwhile, Candy had sat on her bed, as she still held the letter in her hand. From where the address had been sent from, Candy had known that it had been a response to her 60(b) Motion that Tom had filed for her six months ago.

Before Candy had opened the letter, she'd got down on her knees, and had said the various prayers from the Bible that Lisa had often told her to recite. Candy had asked her Lord and Savior, Jesus Christ for forgiveness, especially for every evil thing she'd done in life. Soon after, Candy had sworn to the Lord about her future intentions.

"Dear Jesus, if you help me get through this, I promise, everything I do in life from now on, will all be in good faith. Please, Lord, be with me."

Candy had taken a deep breath before she'd opened the letter. Candy then almost fainted when she'd read the contents. Immediately, Candy had become overwhelmed—the judge had granted an evidentiary hearing on the merits of her motion.

This hadn't been the actual victory, but it had been a very good sign that lead up to one. Most cases had been denied and thrown out without any hearing at all. When a judge had considered the merits in a case, and scheduled an evidentiary hearing, most likely an inmate had a good chance at arguing their case; giving them an opportunity in winning.

"Thank you, Jesus," Candy had said, before she'd fallen onto her knees to pray….

* * * * *

The next morning…

As soon as the correctional officer had opened up the cells, and taken the inmates off of lockdown, Candy had rushed down to the phone to call her cousin, Lisa, and had informed her of the great news.

"Hello," the sweet, little voice had answered on the other end of the phone.

"Hi. Is this Tonya or Latoya?" Candy asked, as she'd still had a hard time distinguishing the voices of Lisa's two younger daughters; who'd been Candy's cousins, and at that time, her new godchildren.

"This is Latoya—is this god-mommy?" Latoya had asked, as her younger cousin immediately thought back to the fun she'd had while visiting Candy.

Candy then smiled, as light tears trickled down her cheeks. At that moment, Candy had fully realized for the first time, that Lisa had accepted her as a full-fledged woman. So

238

much, that Lisa had her own daughters refer to Candy as their godmother.

"Yes, yes it's me, Candy. Is your mommy home?"

"Yes, hold on," Latoya answered, as she'd passed the phone over to her mother.

"Hey Candy, did you get that new *Out* magazine I sent you?" Lisa asked when she'd retrieved the receiver.

"Yes, Lisa, I have it. But yesterday, I've received something even better."

"What's that?"

"Lisa, I got back in court! The judge is going to hear my case next week!" Candy had yelled excitedly.

"Lord, Jesus, thank you," Lisa had replied. She'd then closed her eyes and had sincerely thanked the Lord silently for the blessing. "Give me the date, time and place, Candy. Know that the kids and I, your family, will be there to support you," Lisa stated, as she'd reassured Candy into knowing that she still supported her; just as Lisa had when she and Candy were younger.

Candy had given all of the proper information to Lisa before she'd headed to the Law Library. Candy had wanted to thank Tom for his assistance in helping her get the appeal in motion. Candy also had wanted to remind Tom that no matter what, their friendship would always remain true.

As Candy entered into the Law Library, she'd noticed that Tom and Ke-Ke had been talking harshly to each other, as they'd looked like a romantic couple who'd had a domestic dispute. When Ke-Ke had seen Candy, Ke-Ke had rudely sucked his teeth before diverting his attention back to Tom.

"I *see* you have some sort of *legal* business to attend to— *I'll* be back later!" Ke-Ke replied sharply, as he'd quickly walked away from Tom; and had lightly brushed pass Candy. Ke-Ke had hoped that Candy would've reacted to the shove. Candy, realizing that Ke-Ke had tried to provoke her, wanting to start a fight, smiled back at him; Candy hadn't let the brawny transvestite spoil her joy.

As Tom then frantically sprayed his air freshener again, Candy had come to the conclusion that he and Ke-Ke had had sex in the back, and probably been doing so all along. Going by the foul odor that had lingered from the back area, Candy had also thought that one of them also needed an enema before they'd engaged in sex.

Yet, Candy had been so excited about her great news, that she'd disregarded the thought about Tom and Ke-Ke immediately.

"Candy, can I *help* you with something?" Tom had asked curtly in a nonchalant manner, as he'd indirectly let Candy know that he hadn't wanted to be bothered.

"Tom, I have some *great* news!" Candy had replied thrillingly.

"Oh, really? Well, hopefully it's better than the news I heard about you yesterday," Tom had retorted sarcastically.

"What are you talking about, Tom?"

"I heard what happened down in your unit yesterday. They said the whole unit was on lockdown because your charmingly-prissy butt had gotten smart with that stupid guard. You better stop that *shit,* Candy. One day, somebody may get mad and try to kick your little sassy *ass.*"

"Puh-lease," Candy retorted, as she'd thrown her hands up in the air. "I wish a *motherfucker* in here *would* try putting his hands on me. You *must've* forgotten what happened to the last victim that tried to step to me. I almost popped his eyes out of his head!" Candy snapped, as she'd referred to her scuffle with Jose.

"Well, whatever. There's no need to go on bragging about harming someone," Tom had snapped, being more annoyed with Candy. "Now, what is it that you had to tell me?"

"Well, for your information, Mr. Smarty Pants, I wasn't bragging. Anyway, the judge granted me an evidentiary hearing next week!" Candy had exclaimed, as she'd jumped up-and-down.

Tom then leaned back in his chair arrogantly.

"Let me see that," Tom then responded, as he'd snatched the court order out of her hand. After reading it, Tom had scribbled a name and phone number down on a piece of paper.

"Here, Candy, take this. Now, after you leave here, go down to your counselor's office and show them the order. Most likely, they'll have a copy of one, also. Tell them you need a legal call, and dial up this number. It's the number of my personal friend, Patrick. He'll argue the motion for you. Not to worry, Patrick's a great lawyer, and he already knows about you and what to do."

"You mean to tell me that you knew what the outcome was going to be?" Candy had asked in amazement.

"Candy, please listen to me when I tell you this, and believe that it's true. The *only* case I can't win, is my own...You know why, Candy?"

"No, Tom, why?"

"Because, I'm *not* innocent!" Tom answered back angrily, as he'd stormed out immediately and slammed the door behind him. Tom had been frustrated by the fact that, every case that he'd worked on, other than his own, had enough merit to win in court. There hadn't been a chance of Tom ever beating his case—there had been too much evidence showing that Tom had played an intricate part in the *"Pay-2-Play"* embezzlement scam.

"Damn," Candy had replied softly, as she too, felt bad for Tom, knowing that he'd been hurting. Yet, thoughts of Dewayne changed her mood immediately, as she'd dashed off to the chapel to give him the great news.

"Dewayne! Dewayne!" Candy yelled, as she'd tried to flag down Dewayne; who'd been in a great mood, also. Candy had known that Dewayne was going home in a few days, but it had been something about his smile that made her wonder if Dewayne had already known about Candy's court order.

"Guess what, Dewayne!" Candy cheered, as she'd gasped for air in between her words; Candy had run from the chapel to tell Dewayne her latest update. She'd then tried to catch her breath.

"First, calm down and take a deep breath," Dewayne had suggested, as he'd shown concern for her well-being.

"I'm okay—look at this!" Candy instructed, as she'd excitedly shoved the court order in Dewayne's face. He'd smiled, as Dewayne had told her that he'd been thrilled to hear about Candy's news. Dewayne then sat her down to have a serious talk.

"Candy, you know I'm a man of my word, and that I do *exactly* what I say I'm going to do. Now, I get released in a few days, but I want us to stay in contact with each other. Here's my new cell number, my assistant at my office ordered one for me the other day. I want you to call me the day after I leave here," Dewayne instructed, as he'd handed Candy his cell number on a piece of paper.

"Okay, I'll call to see if you made it back safely."

"Thanks, I'll appreciate that. Candy, I need to talk to you about a serious matter," Dewayne stated, as he'd stared into Candy's eyes.

"Dewayne, is something wrong?" Candy had asked inquisitively. She'd become concerned that Dewayne might've had an important matter on his hands.

"Nah, everything is fine. Actually I wanted to talk about you?"

"Me?"

"Yes, Candy. Baby, I want you to be *totally* happy with yourself. I know you said you weren't fully satisfied with your body, therefore, I'm going to pay for the operation that you need."

"Dewayne, I—"

"And before you try to tell me that you *can't* take my money because you're not able to pay me back, just know that I'm not offering you the twenty-five thousand dollars as a loan—I'm giving you the money as a gift," Dewayne had said calmly and firmly.

Tears immediately had welled up in Candy's eyes.

"You just don't know how happy you've made me feel. Thank you, Dewayne. Thank you very much," Candy replied, as she'd clung on to Dewayne instantly while hugging him. Candy then sobbed on Dewayne's shoulders, as she'd squeezed him even tighter.

"You're welcome, Candy. Now, I'll call your doctor to make the payment arrangement. All you have to do is set up the appointment right before your release date," Dewayne had explained.

"I'll *definitely* do so," Candy answered, as she'd neatly folded the number and tucked it into her homemade bra; Candy then had patted her bra for safe keeping.

"Okay, Candy. Now that we've got that settled and you've shared your news, now's my turn," Dewayne stated as he'd smiled uncontrollably.

"Well, I hope you're not going to just stand there and smile all day—what is it?" Candy joked, as she'd asked anxiously.

"Today, I was called up to medical. They told me I was a *complete* match for my daughter's bone marrow transplant!" Dewayne excitedly indicated, as tears of joy had rushed down his handsome face.

"Oh, I am *so* happy for you, Dewayne. Jesus is *so* good, isn't he?" Candy replied, as she'd known that none of these blessings would've come, if it hadn't been for Candy repenting, and accepting Jesus Christ in her life as her Lord and Savior.

The two then looked into each other's eyes, before Candy and Dewayne had embraced, one last time....

While sitting in the holding cell, waiting for her hearing, Candy's new lawyer, Patrick Nelson, came to the back area and gave the U.S. Marshal a cream, Roberto Cavalli business suit; with a pair of matching Manolo Blahnik low-heel shoes, to give to his client.

Candy wanted to be presentable before facing the liberal judge, Alan Kozinski. Everyone was in the courtroom standing in position. As the marshals brought Candy into the courtroom, she looked to her left, cracked a light smile, and winked her eye at her most trusted cousin, Lisa, and at Candy's two cousins and godchildren, Latoya and Tonya.

Candy then looked to her left, noticing the evil prosecutor, Barbara Kalla, who seemed to hate any and every convict who'd broken the law. No matter how much an inmate had been rehabilitated, she still requested to the judge that the convict be given additional time added to their sentencing.

Then Candy's eyes were fixed on her handsome lawyer, Patrick, in his black Brooks Brothers suit, looking sharp, smart and powerful.

"All rise," said the bailiff, as everyone stood up, as the judge arrived at his desk. Candy's heart raced well above her normal rate, as she looked the prosecutor in the eye; trying hard not to show any signs of weakness. Yet, Candy was distraught, crying internally; she begged the Lord to allow the judge to have compassion for her.

JUDGE: "Okay, now defense, are you ready to present this motion to the court properly?"

PATRICK: "Your Honor, I ask that my client's motion be granted on the sole issues therefore that have been raised during this evidentiary hearing. He's serving an illegal sentence, due to erroneous enhancement."

It seemed as though the whole courtroom shifted their eyes in Candy's direction when Patrick referred to Candy as a "he". Inside, Candy was enraged, but she figured Patrick knew what he was doing while in the courtroom.

JUDGE: "Okay, now does the government oppose?"

PROSECUTOR: "We most certainly do, your Honor. I think we've been over this matter before. But to refresh the court's memory, the Winestock case was the landmark case for the styling of Rule 60(b). It instructs the Court how to distinguish a 60(b) from an attempt to characterize a 2255 in 60(b)'s clothing. Matter of fact, I'd be wasting my breath if I sat here and explained, so I'd like to present the landmark case for you to decide.

The prosecutor then handed Judge Kozinski a copy of the case, as she approached the bench. After reading the case, the judge sat back and looked at Candy and Patrick, then pushed his eyeglasses back on his eyes, shaking his head in a disturbed manner, as Judge Kozinski rendered his decision.

JUDGE: "I hereby deny the motion, pursuant to Rule 60(b), because of the fact that this issue should've been brought before the court on the previous 2255 motion. I also agree with the government, that the Rule 60(b) is just another attempt at filing a Habeas Corpus in disguise. For the reasons set forth, motion denied!"

Judge Kozinski slammed his gavel down immediately after making his decision. Out of everything that the judge said, the only thing that rang into Candy's ears was the word "denied". Instantly, Candy expressed her rage, as she attempted to attack her attorney. Candy almost accomplished her mission, but was stopped by the chokehold of the U.S. Marshal. He then handcuffed Candy before escorting her back to the holding cell, to await the transport van ride back to prison.

"Goddammit, it's about time," said the young inmate who resembled Trigger, as the van pulled up in front of the prison. Candy had stopped reminiscing over her tragic, eighteen-month stay here, looking out the window at the prison Candy would continue to be housed in; realizing that she had three-and-a-half more years of torture left.

As the marshals brought in the convicts, Candy came in with her head held down low in shame, while the new prisoners had their eyes wide open, trying to observe everything they could catch in eyesight.

"Couuugh-couuugh—skwauuught!" once again, Candy coughed two dry, heavy coughs, this time, following with bringing up thick, yellow phlegm, as she spat on the ground.

"You alright, Sweets?" asked the correctional officer, who was now unlocking Candy's handcuffs to place her in the holding cell.

"Nah, not really," Candy answered, as she began to feel the dizziness she'd experienced for a week now. In the past, Candy never had any side effects from her hormone pills. She knew the hormones the prison had provided Candy during her treatment was from a generic brand—assuming that this was the reason why she was having dizzy spells, night sweats, hacking coughs and now, feeling weak and fatigued.

"Okay, Sweets. After we finish processing, I'll call the doctor down to see you," the guard said while taking off her ankle cuffs. As soon as he removed Candy's cuffs and chains, the correctional officer turned around to write something down on his clipboard. As he was writing, the guard heard a loud thumping sound, as if someone had dropped a heavy bag.

When he turned around, the correctional officer almost panicked, as he called the medical office for assistance. Candy had fell unconscious flat on her face, as Candy's body was no longer strong enough to fight off the symptoms that she thought she was having during the hormone treatments.

As the medical response team placed Candy on the stretcher, Candy could hear everything around her, but she couldn't talk or move. Everything was surreal to Candy, it was like she was having a bad dream, one that Candy couldn't end or awaken to.

RAY'S HOUSE IN VIRGINIA
chapter 53

Six months later...

"Hello," Kim, Ray's fiancée answered the phone nervously.

"Hey, baby, it's me," Ray replied, sounding just as worried, as Kim heard the heavy commotion that was occurring in the background from her phone receiver. Kim could tell that Ray was calling outside from a phone booth.

"Ray, where the *fuck* are you at, and what the *fuck* you just do? You know, your parole officer came by here *twice* today with the police looking for your *ass!* They say they got a warrant out for your arrest, and that you left the halfway house?"

"Yeah, yeah, Kim—I know. Look, I can't fully explain everything right now—I don't have time," Ray explained while briefly interrupting their conversation to check his surroundings. "...Look, Kim, I need you to do me a favor."

"WHAT?" Kim yelled, as she immediately became irritated at Ray for making the hasty, unintelligent decision to leave the halfway house. "Look, Ray, this *stupid* shit *gots* to stop!" Kim said, as she was about to loose her control; voicing her opinion regarding Ray's tactics.

"KIM!" Ray shouted through the receiver, raising his voice to let her know that he still was the man in charge. Kim loved Ray's aggressive nature. It was one of the main reasons that turned her on about him.

"Yes, daddy?"

"Look, baby, I need you to go down to the halfway house and get my things, before them *niggas* find out I'm on the run and start stealing my *shit!*"

"Okay, baby, I'ma get right on top of that, soon as I get off the phone."

"Thanks, boo-boo," Ray replied, enticing Kim with his charm. "Oh, yo, Kim!" Ray said, trying to get her attention before she hung up the phone.

"Yeah, baby, what's up?"

"When you go get my *shit,* all you gotta do is call my homie, Ty to the window and tell him to bring down everything to you; but tell Ty to trash all my mail.

"Okay, baby, but why don't you want your mail?" Kim asked suspiciously.

"JUST DO WHAT THE *FUCK* I SAY, WILL YOU?"

"Alright, Ray. Oh, hold up, your daughter want to say something to you before you hang up."

"Aye look, Kim, not right now! Tell her I love her—I gotta go! See you later on tonight!" Ray said frantically before hanging up the phone. The way Ray ended the phone conversation, Kim assumed that the police must've been nearby.

In all actuality, Ray was craving to cop his next blast of raw dope, so badly, that he didn't even care to talk to his own daughter. The only thing that was on Ray's mind was finding a nice spot in the next alley to shoot up his heroin.

After hanging up with Ray, Kim went straight down to the halfway house on *New York Avenue* in *Washington, DC,* doing everything Ray instructed her to do; while waiting for Ty to bring Ray's possessions out to her.

"Thanks," Kim said, as she stuffed the plastic trash bag full of Ray's belongings in the back seat.

"Yeah, tell Ray I said to keep his eyes open because these feds ain't playin'," Ty replied while walking off. As soon as he departed, Kim quickly reached toward the back seat to retrieve Ray's mail out of the plastic bag.

For some reason, she didn't trust Ray. As Kim analyzed her last conversation with him, she noticed that Ray was trying to hide something. Kim decided that she was going to read his mail, opting not to tell Ty to trash Ray's letters.

As Kim sifted through the many letters, most of them addressed by her, she noticed that Ray had received two letters from the *Department of Health* in *Washington, DC.*

After reading the first letters, Kim broke down in tears, as she discovered that Ray was not only HIV positive, but the *Department of Health* had advised him to come in to discuss his options on taking HIV inhibitors, and other medicine alternatives; as well as talk about the update of Ray's recent results which showed a decrease in his T-cell count—a major decline from Ray's first testing nine years ago.

The whole time Ray was in prison, he knew that he was infected. Other than being disgruntled with his imprisonment, this was one of the reasons why Ray had a nonchalant attitude, not caring about himself, or others he engaged with for that matter.

Ray actually became infected by sharing needles which was used to shoot up dope with his friend and cellmate, Lil' Will; the two often using the same filthy works while getting high on dope. Unbeknownst to Ray, Lil' Will became infected by sharing used syringes with other dope fiends within the prison facility, who were infected with HIV without their knowledge.

While others thought that Lil' Will died of a drug overdose, or from a balloon filled with heroin and cocaine bursting in his stomach while smuggling drugs for Ray, Ray and the medical personnel knew otherwise—Lil' Will revealing the unexpected news to him; alerting Ray that he might've passed it on to him, also.

At this point, Kim considered Ray to be a walking time bomb, being reckless and totally irresponsible; jeopardizing his life, as well as hers in the process.

Kim became irate. Not for the fact that he was HIV positive, because she assumed that Ray probably contracted the disease from using heroin in the past before he was incarcerated—long before they connected. That wouldn't be an issue to Kim, loving Ray regardless, with intentions of continuing to love him unconditionally.

Yet, Kim was heated and disturbed by the fact that Ray knew that he was infected all along, and never advised her. Kim immediately thought back to the countless times that they had unprotected sex: oral, vaginal and anal.

Kim became overwhelmed with devastation, but found the strength to continue with going through Ray's mail. She then came across a recent letter mailed to Ray from Candy. Kim's mouth dropped when she read the letter to Ray, reading the paragraph in which Candy asked Ray why did he do all of those devious things to her, especially after Ray had told Candy several times, how he was madly in love with her.

It was at that moment when Kim wanted to commit suicide, not only finding out that Ray was HIV positive, but that he was also gay—a trade having a loving relationship with Candy; a transsexual.

Any thoughts of continuing to love Ray unconditionally was immediately tossed out the window, as Kim's eyes was now intensely filled with complete hatred for Ray; witnessing for the first time in her life that, she was truly sleeping with the enemy. Kim then realized that he never loved her or Raye-Raye, Ray's only daughter and child.

Kim then flipped down the sun visor in the car to look at Raye-Raye's photo.

"I'm so, so, sorry, baby," Kim mumbled as she sobbed uncontrollably. "Don't worry, mommy will fix everything."

Kim then drove to the local supermarket to get groceries, preparing to make Ray's favorite dish of "seafood surprise". Little would Ray know that Kim was surprising him with her adding deadly rat poison to the spicy spaghetti sauce; Kim's new "secret" ingredient.

C-LOW'S HOUSE IN VIRGINIA
chapter 54

"Sit down, please," instructed the medical nurse, as she placed plastic gloves on to examine the terrible rash that recently appeared on C-Low's chest last week.

"What y'all call me back up here for?" C-Low asked curiously, mainly because this was his second visit to the medical office since discovering the rash. The doctor wanted to examine C-Low again before giving him his results.

"There's a valid reason why you've been called to come back here," the doctor said while reviewing C-Low's chart, now signaling the nurse with a head nod for her to leave the room; in order to talk privately with the patient.

"Yeah, well then, what's your valid reason?" C-Low asked eagerly, wanting to make the ten-minute move so he could get to the gym.

"Well, Mr. Davis," the doctor began, addressing C-Low by his last name, "your lab results came back today, and as your medical doctor at this institution, it is my duty to inform you that your results indicate that your HIV test came back positive," he continued mildly.

"What? What the *fuck* you talkin' 'bout? *Motherfucker,* you trippin'! I know for a fact I *ain't* got that bug, *motherfucker!* Your machine *must* be broke! Check this out, doc, I've been *locked* up for ten years now. When I came to this prison, I got tested *three* different times, and each time the results *all* came back negative.

"Now, doc, I swear on my own *mama,* I ain't *never* fuck no *homo* before in my life, or have I gotten any *pussy* since I been here. I don't do drugs and I don't eat after people. Doc, something's *got* to be wrong with your test—I'm *tellin'* you, your results are wrong!" C-Low spat angrily while being confused.

"Mr. Davis, I understand your pain, but we ran your blood sample over-and-over again for accuracy. Are you

252

sure that you've been tested for HIV? Because most inmates believe when they first come to jail and get checked by the medical staff that a HIV test is included in their physical, which is not the case. Unless you *request* the test, we don't voluntarily test for HIV."

"Man, *fuck* that *shit!* I ain't even *tryna* hear that *bullshit* you talkin'! Your *motherfuckin'* ass is trippin'—I AIN'T GOT NO FUCKIN' HIV!" C-Low yelled, as he quickly stood up from the chair; anger now intensifying.

"Calm down, Mr. Davis. You being upset only leads to you having stress, which isn't good for a person with an HIV status," The doctor pleaded.

"*MOTHERFUCKER,* I TOLD YOU I DON'T HAVE HIV!" C-Low shouted irrationally, volatile at this moment.

"Mr. Davis, if you don't sit down and relax, I'm going to be forced to call for back-up," The doctor replied, fearing that C-Low would violently attack him.

"MAN, *FUCK* YOU AND YOUR BACK-UP!" C-Low continued with his temper tantrum, as the doctor now called for the guards to restrain the delirious convict, and to escort C-Low out.

As C-Low continued to with his hostility, he was then cuffed by the correctional officers and dragged to Solitary Confinement. While in "the hole", C-Low's mind raced back to his everyday life and activity since he'd been in prison. C-Low desperately tried to figure out: *How in the world would I be able to catch a disease that mainly homosexuals, intravenous drug users, or people who had transfusions with tainted blood, had caught.*

While feverishly going back to the list of events, C-Low instantly dropped his head into his hands in disbelief, remembering the bloody, brutal brawl he had with Ray in the gym after the basketball tournament.

Under any normal circumstance, C-Low wouldn't have ever imagined that his blood had mixed with Ray's tainted blood during the fight; both C-Low and Ray mixing blood through their open wounds.

At that moment, C-Low thought about how Ray had cut his hand open when he punched C-Low in the mouth, and how he'd punched Ray over his eyebrow and created a huge gash.

C-Low then slumped to the floor of the cell, and hung his head down low while he cried. C-Low was in shock and in disbelief, not being able to fathom the idea that he'd contracted the deadly disease from a fistfight—one over a dope fiend's jealous rage; concerning a transsexual whom C-Low never touched.

"Medical assistance, report to the gymnasium; we have an unconscious male who seemed to have had a stroke," said the correctional officer over his radio, as he looked at the lifeless body of inmate, Keith Harris, a.k.a. Ke-Ke Overness. Ke-Ke fell out while doing a set of power squats with 300-pound weights, trying to keep his butt plump and tight, since he'd lost a lot of body weight.

The amounted pounds of iron from the barbell, along with him not working out regularly, is what the convicts thought was the cause of the stroke, until some observed that the paramedics wouldn't touch Ke-Ke until they all had on rubber gloves. Even then, some of the medical team seemed reluctant to treat him.

By the time Ke-Ke's body reached the hospital, he was pronounced dead. His whole immune system had completely shut down on him. Even though Ke-Ke was taking HIV medications, the inhibitors didn't totally heal him, only helping in preserving his life longer than what the doctors predicted.

Ke-Ke had full-blown AIDS, in which he contracted the deadly disease fifteen years ago at *Levenworth Penitentiary* in *Kansas;* from a gang rape that ultimately determined his fate of becoming a homosexual.

TRIGGER'S HOUSE IN VIRGINIA
chapter 56

"Y-e-a-h, you White *slut,* suck this big black *dick,"* Trigger arrogantly said, while engaging in an Ecstasy and *Cristal*-induced orgy with his male friends and a bunch of female groupies; inside of his plush, oversized mansion, Trigger just purchased in the suburbs of *Long Island.*

Newspapers and magazine articles, as well as the well-known, shock-jock, radio personality, *Wendy Williams,* all reported the new palatial house, having thirty-six rooms, that Trigger recently bought from the youngest, most controversial, *NBA* basketball players.

The young White girl met Trigger's every demand, pleasing him and eventually, his crew of friends with raunchy, explicit sex acts that she willingly and hungrily performed on them. Her parents hadn't a clue of their daughter, a *Harvard Law School* student, being in a house full of Black hip-hop rappers and thugs, giving oral sex to them, and the females; as well as letting the men have their way with the white girl, sexually.

"Damn, White girl, you suckin' on my dick r-e-a-l good, yo. You sure your name ain't *Monica Jewinsky?"* Trigger joked about how well she was performing oral sex on him, as all of his friends burst out in laughter as they watched on. "Alright, hoe, now turn around and eat your girlfriend's *pussy* out, while I *fuck* you in the ass," Trigger rudely instructed, as the White girl eagerly obeyed the new rap superstar.

As she bent over, sticking her ass in the air while licking her friend's vagina, Trigger, lubricated with *Vaseline,* quickly shoved his large penis all the way into her rectum; going as deep as possible, while ignoring the white girl's high-pitched cries for mercy.

The harder Trigger fucked her, the louder the white girl's screams became; which aroused and encouraged Trigger more to powerfully plow faster inside of her. His friends then decided to pull out their personal camcorders and camera phones—recording Trigger having intense anal sex with the hopeless White girl.

After he ejaculated inside of her, Trigger laid back into his *California* king-sized bed, and dismissed everyone in the room in an arrogant manner, as he emulated a big-time Italian mobster. As he popped another Ecstasy pill, and smoked a large blunt filled with "gorilla" marijuana, his phone rang.

"Yo!"

"Hello, Trigger, it's me, Susan—we have to talk!"

"Aiiight, Susan, I already told you, ma, I won't be late for the press release of my next video," Trigger replied jokingly, assuming that Susan was calling to harass him about being on time for his next interview.

"No, Trigger. This doesn't have *anything* to do with no *goddamn* video," Susan replied in a harsh, but melancholy tone. At the sound of her voice, Trigger knew that something was wrong, as he closed his bedroom door for privacy.

"Alright, ma, what's your problem?" Trigger said while being annoyed, letting Susan know by the sound of his voice that she was getting on Trigger's nerves.

"You mean, *our* problem!" Susan snapped. "Trigger, your lil' *rotten* ass need to go to the hospital. *Motherfucker,* you gave me HIV, and in return, I gave it to my husband!"

"WHAT? Yo, what the *fuck* you talkin' 'bout, Susan? *Bitch,* I ain't *got* shit, and I ain't *give* you nothin'! Your old, freak-*ass* probably got that *shit* from somebody else. Don't you *ever* try to front on me like that, *bitch!*"

"You no-good *motherfucker!* Trigger, now, I don't know *how* you got it...but you came home and gave it to me. After I had my lil' fling with you, my husband and I decided to try and work things out. He got some Viagra, and next thing you know, our sex life was a blast. Until recently, when he had to have his blood checked out for his cancer treatment. That's when he was diagnosed with HIV, in which I got tested and my results came back positive, too! My husband and I were *both* uninfected, until I cheated on him with you!

"Now, Trigger, I haven't had unprotected sex in ten years, and that was with my husband. You were the *only* person that I was stupid enough to have unprotected sex with; and multiple times! I was even foolish enough to fulfill all of your *freaky* anal fetishes. Trigger, you *fucked* me raw in my *ass* with *Crisco!*

"…Listen, you need to tell the *motherfucker* you got it from that you have HIV, if you even remember the *stupid* groupie-*bitch's* name. And by the way, *motherfucker,* your *fucking* contract with *Dope Jam Records* has been terminated!" Susan ranted on continuously.

"Wait, hold up, Susan! You can't do—"

Susan hung up the phone on Trigger before he finished his sentence.

"Damn!" Trigger yelled, as he thought back to how he could've contracted the disease. Candy was the last transsexual he penetrated. *It couldn't have been Candy because we always used protection.*

What Trigger didn't realize is that every time he performed oral sex on Candy, licking, sucking and biting on her anus, that there were small tissue cuts in Candy's rectum from the rough sex he loved to have with her; tearing Candy's muscle tissues each time. Trigger licked small droplets of blood, which traveled into his blood stream.

Plus, Candy giving Trigger oral sex, immediately after she came from Solitary Confinement, in addition to passionately kissing him occasionally as she done so, the open wound Candy had in her mouth, due to Jose busting her bottom gum line, allowed blood, saliva and premature ejaculation to mix; Trigger instantly becoming infected.

"FUCK!" Trigger yelled, as he picked up the bottle of *Cristal* from his champagne holder and hurled it across the room, breaking it against his bedroom wall. Trigger then jumped back on his bed and sobbed uncontrollably.

Not only did Trigger ruin his promising career as a platinum rap artist, but sabotaged his own life, as well as others; spreading the disease to Susan, her husband, and a slew of groupies, who took pride in allowing Trigger to have anal sex with them repeatedly without condoms.

TOM'S HOUSE IN VIRGINIA
chapter 57

"Haystack, you have a legal visit," said the correctional officer who came to escort him. Tom knew who the visitor was, he was beyond happy to finally tell Lizzy his deepest secret. Tom made a mental note to himself that, regardless of how much Lizzy tried to quickly seduce him, Tom's mission was to inform her of what he should've, six months ago.

As soon as Tom reached the visiting room, he noticed the long, sad expression upon Lizzy's face, as Tom became worried that something was wrong. He knew Lizzy all too well not to know when something was bothering her.

"What's wrong, Lizzy? Is everything okay?" Tom asked, pulling a chair out for her before he sat down.

"Tom, I have bad news. I don't know how to tell you this, so I'm just going to give it to you straight," Lizzy mildly replied, trying to stop her tears from flowing.

"What's the matter, Lizzy? You're shaking me up here," Tom said impulsively.

"Tom, I'm pregnant, and I don't know who the father is. I was ovulating when we last had sex—I was so worked up from being with you, that Patrick and I had sex as soon as I returned to the office," Lizzy said, taking a deep breath afterwards.

"Lizzy, the baby is Patrick's. You guys are getting ready to be married," Tom said while stroking her hand gently, trying to console Lizzy while clearing her guilty conscious. Tom wanted his two friends to be happy together.

"Tom, that's not why I'm feeling miserable!" Lizzy screamed, as she couldn't hold it in any longer. Tears gushed out of her eyes, as Lizzy looked Tom in the face. "Tom, I'm so sorry," she said sadly.

"Sorry about what?"

"Oh, Tom, I'm HIV positive. I haven't told Patrick yet, because I felt I had to tell you first. I know I couldn't have gotten it from you because you've been incarcerated, plus, I know you're not gay. I think Patrick had an affair and brought it home to me, and now, I've passed it on to my unborn child, and possibly you. Tom, I'm so sorry, I feel so cheated and shameful," Lizzy cried, as she couldn't stand to look at her former lover and best friend.

Tom just sat there in complete shock, amazed and in disbelief, as he wanted so badly to tell Lizzy that she might've contracted the disease from him, but couldn't fix his mouth to utter the words. Tom was ridden with pain and guilt.

After discovering that Ke-Ke died of AIDS, Tom knew he was a prime suspect for the disease. But, from the information that Lizzy just gave him, Tom no longer was a suspect, indirectly, he now became the accuser, as Tom then buried his face in the palm of his hands, and loudly cried out his pain.

Tom not only destroyed his life from having unprotected sex, and from being dishonest, but he also damaged both of his friends' lives; including Lizzy and Tom's unborn child.

DEWAYNE'S HOUSE IN VIRGINIA
chapter 58

"Where are you? How far are you from the hospital?" Dewayne's wife asked, as they both rushed separately to *The Children's Hospital of Philadelphia.*

"I'm pulling into the parking lot right now," Dewayne answered before disconnecting his cell phone, rushing inside of the hospital.

Dewayne was running frantically, as he constantly called upon the Lord for help. After donating his bone marrow to his daughter, Cheryl six months ago, she became violently ill. Everyone was under the impression that Dewayne's daughter would recover quickly.

Even with the doctors' great efforts in trying desperately to save the young girl's life, it was evident that the bone marrow match Cheryl received from her father wasn't working well. After countless surgical tests to see what the problem was, the doctors had no other choice but to recheck the white blood cells in Cheryl's blood.

When Dewayne reached his daughter's bedside, he couldn't understand as to why just yesterday, she was feeling great. Now, all of a sudden, Cheryl went deep into a coma.

"What's wrong, Dr. Lee?" asked Dewayne, as he anxiously wanted to know why the Korean doctor had called both him and his wife on their jobs, indicating that Cheryl's health status had taken a turn for the worse.

"Is your wife here also, Mr. Larkin?" the doctor asked.

"No, not yet. But she's on her way. Now, whatever you have to say to the both of us, you can say it to me, now—I need to know."

"Well, Mr. Larkin, I think you should have a seat," the doctor said while examining his files.

"Look, Dr. Lee, I don't have *time* for any hospital jargon. Now, *please,* tell me what's *wrong* with my daughter!" Dewayne said emotionally.

"Okay then, Mr. Larkin. Since you're the donor, I guess I can tell you first. We just ran a series of tests on your daughter, and everything came back clear, except for one thing."

"What's that, Dr. Lee?"

"Your daughter has tested positive for HIV," Dr. Lee replied, looking at Dewayne with disgust.

"Nah, that *can't* be true, how can that be, Dr. Lee? When I was tested, my blood sample came back non-detective—it came up negative. Dr. Lee, what the *hell* are you trying to tell me?" Dewayne asked, as he grabbed the doctor by his arm.

"Just because you came up non-detective, doesn't mean you don't have HIV. Most likely it wasn't detected, and the hospital that took your bone marrow, evidently, wasn't professional enough to run a series of test. Now, Mr. Larkin, you are your daughter's donor, if she has HIV, then there's *no* other way she could've gotten it, but from you," Dr. Lee stated, as he looked over at Cheryl, helpless; now in a coma.

The doctor then couldn't stand to look at Dewayne, whom he felt was careless enough to give his own daughter a deadly disease. Dr. Lee then left out the room, intending to return, only when Mrs. Larkin arrived.

Dewayne knelt down at his daughter's bedside and begged his Lord and Savior, Jesus Christ to forgive him, and to spare his daughter's life. Yet, no matter how much Dewayne cried, how much he prayed, Dewayne knew that he was being punished—for the lustful temptations Dewayne had for Candy; as the pain of giving his *own* child HIV grew deep into Dewayne's heart.

Now feeling helpless, Dewayne felt that it was nothing he could do to save young Cheryl, yet, Dewayne believed that it was something he had to do; to remedy the damage he caused.

After blowing her horn through traffic and running many red lights, Mrs. Larkin finally entered the hospital;

fifteen minutes after Dewayne arrived. As she entered her daughter's room, Dewayne's wife became curious as to why her husband wasn't there by Cheryl's side.

Mrs. Larkin quickly ran out to get Dr. Lee. After finding the doctor and asking about her daughter's health status, the doctor told Mrs. Larkin that he'd rather Dewayne tell her the new revelation.

"Well, he's not here right now, Dr. Lee," Mrs. Larkin said, looking around the room, focusing her teary eyes on her daughter, Cheryl.

"Maybe Mr. Larkin's in the patients' bathroom. Knock on the door right there," the doctor instructed, as he pointed towards the door on the right side of the room.

Dewayne's wife knocked on the door three times, but no one answered. She then put her ear to the door and heard the sound of water running.

"Dewayne, are you in there?" she asked, voice now low and unsteady. After placing her ear to the door again, Dewayne's wife then looked to the floor, and noticed the overflow of water coming from the bathroom. Her instincts told her that something was wrong.

When Mrs. Larkin opened the door, she received the shock of her life. Dewayne was hanging from the handicap safety rail in the shower by his necktie.

Dewayne's wife hysterically screamed for help, trying to hold his body up in the process; hoping that his noose wouldn't tighten. Unfortunately, she was too late. Dewayne was already dead before his wife discovered him.

There was no way that Dewayne was going to be able to look into his wife's eyes and explain his infidelity. He opted to deal with God for his actions—willing to burn for all eternity in Hell; than to face his wife, and helplessly watch his daughter die. This all came into play because, Dewayne longed for a woman's touch, which too, was artificial.

BEEP...BEEP...BEEP...B-E-E-E-E-E-E-E-E-E-E-E-P!

The last beep from the life support machine was indication that, Candy Sweets was no longer with us. Her soul took flight, as Candy desperately tried her hardest to pull out of her coma. Right before Candy's soul escaped her, Candy overheard the nurses talking about her health status, as they jotted down Candy's information.

Having an out-of-body experience, Candy curiously observed her surroundings and watched the interaction between the nurses, as Candy became very confused as to why she was able to watch over her own body; especially since Candy was actually lying in bed, hooked up to the resuscitator.

"Notify next of kin," Ms. Chase, the head nurse and Candy's former boss instructed.

"What's the cause of death?" asked the assisting nurse.

"Pneumonia, due to complications of AIDS," answered Ms. Chase, while pulling the cool, crisp white sheet over Candy's head. The assisting nurse immediately picked up the phone to call Candy's cousin, Lisa, regrettably informing her of the bad news.

Due to being in a coma, fighting hard for her life before Candy passed on, Candy wasn't in any capacity to know or understand how she contracted the disease. Perhaps if all of Candy's faculties were working properly, and she was still alive, Candy could've assumed that she became infected in prison by one of her ex-lovers, whom Candy had sex with.

Unfortunately, Candy was carrying the disease long before she'd entered the federal prison. It was her first love, Terry who passed the HIV virus on to her, which later manifested to AIDS, after he came home from prison.

Terry himself was unaware that he'd contracted the disease, but the racist, White supremacist, who was a tattoo artist inside the prison, knew all too well. The tattoo artist intentionally tainted the red ink that he used to color in his designs with HIV contaminated blood; blood that the tattoo artist had drawn from one of his *Aryan* brothers, who recently died from full-blown AIDS.

It was the evil White supremacist's way of trying to eliminate as many Black men within the prison, in hopes to make them totally extinct. He conned the Black male inmates into thinking that he wasn't prejudice, and that he got along with them, deceivingly befriending the Black men, as the White supremacist enticed them all; offering discounted prices on tattoos.

In return, the tattoo artist infected them all without their knowledge, in which the Black male inmates thought they were getting innovative tattoo designs for a low price. Unfortunately, the price they paid was their lives.

Candy, originally born Andy Sweets, desperately longed for affection and acceptance, early on in life. From "her" childhood days of innocence, Candy was verbally and physically beaten, disowned and rejected by family members, who ultimately threw "her" out of their homes, and out of their lives—due to Candy's sexual preference and identity.

Never having a fair chance in life, Candy became a victim of circumstance. A tragic victim of abuse, rape, and love, which in the end—ultimately led Candy into being a victim to the deadly disease, AIDS.

JOSE'S HOUSE IN VIRGINIA
chapter 60

As soon as Jose hit the compound at the *USP Atlanta Facility*, all heads turned, as they looked at the gorgeous Puerto Rican with long, silky hair, and the fat, round behind. Jose stopped in front of the unit before resting the heavy belongings onto the floor.

As Jose was about to helplessly pick up the bags and bedroll, a tall, handsome, muscular guy who resembled Ray, came from out of nowhere to aid Jose.

"Let me carry your things for you, ma," the undercover trade said, while effortlessly flinging Jose's belongings over his broad shoulders. "Yo, ma, what's your name, baby?" the guy asked, looking at Jose up-and-down in awe lustfully; not believing what he was seeing.

"Boo, you can call me 'J. Lo'," Jose then responded in a soft, sexy, seductive tone, as "J. Lo" sashayed slowly in front of the guy; the down low brother now having his lustful eyes glued to J. Lo's plump ass, while purposely lagging behind.

Jose Lopez, a.k.a. J.Lo, now committed "herself" to being a full-fledged queen, recently coming out the closet regarding "her" sexuality, and taking hormone treatments; easily transforming into a beautiful transsexual.

With J. Lo already being naturally pretty, and with the way her body took to the Estrogen pills, J. Lo now looked more like a natural woman each day; being graceful, prettier, and much more passable than Candy was when she was alive.

With the exception of the guy who voluntarily helped J. Lo to the cell with her belongings, J. Lo noticed that her wicked beauty instantly mesmerized many men, as J. Lo sensually strutted through the unit. J. Lo then smiled a devilish grin, taking all the advice and insight that Candy had given, now using it to "her" advantage, with plans of now being the new "Queen Bitch" within the prison system.

GLOSSARY

Ahk – Brother

Allahu-Akbar – Allah is the greatest

As-Salaamu-Alaikum – Peace be upon you

Bar-fight – To argue at another convict from a prison cell

Bomb-diggity – Great sex

Bottom – Gay male who only receives during sex

Butch-queen – A gay male appearing to be masculine with female traits

Cell-gangsta – A convict who appears to be tough from his cell only

Cellie – Prison roommate

Cut card – To put up a front

Deen – A system of life where Allah is worshipped and obeyed

Dog food/Dookie/Js/Raw diggity – Dope, heroin

Doin' shows – Being mischief, behaving badly

Down low/On the low/In the closet – Being secretly gay

Do you – A person focusing one himself/herself

Ear-hustlin' – Eavesdropping

E/Ecstasy and Oxycontin – Mind altering drugs

Keep it cute – To not cause problems, to be well-behaved

Fag-hag – A woman who befriends and overly idolize gay men

Femme-queen realness – Passing as a natural woman

Gump/Poo-putt – Faggot

Haqq – Truth

Haram – Prohibition

Imam – Muslim leader

Insha-Allah – Lord willing

Jumu'ah – The Friday prayer

Kufar – Nonbeliever

Lovey-dovey – Being in love, infatuation

Majalees – Islamic committee

Many things – Being uncivilized

One – Good-bye, see you later

Out-of-pocket – Being wrong, inappropriate

Quran – The holy book of Islam

Salat – Muslim prayer

Shady boots – Wicked

Shariah – Islamic Law

Shariefs – Muslim guards

Sunnah – Prophet's example as indicated by his practice of the faith

Sunni – One of the sects of Islam

Top – Gay male who only penetrates other gay men

Versatile – Gay male who both penetrates and receives during sex

Wa'laikum – And upon you, (A reply to others)

What's the tea? – What's new? What's going on?

Wolfing – Hair growing in messy

*HIV/AIDS among African Americans

The HIV/AIDS epidemic is a health crisis for African Americans. In 2001, HIV/AIDS was among the top 3 causes of death for African American men aged 25–54 years and among the top 4 causes of death for African American women aged 20–54 years. It was the number 1 cause of death for African American women aged 25–34 years.

STATISTICS

Cumulative Effects of HIV/AIDS (through 2003)
According to the 2000 Census, African Americans make up 12.3% of the US population. However, they have accounted for 368,169 (40%) of the 929,985 estimated AIDS cases diagnosed since the epidemic began.

By the end of December 2003, an estimated 195,891 African Americans with AIDS had died. Of persons given a diagnosis of AIDS since 1995, a smaller proportion of African Americans (60%) were alive after 9 years compared with American Indians and Alaska Natives (64%), Hispanics (68%), whites (70%), and Asians and Pacific Islanders (77%).

During 2000–2003, HIV/AIDS rates for African American females were 19 times the rates for white females and 5 times the rates for Hispanic females; they also exceeded the rates for males of all races/ethnicities other than African Americans. Rates for African American males were 7 times those for white males and 3 times those for Hispanic males.

WARNING!

Please note that you should only use latex condoms with water-based lubricants, never with petroleum jelly.

*Statistics taken from Centers for Disease Control and Prevention
Department of Health and Human Services
Phone: 800-CDC-INFO   Web site: www.cdc.gov

An excerpt from ***BOY-TOY*** by
DAMON "AMIN" MEADOWS
A GHETTOHEAT® PRODUCTION

Demetrius had just finished watching *Idlewild,* thinking to himself that *Outkast* needed to go back to their original style. "Me and you, yo momma and yo cousin, too," Demetrius then sang the lyrics to *Outkast's* hit single, *"Elevators",* as he made his way to the bathroom to take a shower.

The warm water sprinkling from the multifunctional shower head began to sooth Demetrius' body. He took a quick moment to wash his hair. The *Aveda "Rosemary Mint"* shampoo tingled Demetrius' scalp, as he allowed his fingers to work up a good lather. Demetrius' eyes were closed as he was enjoying the tingly sensation.

Soon after, Demetrius then became suddenly startled by a finger, gently stroking down the center of his muscular back. Demetrius' slightly flinched at the light touch.

Vellicia, he thought, smiling, as Demetrius put his head under the running shower head. He then turned around to face Vellicia. However, when Demetrius opened his eyes, he found Rose, his best friend's mother standing before him; glistening, as the water splashed over her curvaceous nakedness.

"See no evil, hear no evil speak no evil," lightly escaped Rose's lips, before she kissed Demetrius passionately, making it evident that she'd longed for the awaited moment.

Demetrius was blown away. He tried hard to resist but, Rose's soft, manicured hands had began stroking his thick manhood. Within seconds, Demetrius was erect—hard as a rock. He then wrapped his strong arms around the seductress, grabbing Rose's soft, plump ass with both hands, before lifting Rose off of her feet, placing her back against the smooth marble tiles.

Demetrius became stunned when Rose instinctively grabbed his right hand, and guided him to her throbbing pussy to finger Rose from behind; as Rose then wrapped her long legs around Demetrius' waist. He couldn't believe what was happening, but its inconceivability only added to Demetrius' desire, as he then slowly buried his big dick deep into the depths of Rose's wetness.

"A-h-h-h," Rose moaned lightly under her breath, trying not to awaken the rest of the house with her lustful cries. The warm water streaming from the shower head had intensified Rose and Demetrius' pleasures, as the water massaged their naked bodies.

Rose's hands playfully trickled up-and-down Demetrius' muscular back, as he pumped his massive penis inside of her tight soaking slit. Rose then threw her legs around Demetrius' back, waving them about, loving the way his meat rubbed against her throbbing clit, each time Demetrius had thrust himself inside Rose's hot canal.

"M-m-m-m-m-m," Rose murmured, biting her bottom lip while tightening her vaginal walls; Rose contracted her inner muscles, as she steadily squeezed Demetrius' dick inside of her pleasurable pink passage.

Seeing Rose's body quiver, Demetrius then realized that she was about to reached her peak, as Rose's body language spoke directly to him. Demetrius then began to thrust harder and faster inside of her, powerfully pounding his pipe inside of Rose.

Momentarily changing the pace and rhythm, Demetrius rested the side of his face against her soft, silky shoulder, as he then gyrated inside of Rose in a slow, circular motion. Demetrius flexed his ass cheeks, as he throbbed and rotated his huge penis inside of her wet pussy.

The pleasure alone of Demetrius' lovemaking had sent Rose to ecstasy, a feeling that Rose didn't want to end. The passionate sensation felt so great to her, that Rose couldn't believe what she was experiencing. But, instead of not believing what was happening, the realization of how well her young son's best friend was fucking her had immediately set in.

Holding on tightly to Demetrius, as Rose tossed her head back, allowing the water to mix with the joyful tears that streamed down her face, Rose gyrated her hips faster on top of Demetrius, as she felt his body begin to jerk uncontrollably, as Demetrius spewed his hot semen into Rose's love tunnel.

An excerpt from ***GHETTOHEAT*®** by
HICKSON
A GHETTOHEAT® PRODUCTION

GHETTOHEAT®

S-S-S-S-S-S-S!
Can you feel it? Scaldin' breath of frisky spirits
Surroundin' you in the streets
The intensity
S-S-S-S-S-S-S!
That's GHETTOHEAT®!
The energy – Electric sparks
Better watch ya back after dark!
Dogs bark – Cats hiss
Rank smells of trash and piss
Internalize – Realize
No surprise – Naughty spirits frolic in disguise
S-S-S-S-S-S-S!
INTENSITY: CLIMBIN'! CLIMBIN'! CLIMBIN'! CLIMBIN'!
GHETTOHEAT®: RISIN'! RISIN'! RISIN'! RISIN'!

Streets is watchin'
Hoes talkin' – Thugs stalkin'
POW! POW! POW!
Start speed-walkin'!
Heggies down – Rob that clown
Snatch his stash – Jet downtown
El Barrio – Spanish Harlem:

"MIRA, NO! WE DON'T WANNO PROBLEM!"

Bullets graze – I'm not amazed
GHETTOHEAT®!
Niggas start blazin'
Air's scathin' – Gangs blood-bathin'
Five-O's misbehavin' – Wifey's rantin'-n-ravin'!
My left: The Bloods – My right: The Crips
Niggas start prayin' – Murk-out in ya whip!

Internalize – Realize
No surprise – Naughty spirits frolic in disguise
S-S-S-S-S-S-S!
INTENSITY: CLIMBIN'! CLIMBIN'! CLIMBIN'! CLIMBIN'!
GHETTOHEAT®: RISIN'! RISIN'! RISIN'! RISIN'!

Mean hoodlums – Plottin' schemes
A swoop-down – 'Bout to rob me – Seems like a bad dream
Thugs around – It's goin' down
'BOUT TO BE SOME SHIT!
But I'm ghetto – Know how to spit
Gully mentality – Thinkin' of reality of planned-out casualty
I fake wit' the trickery:
"ASS-ALAMUALAIKUM"

"STICK 'EM UP!"

"YO, DON'T FUCK WIT' HIM – HE'S MUSLIM!"

Flipped script wit' quickness
Changed demeanor – The swiftness
Not dimwitted – Felt the flames of evil spirits!
Hid chain in shirt – I don't catch pain – Don't get hurt
No desire gettin' burnt by the fire
Thermometer soars, yo, higher-and-higher
In the PRO-JECTS – Fightin' to protect ya neck
Gotta earn respect – Defend ya rep
Or BEAT-DOWNS you'll collect
The furor – The fever – My gun – My cleaver
Bitches brewin' – Slits a-stewin'
Sheets roastin' – Champagne toastin' – Gangstas boastin':

"The ghetto – Nuthin's mellow
The ghetto – Cries in falsetto
The ghetto – A dream bordello
The ghetto – Hotter than Soweto"

Internalize – Realize
No surprise – Naughty spirits frolic in disguise
S-S-S-S-S-S-S!
INTENSITY: CLIMBIN'! CLIMBIN'! CLIMBIN'! CLIMBIN'!
GHETTOHEAT®: RISIN'! RISIN'! RISIN'! RISIN'!

273

Red-hot hustlers – Broilin' at the spot
Boilin' alcohol – The lucky crackpot
Streets a-scorchin' – Crackheads torchin'
Stems ignited – Junkies delighted
Money's flowin' – Pusherman's excited
The first and fifteenth: BLOCK-HUGGERS' JUNETEENTH!
Comin' ya way – Take ya benefits today
Intoxication – Self-medication – The air's dense
Ghetto-suffocation – Volcanic maniacs attackin'
Cash stackin' – Niggas packin' – Daddy Rock's mackin':

"The ghetto – Nuthin's mellow
The ghetto – Cries in falsetto
The ghetto – A dream bordello
The ghetto – Hotter than Soweto"

BedStuy – Do or die: *BUCK! BUCK! BUCK! BUCK!*

They don't give a FUCK!
In The Bronx – You'll fry – Tossin' lye – WATCH YA EYES!

Walk straight – Tunnel vision – False move – Bad decision
So hot – Starts to drizzle – Steamy sidewalks – Begin to sizzle
HOT-TO-DEF! Intense GHETTOHEAT®

"DO YOU FEEL IT? DO YOU FEEL IT?"
"THE HOTNESS IN THE STREETS!!!™"

So hot – Got ya mase?
Too hot – PEPPER SPRAYIN' IN A NIGGA'S FACE!
The Madness – Sadness
Don't you know the flare of street-glow? OH!
Meltingly – Swelteringly
S-S-S-S-S-S-S!
HOOD IN-FER-NO!
Internalize – Realize
No surprise – Naughty spirits frolic in disguise
S-S-S-S-S-S-S!
INTENSITY: CLIMBIN'! CLIMBIN'! CLIMBIN'! CLIMBIN'!
GHETTOHEAT®: RISIN'! RISIN'! RISIN'! RISIN'!
INTENSITY: CLIMBIN'! CLIMBIN'! CLIMBIN'! CLIMBIN'!
GHETTOHEAT®: RISIN'! RISIN'! RISIN'! RISIN'!
S-S-S-S-S-S-S!

An excerpt from *HARDER* by
SHA
A GHETTOHEAT® PRODUCTION

When I finally arrived back home, Tony was heated. I didn't even realize I was out that long.

"Where the *fuck* you been, Kai?!" he yelled as I walked through the door.

"I went to the range and then shopping. I had a lot on my mind to clear and I just needed to get away. Damn, is there a law against that?"

"Nah, ain't no law, shorty! Just watch yaself, cuz if I finds out different, we gonna have major problems."

Tony was taking on a "Rico" tone with me that I did not like whatsoever.

"Who the *fuck* is you talking to, Tony? I *know* it ain't me. Ya better keep that *shit* in ya back pocket before you come at me with it."

I had never seen Tony like this before, and it made me very upset. I knew I had to calm down, before I said something that I would live to regret.

"Oh word? It's like that, Kai? Fuck you forget or something? This here is *my* house! *I'm* the star, baby girl! You *used* to be the co-star, but now you just another *fucking* spectator! Show over, get the *fuck* out!"

Just when I thought things couldn't get any worse!

"Get the fuck out? You get mad over some *bullshit* and now it's 'get the fuck out'? Tony, think about that shit for a minute." I started talking slowly and softly. "I'm ya 'co-star' alright, but do you *know* what that means? ...It means, everything you own, *I* own. All the work you put in, I put in, too.

"You forget who sees over the cooks and make sure ya deliveries are made on time? That's me, *motherfucker.* You *sure* you wanna have me running the street with all ya info, baby boy?"

That weird laugh echoed out of me again. This time, it set Tony off. He grabbed me by my throat, and *threw* me into the hard brick wall! When I hit the floor, Tony started to strangle me as he screamed, "BABY BOY?! BABY BOY? HUH? YOU FUCK THAT NIGGA?! HUH?! DON'T YOU *EVA* IN YA LIFE CALL ME 'BABY BOY' AGAIN, YOU FUCKING SLUT!"

Tony let go, and I hit the floor again. It took all the air I had in me, but I managed.

"Tony-I-ain't-fuckin'-nobody!"

"Oh word? You come in here acting brand-new, and you ain't *fucking* nobody? We'll see!"

Tony then picked me up by my waist and ripped my jeans off. He proceeded to remove my panties. I didn't know what Tony was up to, until he threw me onto the couch. Tony then spread my legs wide-open, as he stuck three fingers in me at the same time.

I screamed in pain...

Tony bowed his head in regret.

"I'm sorry, Kai," was all that he said, before Tony left the house for the night. I laid there until he came back early the next day. When Tony walked in the house, I'd pretended to be asleep, as he started to play with my hair.

"Kai, I hope you're listening to me. You know shit's been kinda hard since *Five Points.* You know it's hard knowing that I can't make love to you. I be seeing how dudes look at you and shit. I know your type, ma, you got the sex drive of a 18-year-old man."

I stifled a giggle.

"I just be thinking when you're gone, you out there getting the only thing I *can't* give you. I know you've been on my side since I came back home, but I still be bugging. You're a trooper, baby and that's why I love you. Please don't leave me—I need you. All this shit, is 'cause of you. I know that, ma-ma; I love you."

That became my driving force. The man that ran Queens *needed* me. It's true that behind every great man, was a great woman. I wanted to go down in history as being the greatest.

Tony would be my link to the city. I already had him in my back pocket, so that meant I had Queens in my back pocket! All I needed was the other four boroughs to fall in line.

Sure, I would step on some toes, but I would stand to be retired at twenty-five—with enough money to finance my life, for the rest of my life. AJ was right, but I had a point to prove, and money to make! After that was done, I would be game to anything else.

I started stashing away as much money as I could. I told Tony that I would no longer sleep at his house, since he put his hands on me.

Tony begged for me not to.

Instead, we came to the "agreement" that, I would *only* sleep over two or three nights out of the week, and I *had* to be on his payroll.

Tony agreed.

Every Friday morning, I got five-thousand in cash.

I *never* put it in the bank.

I used some of it as pocket money, and had my checks from work directly deposited in my bank account every Thursday. I used my work money to pay my bills and other expenses. I didn't want to give "Uncle Sam" a reason to start sniffing up my ass! Instead, I hid the money that Tony gave me in my bedroom closet at my father's house.

My game plan was clear: I would be the Queen-of-the-NYC drug empire.

I had Tony do all of the dirty work, and I stopped managing the cooks. I became his silent partner, so to speak. With a little coaching from me, and a lot of strong-arming, Tony could definitely have a heavy hand in the other boroughs.

In case the Feds were watching, I had a sound-proof alibi:

I was a student...

I worked full-time, and I lived at home with my pops.

Technically.

The only way I would be fucked was if they ever wanted to search my father's crib. Tony *never* came to my house, so I doubt that would ever happen.

277

An excerpt from *SONZ OF DARKNESS* by
DRU NOBLE
A GHETTOHEAT® PRODUCTION

"They *won't* wake up! What did you let that woman do to our children, Wilfred?" Marilyn nervously asked.

"GET IN THE CAR!" Wilfred shouted. The expression on her husband's face told Marilyn that he was somewhat scared. She hurried into the passenger's seat, halting her frustration for the moment. Wilfred didn't bother to glance at his wife, as he started the vehicle's ignition and drove off at rapid speed.

Marilyn stared silently at the right side of Wilfred's face for ten minutes. She wanted to strike her husband so badly, for putting not only her, but their two children through the eerie circumstances.

"I know you're upset, Marilyn, but to *my* people this is sacred; it's normal," Wilfred stated, while his eyes were locked on the little bit of road the headlights revealed. Marilyn instantly frowned at his remark.

"Andrew and Gary were *screaming* inside that hut, and now they're sound asleep. This is *not* normal, I don't care *what* you say, this is wrong, Wilfred. That *bitch* did something to our kids, it's like they're drugged! Why the *hell* did you bring us out here? WHAT DID SHE DO TO THEM?" Marilyn loudly screamed, budding tears then began to run down the young, ebony mother's face.

Wilfred then took a deep breath, trying his best to maintain his composure.

"Take us to the hospital!" Marilyn demanded.

"They don't need a doctor, they're perfectly healthy."

"How can you say that? Just look at them," Marilyn argued.

"Listen to me."

"I don't want to—"

"LISTEN TO ME!" Wilfred roared over his wife's voice. Marilyn paused, glaring fiercely toward her husband as he spoke. "The Vowdun has done something to them, she's given them gifts we don't yet know. Marilyn, the Vowdun has helped many people with her magic, she once healed my broken leg in a matter of seconds. The Vowdun has brought men and women fame, wealth, and cured those stricken with deadly diseases. It was even told that she made a man immortal, who now lives in the shadows."

"I'm a Christian, and what you're talking about is satanic. You *tricked* me into coming out here to get Andrew and Gary blessed—you're a liar!" Marilyn interjected.

"That is why we came to Haiti, and it has been done—the worst is now over."

As the couple argued, Gary Romulus eyes opened. He remained silent and unknown to his parents. The infant was in a trance, detached from his surroundings. Wilfred wasn't paying attention to the road ahead, his vision was locked on his wife as they feuded. Gary was however. The newborn saw what his mother and father didn't see, way ahead in the black night.

Two huge glowing crimson eyes stared back at the baby. They were serpentine, eyes Gary would never forget. They were the same eyes he and his brother, Andrew had seen in the hut; the Vowdun's eyes. Gary reached across and gently touched his older brother's shoulder, strangely Andrew awoke in the same catatonic state as his sibling.

"Everything is going to be okay, Marilyn. I tried to pay the Vowdun her price, but she refused," Wilfred said. Marilyn gasped.

"A price?" Marilyn replied annoyingly, refusing to hear her husband's explanation.

Andrew and Gary glared at the large red eyes, which were accompanied by an ever growing shadow that seemed to make the oncoming road darker. Lashing shadows awaited the vehicle.

"WHAT PRICE?" Marilyn then retorted, consumed with anger; she could easily detect the blankness of her husband's mind. Wilfred now was at a loss of words, even he had no knowledge of what the Vowdun expected from him, that was the very thought that frightened the man to the core.

The car was moving at seventy miles per hour. The saddened mother of two turned away from Wilfred's stare, at that moment, Marilyn couldn't even bare his presence. When her sight fell on the oncoming road, Marilyn franticly screamed out in terror. Wilfred instinctively turned forward to see what frightened his wife. His mouth fell ajar at the sight of the nightmarish form ahead of them. Filled with panic, Wilfred quickly tried to turn the steering wheel to avoid crashing.

It was too late.

The sudden impact of the collision caused the speeding car to explode into immense flames that roared to the night sky. The creature that had caused it suddenly disappeared, leaving behind its chaotic destruction and the reason for it.

Out of the flickering flames and screeching metal came young Andrew, who held his baby brother carefully in his fragile arms. An illuminating blue sphere then surrounded their forms, which kept Andrew and Gary unscathed from the fires and jagged metal of the wreckage; incredibly, the two brothers were physically unharmed.

Andrew walked away from the crash feeling melancholy. In the middle of his forehead was a newly formed third eye, which stared out bizarrely. Not until he and Gary were far enough away from the accident did Andrew sit down, and the blue orb vanished.

Gary then looked up at his older brother and cooed to get his attention. Andrew ignored him, he was staring at the flaming vehicle as their parents' flesh burned horridly, causing a horrible stench to pollute the air. Through glassy eyes, Andrew's vision didn't waver, the child was beyond mourning.

Finally, Andrew gazed down at his precious baby brother before he embraced Gary. Gary smiled assured, unfazed by the tragic event. With his tiny arms, Gary then tried to reach upwards, to touch the strange silver eye on his brother's forehead, playfully. Gary was as amused by the new organ as he would've been about a brand new toy.

"Mommy and daddy are gone now," Andrew then sobbed, as streams of tears rolled down his young face. He was trying his best to explain his sorrow. "I will *never* leave you, Gary—I promise," The young boy cried. Gary giggled, still trying to reach Andrew's third eye as best he could.

For the price of the Vowdun to bestow her gifts from her dark powers to the children, Wilfred Romulus had paid the ultimate price—he and his wife's lives. Their children were given gifts far beyond their father's imagination, and for this, they were also cursed with fates not of their choosing. The future held in store untold suffering.

An excerpt from **AND GOD CREATED WOMAN** by
MIKA MILLER
A GHETTOHEAT® PRODUCTION

Some people call me a *hoe* because I strip for niggas and hustle for cash.

Yeah, I turn tricks.

I tell niggas, "If the price is right, then the deal is real."

My momma used to say, *"As long as you got a pussy, you sittin' on a goldmine. Never give your shit away for free."*

If that means I'm a hoe, so be it!

None of these *bitches* pays my bills or puts food on my mutha...fuckin' table, so fuck 'em!

God didn't give me the type of brains where I can understand all that "technical" book shit. In elementary school, I was never good at math and, to tell the truth, I was never that good at readin' either.

It's not like I didn't try.

It's just that, when it came to school, nothin' really registered. In high school, I tried to learn the secretarial trade. I figured that if I had some sort of technical skill, that I could at least get a halfway decent gig after I graduated. Well, it turns out that typin' and shorthand was just another thing that I failed at.

So bein' somebody's secretary was out of the question.

With no real education or skill, I had to settle for minimum wage jobs. My first job was workin' as a maid at a five-star hotel. After about two weeks, I got tired of cleanin' after rich bitches that shitted all over the toilet seats, and hid bloody tampons all over the *goddamn* place!

And I wasn't 'bout to work in *nobody's* fast-food restaurant. So I had to come up with a new plan. And that's when I met this f-i-n-e-ass, Puerto Rican *muthafucka* by the name of Ricky.

Ricky was a straight-up thug. He had tattoos all across his chest and stomach like *Tupac* and shit. When I met Ricky, I had two kids. I was single, workin' my ass off as a hostess in a restaurant and braidin' hair on the side.

I was finally maintainin', you know, gettin' money. But I was always workin', so I didn't have no time to enjoy my kids or my money.

Ricky came on the scene and promised me all kinds of shit. He was like, *"Baby, you ain't gotta work that hard, why don't you lemme take care o' you and nem kids."*

Ricky had my head gassed up, for real!

Plus he was layin' the pipe on the regular. Fuckin' me *real* good wit' his fine ass. So one night, after Ricky got finished eatin' my cooch, he was like, *"Baby, I'ma take you to Philadelphia wit' me. You an' the kids can come wit' me, and I'll hook ya'll up wit' errythang."*

Me, bein' naive, I followed his fine ass all the way to Philly and shit, and the nigga started trippin'! Beatin' me up, knockin' me all upside my head, accusin' me of cheatin'...which I wasn't. Ricky started kickin' my ass to the point that I was too ashamed to go to work with black eyes and busted lips, and I eventually got fired.

Long story short. After a while, I finally had enough. I packed me and my kids up and went to a shelter. I didn't know no fuckin' body, I didn't know shit about Philadelphia—all I knew that I was broke and I needed a place to stay for me and my kids.

So I went to the welfare office....

I tried to work within the system. Well, welfare was draggin' they feet, and in the meantime, I needed to make some cash, fast.

That's when Marilyn popped up on the scene. Marilyn was basically a po' white trash version of myself. She was stayin' wit' me at the shelter.

Marilyn told me between puffs of her *Marlboro* cigarette: *"Mekka why don't you strip? You got a beautiful body, and I know you would make plenty of money 'cause you tall, you got them big, perky titties, and you high yellow. You could make some good money and be outta here in no time; you perky titty bitch!"*

I figured what I lacked in the brains department I'd make up for with the "gifts" that God did give me: my pretty face, this small waist and these big ole titties!

So I took Marilyn's advice. I rolled around wit' her, and she took me to some strip clubs. That's how I got this gig where I'm at now. Strippin' at a hole-in-the-wall called *Dutch Gardens*. *Dutch Gardens* is where "Mekka" was born, but I gotta finish this story another time, I think I hear them callin' my name.

"Hey Mekka, you go on in five," Trish hollers from the entrance of the locker room. Trish is a white bitch who *swears* she's black!

Only fucks Black men....

And she can get away wit' it 'cause, Trish got a ghetto-booty and a body like a sista. And some niggas think that "white is right", but they'll be alright. Trish is kinda cool though, as far as white girls go.

"Hey hoe; Mekka, you hear me?" Trish calls again.

"Bitch wait! I heard your *muthafuckin'* ass!"

I check my face in my magnetic mirror hung on the inside of my locker, spray on a hint of *Bulgari* "Omnia Eau de Toilette" body mist, adjust my g-string and tighten the laces on my thigh-high boots. Other bitches wear them tall shoes, but I'm gettin' old, and my old-ass feet and ankles need a lil' mo' support.

Plus, it's easier to slide them dollar bills in your boots and keep it movin'.

I slam my locker shut and take inventory of my surroundings. There's a room full of beautiful bitches all *hatin'* on me!

They wanna know how I make it-do-what-it-do! How I make all dat dough in the course of three hours, and they been in here all night lettin' niggas suck on they titties and finger their coochies...and still comin' up broke?

FUCK BITCHES!

Like I always say: "Money over niggas; bitches, stick to the script!"

An excerpt from **GHOST TOWN HUSTLERS** by
CARTEL: CASTILLO
A GHETTOHEAT® PRODUCTION

It was early in the morning when I heard someone knock
on the door, calling my name. I sat up and reached for my watch
that I'd placed on top of the nightstand.

It was seventy-thirty.

"WHO IS IT?"

"Senor! Lo estan esperando pa desallunar! (Sir! They're
waiting for you to come have breakfast!) I hear the voice of Maria
yell from behind the door.

"Dame unos cuanto minutos!" (Give me a couple of
minutes!"

I hear footsteps going away. I get out of bed, walk over to
a table on the far left corner of the room, where a vase full of fresh
water has been set. Once downstairs, I see the boys sitting down at
the table along with Emilio. I sit next to Pedrito.

"Where's Martha?" I ask.

"She didn't want to eat," Pedrito says while shrugging his
shoulders.

Minutes later after we'd eaten, Pedrito and I got up and
walked out onto the porch, sat down and lit up our cigarettes.
Emilio lit up a cigar, like the one Don Avila used to smoke.

Pedrito then said he wanted to show me something, so we
stood up and walked away from the house. He explained to me
that the two men that were sent to pick Don Avila up from the
airport had betrayed them, and that Emilio had all of his men
looking throughout Medellin; having his connections search the
rest of Colombia for any signs of them. So far, no one was able to
find anything.

We notice that the house was barely visible, so we decide
to go back. When we reach the house, the boys were inside, and
Emilio was waiting for Pedrito with three men by his side.

"Come," Emilio says, gesturing with his hand to Pedrito.
"I want to show you something I found." Emilio had a smile on his
face, but I noticed that it was very different than any other smiles
he'd given before. It was as if Emilio was smiling to himself and
not at Pedrito.

"Can Raul come, too?" I heard Pedrito ask. I stop midway up the stairs, proceeding to go into the house. I look back and see Emilio staring at me, almost as if he was thinking about what to answer.

"Sure," Emilio replied shortly. "He can come." Emilio began walking towards the back of the house, where there were three smaller houses that weren't visible from the front of the main house. One of the smaller houses were guarded by two men. One was holding a rifle, the other had a gun tucked inside the waist of his pants.

"Donde estan esos hijo-eh-putas?" (Where are those sons-of-bitches?) Emilio asked once he, Pedrito and I were before the guards.

"Hai dentro patron!" the guardsman with the gun at his waist answered, as he opened the door for us.

We walked into an unfurnished room, yet, it was well lit. In the center of the room, there were two men on the floor on their knees, with their arms raised above their heads; tied up with rope that had been thrown over a beam and secured to a pole. They're shirtless, and it seems as if someone has been beating them badly with a whip—the two men having cuts on their chest and faces. They were bleeding profusely from their wounds.

"These are the ones that sold out your father," Emilio said, pointing to the two men who are still on their knees. "They're responsible for the death of your father. That's Angel, and that's Miguel.

"Pedrito walked up to the two badly beaten men: "Who killed my father?" Neither of the two men answered. Pedrito then forcefully kicked Angel in his stomach. "QUIEN?" (WHO?) Pedrito shouts.

"Pedrito—" I say while taking a step forward. I immediately stopped when I felt a hand rest upon my shoulder firmly. I look back to see that it's Emilio.

"Leave him," Emilio commands. I turn to look at Pedrito, who's now violently shaking Miguel's head, grabbing him by his hair as he continues to yell loudly.

"QUIEN FUE? DIME!" (WHO WAS IT? TELL ME) Pedrito asks and shouts. Moments later, Pedrito looks around, still holding Miguel by his hair. He then let's go of Miguel and walks toward Emilio and I.

The guardsman who let us inside is now standing next to Emilio. Pedrito walks up to him, snatches the gun from his waist, cocks it, and runs back to where Angel and Miguel is. I see that Angel and Miguel's eyes are dilated before Pedrito blocks my view of the two men, now standing in front of them.

"Por f-f-f-avor no-no-no-no me maates!" (P-l-e-a-s-e don't kill me!) Angel begs for his life. "Yo no fui quien le mato." (It wasn't me who killed him."

"Entonce fuiste tu, eh?" Pedrito says, turning the gun to Miguel.

"N-O-O-O-O-O-O-O!" Miguel screams.

An excerpt from **GAMES WOMEN PLAY** by
TONY COLLINS
A GHETTOHEAT® **PRODUCTION**

A woman always sees a man before he sees her. Then, in a blink of an eye, she completely checks out everything him about him from head-to-toe—without him even knowing what the woman is doing. Even faster than her lightening quick assessment of him, she studies very swiftly, all of his surroundings; including any other woman who is interested in him.

Yes, a woman notices every little personal detail about a man. That's right, not one thing about him escapes her laser-like focus. So, as she studies him, at the same time, the woman makes a complete mental list of the number of turn-ons and turn-offs regarding any or all of his personal details. These turn-ons or turn-off may include: details about his personality, his looks, a man's level of personal grooming and cleanliness, body type, clothing, shoes and accessories, financial status, a man's relationship status, and so on.

However, a woman doesn't just stop at this point, the level of merely making a "check list" of superficial observations about a man. She doesn't stop her analysis of a man at the point that most men would end their analysis of a woman. A woman looks beyond the surface of a man's visible details, when she considers whether or not to pursue him. A woman analysis of a man is more complex.

Not only does a woman make a mental check list of all the personal details that a man possess, but also, she notices how well he maintains his personal details. Yet, a woman doesn't stop even at this point in her study of him. She is still not done putting him under her mental microscope. She takes her analysis of him to an even deeper level.

A woman notices if any of his personal details lacking, and she observes which personal details a man should have, but are completely missing. Why does a woman go through all these levels of observation regarding a man's personal details? Well, a woman makes such an in depth study, because she knows that by analyzing the presence, and/or the absence, and/or the condition of a man's personal details, that these three factors raises questions in her mind about him, making the woman go "Hmmm, I wonder why that is?"

Once she begins to ponder, then her naturally-analytical mind, kicks right into high gear. Instantly, a woman starts trying to figure out what's the most probable answer to each of the questions raised in her mind—from studying a man's personal details; putting two-and-two together.

By taking this approach, and backed by a lifetime of observing men, combined with her training from the "Female Mafia", a woman knows that what she can come up with quite a lot of accurate information about a man. Although she may not always be exactly correct with all of her on-the-spot analysis, and "guesstimates" about him, usually a woman is very accurate with most of her breakdown regarding him.

Even more amazing, and usually to a man's complete bewilderment, a woman's reading of him, using his personal details, can be so on point, that she even figures out things about a man that he was purposely trying to conceal.

So, from studying the presence, the absence, or the condition of a man's personal details, and then "guesstimating" the most probable answers to the questions raised by studying them, a woman gets not only a superficial understanding of him, but also, she gets a deeper insight into who this man really is, and what he is really about; at the core of his being, beyond the image that he is presenting to the world.

Therefore, given this scenario, let's follow along as she studies, analyzes, questions, and then figures out, everything about a man without him even knowing what she is doing; all of this taking place in a blink of an eye.

An excerpt from **LONDON REIGN** by
A. C. BRITT
A GHETTOHEAT® PRODUCTION

Back in Detroit, Mercedes was bragging to her sisters about how good the sex was with London. She was truly falling in love with London, and wanted to do something really special for "him". One night towards the end of the week, Mercedes went over to the *Lawrence House*, and convinced the landlord to let her into London's room.

She had all kinds of decorations and gifts for London, wanting to surprise "him" with when London came home.

"I can't *believe* you're going through all this," Saiel said, before she started blowing up some balloons.

"I know...I can't believe I'm feelin' this nigga this hard. I think I'm just whipped," Mercedes replied.

"From what? ...You two only did it once."

"But London can eat the *fuck* out of some pussy though! That nigga stay havin' me climbin' the wall. You know, I ain't never been in here when London wasn't home. I wonder what he got *goin'* on around here that he doesn't want me to see," Mercedes said, as she began going through London's things.

"Mercedes...don't go through the man's *shit!* You might *find* something you *don't* wanna see...and then what?" Saiel asked.

"This nigga, London keeps talkin' about how there's *shit* I don't know about him anyway, so I *might* as well play detective... He's takin' *too* damn long to tell me." Mercedes then picked up a pile of papers out of a file cabinet, and started flipping through them. "Pay stubs...bills....bills...more bills," Mercedes said to herself.

"Mercedes, you *really* need to stop."

"Perhaps you're right," Mercedes answered, as she put London's papers back and opened his closet door. Saiel then looked in the closet as well.

"Mercedes, why you leave so many *tampons* over here? That's weird."

"...Yeah it is...because those *ain't* mine." Mercedes pulled the box of tampons out the closet, and looked in it to see how many were missing. "I don't even use this kind, must belong to some other bitch." Mercedes then put the tampons back where she

289

found them, yet, Saiel picked up a stack of medical papers that had fallen when Mercedes opened the closet.

Saiel read the contents of the paper, and her mouth practically *dropped* to the floor. Mercedes noticed her sister's reaction, so she immediately walked over to where Saiel was.

"What, Saiel? ...What does it say? What is that?"

"U-m-m-m...doctors' papers,"

"What? London ain't go no disease, do he? Because I don't even know if London used a condom," Mercedes said. Saiel looked at her sister again and shook her head.

"Naw...no disease...and whether London used a condom or not, doesn't matter," Saiel answered, as she gave her sister a traumatized look. "Mercedes...I think you better sit down."

"Why? What that *shit* say?" Mercedes asked anxiously.

"London   ain't...Mercedes,   this   nigga...damn!
...Mercedes...ha...London *ain't* no dude!" Saiel said emotionally; completely shocked.

"WHAT?" Mercedes asked with much confusion.

"London...Mercedes, London is a girl!"

Mercedes could tell by the look in her sister's eyes that she wasn't kidding. Mercedes immediately snatched the papers out of Saiel's hand, and read everything from the name, to the diagnosis of a urinary track infection.

"A girl? ...But I fuckin'...I fucked him! Her...it! We had sex, Saiel, how the *fuck* is London a girl?" Mercedes was hurt at first, but it quickly turned into anger. "THAT'S WHY THAT *MUTHAFUCKA* NEVER WANTED ME TO TOUCH DOWN THERE! ...And why he...she, whatever, didn't want to have sex!

"I am so *fuckin'* stupid, he made me, she made me wear a blindfold. Said she wanted to try somethin' new. I don't understand Saiel, I've seen London's chest, and she ain't got no breasts. I mean, there were nubbs, but I ain't think nothin' of it," Mercedes said as she began to cry.

"Mercedes...sweetie, she had us *all* fooled! London don't *look* like no girl! She doesn't *sound* like no girl, and London *sure as hell*, doesn't *act* like no girl! We had no reason to think otherwise. Sweetie, just leave this *shit* alone and let's go!" Saiel said, taking the items out of her sister's hands while ushering Mercedes to the door.

An excerpt from *SKATE ON!* by
HICKSON
A GHETTOHEAT® PRODUCTION

Quickly exiting the 155th Street train station on *Eighth Avenue,* Shani, walking with her head held down low, decided to cross the street and walk parallel to the *Polo Grounds;* not chancing bumping into her parents. As she approached the corner, Shani contemplated crossing over to *Blimpie's* before walking down the block to the skating rink. She craved for a *Blimpie Burger* with cheese hero, but immediately changed her mind; fearing of ruining the outfit Keisha gave her.

Shani then headed towards *The Rooftop,* feeling overly anxious to meet with her two friends. As she walked down the dark and eerie block, Mo-Mo crept up behind Shani and proceeded to put her in a headlock; throwing Shani off-guard.

"GET OFF OF ME!" Shani pleaded as she squirmed, trying to break free. Already holding Shani with a firm grip, Mo-Mo applied more pressure around her neck.

Trying to defend herself the best way she knew how, Shani reached behind for Mo-Mo's eyes and attempted to scratch her face. Mo-Mo pushed her forward and laughed.

"Yeah, *bitch,* whachu gon' do?" Mo-Mo teased. "SIKE!" Startled, Shani turned around with a surprised expression on her face.

"Mo-Mo, why are you always *playing* so much? You almost scared me half-to-death!" Shani said while panting heavily, trying hard to catch her breath.

Mo-Mo continued to laugh, "Yo, I had ya heart! You almost *shitted* on yaself! I could've put ya ass to sleep, Bee!"

"Mo-Mo, please stop swearing so much," Shani replied, as she smiled and reached out to hug Mo-Mo. Mo-Mo then teasingly tugged at the plunging neckline of Shani's leotard, pulling it down to reveal more of Shani's cleavage.

"Since when you started dressin' like a lil' hoe?"

Shani, quickly removing Mo-Mo's hand from her breasts, became self-conscious of what she was wearing.

"I knew I shouldn't have put this on. Keisha made me wear this. Do I *really* look sleazy?"

Mo-Mo frowned. "Whah? Shani, stop buggin'! You look aiiight. I'm just not used to seein' you dressin' all sexy and shit."

Shani then looked towards *Eighth Avenue* to see if Keisha was nearby.

"Mo-Mo, where's Keisha? I thought you two were coming to *The Rooftop* together."

Mo-Mo then pointed across the street, as she loudly chewed and popped on her apple flavored *Super Bubble* gum.

"Yo, see that black *Toyota Corolla* double-parked by *The Rucker?* She in there talkin' to some Dominican *nigga* named, Diego we met earlier. We made that *fool* take us to *Ling Fung Chinese Restaurant* on Broadway. Keisha jerked him for a plate of Lobster Cantonese—I got chicken wings and pork-fried rice."

Shani shook her head and chuckled, "You two are always scheming on some guy."

"And you *know* it! A *bitch* gotta eat, right?!" Mo-Mo asked, before blowing a huge bubble with her gum, playfully plucking Shani on her forehead.

Mo-Mo was a belligerent, lowly-educated, hardcore ghetto-girl who was extremely violent and wild. Known for her southpaw boxing skill and powerful knockout punches, she'd often amused herself by fighting other peoples' battles on the block for sport. That's how Mo-Mo met Shani.

Last January, Sheneeda and Jaiwockateema tried to rob Shani of her *Bonsoir* "B" bag near Building 1. Mo-Mo observed what has happening and had rescued Shani, feverishly pounding both girls over their heads with her glass *Kabangers.*

She didn't even know Shani at the time, but fought for her as if they were childhood cronies. Since then, the two have become close friends—Mo-Mo admiring Shani's intelligence, innocence and sincerity.

In addition to her volatile temper, ill manners and street-bitch antics, Mo-Mo was rough around the edges—literally and figuratively. Eighteen-years-old and having dark, rich, coffee-colored skin, Mo-Mo's complexion was beautiful, even with suffering from the mild case of eczema on her hands—and with her face, full of blemishes and bumps from the excessive fighting, junk food and sodas she'd habitually drank.

Bearing a small scar on her left cheek from being sliced with a box cutter, Mo-Mo proudly endured her battle mark. *"The Deceptinettes"*, a female gang who jumped Mo-Mo inside of *Park*

West High School's girls' locker room last year, physically attacked her. Mo-Mo took on the dangerous crew of girls all by herself, winning the brutal brawl, due to her knowing how to fight hard and dirty.

With deep brown eyes, full lips and high cheekbones, she highly resembled an African queen. Mo-Mo wasn't bad looking, she just didn't take care of herself; nor was she ever taught how. Because of this, Mo-Mo was often forsaken for her ignorance by most.

Awkwardly standing knock-kneed and pigeon-toed at five-foot-seven, big boned with an hourglass figure, Mo-Mo was a brick house! Thick and curvaceous with a body that wouldn't quit, she had ample sized forty-two D breasts, shifting wide hips, big legs, with well-toned thighs. Having the largest ass in Harlem, Mo-Mo's behind was humongous—nicely rounded and firm. It automatically became a sideshow attraction whenever she appeared, as everyone, young and old stared in disbelief; amazed at the shape, fullness and size of Mo-Mo's butt. A man once joked about "spanking" Mo-Mo's rear, claiming that when he'd knocked it…her ass knocked him back!

Her hair length was short, in which Mo-Mo wore individual box braids, braiding it herself; having real, human hair extensions. Often, her braids were sloppy and unkempt, having naps and a fuzzy hairline. Mo-Mo's coarse, natural hair grain never matched the soft and silky texture of her extensions, but she always soaked the ends in a pot of scalding, hot water to achieve a wet-and-wavy look.

Mo-Mo never polished her nails or kept them clean, having dirt underneath them regularly. Rarely shaving the hair from under her armpits or bikini line caused Mo-Mo to have a rank, body odor. Someone even left a package at her apartment door one day, filled with a large can of *Right Guard, Nair* and a bottle of *FDS Feminine Deodorant Spray* with a typewritten note attached. It read: *"Aye, Funkbox, clean ya stank pussy and stop puttin' Buckwheat in a headlock—you nasty bitch!"* Mo-Mo assumed it was either a prank from Sheneeda and Jaiwockateema, or Oscardo—still sulking over Mo-Mo kicking his ass six years ago.

She'd now lived alone in the *Polo Grounds,* due to her mother's untimely death six months ago—dying of sclerosis of the liver from her excessive drinking of hard alcohol. Just days after

293

Mo-Mo's mother's death, she'd received a letter from *Social Services,* stating that they were aware of her mother's passing, her only legal guardian, and that she would receive a visit from a social worker; one who would be instructed to place Mo-Mo in an all-girls group home in East Harlem.

Mo-Mo had begged her other family members to allow her to live with them, but they refused, not wanting to deal with her nasty disposition, constant fighting and barbaric lifestyle. Nor did they wish to support Mo-Mo emotionally or financially, resulting her to rely on public assistance from the welfare office. At that point, Mo-Mo hadn't any relatives whom she can depend upon—she was on her own and had to grow up fast.

Luckily Mo-Mo's eighteenth birthday had arrived a day before she was accosted in the lobby of her building by a male social worker, having the rude investigator from *Social Services* antagonize her with legal documents; indicating that she was to temporarily be in his custody and taken immediately to the group home.

"SUCK A FAT BABY'S ASS!" was what Mo-Mo yelled at the social worker before defiantly slamming the door in his face.

Failing most of her classes, Mo-Mo barely attended school. She was in the tenth grade, but had belonged in the twelfth. Mo-Mo was still a special education student, now having a six-grader's reading and writing level. Her former teachers passed her in school, being totally unconcerned with Mo-Mo's learning disability. Their goal was to pass as many students as possible, in order to avoid being reprimanded by superiors for failing a large number of students. The school system had quotas to meet and didn't receive the needed funds from the government for the following term—if a large amount of students were held back.

Along with other personal issues, Mo-Mo was hot-in-the-ass, fast and promiscuous, having the temperament of a low-class whore. She was a big-time freak, a sex fiend with an insatiable appetite for men with huge dicks—becoming weak at the knees at the sight of a protruding bulge.

Mo-Mo's self esteem and subsidized income was low, but her sex drive was extremely high, having sex with men for cash while soothing her inner pain. She didn't sell her body for money due to desperation and destitute—Mo-Mo did it for the fun of it. She *loved* dick and decided to earn money while doing what

Mo-Mo enjoyed the most—getting fucked! She was going to have frivolous sex regardless, *"SO WHY NOT GET PAID FOR IT?"* Mo-Mo often reasoned.

Academically, she was slow, but Mo-Mo was nobody's fool; being street-smart with thick skin. A true survivor, who persevered, by hook-or-crook, Mo-Mo was determined to sustain—by all means necessary.

"AYE, YO, KEISHA, HURRY THE *FUCK* UP!" Mo-Mo beckoned.

"Hold up! I'm comin'!" Keisha replied with irritation in her voice; concluding her conversation with Diego, "My friends are callin' me—I gotta go."

"Can I see you again and get ya digits, mommy?" Diego begged, talking extremely fast with his raspy voice.

"Maybe! And *no* you can't get my number—gimme yours," Keisha snapped.

Diego immediately was attracted to Keisha's good looks, snootiness, nonchalant attitude and bold behavior. He smiled as he wrote his beeper number on the flyer he received for an upcoming party at *Broadway International*—while exiting the Chinese restaurant with Keisha and Mo-Mo an hour earlier.

While handing Keisha the flyer, Diego attempted to wish her goodnight, but Keisha interjected: "Can I get three hundred dollars?" she said, looking straight into Diego's eyes.

"Damn, mommy, what's up? I just met you an *hour* ago and you *askin'* me for money already?"

Keisha paused for emphasis.

"...Are you gon' give it to me or *not?*" Keisha coldly asked, still looking into Diego's eyes—not once she ever blinked.

"Whachu need three hundred for, mommy?"

"First and foremost, my name is *Keisha,* not mommy! And I don't *n-e-e-e-e-e-d* three hundred dollars—I want it!"

Diego sat silently, bewildered and turned on by Keisha's brashness.

"Diego, don't you want me to look cute the next time you see me?" Keisha asked innocently while batting her eyelashes; deceiving Diego with her fake, light-hearted disposition.

"So I'm gonna see you again huh, mommy?" Diego nervously asked, smiling as he pulled out a wad of cash from his pocket. His large bankroll, wrapped in jade-green rubber bands caused Keisha's eyes to widen.

LADY SPEAKS THE TRUTH, VOLUME 1
Essay written by SHA
A GHETTOHEAT® PRODUCTION

Growing up in Urban America isn't easy. Throw in the race, gender and age cards. You walk through life with iron-filled crates shackled to your ankles. How can you climb the ladder of success with so much holding you back?

This isn't about me outlining how to live your life or what's right and wrong—I don't know the answer to that. This is about me asking you to wake up! What's up, Urban America? Have we've become so complacent as to stop our complaining because we've been reassured that everything is new and approved, and comes backed with a money back guarantee if we're not satisfied?

I don't know about you but, I'm not satisfied! I'm not a part of the "walking dead" that rest assured in what they've been spoon-fed, that would've been the easy way out: I like it hard.

I don't think you understand me. As my third-grade teacher put it, I wasn't "born with a silver spoon in my mouth." I was born in Kings County Hospital in Brooklyn, New York. It happened sometime after the birth of "THE MONSTER" (HIV/AIDS) and just before the Crack epidemic hit hard.

Though my father owned a bodega and I attended parochial school, I was far from rich. It wasn't steak and lobster; 34th Street Miracle Christmas' and such. However, what we lacked in finances, we made up for through love and unity.

No money meant a closet filled with out-of-style clothes and ridicule from my peers; it was whatever! I was too focused on school to really give a damn. Then my body decided it wanted to start puberty at nine-years-old. Don't think that made me special, there were other girls in the fifth grade with bangin' bodies.

While they were using what they had to get what they want, I stayed in my books. Of course I wasn't popular with the boys, but everybody knew my name. Rhymes were my reason and Hip Hop saved me from the cruelty of the bullies. Well, at least, some of the time.

Being from BK, my ability to write poetry and to get lyrics from any song off the radio, made me tolerable. My strict Haitian father didn't allow me to hang out after school, go on go-away trips or participate in any of the bullshit that happened in my neighborhood. If it didn't happen on my stoop, I wasn't able to go.

Soon after, I was in Queens and desperately wanted to go back to Brooklyn. I thought I'd be much more popular back "home", but the reality was if I wasn't "doing it", I was wack. I accepted that. I had no choice but to be wack and watch every single move that everybody made.

Then I reached high school. I attended a school that made headlines for acid-throwing, gun-toting, monster-infected students! It was the closest one to my house, so I really didn't have a choice. It was then when I got the fever for the fast life. I wanted to be that chick with the fly dudes that pushed the baddest cars, dipped in jewelry of every caliber.

I started asking around for the fly boys from elementary school. Surely by then, I thought, they had to be on top of the game. Dudes were either in Spofford, just recently released from juvenile detention, dead or strung the fuck out on crack-cocaine. Real talk, a sixteen-year-old junkie is not a joke.

Then I started watching the older dudes. This was the era of *The Sleepwalkers*, *The Lost Boys* and others. My young self got a thrill walking through the neighborhood with the older boys checking for me, because of my over-developed body; that made the girls hate me even more. I was already catching hell because of my hair and swagger. Yet, that was dealt with accordingly. I'm not saying I won every battle, but you damn sure won't be able to call me cara cicatriz (Scarface)!

It was all fun and games until someone got his head blown off in Brookville Park one hot summer night...That brought me to the reality of things. I sat back and started making connections. It didn't take too long to figure out who were the major drug dealers, the minor drug dealers, the wanna-be drug dealers, the stick-up kids, the car thieves and the wankstas (Suckers). Before long, I had them all figured out and knew most of their modus operandi; it was too easy.

For the rest of high school, I met a whole slew of characters. I met guys who were predicate felons at the age of twenty; guys who snapped their fingers and made anything you desired appear like magic. I'll admit, crime life is very enticing! But the end results are not.

I played my cards well, at that time, holding them close to my chest. I was very careful about who I was seen with and where. Undercover detectives were all over the place all the time. Every other day, somebody was getting locked up, and females were getting caught out there on technicalities.

That right there was what *really* made me think twice about all my moves. I lost count of how many females I've seen get charged with years and decades, just because they were at the wrong place at the wrong time. Damn those RICO and Rockefeller laws! They will get innocent people and first-time offenders caught up in the system every time.

Besides the jail time aspect of a hustler's life, I realized that Uncle Sam makes fun and games out of hustlin'. That's another reason I just observed the business of drugs. Tell me why a black man getting caught with crack rocks in BK will get at least ten years, but a white man getting caught on the island with cocaine will get a much lesser sentence? Doesn't crack come from cocaine? Wake up, Urban America!

Why is it that Caucasians dominate the welfare system, but yet African-Americans and Hispanics are portrayed as being the dominate races in the system? Isn't it strange how families stay stuck in the same situation generation after generation? Your momma had you at sixteen, her momma had her at fifteen and her momma had her at fourteen! Yet, all of you still live in the same project apartment? F.Y.I., the projects, no matter how "luxurious" some may seem, are designed to keep the masses psychologically disabled so we can perpetuate the cycle, over-and-over again.

Uncle Sam put up the projects. Uncle Sam allows drugs to come into the country. Trust that if America really wanted to be drug free, then we damn sure would be! Then what would the DEA do? Do you realize how many federal, state and city jobs would be lost if there wasn't any illegal drugs in America?

Thousands of people would be out of work and the economy would fall apart. The Great Depression wouldn't be able to compare to the economic state of America if drug money wasn't in circulation. Uncle Sam can keep his VESID vouchers and his rehabilitation programs: I know the score.To my young people of Urban America: hustlin' is what it is. We all do it in one shape or another. For most of us, it's a part of life. Victims of our socio-economic status, we have to do what we have to do; just do it wisely. Know when to hit *HARDER,* know when to ease up. I thank God for that ability. Too many times I've come this close to being state property...I'm free. Wake up and you'll be too.

An excerpt from *SOME SEXY, ORGASM 1* by
DRU NOBLE
A GHETTOHEAT® PRODUCTION

BIG BONED

"I need you, Melissa; oh I *love* your body! Let me taste you, mmmph, let me *love* you—just give me some sexy!" Jezebel begged while still squeezing the woman's luscious crescents. Melissa had no hope of resisting this sudden passionate impulse that flooded her.

She felt Jezebel's grip tighten on her, then a finger slowly traced between her curvaceous legs. The unexpected jolt of excitable pleasure caused Melissa to rise on her side, throwing Jezebel off of her. She palmed between her own thighs, trying to silence the rest of the roaring waves threatening to overcome her preciousness.

Jezebel couldn't take her eyes off of Melissa, as she breathed erratically, while Melissa couldn't help but to stare back with conflicting desperation. Melissa's hand reached out and grasped the back of the Native-American woman's neck, as she pulled Jezebel towards her forcefully.

Their lips touch, melded, then opened. Jezebel's tongue dove into Melissa's mouth, finding the versatile muscle was eager to wrestle her own. A groan vibrated down Melissa's throat. Her hand came up, and two fingers strung like guitar strings on Jezebel's upturned beady nipple—first playing with it, then catching Jezebel's hardened nipple between her index and middle fingers; closing it within tight confines.

Jezebel then straddled Melissa, the two women's hands meeting, immediately intertwining before their kissing ended.

"I wanted you since I *first* saw you; I've been wet ever since that moment. You're so *fucking* sexy, Melissa. I *need* you, can I have some sexy? Give it to me," Jezebel said in a low, hushed voice.

The twinkle in her beautiful brown eyes affected Melissa like an intoxicating elixir. Melissa watched on, as Jezebel took her captured hand and began to suck on two fingers with her hot, steamy mouth. Jezebel's checked hollowed, as she continued to close in on Melissa's dainty fingers.

Melissa, voluptuous and womanly, petals became slick, and damp—natural juices now running down towards her rounded rear end.

"I want you, too Jezebel, come get some sexy!" she pledged. Jezebel smiled as Melissa's fingers slid from her mouth, leading them down her body. With her lead, Melissa allowed her hand to enter into Jezebel's bikini. A glimpse of her fine, black pubic hair came into view, as Melissa then felt the lovely grace of Jezebel's vagina.

A soothing hiss breathed out of Jezebel. The moistness of her internal lake coated the fingers that ventures to its intimate space. Melissa then bent her hand so the bikini could come down, and she was grand the delightful vision of where her fingers ventured.

Jezebel's outer labia had opened, as Melissa's fingers split between her middle, like tickling a blooming rose. She tipped her hand up, and used her thumb to peel back the protective skin over Jezebel's engorged clitoris. The pink button revealed itself exclusively, and Melissa used her thumb to caress it; stirring up Jezebel's burning desire.

Melissa had never seen or touched another woman's pearl, but found that she'd loved it completely. Two of her fingers then slipped within Jezebel's hot, oily insides, and the Native-American woman had thrust her hips forward to take all Melissa had to offer.

"You're so *hot* inside; burning up my fingers, baby."

"Just don't stop; *please* don't stop what you're doing," Jezebel instructed. Her hips began to undulate, rocking herself to a sweet bliss. Jezebel rode Melissa's fingers like she would her fiancé's long, pleasure-inducing dick.

Melissa then curled her wet fingers back slightly, as she would if she were touching herself, searching inside for that magical area most women long to discover—the G-spot.

Melissa felt Jezebel's tunnel pulsate, and a shock ran through the humping woman, giving Melissa total satisfaction that she'd found Jezebel's spot; now also realizing that, by her being a woman, she had full advantage to knowing another woman's body, better than any man could.

An excerpt from ***SOME SEXY, ORGASM 2*** by
MIKA MILLER
A GHETTOHEAT® PRODUCTION

Oh God, I think I broke my clitoris...or at least fractured it. After eight months of non-stop intense and dedicated masturbation, my fingers have grown tired, my wrist threatens me with the dull twangs of carpal tunnel and, as of lately, there is no climax in sight. It's as if over the last eight months during my lack of satisfying dick, and therefore, subsequent mounting sexual frustration, I have *masturbated* myself into a physical catastrophe. My clitoris just...died. There's no longer a satisfying crescendo of orgasmic waves rushing through my pelvis. Nothing's happening South of the border. Nothing. Nada. Zilch. Not a *fucking* thing!

I flop my head back into the plushness of my Versailles jacquard-woven comforter with golden hues, and bury my head beneath the 1200 thread count, matte-satin finish bed sheets, and pray to *God* that I haven't destroyed the most powerful sexual organ on my body. I should have seen this coming.

Over the past four weeks, it's become increasingly harder-and-harder for me to reach the point of orgasm. I have *exhausted* my stash of pornographic movies, and just about bored myself to death, trying to rely on the secret sexual fantasies that I keep imbedded in the "freak" quadrant of my brain. My pornographic movies and imaginative sexual illusions, have all become doldrum. I mean, who can get off to the same *shit* night-after-night? Certainly not me.

When those efforts failed, I resorted to mechanical assistance. One evening, like a sex-addicted junkie, and in a complete state-of-desperation, I hopped in my silver, convertible *BMW Z4 Roadster*, drove forty-five minutes down Highway 35, until I saw the three, brightly-beaming red, neon letters that I sought, peering at me from the exit near the movie theater in Pluergerville: "XXX".

I parked my "Beamer" in the back of the ex-rated, adult video store, and in an attempt to be "incog-negro", I flipped the hood of my *Azzuré* tracksuit over my head, hid behind my *Oliver Peoples* "Harlot" sunglasses, and tried to nonchalantly mosey my way inside.

An hour later, after consulting with the bubblegum-popping female sales clerk; dressed in a tartan plaid, pleated ultra-mini skirt, and red, thigh-high patent leather, platform lace-up boots, I left the store with a plethora of sex-toy treasures and erotic devices: personal lubricants, battery vibrators, electric vibrators, G spot stimulators and orgasm books.

I even bought the infamous two-hundred dollar vibrator called *The Rabbit,* that I heard mentioned on *Sex in the City.* I had just partakened in an erotic shopping spree, one that would even cause *Kirk Franklin* to blush.

Needless to say that, after I tried all of my treasures (and sometimes even twice) I was still no closer to an orgasmic experience than before. So, when my orgasms began to steadily decline and weaken, and when it seemed that I had to *work* harder to implode, I blamed it on a lack of…"inspiration".

The "clitoral" truth is that, I had become a woman obsessed. What I needed to do was pump my brakes. I needed to take a sebaticle from my not-so-good vibrations. My "pussy problem" was fast becoming a perplexing conundrum.

ghettoheat.

THE GHETTOHEAT® MOVEMENT

THE GHETTOHEAT® MOVEMENT is a college scholarship fund geared towards young adults within the inner-city, pursuing education and careers in Journalism and Literary Arts.

At GHETTOHEAT®, our mission is to promote literacy worldwide. To learn more about THE GHETTOHEAT® MOVEMENT, or to see how you can get involved, send all inquires to: MOVEMENT@GHETTOHEAT.COM, or log on to GHETTOHEAT.COM

To send comments to DAMON "AMIN" MEADOWS and/or JASON POOLE, send all mail to:

GHETTOHEAT®, LLC
P.O. BOX 2746
NEW YORK, NY 10027

Attention: DAMON "AMIN" MEADOWS/JASON POOLE

Or e-mail them at:

AMIN@GHETTOHEAT.COM

JASON@GHETTOHEAT.COM

Artists interested in having their works reviewed for possible consideration at GHETTOHEAT®, send all materials to:

ghettoheat.

P.O. BOX 2746
New York, NY 10027

Attention: HICKSON

GHETTOHEAT®: THE HOTNESS IN THE STREETS!!!™

ORDER FORM

Name_____

Registration #_____(If incarcerated)

Address_____

City_____ State_____ Zip code_____

Phone_____ E-mail_____

Friends/Family E-mail_____

Books are $15.00 each. Send me the following number of copies of:

___ CONVICT'S CANDY .   ___ GHETTOHEAT®

___ AND GOD CREATED WOMAN   ___ HARDER

___ SONZ OF DARKNESS   ___ LONDON REIGN

___ GHOST TOWN HUSTLERS   ___ BOY-TOY

___ GAMES WOMEN PLAY   ___ SKATE ON!

___ SOME SEXY, ORGASM 1   ___ HARDER 2

___ AND GOD CREATED WOMAN 2

Please send $4.00 to cover shipping and handling. Add a dollar for each additional book ordered. *Free shipping for convicts.*

Total Enclosed = _____

Please make check or money order payable to GHETTOHEAT®. Send all payments to:

GHETTOHEAT®
P.O. BOX 2746
NEW YORK, NY 10027

GHETTOHEAT®: THE HOTNESS IN THE STREETS!!!™